EVIL FROM THE SEA

It was while he gathered Ruth's slight form into his arms that the fear, forgotten in the confusion of the moment, arrived again, clutching at the very pit of his stomach, catching at his breath so he could feel himself tremble. He suddenly felt a certainty that he and Ruth were not alone in that small earthen chamber, that the room swarmed with...something, something both unknown and terrible.

And it was just at this same moment that he heard the sea. Not only the sea that had become a background for their every moment in this house, but all the seas of the world, suddenly rushing in upon his hearing as though all the tides of the earth were being poured into that one little chamber, drowning out the sounds of the storm, filling the vacuum of space with a tremendous, pounding roar that seemed to drive a burning wedge into his brain...

UNDERTOW

DRAKE DOUGLAS

LEISURE BOOKS   NEW YORK CITY

With deepest appreciation
to Stephen David Kent.

Nothing is every really done alone.

A LEISURE BOOK

Published by

Dorchester Publishing Co., Inc.
6 East 39th Street
New York, N.Y. 10016

Printed in the United States of America

PROLOGUE

I first saw the painting in the window of a small art gallery I occasionally visit on Fifty-Eighth Street in New York City, just across from the side entrance of the Plaza Hotel. I probably would not even have noticed it, were it not for the fact that it looked so completely out of place there, a dark and gloomy canvas placed, almost as though with an after-thought, at the side of a display filled with far more cheerful subjects. My first reaction was one of displeasure and wonderment that my friend Tetrollini, manager of the gallery, had set it there. At first it appeared more like a Hallowe'en cartoon than the work of a serious artist, and it occurred to me that this might be one of Tetrollini's curious little jests, since we had just entered the autumn season and merchants were already beginning to display their garish Hallowe'en wares; if so, the joke was in very poor taste. It was only when I peered more closely that I realized there was, perhaps, something more here than met the casual eye.

There was nothing particularly remarkable about the subject of the canvas. It was simply a painting of a very old house, a tall and sombre wooden structure set upon a cliff overlooking the sea, a house such as would have been dear to the brooding appreciation of a Nathaniel Hawthorne. The brief shoreline in the lower left corner of the canvas rose abruptly to the cliff upon which the house stood, its facade facing the viewer. The left side of the house formed an unbroken wall with the cliff itself, whose sheer face fell in a jagged line to a mass of pointed black rocks glittering with the foam of an angry sea. The twin pointed gables of the house rose sharply against a gloomy sky covered with tumbling gray cloud; between them was a barren Widow's Walk enclosed by a low iron railing. A broad veranda which seemed to circle the house, save for its seaward side, cast the tall, empty windows into dark shadows; I peered more closely, but decided I was mistaken in my initial impression of figures lurking in the shadow. The earth upon which the house stood was dry and hard, marked here and there with clumps of hardy scrub clustered almost defiantly upon the yellow-brown soil, and beside the veranda to the right stood an ugly dead tree, its bare branches agonizingly etched with harsh black strokes of the brush. A dirt roadway, its center only slightly rutted, made an arching curve before the house, and then again descended down towards the beach.

The painting was a rather depressing mass of unrelieved grays, blacks, browns and drab yellows, save for one startling burst of color. At first I thought this was an unfortunate accidental smear upon the canvas, but as I bent closer to the gallery window I could see that this was not the case, that the smear had been deliberate and was actually an integral, if inexplicable, part of the whole. It expressed itself in a curious brilliant flow of green issuing from what was probably a window in the cellar of the house, seeming to seep almost with living motion from the seaward side of the structure, and down to the turmoil from which rose the black pointed rocks. There seemed neither rhyme nor reason for this curious seepage, and yet there was about it something distinctly disturbing and almost ominous; it had been carefully drawn with a heavy touch that made the paint appear fresh and still wet.

6

It was not a pleasant work. The house spoke of abandonment and desertion, the entire atmosphere of loneliness and, somehow, of fear. I thought it could never have been a happy house.

And yet there was something vaguely familiar about the work, about the strong curling brush strokes of those gray clouds that seemed to tumble over each other in their impatience to leave that lonely scene, in the strong angular lines of the gables pointing to the coldly unfriendly sky. It was when I again bent closer to examine the small portion of sea visible in the lower left that instant recognition came; I knew of only one contemporary artist who could paint the sea in so lively a fashion. I was not surprised to see the name of Ruth Kendall inscribed in small, almost dainty signature at the right bottom of the canvas.

I had long been something of an admirer of the works of Ruth Kendall, of which I then possessed two rather striking examples. Yet although painted in her distinctive style, I knew this canvas was totally unlike any other work of hers that I had ever seen. Kendall was an unfortunately little-known artist of considerable ability, although her work always seemed to lack the full maturity that would reveal the true extent of her talent. She generally worked in brilliantly colored and richly realized seascapes. Admittedly the plethora of seascapes constantly turned out by aspiring artists are generally rather dull and uninspiring works . . . after all, how much can you do with masses of water? . . . but Kendall's work was considerably above the usual sunset-on-the-sea or tumbling billows; they were studies that, more than any other current painter of the genre, seemed to express to the full the depth and the mystery of the sea, canvases that held the viewer through the sweep of motion and the play of color.

I had heard nothing of Ruth Kendall for some time, and had assumed she had abandoned an unfortunately unrewarding career as an artist for other perhaps more mundane but also more lucrative pursuits. As I gazed at the painting in the gallery window, I decided she had probably done well in seeking her livelihood elsewhere, if this were an example of her later work. At the time, I had no wish to become the owner of what seemed something of a curious bastardization of her promise and talent.

The painting remained there in the gallery window for some weeks, until it seemed to me to have gathered a slight patina of dust that somewhat softened the harsh contours of the subject; apparently it no more impressed others than it had me. It irritated me, and yet, somehow, I could not pass that window without pausing to peer at it. It was unpleasant and unattractive, but I found myself wondering at the drive that had created it, and perhaps I sensed some hidden purpose behind it all. I had no dealings with Tetrollini at that time, or I would undoubtedly have questioned his wisdom of marring his display with such a canvas.

When the work was finally removed from its place of exposure, I quickly forgot all about it; the window unquestionably looked much improved for its absence.

Some months after its disappearance from the window, I stopped at the gallery to view a fine Tinteretto that Tetrollini had managed to secure for me at an excellent price, and after agreeing to its purchase, I strolled about the small but elegant gallery and rather wryly gazed at the gaudy smears on the walls that passed for the day's examples of art. To my surprise, I found the Kendall canvas propped against a rear wall, apparently awaiting either removal or placement in a new location. I paused before it for some moments, again struck by a curious sense of power whose origin I could not determine. It looked somehow darker and drearier than before, and it occurred to me that this was its proper setting, away from brightening light and coated with the softening effect of shadow. It was then that I heard a soft and gentle voice behind me.

"The painting interests you, sir?"

I turned to find standing behind me a charming little old lady, elegantly dressed in the fashion of some years ago which seems always just right for gentle women of this kind, leaning lightly on an ebony cane with a rounded silver top. She wore a black dress of the finest material, superbly fitted to her small and slender form, with a single strand of marvelously matched pearls; there were small pearls of equal calibre in the lobes of her delicate ears. Atop her lovely white hair was perched a small toque hat such as was favored many years ago by England's late Queen Mary; the veil of the hat had been raised to reveal a sweetly lovely face only lightly lined by her years, brightened by light blue eyes whose sparkle and liveliness might well have been envied by a woman half her age. She was surely well into her seventies, if not beyond, but the firmness of her carriage, save for the slight infirmity that apparently forced her to depend on occasional support of the cane, belied her years.

"Forgive me for disturbing you," she said in a pleasantly soft and friendly tone. "I could not help noting your preoccupation with the work. Yet it is not exactly an attractive painting is it?"

I smiled in return, feeling quite at my ease before this stranger. "Certainly not. But it does have something of a . . . a curious power about it. It's very different from any of the work of this artist I have ever seen."

"Then you are familiar with the work of Ruth Kendall?"

I nodded. "Yes. I own two of her paintings."

"But you would not care to own this one?"

I turned again to look at the canvas, felt the chill of its barren grayness, and shook my head. "No. I don't believe so. I can recognize the artist from the technique, but this lacks all the ebulliance of her work, the sharp vibrancy of her seascapes. This is . . . unsettling. I wouldn't quite know what to do with it."

"I had planned to have it destroyed," the woman said softly, then adding, almost to herself, "but then I remembered all that had gone into its construction . . ."

I raised my eyebrows with interest. "You were acquainted with the artist?"

"Oh, yes. Ruth Kendall was the wife of my grandson. I knew her very well, indeed. A fine young woman." The last words were said almost defiantly.

"I have seen no recent work of hers," I mentioned. "Other than this, that is. I assume this is a later work."

"It was her last."

"That's a pity," I commented. "She had a very real talent that might well have developed into something important. Has she abandoned art?"

"She is dead."

"Oh. I'm sorry. I hadn't heard."

The old woman stood silently for a moment and stared at the canvas, and I was struck by the sorrow in her eyes that seemed suddenly to emphasize her years. as though a protecting veil had been removed from her face to reveal the harsh reality of her age.

"This canvas had much to do with her death," she said softly. "I can not see it without remembering." She turned to me again and looked intently at me for a moment before continuing. "Since you seem interested in Ruth's talent, perhaps you would care some time to hear the story behind this work. You might better understand what she has done here."

"I would be delighted," I assured her, adding abruptly, "Why not now?"

The old woman looked about her and smiled. "I believe the gallery is about to close."

"That's no problem," I said. "Would you consider me too forward if I invited you for a cocktail at the Plaza? It's just across the street, you know."

"Yes. I am staying there." Her smile was genuine and pleasing, again lighting her gentle face and removing the slight cast of sorrow. "It is a long time since I have received such an invitation, young man. I should be delighted."

I quickly completed my business with Tetrollini, arranging for shipment of the Tintoretto to my apartment, and then carefully guided the little old woman across the narrow street to the hotel. She winced slightly as we started up the steps into the hotel, and mentioned with a rather delightful touch of embarrassment that an attack of rheumatism had slowed her down and made necessary the temporary use of the cane. Several moments later we were seated at a window table in the Oak Room of the Plaza, she with a brandy and I with a martini.

It was a brilliantly sunny autumn day, and the leaves of the great trees in the park just across Central Park South were beginning to turn color. The sky was a light blue with only the occasional whisp of a powdery white cloud. There was already a bit of a nip in the air, and people walked past our window with brisk and determined strides. A hackney coach drove by, its two young occupants, warmed by a lap rug, sitting very close together. A tree directly opposite, its green leaves already edged with yellow, bowed slightly in obeisance at the touch of a gentle breeze.

"How very pleasant and lovely it is here," my aged companion mused softly. "I often think that this world of ours must surely be one of the greatest jewels in the heavens, with its tumbling blue-green seas, soughing green forests, purpled mountains, magnificent cities and sweeping vistas. I wonder if we are unique in the great expanse of the universe."

"That is perhaps something we may never hope to learn," I remarked, and she again turned that enchanting smile upon me.

"I am Ellen Pirenne," she said, "and it's very kind of you to ask me here."

"It was very kind of you to come," I countered, introducing myself.

The smile saddened. "The world may have changed, but old women still often become lonely. I sometimes like to talk about Ruth to those who are interested. It eases me, somehow."

She seemed to slip into a reverie, and for some moments she sat silently, occasionally sipping her brandy as she stared across to the park. Her next words were not at all what I expected to hear.

"How long do you suppose *Evil* endures?" she asked.

"I . . . I don't know," I responded lamely, caught off guard. "I've never really thought about it."

"The subject of *Evil* intrigues me," she confessed. "Are you a religious man?"

"I'm afraid not," I said with a shake of my head.

"Why should you be afraid to confess it?" she asked with a slight smile. "When you realize *Evil* exists only with the permission of God, it makes one wonder, doesn't it? I've often wondered how many years or centuries must pass before the remembrance of *Evil* fades from a man's mind. I have wandered much about the world, young man, and I have seen many strange things in which perhaps you would not believe. I have learned it is the remembrance of evil that causes insubstantial shades to roam ceaselessly through the dark and silent corridors of haunted mansions. Do you know there are places where the memory of *Evil* is as strong today as it was centuries ago? The tumbled, dust-covered dungeons of the Inquisition still echo with the screams of those placed on the rack for the greater glory of God, and the sun-splashed squares of the old Spanish cities sometimes still ring with the remembered agonies of those whose stake-bound bodies were given to the flames for the perpetuation of the True Faith. Battered and terrified Negroes may still raise their ghostly voices in the darkness of the barraccoons of western Africa, and I would imagine the agonized voices of Israel can be heard in the cold concrete silence of the great death camps. No, Evil does not die easily."

"There has always been *Evil*," I commented, wondering what all this had to do with the story of Ruth Kendall. "The great tragedy is that it appears an inherent part of the human race." It was somehow disconcerting to hear this gentle old woman speak of such horrors.

She nodded. "Yes. And unfortunately as well, Evil is stronger than good and has a longer life in the remembrance of man. The good often take their goodness with them when they leave, but the evil will permit their wickedness to remain behind as a lasting legacy of their hatred and malice. Man abhors *Evil*, but he refuses to banish it from his memory, and it is perhaps this that keeps it so constantly alive." She looked up at me. "You are wondering what all this has to do with a rather curious canvas in a small Manhattan art gallery."

I nodded. "Yes."

Darkness crossed her face again. "That painting is the final agonized expression of the greatest *Evil* I have ever encountered." Her eyes were sharp and brilliant as she looked at me. "Have you ever heard of a place called Fowles House?"

I shook my head.

"There was an *Evil* there that lasted for two centuries, hovering like a poisonous miasma over its pointed gables even after the house had long stood empty and deserted, shunned by all who knew its dreadful story. It was part of the arid, bloodless land upon which the house stood. It seeped into the walls and the floorings, and it festered for two hundred years in the dusty cellar where the silence was disturbed only by the muffled roar of the surf . . ."

CHAPTER ONE

THE house was situated somewhat precariously on the very edge of the naked, ragged bluff that rose precipitously from the sea like an arrogant finger of stone thumbing its nose at the sky. If you stood on the harsh, weed-spotted precipice just before the house when a bitingly cold wind roared down from the north and angrily dashed the churning gray-green and white encrusted waters against the glittering spume-covered jagged purple-black rocks, you could taste on your lips the tangy salt spray that had traveled to this lonely spot across all the mysterious seven seas of the world. The skies here seemed always thickly blanketed with tumbling dirty gray clouds through which the sun occasionally cast a questing golden ray that lightly burnished the heaving breast of the ever restless sea. The only sign of life in this lonely world was the occasionall white gull with gray-tipped wings that dared to swoop over the stabbing gables.

For more than two centuries, the large, rambling old house, its time-pitted boards now snow-whitened by the many long years of exposure to the heavily salt-laden atmosphere, had pointed its sharp gables at the darkly leaden sky, as though trying to pierce the soft underbelly of the clouds and release the imprisoned warming light of the sun upon a cold and lonely world.

The wood-framed windows were tall and narrow, but as empty as the sadly emotionless eyes of the blind. Small fancily grilled balconies overlooked the sea from the second floor. Between the two narrowly pointed gables, the black platform of a Widow's Walk crowned the flat roof with speared iron railings that gleamed a dull reddish shade of rust; many storm-tossed seasons had passed since last that melancholy platform had echoed to the restless sound of anxious pacing feet. One side of the house was like a wooden extension of the cliff itself, and black stone and weathered boards rose in an unbroken line from sea to sky. A broad shadowed veranda supported by narrow spaced wooden pillars completely encircled the first floor of the structure, save for that side facing the sea.

The grounds about the house were barren, hard-packed and bloodless yellow-brown earth, with here and there a straggly tuft of coarse, hardy, salt-encrusted scrub grass as evidence that nature had never completely abandoned her battle to obtain possession of this seared piece of land. A sadly solitary tree raised its contorted, leafless arms in mute supplication near the end of the veranda.

There was about the bluff an overwhelming melancholy air of solitude, neglect and mournful decay as though time, in its hurry to move on to more amenable sites, had abandoned the cliff to the silent past.

And yet, both Ruth and John loved the old house from the very first moment they saw it, looming so dark and empty against the heavily clouded sky just before dusk, on a day when early autumn winds blew a sharp chill and the waves crashed noisily against the pointed rocks below. Ruth stood very near the cliff's edge, shining wet with spray that seemed to have swept away the finely etched lines of care and sorrow that had been there for too long a time; her eyes seemed to dance with excitement as she looked out to the sea and the empty horizon.

"Oh, John, it's absolutely perfect! It's enchanting," she enthused, her voice unsteady with excitement. "Will you just look at that wonderful sky, the light touch of amber on the under-bellies of those black clouds, the play of black and gold on that tumbling gray sea! I just know I could do some really good work in this place, John, I just know it! It cries for a painter's brush!"

John, who was encountering considerable . . . and, in view of his wife's apparent firmness of stance, rather embarrassing . . . difficulty in maintaining his footing as the wind flapped the legs of his trousers with a noise like the spattering of pistol shots, looked back toward the house, standingly stolidly behind them as though defying the enemy winds to topple it from the dominating perch it had proudly occupied through so many long years. A few errant leaves with brilliant red and yellow bodies chased each other aimlessly down the length of the veranda, and the tall windows were like vacant eyes staring eternally out to sea, watching for a ship that never appeared on the horizon.

"I suppose I might even be able to finish that damned book the publisher's been hounding me about," he confessed.

He looked at the dry, achingly arid landscape about them, and then glanced down to the smooth yellow-white beach below, darkly stained here and there with twisted, trailing masses of green-black seaweed, like disjointed corpses vomitted up by the sea from some long forgotten, barnacle encrusted sunken derelict. He stepped quickly back from the cliff's edge as a wave of vertigo swept over him, and involuntarily lowered his head as a large white gull swooshed past them on a current of air.

"At least it would take us away for a while from those damned constantly jangling telephones, insipid television entertainments, and mindless cocktail parties where we've been wasting so much of our time. Who knows," he said with a slight touch of wistfulness, "perhaps we would even have a chance to regain our lost sense of values."

He looked at Ruth, standing alarmingly close to the very edge of the weed-lined bluff, and for a moment her stance reminded him of the painted wooden figureheads on the old sailing vessels, her head boldly held high, the graceful profile sharply outlined against a tumbling gray bank of clouds, her hair streaming behind her, the firm small breasts defined by the wind that pressed her white blouse against the slender body. He could almost visualize her dipping into the sea and then triumphantly rising again like a nereid with the salt spray streaming from her body and glistening in her hair; only the incongruous tight faded blue jeans that encased her shapely lower form destroyed the fanciful image of an older time.

He felt for her again that sudden rush of love, that almost overwhelming desire to protect her with which sight of her always filled him, and the sense of shame and guilt at his failure to provide her with what comfort she needed most.

She turned to him, and he saw the agreement already shining in her lovely dark green eyes. He scarecely needed to ask the question.

"Well, what about it? What do you think?"

"Oh, yes, John, yes! Do let's take it!" The words tumbled from her lips like those of an eager child impatiently awaiting its gaily wrapped gifts at a birthday party.

He smiled at her enthusiasm; she had shown so little of it during recent months. "But we haven't even seen the inside of the house yet! It may be dirty, tumbled down, and not fit to live in!"

She laughed in her peculiarly infectious way, and his own smile broadened at the happy, healthy sound; he wondered when he had heard it last.

"Oh, no," she insisted. "It has to be every bit as perfect

as the outside! Anyone with the imagination to build a house like this in a spot like this would know just what to do with it. You have the key, John; let's go in and see.''

She grasped his hand and, both laughing in their sudden almost juvenile excitement, they rushed over the hard, wind-swept earth and mounted the sagging wooden steps to the veranda. The wind blew here somewhat less violently, and Ruth ran her slender artist's fingers through her thick black hair to repair the damage done, while John fished impatiently in his various pockets for the key they had secured at the real estate office in the sleepy little fishing village some two miles or so down the narrow, dusty road that ran parallel to the beach.

Ruth had first spotted the house from the roadway as they drove past, and had immediately commanded John to stop while she stepped out of the car and stared with fascination at the harshly angular structure looming against the sky; a pair of seagulls seemed to dip their wings in obeisance as they flew over the gables. Something had immediately drawn Ruth to the house, perhaps the air of loneliness or of arrogance with which it stood so starkly outlined against the horizon, the only sign of habitation in that silent and peaceful seaworld.

They had no reason to suppose the house was unoccupied, save for a certain undoubted air of vacancy, but Ruth would give him no peace until they determined this for themselves. To John's surprise, and Ruth's I-told-you-so attitude, the pleasant, sandy-haired agent in the town's only real estate office had confirmed that the house had stood completely vacant for a number of years and was now being let for the summer, completely furnished, by its owners who lived in quite another part of the country and never even bothered to visit their property; almost as an afterthought, he mentioned that the renter would also be given an option to buy, should he feel so inclined.

While John now fumbled angrily for the key . . . he

never could remember in which pocket he placed such things, and invariably found what he sought in the very last pocket he explored . . . and then struggled with a lock whose native stubbornness was angrily increased by the years of total neglect and disuse, Ruth strolled along the veranda, delightedly testing the squeaking, sagging floorboards, kicking at the dried leaves, using her handkerchief to swirl little portholes in the grime-covered window panes so she could peer into the dark interiors filled with shadowed corners and massive hulks of old furniture covered with yellowing dust sheets, all suggesting a shadowy, mysterious world of the past. Resting her hands carefully on the somewhat shakey and rather insubstantial wooden railing, she examined with intense interest the sharply dramatic contrast of the gauntly black bone-like branches of the bluff's single tree twisted against the background of the yellow-gray clouded sky.

"John, what kind of tree do you suppose this is?"

Struggling with the lock on the front door, John made no reply, merely muttering an exasperated "God-damn," which Ruth quite correctly assumed did not refer to any particular classification of flora.

"I don't believe I've ever seen a tree quite like this one," she continued as she moved further along the verandah to view the tree from another angle. The scarred trunk was the color of ebony glowing dimly in the fading light, and the bare branches had the look of petrification. A deep scar cutting along the center of the trunk might have been caused by fire. "It looks something like an ash, doesn't it? Or possibly a birch. I didn't know they grew in this part of the country."

"The only tree you've ever been able to identify correctly is a fir tree," John muttered, "because it reminds you of Christmas. You don't know a damn thing about trees."

Ruth sniffed and made a moue of distaste. "It smells, too. Unpleasantly. Sort of . . . I don't know what it is. It looks like it's been burnt. It seems . . . sad, somehow."

Crouched rather uncomfortably before the door, stabbing at the intransigent lock with the large metal key that he was beginning to suspect had never been intended to mate with this particular keyhole, John still didn't bother to glance up at his wife.

"That particular tree happens to be dead," he commented rather wryly. "Wouldn't you be sad?"

"I think that perhaps the sun came out from behind the clouds on one particular morning, and the tree died in the sheer ecstacy of raising its arms up to it in greeting," Ruth mused in that dreamy tone that always told John it was the impractical artist speaking.

He glanced now at his wife with a slightly distasteful expression; she looked almost like a slender young boy leaning with her hands against the railing. He suppressed a surge of yearning; no, not yet, not yet.

"Christ!" he swore. "If I ever put a line like that into one of my books, you'd laugh it right smack off the page."

"Perhaps it sounds better when I say it than when you write it!" Ruth kicked at a few of the scattered crimson-gold leaves that rustled along the veranda with a fragile sound like dried vegetative bones. "And where do you suppose these leaves have come from? There isn't another tree anywhere in sight."

"The sea wind isn't necessarily troubled by distance," John explained, returning his attention to the God-damned door.

There was a sudden sharp clicking sound, and John straightened himself with a smile of intense gratification as the heavy door with its decorated frosted glass panel swung slowly inwards.

"And now, Madame, if you can manage to bear up under the intense and woeful sorrow of mourning a dead tree and inspect our possible future abode . . ."

" 'Woeful sorrow' is a redundancy," Ruth commented as she quickly slipped past him and into the house.

"You'll never sell your books if you don't learn such things."

John followed her into the house, closing the door behind him, and they stood, suddenly silent, in the large spacious foyer, an elegant chamber composed of a solid dark wood which, despite the passing of time and the neglect of many years, still bore some of the high polish that had burished it a deep reddish brown that would surely have cast a warm glow of welcome to those entering the house.

"Oh, John, it's lovely!" Ruth sighed.

John could only agree with her as he swept his eyes over the burnished wood of the walls and the blue-veined white marble of the flooring. Against the far wall, a broad staircase curved its way to the second floor, lighted here and there by small circular windows like portholes set into the wall; the wooden bannister was delicately carved with twisting sea motifs. In the wall formed by the stairway depended a large chandelier whose crystals were dimmed by a thick coating of dust, strands of which dangled like a forest of white lianas in the motionless air. A large bare table, leaning somewhat because of a splintered leg, stood in the center of the foyer, and against one wall was an enormous grandfather's clock, its pocked face concealed by grime, its golden pendulum frozen in time in its glass case. On the wall beside the clock was a hatrack made of a massive solid piece of contorted driftwood whitened by the sea and spotted with sand and insect runnels; a small table stood beneath the rack. On the left side of the foyer two doors, slightly ajar, led to other rooms, with another single door to the right, at the foot of the stairs. A portrait-lined corridor running past the staircase reached to the rear of the house.

The effect was one of spacious elegance, of taste and a strongly masculine sense of beauty. The silence here was almost tangible, broken only by the strangely muted sound of the sea. The air was as stuffy as that of a long-sealed attic, and John felt an almost irrepressible desire to sneeze, created by floating motes of disturbed dust. Ruth embraced herself as against a chill, and suddenly realized she was shivering slightly.

"You can almost feel the past, can't you?" she asked softly. "You can almost reach out and touch it. You expect to see someone coming down those stairs."

"I imagine it's been quite some time since anyone's used those stairs," John whispered, looking at the thick carpet of dust on the wooden steps. Then he suddenly laughed, and his laughter resounded up the stairway and echoed through the well, effectively dispelling the sudden air of strangeness that had fallen upon them. "What are we whispering for? There's no one to hear us! Come on, let's see the rest of the place!"

There were large, airy, heavily panelled rooms with dark walls and loftly ceilings, again speaking of the artistic tase of the builder, cluttered with heavy dark furniture of a bygone era, some of it covered with yellowing dust sheets that provided an added touch of melancholy, as though they were attempting to conceal all the joys and sorrows that had been experienced here.

Everywhere the walls bore the expected framed paintings of swan-like clipper ships in full sail and sweeping seascapes which Ruth, having brushed away some of the coating of dust that covered them, declared rather patronizingly following a perhaps too perfunctory examination to be quite acceptable, although distinctly inferior to her own work in the genre. There were also numerous huge portraits in heavy gilt frames of bearded sea captains with full red lips and hawk-like noses posed in the time-honored costume of brass-buttoned coat and blue captain's cap; their piercing eyes seemed to follow them through the heavy layers of grime, dust and dirt, as they moved from room to room. There was sufficient resemblance in all these portraits to justify the assumption that they were all past members of the family that had built and apparently still owned the house. An impressive breed, John thought as he looked at the stern, iron-faced bearded visage in the large dusty portrait hanging over the living room mantel. Even through the gathered crust of an unknown number of years, there was a harshness, even something of a brutality in the face that stared back to him as though angry at this intrusion into the musty silence of the long-vacant house.

"I wonder what the current generation looks like," John mused as he stared into those steely eyes. "Strong families have a sad habit of decaying in later generations."

The living room was entered through the first door on the left side of the foyer and connected with the dining room, an impressively vast shadowed chamber boasting an enormous solid oak table lined with half a dozen heavy high-backed arm chairs; a massive silver candelabra, turned green with age and neglect, stood at either end of the table before an ornately carved centerpiece too thickly shrouded with dust to permit them to decipher its subject. The dining room could also be entered directly from the second foyer door, and there was another connecting door to the kitchen.

Feeling like wraiths from the distant past, they ascended the stairway to the second floor, kicking up little clouds of dust at every step. The master bedroom, largest of the three bedrooms on this floor, was situated on the side of the house that was flush with the very edge of the cliff itself. They stepped out onto the bedroom balcony, seeming to float freely in space, and felt an unnerving touch of vertigo as they looked down into the heaving, tumbling sea far below them.

"A perfect spot for a suicide leap!" Ruth muttered.

"You sound like Mrs. Danvers!" John retorted as he quickly stepped back from the dangers of the precipitous perch, grasping his wife by the arm and pulling her to safety, although Ruth had never shared his rather unmanning fear of heights.

At the end of the second floor corridor was a small, narrow door apparently leading up to the Widow's Walk; to their disappointment, the door was locked.

Their examination of the house confirmed the statement by Sanders that it had long been vacant. Wherever they looked the old-fashioned aspect of a more distant time was sharpened by the thick layers of dust that covered everything. Time had stopped here and been too weary to move on.

Yet both John and Ruth felt instinctively that here they had found exactly what they wanted for the several months they had determined to devote exclusively to themselves and their work, away from the chattering friends and the constant distractions and irritations of big city living, in hopes of realizing those achievements of which they both felt themselves capable, and of recapturing the happier early years of marriage . . . a marriage that, they both secretly admitted to themselves, was showing signs of disintegration.

The single door to the right of the foyer led to what had been a man's study, where dust had turned into sandy deserts the blue seas of a massive floor-standing globe and where a telescope, its brass green-tarnished with neglect, still pointed its single, sightless, dirt-encrusted eye towards the empty sea. John leaned on the tube and surveyed the handsome, masculine room with its heavy, stolid furniture, rows of dust-covered books on sagging wooden shelves, and a large, superbly crafted model of a sailing vessel whose sails had turned yellow with age and whose weakened rigging was hung with dangling strings of dust.

"Seems strange that all this stuff should have been left here like this," he muttered. "Why do you suppose this place has been abandoned for such a long time?"

Ruth was admiring the intricacies of a dull brass

sextant on the massive oaken desk, holding it in her hands in various positions to her eyes in hopes of seeing something of interest; she had always had the sneaking suspicion that captains claiming to shoot the sun as they looked through such complex instruments were actually looking at something quite different, like those watch-fobs men looked through to see a picture of a naked woman. She wondered vaguely, as she abandoned the effort and replaced the sextant amid the dusty clutter of the desk, if men still carried watch fobs, or if they had gone out with spats and golden watch chains.

"Some people just don't like living near the sea," she idly replied to her husband's comment. "I think it has something to do with the psychological effect of the constant rhythmic tidal roar, or something of that sort. Or maybe the owners just couldn't afford to keep up the place. Maybe their business keeps them away. Oh, there could be any number of reasons."

"But then why would they just leave everything here as it is?" John wondered. "All of this stuff may be outmoded today, but it's still good, solid material; the family obviously had excellent taste, and the means to indulge it. This place is filled with antiques from the days of sail. Some of it should bring a pretty good price. At least, it should be stored in a safer place, or be given to a seaport museum or something."

"Storage can be expensive, and not everyone is a philanthropist," she responded. "Could be the owners simply don't realize what they've got here. There may not be any seafarers in the family any longer."

"But still. . ." John said hesitantly.

Ruth wandered idly about the room, peering through the gathered grime at the paintings and blowing decades of accumulated dust from the books to gaze at their titles; not surprisingly, most of them dealt with the sea and sailing. She was impressed by the fine rich leather of the bindings.

"It's probably just cheaper to keep everything where

it is," she concluded.

"And accessible to thieves?"

She shrugged. "It's an isolated spot."

"All the more inviting to thieves."

"I don't imagine very many people come out this way. And I don't see any signs of attempted forced entry. The dust on the floors hasn't been disturbed for a very long time."

"Now you sound like Agatha Christie," John said. "Isn't that rather strange in itself?"

"Apparently they simply aren't very much concerned about thieves out here. Why else would the agent have merely given two complete strangers the key to the house so they could wander about at their leisure, instead of coming along to keep an eye on us and avoid any possible pilfering?"

"And that's another odd thing," he suggested.

She turned to him with a smile as she carefully leafed through the yellowed pages of an over-sized, weak-binded book on the Carribbean.

"How should I know all these things?" she asked. "I believe you're just trying to create a mystery for yourself. We should get out of the habit of big-city thinking. Maybe it just hasn't occurred to anyone to break in here."

John blew the dust from the large globe and peered at the African continent in order to determine the approximate date of the globe's construction; the mass of pink and purple that covered the Dark Continent took him briefly back to his school days. When he looked at his wife again, Ruth was staring at him with a wistfulness he well understood. He smiled again.

"It's really much too large for just the two of us, you know."

She nodded. "Of course it is. That could have its compensations too, I suppose. We would be able to keep out of each other's way during our periods of creative funk. And don't you dare deny that you have them as well as I do!"

"It's awfully dusty and old-fashioned," he continued, sweeping with his hand at a long string of dust trailing from the ceiling like a displaced light chain.

"Dust is easily removed with just a bit of elbow grease," she assured him, "and there's nothing terribly wrong about being a bit old-fashioned; I understand it's considered quite charming nowadays. If we insist on all the modern conveniences, we should never have left the city in the first place."

He looked at her over the globe, and they both grinned.

"You do want it, don't you?"

She nodded.

"No use arguing about it?"

She shook her head and crinkled the end of her small, slightly upturned nose. He quickly kissed her on the lips.

"Well, I know when I'm beaten. Okay. Let's go into town and see about the arrangements."

Suddenly fired with excitement and ambition, Ruth untied the red silk kerchief from about her throat and quickly and deftly converted it into a quite functional dust cap.

"You go and take care of that," she urged, stuffing her hair beneath the silk covering. "You don't really need me, and you know how hopelessly dense I am when it comes to business matters. I'd much rather start in on the cleaning. If we want to make this place liveable, there's a lot to be done. And you'd better pick up some groceries and things. Nothing very elaborate; I'm afraid the stove's capabilities are going to be severely limited, to say nothing of my own. I can go into town with you in a day or so to stock up on what we really want or need."

As she turned to leave the study, her eye was caught by the colorful spine of a book on the shelf near the door, and she took it into her hand, staring at the brilliant scarlet flames on a black background. She opened the cover and stared with surprise at the title.

"What do you suppose this book is doing here?" she asked.

John, preparing to leave for the village, rather indifferently asked. "What book?"

Ruth held the book up in her hand. "This one. Not what you would expect in this sea-faring library. It's the old *Malleas Malificarum. The Hammer of Witchcraft.*"

CHAPTER TWO

RUTH stood on the veranda and waved as their little red sports car disappeared in a swirl of yellow dust from the narrow road, and as the sound of its progress faded into silence, she became aware again of the utter stillness of the bluff, disturbed only by the distant sound of the sea which seemed here merely another part of the silence. There was no movement save for an occasional gull sweeping about the bluff on a current of air that soon carried it from her view. She missed the sound of birds, then realized there was nothing to bring them here.

She leaned for a moment against one of the veranda posts, her arms crossed, and looked at the seared dryness about her. Why had the house been placed in this particular spot, so alone, so far from all others, in the midst of this rather depressing aridity? The view, probably, yet the sweep of sea and sky, the yellowed sands almost totally unmarked by greenery, all merely emphasized that sense of loneliness. Perhaps that was the answer, after all. There are people who prefer loneliness. She was one of them. She felt a momentary rapport with the builder. Yes. He had understood. The sea was companion enough.

Her eyes were caught by an unexpected movement on the dry earth before her, and a small sand creature scampered quickly by on too many legs. How had it got up here, so far above the sea? It reminded her again that even in the driest lands, there was always the often unexpected sign of life. A slight breeze did not disturb the dark branches of the tree at the side of the house. She licked at the moisture on her upper lip and realized it had suddenly become considerably warmer. The sun was lower on the horizon, concealed by the bank of gray clouds, and the sea was like a mirror of heated glass. A storm approaching?

She stirred herself, muttered, "This is no way of getting anything done!" and re-entered the house.

For a moment she paused in the foyer and listened to the intense silence. The gathered stillness of unknown decades seemed to move in upon her. The house seemed to have been made for silence. It was difficult to imagine its rooms filled with the sounds of music and laughter. Had richly gowned women ever descended that sweeping stairway to preside as hostesses at dinner in that rather formidable dining room with its baronial chairs and dark wood paneling? Could a home once filled with life ever become so completely silent? And once so silent, could it ever be filled with life again?

She suddenly felt depressed by the total absence of sound. Her eyes moved to the grandfather's clock, and she wondered at what precise moment its pendulum had ceased to swing and the absence of its ticking had added to the quiet. She suddenly wished she could hear a sound, any sound, the barking of a dog outside, the swish of traffic on a wet street, the creaking of wooden timbers, the whistle of the wind around the corner of the house. It was simply too silent here. She shivered slightly.

"Oh, how ridiculous!" she scoffed at herself. "I came here to get away from all the noises that fill our air, and now I'm already complaining about the silence!"

She entered the living room and stood for a moment in the midst of the dustscape with her hands on her hips. This was going to be quite a task! There was dust everywhere, covering the protecting sheets, dangling from the darker corners, depending in lace-like streamers from the chandelier. Tiny motes of dust floated lazily on a weak sunbeam that did little to brighten the dirt-covered portrait over the mantle. The sheeted furniture seemed like massive alien forms ready to pounce upon her. A large lamp on the table near the windows boasted a shade of red glass from which dripped ruby pendants; its light would have provided a pleasant glow on the long, dark cold evenings of winter. The room would have been quite comfortable then. She blew lightly at the dust on the mantle, and her fingers traced the blue veins in the white marble.

She tried to imagine what this place would have been like in its earlier days. This had once been a home. People had lived here, been born here, probably died here. They had laughed and cried here, had known joy and pain, sorrow and happiness. Could it become a home again, for herself and for John? Perhaps old places like this, filled with the memories of those long gone, resented the intrusion of newcomers.

She and John had never really had a home of their own. They had lived since their marriage in a series of quite comfortable but totally anonymous apartments. No matter how long you lived in them, apartments could never really develop a personality as a house did. There was something too transitory about them. They always seemed to be waiting for the next occupants, and even those personal touches that everyone brings into his own home seemed temporary and never really accepted as a permanent part of the place. They would leave when you did. You left nothing of yourself behind in an apartment.

City living had been bad for them, proving deleterious not only to their artistic growth and achievement, but also placing a considerable strain upon their marriage. When their only child, the golden-haired Elinor, had met her death in a street accident . . . so recently that even now the remembrance of that sweet, now ever silent face clouded her vision with the mist of tears . . . they had determined to alter their mode of living, at least for a short time, and attempt to discover where they had gone so seriously wrong in their careers, in their marriage, and in their status as human beings.

It was surely even now not too late, she told herself again, as she had so often whispered to the concealing darkness of the night when she lay wakeful in bed and listened to John's even breathing. The love was still there between them, the passion that had ultimately expressed itself in the birth of their daughter. On how many dark nights had she tried to convince herself of that?

But love can not be lost. It may lie hidden, concealed by the detritus of their lives, but it was surely still there. And now it had been tragically rediscovered in the sudden loss of their only child. They needed each other now more than ever before. The old love needed only to be nurtured and treasured in order to regain all the golden splendor of those first wonderfully happy years when they were still young enough and perhaps foolish enough to believe quite sincerely that love really could conquer all. They were wiser now, and that would help. There was no need to speak of conquering anything but their own failings and shortcomings. Love must be strong enough for that. No, it could not be, it must not be, too late.

Having at last a home of their own would be something of a challenge for them, a test of their mutual affection and understanding. New surroundings, perhaps new standards or just revival of the old forgotten ones, new friends or no friends at all, just their own company and their reawakened love. They needed nothing more.

"No. Nothing more," she murmured to herself again. "That's all we need, John and I. Just each other. Nothing more, now or ever."

Ruth shook her head, as though trying to dismiss these thoughts from her mind. She did not like to think of the past. Since that terrible day, she had determinedly barred the past from her mind, and she was not going to let it return now. There was only the present and the future to think about now.

With some determined hammering of her fists and a bit of quite unlady-like cursing when a small but painfully sharp splinter of wood viciously drove itself into the soft palm of her right hand, Ruth managed to throw open the large windows. Sucking at the slightly bleeding wound in her palm, she breathed deeply of the fresh sea air, admitted once again into this world from which it had for so long been excluded, quickly replacing the musty stuffiness of the long-shuttered room. Coughing considerably at the disturbed clouds of long recumbent dust, she removed the furniture coverings and was pleased to see that the furniture, for the most part, was still in serviceable condition. Many of the pieces were hideously ugly, overstuffed chairs with lumpy cushions and wine-colored divans with faded braided designs, all dating from a distant time when esthetic value counted for considerably less than stolidity and permanence, but they could gradually replace these pieces when and if . . .

She brushed the dust from her jeans . . . luckily she had not surrendered to John's insistence that she should wear a dress when they first entered the village . . . and looked about her, wondering where to begin. Her most immediate need was a broom to sweep out those dark corners in which the dust had already piled itself into small desert sand hillocks.

The kitchen was easily the most depressing room in the house, quite obviously looked upon by its owner as a necessary utility, but not part of the living quarters of the house. The windows were smaller here and as a result the room was poorly lighted. The bare wooden chairs and table were like something from an army barracks. The enamel sink was badly stained and discolored, and in place of the refrigerator was an old-fashioned wooden icebox with two doors and a battered pan beneath, which now contained nothing but dust. One entire wall was occupied by the huge black iron bulk of the wood-burning stove, and she wondered where on earth, in this blasted area, one could possibly find enough wood to feed such a monster. The musty pantry was just as dreary, a small and narrow windowless room lined with dust-laden shelves and empty of all but a few rather badly battered pots and pans. Whatever modernizations had been made in the house had obviously not seeped over into the kitchen area.

And there was no broom anywhere in sight.

Ruth looked with a bit of uneasiness at the scarred, paint-peeling white door that obviously led into the cellar. She had always felt a most decided aversion for cellars. As a child, she had loved the attic in her old home, warm and comfortable and quiet, a bit musty and smelling of wood, filled with large wicker baskets that held faded reminders of the past. It was a childhood haven that became a perfect playground when the rain beat a lulling tatoo upon the roof, or when it was too cold to play out-of-doors. Then the attic had become her own mysterious world of grownup make-believe, where she would dress up in the old style, worn gowns stowed there, parading before the large dusty mirror that reflected a fabulous chamber of her own imagining. That was what an attic was for.

Cellars were something very different; they were darker, colder, less comfortable and reassuring worlds, the domain of the man of the house, where he descended for his mysterious hammerings and little 'odd jobs' that had to be done. Ruth had always had the feeling that unpleasant little crawling creatures with too many legs lurked everywhere in the dark, dank, neglected corners, just waiting to pounce upon her as she passed.

She put her hand uneasily on the cracked porcelain knob of the cellar door, finding it rather unpleasantly cold to the touch. She drew her lips into a firm line of determination and straightened her form, much like a child about to enter the frightening office of the school principal. This was all really too foolish. A cellar is, after all, only a cellar, and this one was undoubtedly as completely deserted as the rest of the house. Besides, she had to have a broom, and the cellar seemed the only likely place to find one.

Ruth opened the door very slowly, absurdly grateful that it did not creak on its hinges, and cautiously stepped onto the top of the stairs, bending slightly to peer into the gathered gloom. Her hand reached for and pressed the light switch just beside the door before she remembered there would be no power, and the thought of the darkness was an added discomfort; hopefully, restoration of the electricity would be one of the first matters John would attend to while in town. Holding onto the shakey wooden bannister, she started slowly down the rather steep wooden steps, narrowing her eyes against the darkness; the light coming through the small, encrusted, grimy windows was extremely limited.

There seemed nothing in the least unusual about this particular cellar, and that was somewhat heartening. Dusty gray asbestos pipes criss-crossed directly under the low ceiling, and the single chamber was filled with that confusing paraphernalia that always finds its way into such places. There were bits of heavy tackle, broken chairs, wooden crates, even a large rusted ship's anchor leaning against the far wall. To the left rear a large black pot-bellied furnace obstructed her view of the furthest corner; she assumed that corner was as dirty and cluttered as the rest of the cellar. Several white-painted iron stanchions supported the great weight of the house.

Why did the term 'ominous' come to mind, she wondered? And why was it she could not even hear the sea? The stillness was almost tomb-like, and the comparison did nothing to soothe her sudden uneasiness.

But at least there was a broom. She spotted the rather sorry-looking implement leaning against the wall near the furnace. Instinctively making herself as small as possible, so as to avoid coming into physical contact with anything that might depend from the ceiling . . . she had never been able to distinguish between a cobweb made of dust and one produced from a spider's nasty entrails . . . she walked past the furnace and picked up the broom.

She shook her head; this would not be of much use. It looked like something that had outlived its usefulness and crawled down into the cellar to die, or like the upper gum of an old haradin who had lost most of her teeth and could now only gum her way through what remained of her life. Always a bit frightened that she might happen to espy some kind of little creature scurrying for protection in some dark corner, she glanced about in hopes of finding something a bit more serviceable.

It was only then that Ruth noticed the small door on the other side of the furnace, and realized that this rear portion of the cellar was quite different from the rest of it, completely clear of debris of any kind, save for the coating of dust on the level earthen floor. The shape of the furnace had concealed from her the fact that there was a second room here, effectively partitioned off from the rest of the cellar by an earthen wall. There was a heavy door made of unusually dark wood reinforced with strips of rust-tarnished metal; the door stood only very slightly ajar.

Curious, still holding onto the woebegone broom, Ruth approached the door and attempted to push it open, but all her efforts were unable to budge it; it either was simply too heavy for her or it had become warped by time and damp and settled into the hard dirt of the floor. She placed her eye to the small opening, but she could see nothing; she had no more success in trying to peer through the narrow slit between the door and the jamb. There was very little light in the room, that probably coming through a single small window as thickly covered with dirt as were all the others in this vacant house, and from what little she was able to discern, the room appeared completely empty. She had a distinct impression of a greenish hue, and wondered if the window had been painted over, or perhaps was covered with a green fabric; people sometimes did that to cellar windows, although she could never understand why. The window would overlook the sea; the room must be immediately beneath the master bedroom, with the first floor of the house between.

It was at this moment that the first light touch of fear came to her like the unexpected, delicate flicking of a feather across her face. A strange, nauseating odor seemed to emanate from the small room, and Ruth was suddenly aware that the door on which her hand rested was almost painfully cold to the touch. A peculiarly drawing undercurrent of cold air seemed to be trying to pull her into the room, prevented from doing so only by the solidly fixed position of the door. A knot of fear twisted in her stomach, and she felt suddenly seized by an almost retching nausea as a wave of faintness passed over her; she was revived when her forehead made rather sharp contact with the door.

Ruth stepped quickly back from the strange door and the peculiar sensation passed as quickly as it had come. When she again carefully and gingerly placed her hand upon the surface of the door, it was no longer quite so cold.

Then she suddenly realized that the intense, morgue-like silence of the cellar had been broken. It was as though the sea had discovered some unsuspected flood. She heard the shattering crash of the breakers, the gurgling of the tide, the swish of foaming waves crashing upon a hard sanded beach. The sounds of all the seven seas of the world seemed to surround her, sweeping into her mind and casting her into a whirling maelstrom of fear.

And yet, she could see nothing. When she whirled about, fearing to see a massive wall of green-white water cascading down upon her, she saw nothing whatever. There was only the cellar, dark and empty and undisturbed save for her own presence. Yet still the air screamed with sound.

With a sharp cry of fear, Ruth dropped the mis-begotten broom and rushed for the stairs. She stumbled on the first step and fell heavily against the wood; ignoring the sharp pain where the edge of the step dug into her right side, she picked herself up and dashed up the remaining steps and into the kitchen, quickly and heavily slamming the door shut behind her.

For several moments she stood with her back pressed to the closed door, her eyes shut, perspiration beading her forehead, breathing heavily and trembling slightly, while the tumultuous sea noises slowly faded from her mind and the deep silence returned, broken only by the more muted, natural sounds of the surf outside. Slowly, she opened her eyes. Nothing in the kitchen had changed . . . the time-scarred table, the ancient stove, the barren shelves, the cheerless gloom. There was not the slightest sound save for the ever-present rolling of the sea, somewhat more distant in this back part of the house.

With a quick, startled gasp, she stepped away from the cellar door, as though its touch had suddenly burned her, and looked at its bare, innocent, streaked whiteness for a moment. No sound, no emanation came from behind it. Very carefully, as though fearing something might wait just behind to leap out at her, Ruth opened the door just a crack and placed her ear to the narrow aperture.

She could hear nothing. There was only the intense silence; she should have become accustomed to that by now, for silence was part of this old house. No waves, no breakers, no roaring surf. Not the slightest sound of any kind. Nothing on the other side of the door but the always somewhat ominous stillness of a strange, dark cellar. That's all it was, after all, she told herself. Just another dark cellar, containing nothing more dangerous or alarming than a small, long-legged spider weaving its sticky web in the dark corner, or a cricket briefly shattering the stillness as it rubbed its hind legs together, or a millipede rippling over the asbestos of a covered pipe. Only that and the figments of her own imagination.

"This is just plain ridiculous," she muttered to herself with considerable irritation as she brushed a fallen lock of hair back from her forehead. "Absolutely ridiculous. I'm acting like a frightened child."

Nervously running her hands over her jeans to efface the dusty marks of her fall on the stairs, Ruth warily walked from the kitchen and through the dark, narrow hallway lined with paintings of bearded sea captains whose eyes had not yet completely lost their lascivious glances, and out onto the veranda.

The slightly cooler air blowing across the bluff reached her at once as she sat, still trembling with remembered fear, on the top step, wrapping her arms about her raised legs and resting her chin on her knees, and tried to compose herself while attempting to understand just what had happened.

The solution Ruth naturally wanted most to accept was that actually nothing had happened at all. Surely all of this could easily be rationalized. It was probably merely the result of her own overly active imagination, combined with the events of the day. The excitement of finding this marvelous old house by the sea, an unsatisfactory dream-haunted sleep the night before (her nights now were seldom really restful), and the fact she had eaten nothing really substantial all day long save for a very light breakfast and it was now approaching evening . . . all this could very easily explain away those peculiar sensations she had experienced in the cellar.

"There's really nothing to it at all," she told herself. "All I have to do is think about it cooly and sanely."

She obviously had rested her head against the naturally colder metal strips on the door rather than on the wooden frame itself, hunger had brought about that brief touch of nausea, increased by the foul air of the long-closed cellar, and the imagined sounds of the roaring seas had been nothing but the blood rushing to her ears, undoubtedly caused by the touch of nausea.

"There it is," she told herself with some satisfaction, rather pleased at her little exercise in common-sense reasoning. "That's all there was to it;' very simple. The mind can do mighty peculiar things to you, but a rational explanation can be found for all phenomena if you just look hard enough." She nodded again with deliberate firmness. "Of course. That's all there was to it."

She shook her head and smiled as she rose again to her feet, leaning against the pillar as she rubbed the soreness of her side where she had come into such sudden contact with the hard edge of the cellar step; there was also a slight discomfort, beginnings of a headache, from striking her head against the door. It all served her right. She had surrendered to unreasoning panic. It was ridiculous to be so foolish. She would really have to get hold of herself.

Slowly, the uneasiness of her few moments in the dark cellar began to fade, and the knot in her stomach unwound itself. It was difficult to be afraid out here. The world seemed so calm, so serene, so at peace; fear had no place here. She looked about, seeking the further comfort of these thoughts.

The sky had become somewhat darker than it had been. Was it the approach of evening? She glanced at her watch. No, it was still a bit too early for that. An approaching storm, then? It had been threatening all day. The sea and horizon had merged into one almost solid gray wall, and she found it difficult to determine just where one began and the other ended. If there was a storm coming, she hoped John would be back before it broke. She feared electrical storms, with all their noise, flashing brilliance, violence and possible danger. She smiled again. Another of her many fears. John did not always have an easy time of it.

There was no sign of gulls about the clifftop now; didn't they generally move further inland at the approach of a storm? For the first time, she noticed a small black speck on the horizon, probably a fishing vessel returning to its home, also running ahead of the storm, and she wondered fleetingly about the lives of those on board. A sudden gust of wind swept across the veranda, and the sad tree moaned in sorrow as it bowed before its touch.

Ruth sighed and stirred herself. John would at any rate be back before long, and she had made absolutely no progress in her cleaning. Perhaps it would be best to start in the kitchen. John would surely be as hungry as she, and they should at least have a clean table on which to enjoy their first meal in this new home. She had better examine the stove more closely, too; it would undoubtedly present numerous little problems of its own to a rather indifferent cook accustomed to the most modern of kitchen equipment. She wondered again why the obvious modernizations in the house had not been extended to the kitchen. Perhaps the owners considered the kitchen not a part of their own domain; it belonged to the servants. How many servants had there been here during the heyday of the house?

Oh, and what about the bedroom? Somehow, there seemed to have been a tacit agreement between them that they would be spending the first night here at the house despite its temporarily rather primitive arrangements, rather than at the hotel in the village. (She vaguely recalled there was such a place, a rather unimpressive three storied structure somewhere in the rather unimpressive little square of the rather unimpressive little town.) For the first time, she became curious about the bed clothing on the shelves in the huge closets upstairs; when you leave a place, you generally take such things with you, no matter what else you may leave behind. It all looked clean enough, but it would surely require at least an airing, and that had better be done before the breaking of the impending storm.

She ran her hands through her hair, stretched herself, and sighed again, breathing heavily of the sharply bracing air before returning to the lingering stuffiness of the house. A breath of sadness touched her when she suddenly thought how Elinor would have loved this place, how she would have run along the beach, played at tag with the breaking waves, squealing with delight as she danced back from the cold salty touch, examining with the insatiable curiosity of the very young the minute aspects of marine life tossed upon the beach, holding shells up to her ear and thrilling to the mysterious sound of the sea . . .

No, no, she mustn't think of Elinor. Not yet. At some future time, when she could remember only the happier days they had known together and push to the back of her mind the darkness of her little daughter's end, and the terrible knowledge that there would be no future happiness for her, then it would be all right to think of Elinor, but now there must be only John and herself.

She wouldn't mention anything to John about her foolishness in the cellar. He would only laugh at her. And worry, too. Her nerves had been very bad since Elinor's death. There had been too many nights when she had awakened from her nightmares, crying out with vaguely remembered fears, and John had been forced to spend the remainder of the night lying uncomfortably with his arms around her weeping form, trying to bring her the peace and comfort that seemed to have departed forever from their lives. It was partly John's concern over this aspect of her health that had led to his suggestion of a brief hiatus away from the city. There was no point in reminding him. The fears were still there, but they must lie concealed, for another greater fear had been added. It was the fear of losing John.

Fear, fear. Her life was composed of fears, a destructive force that preyed constantly on her mind and nibbled like a cancer at the marriage she could now, more than ever before, not bear to lose.

As she started into the house again, Ruth remembered that she was still without a broom; the only one in the house still lay in the cellar where she had dropped it in her panicky flight. Well, she would manage without it.

CHAPTER THREE

FOR the first time in too many months, John felt reasonably satisfied with life as he headed the car down the narrow dirt road and toward the village, and undoubtedly his surroundings were largely responsible for this surprising sense of euphoria. He breathed deeply of the fresh sea air and glanced at the broad expanse of ocean to his right. It felt good to be here.

A strong love for the sea was a deeply ingrained aspect of his basic nature. Several of his ancestors had been seafaring men . . . some of the more distant members from the English side of his family, he strongly suspected, had not always been too careful or particular about the color or the composition of the flags under which they sailed . . . and he himself had served as a naval officer for a period of three years.

In retrospect, John often thought of those three years as perhaps the happiest and most satisfying time of his life. During that rather colorful and masculine time, he had never shared in the constant grumblings and complaints of his companions about the rigors and restrictions of sea duty as compared to the greater freedom and the practically unlimited sexual opportunities of being shore based, for he had always loved the gentle rolling of a good ship beneath his feet, the dashing of salt spray into his flushed face as he stood in the dipping prow during a North Atlantic storm, the soothing shooshing sound, almost like the gently amorous whispers of a lover, that the sea made as it swept carressingly along the smooth metal sides of a swiftly moving vessel.

The sea seemed to take him back to a much simpler time when, for a short period, he was able to put behind him the increasing irritations of a constantly more complex and nerve-straining society. He found a mind-soothing restfulness in a calm, clear night at sea, with a sky ablaze with stars whose brilliance was undimmed by the haze and smog of a big city, with the silver platter of the moon reflected in the gently rolling swell that concealed a myriad of life totally alien and apart from that of civilized man. Surely at one time all the world must have been like this: calm, quiet, uncluttered. How different the world must have been before the explosion of population had converted Earth into a circular Tower of Babel filled with constant noise where it became almost impossible for man to get off by himself and make an attempt to come to grips with the truly important basics of life. A quiet forest could provide that opportunity to some extent, yet even the small sounds of nature, the soughing of a breeze through the trees, could be distracting. The land was never the same, ever changing or being changed by the arrogance of man, but the sea remained an unchanging constant, and he could feel a kinship with the great sea travelers of the past, for the sea upon which they had traveled was the same that now carried him . . . the Phoenicians and the Greeks sailing about their blue Mediterranean and afraid of the unknown terrors beyond the fabled Pillars of Hercules, the hardier and more daring Vikings reaching tentatively across the great unknown oceans, the adventurers to the mysterious New World.

He had often regretted not having lived during the more exciting days of the great clipper ships, with their billowing canvas like man-created cumulous clouds against the blue sky, the creaking of the rigging and the dipping of the painted figurehead at the prow, the tall sturdy masts pointing the way to adventure.

He smiled at his own thoughts. He was only another man born out of his time, a constantly increasing breed in the uneasy modern, mechanistic and materialistic world. Certainly it was rather a foolish attitude.

"People are never fully satisfied with their time," one of his more learned shipmates had once said, somewhat irritated by his constant glamourizing of the past. "It's a matter of looking at the past through the wrong end of a telescope. Your beautiful sailing vessels were small and cramped, often officered by sadistic brutes and manned by seamen of the lowest caliber, dirty and filled with vermin. To a romantic, the past is always more beautiful than it actually was. There's really no such thing as the good old days; it's only today that matters. Christ, how can you be so God-damned romantic and still write such garbage?"

No matter. Reason has no place in a man's fantasies.

It was, in a sense, the sea that had given him Ruth, for they had met for the first time against the soothing background of waves lapping slumberously upon a sandy shore. John's doctor, concerned over a too lengthy period of persistent illness, had been responsible.

"I'm warning you, John," the grim doctor had said after a lengthy examination. "You've got to get away. You're working yourself much too hard. You worry a lot, don't you? Well, we all do these days. You become too easily irritated. You're tight as a drum. You've got to chuck it all, have a really long vacation, or I won't answer for the consequences."

"I can't get away just now," John complained as he rebuttoned his shirt, still irritated by the medical fact that a stethoscope must always be apparently chilled before use. "Too much to do. There's a new book . . ."

The doctor almost threateningly pointed the cold instrument at him again, and John quickly completed the task of covering his chest. "You either get away, or you won't have to worry about that new book. Hypertension's nothing to play around with, John, and you've got a grade A case of it."

John paused, despite himself impressed by the seriousness of the doctor's tone. "But where would I go? I've just come back from Europe . . .

"Europe's no good for you right now," the doctor insisted. "I don't mean that kind of getting away. In Europe you'd do exactly the same things you do here, only in different surroundings. You'll spend most of your days poking around in cluttered museums and dusty palaces, and most of your evenings in a cocktail lounge. You need something completely different. I mean you have to get really away, where there's nothing special to see or do but relax. Someplace quiet and peaceful. The islands, maybe."

John had never really cared for the warmer southern regions and seas, with their strangely phosphorescent turquoise waters so clear that you could hover in a boat on the surface and watch the gliding, spastic life beneath you, somewhat like a space creature hovering over the strange planet Earth to observe the curious pattern of life on an alien world. The southern seas were too deceptive, the waters always so calm and beautiful, like the mirrored marble pools in a tale from the *Arabian Nights*, until treacherously whipped into dangerous maelstroms of fury by the angry breath of a hurricane.

No, he much preferred the more northerly waters, green seas flecked with touches of white, moving in great, swelling rollers, never concealing their strength behind the beautiful vapid facade of a tropical night. There was excitement in such waters, daring, a challenge that did not exist in the waters to the south.

But the doctor refused to listen to any such arguments. "I don't care what you say," he responded in a no-nonsense tone. "There are lots of smaller islands where you won't be joining a tourist innundation. You do as I suggest, or within a year's time, I'll be looking for another patient, and you won't be needing another doctor."

And so, reluctantly conceding that the slow and lazy life of the tropics probably would be more conducive to recovery than the more rapid and pressurized areas of the more northern climes that he preferred, John had obeyed his doctor's orders and turned his way south.

He had no reason to regret that decision, for it was their mutual love for the sea that had first brought him and Ruth together on that peacefully beautiful tropical night when he sat all alone on the dark and deserted beach, his back resting rather uncomfortably against the rough bole of a slender curved palm tree, one hand idly tracing meaningless figures in the soft warm sand, his gaze fixed unseeingly out to the star-brightened horizon, as he fell into a deeply melancholy reverie, pondering upon his unhappy past and his uncertain future.

Although his life could not be considered a failure, John had little enough reason to be satisfied with himself. He had found a modicum of success as a writer, but he was the first to admit that his work was shallow and impermanent, and he knew himself capable of better things. Somehow, he had never found the time, nor the necessary concentration, nor the driving ambition to do the work he sensed he could accomplish. When he completed another of his rather tawdry little sex-spiced spy thrillers, he always determined that this must now be the line of division; now he must get himself down to some more serious writing.

But always it had been postponed still further. Another book was demanded by his publishers; another book was needed by himself in order to maintain the strangely continually fluctuating bank account. He lived well, and he was not willing to lower his standard of comfort for the strictly egotistical sense of artistic achievement. Just one more crude money-maker, one more pot-boiler, one more of that bit of claptrap so popular with the largely unschooled reading public who haunted the lurid racks of the paperback displays. Just enough to get his balance to a certain comfortable figure, and then he would concentrate on something really important.

But one comfortable bank balance pointed the way to another even more comfortable, and he would decide to wait just a bit longer. He wasn't really fooling himself. He realized fear was responsible; he just did not want the flow of royalty checks to run dry. Right or wrong, he felt that dry critical appraisal could not take the place of the approval of the money-spending public.

Perhaps there was another fear as well: the fear that he might discover he was not really capable of the achievement he planned. He refused to think about that.

But his doctor's warnings had frightened him. He was one of the hardy breed, unaccustomed to poor health, who have little use for doctors until 'something goes wrong,' and then feel a sudden sense of panic when they are informed there really is something wrong. A few weeks of hiatus from the boredom of his own writing would do him no harm.

What he actually did was merely to change one form of boredom for another. After only two weeks, he'd already had more than enough of whispering palms, of sex-starved beauties with their breasts cascading from their prisons of too small halters, of perspiration trickling down to the small of his back, and of over-sized hard-shelled bugs crawling into his bed and sinking their fire-tipped fangs into his tender flesh.

He simply had to do something to ease the boredom. It occurred to him that, despite his doctor's insistence on total relaxation, he might use this time to make at least a beginning at last on the work he had for too long postponed. It wouldn't have to be much. Just a beginning, an outline, a first draft. There would be no pressure, he could work slowly and thoughtfully, and thus not really go counter to his doctor's orders.

He enthusiastically ensconced himself on the small terrace of his hotel room, overlooking the calm blue sea, with a cooling drink at his elbow and the typewriter before him, and with a sense of renaissance settled himself to begin work.

It was just no good. Even his fingers seemed clumsy and unable to find the right keys. His thoughts were muddled and refused to sort themselves into any recognizable form. His eyes wandered constantly to the sea and he found himself thinking of fantasies that had no connection with what he was trying to do. His mind was benumbed in this stifling, enervating atmosphere, and he finally admitted he could hope to accomplish nothing until he returned home again.

And that, of course, would only mean the resumption of that same round of waste, the same vacuous social activities to which he was obligated by his position and his profession, the same comfortable but empty apartment, the same hours spent at a typewriter churning out meaningless words while attempting to ignore the nagging ache in his head left as a scolding reminder of the previous night's activities.

And for the first time, John now suddenly found himself suffering from a sharp sense of loneliness. He had never minded it before. At thirty years of age, he was still a bachelor and seemed likely to remain so. With the sole exception of a marvelous, aging, but still continually active maternal grandmother, he was quite alone in the world. That had never really bothered him. For the young, the term "loner" has a rather rakish connotation, one that brought knowing leers into the eyes of erstwhile bachelors and slight reprimands from hopeful mothers with marriageable daughters. He had always been rather proud of his independence and his rejection of the social regulations that insisted every man must abide by the mores of his time, must select one person to whom he would supposedly remain faithful throughout the remainder of his life, purchase a home, raise a family, and become a respected, stolid citizen of the community. It was part of the rules of being a member of the human race.

Well, that just wasn't the kind of life for him. No, sir. So he had always thought. Now, quite suddenly, perhaps spurred by this totally unexpected illness, the word *alone* hammered at his mind. What would happen to him once the social life began to pall, when the readily accessible sexual partners turned to younger and more active men, when it was too late to find that one special person with whom to spend his approaching twilight years? What would happen when the wellsprings of his imagination ran dry, and he no longer had the catharsis of work (no matter of what value) to relieve the encroaching boredom? He was thirty years old, for the first time his health had gone back on him, and who could tell what lay ahead? The sudden, unexpected spectre of middle age frightened him, and he was suddenly afraid of being alone.

Sitting on the beach that night . . . alone again, when all about him were younger couples with clasped hands and dreamy eyes . . . he ran the sands through his fingers and made the rather banal comparison of the swiftly running sands of his own life. He sensed there was something a bit foolish in his attitude, but that provided no comfort. Was that great novel of his really nothing more than an empty egotistical dream, one shared by hack writers throughout the world and all time? He could not write it here and he could not write it at home. Perhaps he was incapable of writing it at all. How long could he continue to fool himself? In a sudden self-pitying glimpse of the future, he saw himself humped over his typewriter beside piled reams of paper, his arthritic fingers moving slowly over the keys, old, embittered, and alone.

He was in this deeply depressed state of mind when

Ruth entered his life, strolling slowly along the beach towards him, walking with measured steps right at the water's edge, letting the dying surge of each wave lick weakly at her feet as though in hopes of finding renewed life there, pondering her own considerable unhappiness and dissatisfaction with her career as an artist.

It was very late, and the beach had become deserted. He was rather startled when she came unexpectedly into view. She was wearing a simple white dress, and at first as she approached him out of the darkness, he had mistaken her for the white moonlit curling of an incoming wave. As the spot of white came closer, he recognized the unmistakeable feminine figure that was outlined, although not overly emphasized, by the gold mesh-belted dress she wore. She walked with bare feet, carrying her shoes in one hand draped over her left shoulder, and her dark hair framed her face as she ambled with her head down, her features etched in silver by the sharp moonlight. He was reminded of a nereid rising from the sea, of a clothed Botticelli Venus. The waves behind her were tipped with a phosphorous glow, and he wasn't quite certain if the stars twinkled in the clear sky or in her hair.

She paused at the edge of the surf and looked out to the star-sprinkled horizon, searching there for something or for nothing. There was in her a deep sense of lack of fullfillment that made her rather minor achievements in the difficult world of art seem empty and unimportant. She wanted . . . something . . . yet even she could not say just what that something might be. Like John, she had often turned to the calmness of the sea in times of trouble, finding its peace and grandeur conducive to clear thinking, but somehow even that had failed her this time. The answer was not out there. Perhaps there was no answer.

It was not until later that John learned how closely her attitudes matched his own, but he sensed them even on that first night of their meeting. There was in her slight figure, as she stood motionless staring at the vast rhinestoned emptiness of sea and sky, a touching aura of loneliness that reached out to John and instantly made them seem less like strangers.

She sighed and seated herself on the scanty grass at the beach edge, unaware of John's presence until he brought himself to her notice with a slight embarrassed cough.

Somehow . . . they could never quite recall how it had happened, or who had made the first move, for it was unlike either of them to become so immediately involved with strangers . . . they had fallen into conversation and discovered those various aspects of life that they shared in common . . . a love of beauty, a desire for achievement, a dissatisfaction with the status of their lives, and the loneliness of the creator that places him always apart from others.

They talked for hours on that first evening, while the great silver tropical moon etched the fronds of the palm behind them against a deep blue cloudless sky over which some giant had tossed a double handful of diamonds. They discussed life, art and dreams; they talked of hope and futility. They were two suddenly lonely people reaching out for reassurance that they were not truly alone. John found himself extending an invitation to dinner for the following evening, and Ruth just as surprisingly found herself instantly accepting.

That next evening John found his lonely barefoot beach girl transformed into a quite strikingly lovely young woman with shimmering chestnut hair and deep eyes, a slightly curved nose and a quick, dimpled smile, while she saw a trim and slender fair-haired man, attractive rather than handsome, several years older than herself, who was both charming and comfortable to be with. She wondered at the uneasiness that so often appeared in his blue eyes, and he caught the lines of strain that occasionally creased the corners of her mouth.

That first dinner was just the beginning, and soon they were spending all their time together, strolling through the gaudy, crowded areas of the colorful native quarters, applauding the pleasantly twanging music of the steel bands which neither had cared for until the moment they first heard them together, for the first time sensing the genuine warmth in the friendly brown faces so often slashed with the whiteness of a toothed smile. Quietly, they shared the beauties of the sea and sand world about them, and gradually they began to feel a lessening of the loneliness that plagued them both.

John vaguely recalled seeing some of Ruth's sea paintings in a small art gallery off Fifth Avenue in New York, and he was relieved by her guileless admission that she had never read any of his work.

There was more moonlight, the very special romantic moonlight that is the provenance of tropic nights, long evenings refreshing themselves with fruit-filled tropical drinks on the seaside veranda of the hotel, midnight walks along the beach, the somewhat guilty relief of both when they first saw each other in bathing costume. There came the seemingly casual clasp of hands and the first unexpected kiss. Neither was particularly interested in the fleeting romance that was so attractive to most of the visitors to the island, and it somehow never occurred to either to extend what now appeared a budding romance into sexual exploration. His illness had dulled John's normally strong sexual drive, and Ruth's own inclinations had been chilled by a very brief, extremely tumultuous marriage whose scars had not yet completely faded.

And yet, both somehow knew they could not return to their old world without the comfort, warmth and understanding they had suddenly discovered in each other, and by the time they finally left the islands for the more mundane society in which they were required to seek their livings, they had suddenly and, again, quite unexpectedly, become man and wife, brought together by their mutual loves, emotions, and needs.

It had started as a very promising marriage, despite the rather snide and sarcastic remarks of John's friends that he was simply not the marrying kind, and of Ruth's friends that he was really far too old for her, and there were perils in marriage with a man nearly six years her senior. For the first few months they had enjoyed the shared experience of discovering each other. Perhaps more important, for the first time they felt themselves no longer alone. A new richness had entered John's life, a warmth and happiness he had never thought possible, and he wondered how he could have lived so long without it.

They traveled a great deal during those first months, to the museums of Paris and the palaces of Vienna, to the silence of departed Rome and the honey-colored columns of Greece, filling their lives with the beauties of the past and the happiness of the present. They both put aside their work for a time and sought some of the enjoyment of life which they had always been too busy to grasp. They thrilled anew to the treasures of the Louvre, the peaceful beauty of the Greek isles, the rich panoply of British monarchy. Life took on a new golden patina, and all the world was more richly colored.

While they were in London, John with some trepidation introduced his wife to his Grandmother Ellen in her suite at the Savoy. There was no need for concern. The *grande dame* and the young artist took to each other at once, and became friends.

But life cannot be composed of pleasure alone and, inevitably, the time came at last when they had to return to the corrosive pressures of their artistic social world, which they both claimed to despise and for which they both found it constantly necessary to prostitute themselves, and the insidious erosion began, eating at the very foundations of their mutual love and trust, and their so bright and happy world became darkly shadowed.

Perhaps they both tried too hard in their respective chosen fields; real success, as opposed to the slipshod achievements of sex-filled paperbacks and lurid magazine illustrations, seemed to elude them. The ability was unquestionably there for both of them, but more and more it became apparent that time and inclination were not. They were kept too busy with other things, too involved in making those supposedly invaluable contacts that ultimately proved quite useless, too intense about convincing others (and perhaps themselves most of all) that they were really greater and more gifted than anyone believed them to be, and would someday reveal their genius to the world. They were too concerned about being seen in the right places and with the right people, too involved in enjoying the very vapidness of their lives. All of this was of inestimible value to their careers, they insisted, knowing the misstatement was only a lie they simply lacked the courage to face. As time passed without the expected achievement, fear returned to both of them, and their activities became an almost hysterical frenzy in which neither could bear the time to be alone and face the truth.

Their work suffered, and soon so did their marriage. Certainly they still loved each other just as deeply if not quite as gloriously as they had under the bewitching moon of a tropical island, but they no longer seemed to find the time to express that love in the many little, meaningful ways they should. John was always too immersed in the complex plot entanglements of his latest spy thriller, then Ruth was too concerned with the exactly proper delicate shadings of another painting, and then they were both simply too preoccupied with other things and too frightened by their own un-certainties. The necessary words remained unsaid, life began to resemble little more than a still fairly comfortably habit, and the love began to turn stale. They began to feel a sense of mutual boredom. Worse, they began to quarrel. There were recriminations, tears, re-conciliations, and irreparably damaged feelings.

The birth of Elinor came as something of a surprise for both of them. It seemed to startle them into realizing they had still occasionally found the time and the inclination for the kind of intimacy that could result in the birth of a child. John perhaps felt a slight embarrassment at becoming a first time father at his age, while Ruth resented the necessary curtailment of activities caused by her period of pregnancy.

But their little daughter, that winsome child with curled blonde hair and twinkling blue eyes, looking so much like an illustration from a book of tales by the brothers Grimm, or the model for a Hummel figure, had helped, at least for a time, to bring them together again, but even the small hands of this sincerely loved child could not quite fill the emptiness of two hearts that could exist on love only with the added spice of creativity.

And then, one bright sunny afternoon, Elinor had stepped out into the street—toddled would be a more accurate term, for she was still so little more than a baby, incurably inquisitive about that great noisy world just beyond her nursery window—and sudden death had rushed upon her on burning rubber wheels. The screeching of the brakes, the shrill screams of the horrified bystanders, the sharp frightened cry of their only child suddenly facing a terror and pain she could not begin to understand, tore into the tenuous fabric of their empty lives and brought them a terribly sharpened sense of reality.

They both blamed themselves for what had happened, but quietly and tacitly avoided blaming each other. Again, they had simply been too busy, too completely involved in their own creative problems, too withdrawn into their own so-called artistic worlds to heed the very real world about them. Each had thought the other was looking after their child, and so Elinor had freely wandered alone to her death.

Over their poor child's grave, that pitifully small, flower and ribbon bedecked mound of fresh brown earth concealing those little white hands that had been unable to hold them together, Ruth and John had sworn to abandon this aimless existence that was destroying their lives, their creativity, and their marriage, and seek a renewal in a more peaceful and ordered existence. As they walked away from the fresh grave, a light breeze stirred a white gauze ribbon bearing the words REST IN PEACE in glittering letters of gilt, and it was like Elinor's little hand waving them goodbye.

The weeks that followed had been extremely difficult for both of them. Even attempts at creativeness came to a complete stop, while they both moved dreamlike through a world that had so suddenly changed color, that no longer contained the light laughter of their daughter, as they desperately tried to understand what had happened to them. Hadn't they realized before it was too late how deeply they had loved their little girl?

Ruth found it impossible to believe that the little blonde child called Elinor no longer existed, not anywhere in this world, that this beautiful entity who had just begun her life was no longer there, that all the long years of promise, of happiness, of sorrow that were her human birthright had been so abruptly discarded and would now never be experienced. They could find neither relief nor solace in the benumbing trappings of religion, for how could they believe in a God who punished the erring parents by taking the life of an innocent child? Driven by guilt as much as by sorrow, Ruth's nerves threatened to give way, and in the suddenly lonely and frightening nights, she lay in John's arms and wept away the dark hours, fearful of sleep because of the terrible nightmares of her beautiful child straining against the dark earth that covered her grave.

John, himself suffering from remorse and a deep sense of shame, attempted to console his wife as best he could, and they knew in those terrible days and nights a closeness that had been gone from them for too long a time, and which had been returned to them in exchange for the life of their daughter.

True to the oath sworn at Elinor's little grave, they had then abandoned their manner of living. They saw none of their friends, they went nowhere. They cast aside their meaningless work and, immured in the rooms haunted by the presence of their dead daughter, they attempted at last to bring some meaning into their lives, but both soon realized the effort was useless. They had merely entered into a solitary existence in its own way every bit as empty and pointless as that they had voluntarily put behind them. They could not hope to change what they were, only what they might become.

In desperation, John had then suggested a more complete alteration in their lives. They should leave the city for a time, get away from all the too familiar sights and sounds, the often painful reminders. They would find totally different surroundings, where they and their sorrow were known to no one, where they could attempt to rebuild their lives and find the fulfillment they both so desperately needed. Ruth had at first been quite indifferent to the suggestion, as she was indifferent to everything since Elinor's death, but once John had pointed out to her the possibilities and the advantages of the move, she had gradually become more enthusiastic. It had at least for a time taken her mind off other, more painful matters.

John smiled slightly to himself as the car now moved through a cloud of billowing yellow dust down the narrow dirt road, away from the tall gabled house and towards the small fishing village nestled so picturesquely in the sheltered cover. He glanced back at the old house through the rear-view mirror . . . the whitened boards, the tall windows, the broad veranda, the Widow's Walk where often on stormy nights anxious eyes long since closed in permanent sleep had peered so hopefully or despairingly into the violence of a storm-lashed sea in the fervent hope of spotting a while sail. He could see Ruth standing on the veranda, leaning against one of the narrow stanchions, and her small figure already seemed to belong there. The house was warm, friendly. It was ready to make them welcome.

It already promised well. Since they had left the city just two days earlier, Ruth had suddenly become much more like herself, more interested in what went on about her; the beginnings of laughter danced again in her eyes. The fears still returned to her in the darkest hours just before the dawn, but these were now more easily calmed, and she was sleeping better. The possibilities of this new adventure had done this for her. In this new house, she would have more to do, something different, far away from the memories of the painful past. Elinor had never seen this house; that would help. They would do their best, he and Ruth, to rebuild their lives. This was what they owed to a dead child.

John licked at his lips and tasted the pleasantly tangy saltiness of the sea air, taking him momentarily back to the heaving deck of his old ship and those stirring days of cameraderie and closeness to the sea. He breathed deeply and exulted in the total absence of the city's ever present noise and throat-choking pollution. The very sounds of big city living, the irritating honking of harsh auto horns, the jangling of telephones demanding immediate attention, the obscene racket of transistor radios forever carried in the grubby hands of mindless idiots who could not tolerate a single moment of silence for the painful and unaccustomed processes of thought, the insipid shadowplay of figures on a television screen, the bastardization of great music to sell detergent and beauty aids, the shouting of constantly angry, frustrated people.

Here were only the pure, clean sounds of nature, the sounds that belonged, that dated from the very beginnings of life on a slowly cooling and evolving planet, placed here by the hands of nature herself, and not created by that overbearingly egotistical two-legged creature that somehow found it necessary to conceal his own basic sense of inferiority by creating a constant barrage of unpleasant, jarring noises that only he was able to produce.

The road John traveled from the bluff into the village was little more than a dusty country pathway, whose only slightly rutted center (perhaps indicative that the road was little traveled) and sand-concealed depressions were yet troublesome enough to toss and bounce the small sportscar from side to side as it traveled in the center of its own choking cloud of yellow dust, and on more than one occasion, forced a strong four-letter word from John when his head was brought into rather violent contact with the roof, as he descended the gentle rise from the bluff and headed for the town.

On John's left was a harshly barren series of gently rolling sand dunes shaped into graceful ocean swells and ripples by the artistic hands of the constantly carressing and moulding winds, sunwhitened sand spotted here and there with almost buried growths of stunted, scrabbly, yellow-green grass which only managed to increase the impression of aridity, of a world that had once known fertility but had long since run dry. To his right was the sea itself, with the gray water stretching unhindered to a yellow cloud-covered horizon. It was, indeed, a world of grays and yellows, yet there was about it nothing that was unpleasant or depressing. It had a peculiar beauty of its own.

The beach was completely deserted, an empty stretch of hard packed sand, except for the flotsam that the sea often finds necessary to spew out of its disturbed, tragically over-filled bowels. There were dark twisting strands of kelp which disturbingly resembled recumbent corpses . . . why did he always make that comparison, he wondered? . . . and brittle, insect-riddled snow-white bits of tormented driftwood that once, many long forgotten tides ago, might have formed part of some Spanish galleon loaded with New World treasure for the coffers of the gold-hungry king, or an over-crowded passenger vessel filled with hopeful immigrants looking for a new life in another, younger world. The shushing of the waves casting themselves . . . was it lovingly or despairingly? . . . onto the beach was broken by the harsh and strident cacophony of seagulls in constant search of food. There were no other signs of life, although John sometimes thought he could discern the faint, erratic scratchy traces of small scurrying sand crabs on the wet sands.

The heavy covering of the sky, a billious yellow shot through with streaks of midnight black and swollen purple, made him think of the underbelly of the sea itself as seen by a diver from beneath the surface. Both sea and sky were calm and serene, but both seemed pregnant with ancient mysteries they alone could reveal, were they so inclined.

The road made a wide curve, around another promontory jutting out into the sea, awash with the hissing confusion of breaking waves, upon which stood a sturdy, thick-based, tapering lighthouse. Gulls swooped about the tower's top; panes of broken glass and the peeling paint of its white walls indicated the lighthouse had long been abandoned, another deserted momento of a colorful past. For a moment, John felt the old romantic tug of such structures . . . he had alway thought a lighthouse the perfect place of seclusion for a struggling writer . . . and then he laughed it off; it was probably filled with dust, cobwebs, rats and useless equipment.

As he descended the gradual rise and entered the rather somnambulant main street of the little fishing village, the thought came to John that here, at least, he and Ruth would find very little to distract them and keep them from their more serious pursuits.

The simple wooden structures of the village, few of them more than two stories tall, were gathered in a tight cluster between the sand dunes and the pilings of the fishing wharfs. They were either unpainted or whitened by the touch of the sea air, or painted a white color that had long since faded through exposure. Here and there some daring innovator had daubed a wall with red or blue paint that was losing its battle to retain a once brilliant hue against the paint removing effect of the salt-laden atmosphere. Curved along the sheltered cove against the background of low, barren hills, the village was typical of numerous other such towns along that particular stretch of coast, which were now more concerned with boating and fishing than sea bathing.

Gulls wheeled and swooped in considerable numbers about the harshly pointed masts of the small fishing vessels that rose like wooden needles from the pin cushions of the wharfs, and the plankings of the wooden runways leading to the boats were white-spotted with their excrement.

There was very little activity in the village as John drove slowly down its main street, past homes heavily decorated with carved wooden curlicews, with broad verandas holding rocking-chairs and porch swings, small circular flowerbeds on heat-seared lawns, and driveways of beach sand. There were few people to be seen: several men either bearded or at least unshaven, casually clad in open shirts, slacks whitened by salt or paint-streaked faded jeans, with blue or white captains caps with golden anchors sewn above the black visors, and a few women who had encased their too frequently overflowing buttocks into tight trousers of pink, canary yellow or kelly green, with halters invariably (perhaps hopefully) too small for what they contained. Here and there a tired looking woman in a simple print dress sat on the veranda rocking chair, lazily wafting a bamboo fan at the warm air. There seemed few children about which, at least for the present, was all to the good; there would be few reminders of the unhappy past when Ruth came to town.

The business district centered about the inevitable village square, an unimaginative civic construction with at its center a small park with poorly planned flower beds, gravel walks, a few wooden benches, and a gull-spotted ancient cannon. A single church spire, topped by a tail-frisking black whale, was the tallest structure in town, standing at one side of the square directly across the street from the square red brick structure serving as combination town hall and police station; its tower held a white-faced clock which, he later learned, had frozen in time some forgotten moment of fear at twenty minutes past three and, through civic indifference, had never been repaired. The shops that lined the square were heavily nautical both in appearance and in their wares; various kinds of fishing tackle and boating equipment seemed to predominate. There were few cars to be seen, and the loudest noises were made by the ever-present swooping gulls. A thin layer of soft white beach sand seemed to cover everything; he was pleased to note the absence of litter. It all seemed peaceful, pleasant, and quite reassuringly dull.

John drew up before the single storied real estate office and paused for a moment as he glanced at the grocery store just across the square where the thin, bespectacled, white-aproned clerk with a slight whisp of gray moustache was busily piling deep red apples into a totally unimpressive triangular display. It struck John that he was quite ravenously hungry, his appetite sharpened by this sight of food, and he remembered Ruth's instructions to bring back something that was not too complicated for the antiquated stove that had now become their temporary property . . . or would, once the necessary arrangements had been made.

He hesitated a moment longer before deciding that the firm securing of the said property should be the first order of business. He peered through the one large plate glass window of the real estate office which bore letters in chipped gold reading SANDERS REAL ESTATE AND INSURANCE. Leaning against a wooden backdrop was a fly-specked bulletin board on which had been thumbtacked several unattractive and ordinary black and white photographs of saleable properties that were beginning to curl and yellow with age, indicating that business was perhaps not very brisk. The office appeared to be empty, but he corrected that impression just a second later, when a young woman suddenly appeared from behind a small desk, momentarily lost to sight when she bent to retrieve something from the floor.

John entered the office, wincing slightly at the crass jangling of a small aluminum bell that dangled just above the door and was stirred into vibrant, almost joyful life as she opened the door.

The single occupant he had glimpsed through the window proved to be a quite shapely and un-questionably attractive young lady with loose hanging brown hair, well-clad in a smart white dress with blue trim. Apparently in the process of departure, she was standing before the small mirror on the wall behind her desk, fluffing her hair, when John entered. She turned, looked at him with some surprise, quickly and quite thoroughly examined him with a single sweeping glance of her large brown eyes, and smiled.

"I'm terribly sorry," John apologized, automatically glancing at his watch, but completely failing to register the position of the small golden hands. "I'm afraid I didn't realize the time; it's later than I'd thought. Are you closing?"

"I was just about to leave," she admitted in a pleasingly low and melifluous tone as she absently repositioned the various articles on her desk, "but mostly because I've really nothing else to do. A few moments longer won't really matter. My I help you?"

"My name is Kendall. I would like to make

arrangements for renting that old house on the cliff just outside of town."

She looked at him again as she slowly seated herself behind the desk, and this time her expression carried some surprise and considerable more interest.

"The old Fowles House?"

John smiled. "I'm afraid I don't know its name. I'm a stranger here. But if that's what they call that big place on the bluff about two miles down the coast, then I suppose it's the one I mean. I was here earlier today, and picked up the key from Mr. Sanders."

"Oh, I see. I must have been out to lunch." Her face was briefly shadowed by the slightest touch of displeasure at this revelation of something of which she had not been previously advised. "Mr. Sanders really should have told me," she added almost to herself, with just enough irritation to imply some kind of special relationship between herself and her employer. "Well, I do believe Mr. Sanders is still here. Would you mind waiting for just a moment, and I'll see?"

She disappeared through the door beside her desk, softly closing it behind her. John lighted a cigarette, smiling with slight amusement at what he considered the obvious big city business tactics of having the secretary advise a prospective client that she *believed* Mr. Sanders was still available. The office apparently had only two doors, the one leading to the street and the other into the inner office; Sanders could not have left the place without being seen by his secretary/receptionist. He would undoubtedly be extremely busy when John entered the inner sanctum, but there's always time for a client, isn't there?

Well, he supposed they had to do something here to give themselves the illusion of business; he didn't imagine there was really very much of a real estate boom here. He wondered how long it would be before they took the next step upward and installed an intercom.

He glanced idly about the office, whose small size made it appear more cluttered than it actually was, with its row of green metal filing cabinets, the old-fashioned well-polished wooden arm chairs lined up before the window, the half-filled water cooler near the door, the large wall calendar from the local bank bearing a poorly developed print of Whistler's rather dull mother, under which was inscribed a pithy and supposedly very clever little comment about the desperate need of saving up for your own rocking chair days while there was still time. The secretary's desk, perhaps significantly devoid of the usual business clutter of papers, bore a single red rose in a tear-shaped vase and a framed photograph of a pleasant looking elderly couple standing with somewhat forced cheerfulness before a small white frame house; the picture's glass was cracked and the photo was slightly faded.

He bent slightly to stare under the half-lowered shade through the window and into the quiet square; a large blue fly had imprisoned itself in a corner of the glass and the room buzzed with the sound of its stupid fury.

A very young mother, her excessively blonde hair tangled in massive pink plastic curlers, strolled by wheeling a baby walker in which a still sexless infant slumped with its head fallen over the side, in a deep and innocent sleep. A tightly-dungareed youth on the opposite side of the street eyed with an open lascivious appreciative stare the young woman's bouncing, over-flowing breasts. The bespectacled grocer emerged from his store and again began to redistribute the dust and blown beach sand on the walk with a broom sadly lacking in bristles; he paused to readjust his earlier work of art, the pyramid of apples, about a quarter of an inch to the left, and wiping his hands on his apron, looked proudly at his handiwork and then returned into the store. Two small boys in bathing trunks walked down the street with fishing rods slung over their shoulders. A retired sea captain . . . or a reasonable facsimile thereof . . . sat lazily smoking his pipe before the fishing tackle store beside the grocery. Two plainly dressed housewives sat on a bench in the small park, both talking at the same time; on a nearby bench a portly middle-aged man with suspenders over his open-throated white shirt sat dozing with a forgotten newspaper on his lap.

Life obviously moved at somewhat less than a snail's pace in this little village, John mused. Well, wasn't that exactly the sort of thing he and Ruth were looking for? No theatre going, no cocktail parties, no telephones. Nothing but total peace and quiet. They would have a good deal of that here.

John sighed, again sensing that nagging dissatisfaction at the back of his mind, that sense of something missing. That was a bad sign. He had not yet been here a full day, and already there was just the smallest seed of discontent. After all, the entire business had been his idea. He crushed his cigarette in the tray between two of the chairs. Oh, what the hell; a little boredom wouldn't hurt either one of them.

The inner door opened and the secretary, pushing it wide for him, smilingly indicated that Mr. Sanders would be most happy to spare a few moments for Mr. Kendall to discuss the necessary arrangements for his taking a rental of the old Fowles mansion. As he passed the young woman, John caught a delicate scent of lilac; it pleased him. There was a slightly nervous smile in the woman's eyes as she closed the door behind him, and he rather liked that, too.

It did not surprise John to find Sanders slouched back in his overstuffed black leather armchair behind the desk, with the telephone cupped professionally against his shoulder to his chin, apparently deeply engrossed in a most important conversation.

Sanders was a young man certainly not yet beyond his twenty-fifth year, quite masculinely attractive, slender, with sandy hair tumbling freely and rather fetchingly about his well-shaped head; he had intensely blue eyes and a firm, strong jaw line. His clothes, although obviously not very expensive, fit him well. He wore tan slacks, a white shirt and a striped necktie whose knot was just the slightest bit off center, and John wondered if it had been hastily reknotted just before the door had opened to admit him. Did Sanders knot it himself, or was it one of those little services performed for him by the young lady outside? Sanders struck him as the type who wouldn't mind having his necktie knotted by a woman, something John had never tolerated. A large, strong hand on which glittered a single gold ring with a dark blue stone waved him casually to a seat across from the desk.

Watching Sanders with amusement, John seated himself in the heavily overstuffed red leather chair that sighed with surprise and displeasure when he lowered himself onto the rounded cushion. The room was rather sparsely furnished and was not much larger than the receptionist's chamber. There were three rows of wooden bookshelves on which were some rather dusty looking large tomes carrying extraordinarily uninteresting titles dealing with real estate and insurance; the books seemed to lean with exhaustion against each other, undoubtedly overcome by the sheer weightiness of their contents. A number of framed photographs no more imaginative than those that were silently rotting in the front window, a tall coatrack on which dangled the lifeless shape of Sanders' rather natty sports jacket, and a small glass case upon a table against the wall, filled with a fairly colorful display of local seashells, made up the bulk of the room's furnishings.

The desk behind which Sanders was seated with such aplumb was a bit too large for the room, as though it had been selected in high business hopes that had never quite materialized. It bore a highly polished aluminum carafe of water (at least, John assumed it held water), and two somewhat hazy glasses on an aluminum tray.

There was an inexpensive ball-point pen set of black and gold, with two pens pointed in opposite directions, a rather ornately carved wooden humidor, a large empty glass ashtray, the telephone, and a wildly loose arrangement of papers, perhaps a bit too loose and wild to be quite convincing, John thought as he smiled again at a mental picture of Sanders and his Girl Friday desperately spreading the papers and knotting his necktie in an effort to impress a possible new client with the busy tone of the office. He mentally chided himself for the ungenerous, patronizing attitude he had adopted since entering the office.

The rear of the office hung over the embankment and directly over the waters of the harbor, probably shored up by heavy timbers. The desk was placed before two fairly large windows overlooking the water; John could see two small fishing vessels chugging slowly toward the wharf. There was a leadenness about the water, and the sky had grown darker.

"Yes. . . Yes. . ." Sanders was saying into the phone. "But of course, I understand your position perfectly. No, no, I assure you. It's no trouble at all. The deeds will be ready when you want them . . . Certainly . . . Very happy to be of service to you. sir . . . Yes . . . Goodbye, now."

With a heavy sigh, Sanders dropped the phone back into its cradle, shook his head in exasperation over the almost unsurmountable difficulties with which he was daily forced to cope, and suddenly seemed to become aware that there was a visitor in his office. His face broadly wreathed in a superbly professional smile, he turned to John, swinging the large, heavy chair about in an expert manner that indicated long hours of practice.

"Ah, Mr. Kendall, I believe. Yes. Very good to see you again, sir." He waved a hand at the telephone. "These little irritations . . . Well, we must try our best to please our clients, of course, regardless of how small or demanding they may be. Yes. Uh. . . You were here earlier in the day. Now, let me see. . ." He sucked in his cheeks and stared up at the ceiling, as though part of his filing was kept up there out of the way. "Oh, yes, Fowles House, I believe."

Amused, John nodded; he liked this young man. "Yes. Fowles House. At least, I understand that's what it's called."

"Yes. Yes." Sanders opened the humidor and offered John a cigar, which John refused with a smile and a slight wave of his hand. "The old Fowles House," Sanders muttered. He took a cigar from the box and, with obvious inexpertise, encountered considerable difficulty in lighting it; his face then briefly disappeared behind a cloud of blue-white smoke, from which John could hear coughs Sanders desperately attempted to suppress. "A fine property it is, too, that old Fowles place. Oh, I suppose there are some who might find it just a bit old-fashioned, but it is a solidly built edifice . . . don't build 'em that way any more, like they say . . . and I suppose there really isn't anything particularly wrong with being a bit old-fashioned, is there? It also has a really splendid view of the sea . . ."

Sanders was beginning to stumble badly in his sales pitch, and John decided it was time to bring this useless, if amusing, charade to an end and put the over-anxious young agent at his ease.

"My wife and I have decided to take the place for a four month period," he interrupted.

Caught in mid-sentence, Sanders quickly, and with a decided air of relief, lowered the large black cigar into the glass ashtray and the smile became a trifle more sincere. He seemed rather surprised by John's decision.

"Why . . . fine. That's just fine, Mr. Kendall. You've really made an excellent decision. Yes, indeed." His voice became firmer, now that he was on somewhat more familiar ground; John decided charm was more his forte than business. "I'm very glad to hear it. You will want to take immediate possession?"

John smiled. "I think we had better. My wife has

already begun her cleaning, and if I know her, there's no telling what she may have done to the place by this time."

Sanders had now become quite relaxed and permitted his natural friendliness and good nature to reveal itself. "Well, I have the papers right here and ready for you."

He instantly opened the center drawer of his desk and drew out the lease, then belatedly realizing he had thus destroyed his own carefully constructed business image by failing to spend at least some sixty seconds of irritated mumbling while rummaging noisily through the mass of papers that had been placed on his desk for just that specific purpose. He glanced somewhat shamefacedly at John, and this time the smile was natural and friendly as he waved at the papers on his desk; there was a rather infectious lilt to his chuckle.

"All these papers . . . well, they're really just for show. Actually, I've been holding onto this lease all day, hoping you would come back. Appearances. You understand." He smiled again, shaking his head. "It's my secretary; she thinks it looks good."

John nodded, smiling. "Of course. Like the telephone."

Sanders flushed slightly, then laughed aloud. "Yes. Actually, I was just talking to Mildred, the town switchboard operator. She's used to it be now, and it gives her something to do. I present her with a big box of chocolates every Christmas; she puts them on the switchboard and munches on them all day long; they don't last beyond the holiday season. Business happens to be a trifle slow just now." He again laughed slightly. "What the hell, business is always pretty God-damned slow around here. Don't know why I stick it out. We're a small out-of-the-way village, and there aren't many properties available and fewer people to buy them. Things pick up a bit during the summer season, bu even that doesn't amount to very much. Insurance is what keeps me going, especially on the boats. Nice of you to give me something to do."

He quickly brushed aside the useless, unheeded papers to one side, disregarding the few that fluttered to the floor, and cleared a space in the center of the desk for the lease.

"Now, then, You do understand the terms of the lease?" he asked, his voice becoming a bit more concerned with the uneasiness that something might yet go wrong. "I hope I made them clear to you when you were here earlier?"

"Yes, of course," John assured him with a nod. "You made everything perfectly clear."

Pleased by what he apparently chose to regard as a compliment, glancing over the few pages of the lease, Sanders said, "Well, it doesn't hurt to go over them once again, does it, just to be sure? Now. You'll make yourself fully responsible for the house and for everything in it, for the length of your tenancy."

John nodded.

"The lease cannot be broken without payment of a penalty."

Another nod; Sanders, who had looked up cautiously at this rather sticky condition, looked considerably relieved.

"And you have an option to buy, of course."

A third nod.

Sanders hesitated when he reached what he considered the most crucial point in the agreement. "And there will be a month's rent paid in advance, together with an additional month for security."

"Yes. You'll take a check?"

The smile returned immediately. "Of course."

After the lease had been signed and countersigned and John had pocketed his copy while Sanders placed the original very carefully back in the center drawer of his desk as though it were his own personal copy of the *Bill of Rights*, the agent leaned back in his chair, considerably more at his ease and obviously well pleased with the transaction. He spent a few more difficult moments trying to relight his cigar, then finally gave it up as a bad job, and with a sigh of pleasure, loosened his necktie, opened the collar of his shirt, and lighted a cigarette.

"I really don't at all go in for cigars," he explained. "They make me a little sick to my stomach. But it looks good for business, so I've tried to cultivate a taste for them. Cigar's supposed to give businessmen a touch of solidness, or something like that."

"I've never really cared for them myself," John confessed, as though trying to please a child by telling him he completely agreed with him.

"Well, now, I'm afraid you and your wife will find our little town just a bit dull and uninteresting after the big city," Sanders continued; no need for caution now that the signed release rested safely in his desk drawer. "It's a nice enough little place we have here, but there isn't a hell of a lot doing, especially once the summer season is over. City dwellers might find themselves just a little . . . well, bored."

"We haven't come here to involve ourselves in a new social round," John assured him. "If that's what we wanted, we might just as well have stayed where we were. We're looking for some place quiet, where we can keep to ourselves."

"Yes, of course," Sanders nodded, toying with a plastic paperweight in which were imprisoned five golden coins. "Well, I don't want you to get the idea that we're strictly backwoods, either. We do have a movie house, with one performance a day and two on Saturdays. Closed all day on Sundays. Strictly family entertainment, of course; we haven't yet come up to your X-rated films. There's a pretty good hotel, with a restaurant that isn't half bad at all; seafood mostly of course. A lot of passers-through stop there on their way;

the swordfish is 'specially good. Got a Congregational Church, if you're of a religious turn. A really pretty fair little library, couple of bars, and a school, although I don't imagine you'll be too much concerned about that; you haven't mentioned any children.''

''No. We did have a daughter, but she died quite recently,'' John added, and then wondered why he had wished to embarrass Sanders by making mention of his personal tragedy. He was pleased when the agent failed to make the usual vapid and meaningless expressions of regret for the death of someone he had never known.

''We do have plenty of really good fishing hereabouts, though.'' Sanders turned his chair to the windows; the two vessels John had noticed earlier were now tied up at their berths, and there were no other ships in the darkening harbor. ''The beaches aren't too bad, although frankly they are a lot better a few miles further down the coast. Actually, we used to be quite a thriving little village. Pretty big in the days of piracy, though maybe you wouldn't think so, far north as we are. Then we were a major fishing port for a while, even some whaling. The death of the old clipper ships finished us, though; harbor isn't deep enough for the really big steam vessels. Well, times gotta change, I guess. Now we survive mostly on the summer tourist fishing trade. Lot different from the old days.''

John smiled. ''You sound like the *Ancient Mariner*. You could hardly remember those old days.''

Sanders turned in his chair to face John again. ''That's true, but I was born here and brought up on the old legends and stories. That's one of the real charms of these little old coastal villages, I suppose; the old legends.''

''And are their any legends about Fowles House?''

Something flitted over the young agent's face when John made mention of the house that had brought him to this office. It was the merest shadow, a brief darkening, an almost unnoticeable tightening of the lips and hardening of the eyes. Perhaps it was not really there at all; it may have been John's imagination. Sanders hesitated for a moment and his hand rather nervously reached out to place the ballpoint pens in proper position. Was he avoiding John's eyes?

"I'd be interested in hearing it."

It had not been John's imagination at all. The darkness returned, more noticeable this time, and from it Sanders's eyes seemed to gleam with a peculiar intensity. Still but the impression of a moment, it quickly passed.

"Oh, I daresay you'll hear them all," Sanders said with a light, somewhat uncomfortable laugh, "if you're in these parts long enough, but for now, I really mustn't keep you any longer, Mr. Kendall. I imagine you're anxious to get back to your wife and begin settling in."

The agent seemed suddenly anxious to bring their discussion to a close and, rising, reached his hand to John across the cluttered desk, still seeming to avoid looking directly at him.

"Yes, I suppose I had better be getting back," John agreed, rising.

"I wish you every happiness in your new home," Sanders said in an obviously sincere tone. "Who knows, maybe you might make it a permanent one; we're always glad to have new neighbors here. If there's anything I can do for you, at any time, please don't hesitate to call on me."

"I'll be sure to do that," John promised, and he suddenly had the feeling, despite the brief moment of strangeness, that Sanders meant what he said.

His business at the local grocery took John even less time than at the real estate office. John was never a careful shopper, nor a wise or selective one. He disliked the chores of shopping, which he considered to be the woman's side of marriage, and he was quick to pick up whatever drew his eye, regardless of the posted prices of any other alternative possibilities. By this time he had become extremely hungry, and he was interested only in returning to the house over which he now felt a quite decidedly proprietary interest; he didn't like to leave Ruth alone for too long a time.

The grocery store was a small one, its shelves and display cases quite well stocked and traditionally arranged, with a decided preponderance of produce from the sea. Two middle-aged spinsters eyed him closely from behind the piled canned goods and exchanged whispers as he examined the wares, and even the white-aproned clerk could not quite conceal his curiosity at the presence of this tall stranger in his little store during the off-season. John carefully fenced off any attempts at dragging him into conversation. That was one sure way of starting that round of socializing that both he and Ruth were anxious to avoid, at least for the present time; with an eye to the possible future, however, when their attitudes might change should they decide to stay here, he would not be rude to any of the villagers, while still carefully maintaining his distance, and he was extremely proper and polite in muttering *excuse me*, *please* when the curious women quite accidentally blocked his passage.

Reasoning Ruth would hardly be in the mood for cleaning and filleting fish, John purchased some hamburger patties, eggs, bread, and an assortment of cold cuts; not very imaginative, perhaps, but they could both come into town tomorrow or the next day for some full-scale provisioning. He bought quickly, monosyllabically responding to the clerk's banal comments regarding the weather, and smiled noncommittedly as he deftly slid between the two gossips who through some nifty maneuvering of their own managed to reach the door just before he did, and had already opened their mouths to speak to him; returning to his car, he dropped the parcels into the rear seat.

He had opened the door of the car and was about to slip behind the wheel when his eyes happened to fall upon the three-storied building just two doors down from the grocery store. It was a plain structure of white wood, attractive in its simple seaside way; four steps led up to the entrance where, hanging between two rounded pillars, a sign decorated with whales and dolphins announced it to be THE SEAVIEW HOTEL. What particularly caught John's attention, however, was the smaller door just to the left of the main hotel entrance, opening directly from the sidewalk, advising the world of the presence of a restaurant/bar called THE WHALER'S REST, by means of a wooden sign in the shape of a whale hanging out over the sidewalk. John licked his salt-stained lips, suddenly aware that he had developed a quite respectable thirst. Anxious though he was to return to Ruth, he realized an overpowering desire for a drink. It would take only a few moments, and he could drive that much faster to make up for lost time. It would be in the nature of a celebration.

The restaurant was exactly what he would have expected to find in such a village—cozy, small, comfortable, strictly nautical. The tables were covered with red-checkered tablecloths and equipped with large, comfortable captains chairs. Wicked-looking harpoons decorated the walls that were spotted with old-fashioned brass lanterns and coils of looped rope and tackle; here and there were paintings reminiscent of illustrations from an edition of *Moby Dick*. At the far end of the room was a small bar over which hung a huge fishing net supported at strategic points by harpoons set into the bar itself; over the bar's liquor supply was a large mural of a monstrous whale in its death throes, surrounded by small whale boats filled with a motley crew in old seamen's outfits. A door at one end of the bar apparently opened directly into the lobby of the hotel.

In addition to the portly, grizzle-haired bartender with his blue-striped whaler shirt, there were perhaps a dozen people in the restaurant, occupying four of the tables, with a waiter dressed as a sailor moving among them; it was the largest gathering of people John had yet seen in the village.

But what immediately caught John's attention was the young woman seated alone at the bar, slowly sipping her drink. It was the secretary from the real estate office. She looked up when he entered, apparently expecting someone; she smiled and beckoned to him.

"Well, hello again," she said. "Welcome to the Whaler's Rest."

He returned her welcoming smile. "Thank you. Nice to see you again."

"Finished your business?" When he nodded, she added, "Won't you join me?"

John hesitated for a moment, thinking once again of the groceries in the rear of the car and the wife waiting for him in a strange house, but decided since he had planned on having a drink in any event, he might just as well enjoy it in pleasant company. He seated himself on the tall wooden stool next to her, as she motioned to the bartender.

"Frank," she introduced, "this is Mr. Kendall. He and his wife will be spending a little time with us."

Frank wiped his hands on his apron and extended a large red paw with blue tattoo marks coiling snake-like around the thick stubby fingers. "Hi. What'll you have?"

"Scotch on the rocks," John replied.

"You got it."

"You really were about to leave, then, weren't you?" John asked, turning to his attractive companion.

She nodded, smiling again. "I like to come in here after a hard day's work and unwind. It's pleasant and relaxing, and Frank's a real friend, always ready to listen to my little feminine problems." Her smile broke into a pleasant, throaty chuckle. "You probably find it difficult to believe we ever do a hard day's work, don't you?"

"Well, I did notice an empty chair or two in the

waiting room."

"And a chair or two too many, while you're at it. Actually, we originally did have one chair less, but two summers ago, the fishing here became quite spectacular, and business boomed so, we hopefully ordered a third chair. Besides, Paul felt there was something wrong when he realized the barbershop had more chairs than we did."

"In that case, it was good of Mr. Sanders to find the time to see me," John said, with just the slightest touch of sarcasm, as Frank placed a drink before him.

"Oh, please don't mind that little charade," she pleaded. "Confidentally, that extra chair has never even been used, and we could just as easily go back to the original pair, but Paul doesn't like to admit he was wrong. The very good fishing didn't last beyond that freak season, and things then dropped back to their more normal leisurely pace. Paul likes to feel he's running a small empire of his own, and he insists I handle all prospective clients accordingly. He doesn't mean anything by it; Paul is really quite a dear."

John was instantly confirmed in his fleeting impression of some kind of special relationship between them, while amused by each passing onto the other the responsibility for the attitude of big business.

"Well, I'll have to take your word for that," he remarked.

She stared for a moment with somewhat too much concentration into her ice-chilled drink. "So, you've really decided to take the old Fowles place?"

"Yes, I have, Miss. . ."

"Oh, I'm terribly sorry." Her smile was quick and friendly. "But please, just call me Linda."

"You seem surprised by the fact, Linda."

"Somewhat. We've never rented the place before. It's been on our books for the past few years, but no one has ever shown any interest in it."

"I imagine it's a bit far out for most people, and then it lacks a good portion of the supposedly vital modern conveniences. Besides, as you can see, we don't really get very many tourists out this way any longer, particularly those who stay. Actually, I've never even seen the house myself."

"Isn't that a bit unusual for a renting agent?" John asked.

"Paul's the agent, not I," she reminded him. "I'm strictly the office handywoman . . . sorry, handy-person."

"Quite a good one, I should think."

Again she smiled and tipped her head in acknowledgement of the little compliment.

"And you really never have seen the house?" he asked after a moment.

"Oh, I've seen it, of course. You can't go far from town without seeing it, perched like some kind of giant albatross on the cliff out there. What I really mean is I've never been inside. But then, I really haven't been here very long myself, and the house has been empty for many years."

"You're not a native?"

She shook her head. "Oh, no. My husband spent most of his life here, though, and I came to know it through him. Oh, I know the village seems very dull and provincial, but it's really a very pleasant, uncomplicated little town, once you get to know it and to accept the rather unsophisticated attitude of those who live here."

"Not very many of those, are there?"

She laughed slightly. "Just about enough, I think." Her face became suddenly shadowed with sadness, and an added mantle of years seemed to fall upon her like someone whose experience with life belies her youth. "We had many wonderfully happy times here, Richard and I, boating, sailing, swimming, just walking hand-in-hand down the beach. This is a really beautiful part of the coast. Especially after a storm, and we have many of them, there's an almost overwhelming sense of power in the sea. . ." She smiled off her sadness. "Anyway, when Richard died, quite recently, I was at loose ends, and I came back here. I suppose I was looking for something. What? Memories, perhaps. I don't know. I've never been afraid of memories, as so many people are. I find them wonderful company. I was going to be here for just a short time, until I could adjust myself to being alone again. But I found myself very much at home here. Paul was Richard's oldest friend, and when he needed a secretary, I offered my own services, although I do still have a sneaking suspicion that the need for a secretary was created solely for my own benefit. It's worked out quite well. I may stay."

"Then you probably don't know very much about Fowles House, do you?" he asked.

"Is there anything to know?" she countered, after an almost imperceptible pause.

"You tell me. Isn't there always a story in old houses? Your boss was expounding on the delights of local legends, and then became strangely evasive when I asked about any legends connected with Fowles House. It did make me wonder a bit. I don't even know who this Fowles person was. I assume there actually was someone by that name?"

"Oh, yes, indeed, and from what I understand, he was one of the most colorful and disreputable characters in these parts, about two hundred years ago. I have an idea the memory of the man still embarrasses the villagers, and that's why they don't care to talk about him. There are rumors that he was a pirate of the most unpleasant kind. Quite a scoundrel, apparently."

"You mean one of those scalawags with one eye and a wooden leg who always carried on one shoulder a parrot with an obscene vocabulary, and was in the habit of committing all kinds of dastardly crimes for treasure that he never used, but simply buried away somewhere with a body or two for good measure, as sort of a guarantee for his old age, when his swashbuckling days were over, provided, of course, that he managed to evade the sword and the hangman's noose?"

She laughed. "I didn't know there were people any longer who still remember *Treasure Island*!"

"Say, maybe the house has secret passages and panels, and a buried treasure trove of its own!"

She joined in his easy laughter; the brief moment of sorrow had passed just as quickly as it had touched her.

"Oh, I rather doubt that. If there were any possibility of hidden treasure, you can be certain there would be considerable more interest shown in the old place than I've noticed since coming here. You know, that might have improved our chances of renting the house. We could have spread rumors to that effect. Rent the house for four months and see if you can find the hidden cache of pirate's gold. I'm surprised the possibility never occurred to Paul." She shook her head. "No I'm not, really; Paul is far too ethical for that sort of thing."

"What about the owners?"

"As far as I know, they've never even seen the place. They seem anxious to have no connection with it whatever . . . aside, of course, from collecting possible rentals. They're direct descendants of the rascally old Fowles, so they probably have sufficient reason to want to live down the name and the reputation."

"After all these years?"

She shrugged. "People can be ridiculously small and moral. The sins of the fathers are not quickly forgotten."

"The house is filled with some rather valuable antiques, you know. I'm surprised it was left without even so much as a caretaker."

"I don't recall a single case of theft in these parts since I came here," she mused. "The owners probably haven't the slightest idea of what the place is like or what's in it. You know, a house by the sea . . . they may picture it as some kind of run-down bungalow used for somewhat questionable romantic purposes."

"The amount of rent being asked would seem to indicate they have at least some understanding of its value; they're not letting it cheap, you know."

"Yes, that's true," Linda agreed. "I should think you would find the house a bit too large for . . . well, for your purposes, Mr. Kendall."

"Please. If it's Linda, it has to be John."

"Okay."

"Yes, I guess it is rather large. That's one of the points I mentioned to my wife just before I came into town."

She drank, smiling slightly. "I could have asked, you know."

He nodded, returning the smile. "Of course."

They both dismissed the subject, and Linda asked, "I suppose Paul made it clear there is an option to buy?"

"Oh, yes, a very important point. It's a bit too soon to think about that."

"Of course." She sighed a trifle wistfully. "It would be nice to have a new face about Main Street; the old ones become rather too familiar after a while, particularly when they're not really particularly interesting to begin with."

"That doesn't quite square with your earlier comments about this being a nice place to live."

"Oh, I still mean that," she insisted, "but change is always pleasant." He leaned forward to light her cigarette. "I find myself wondering what brought you here in the first place."

"Oh, a lot of things," he replied vaguely.

"You don't mind my asking?"

"Certainly not. I guess there was just a need for Ruth and me to get away for a while." He hadn't hesitated to speak to Sanders about Elinor; why did he say nothing now? "The well-known rat race can get exhausting and disillusioning after a while, and you feel the need for a little less artificiality in your life. Professional reasons had something to do with it. I'm a writer, and my wife is an artist. We felt a change might help us."

"I'm sorry; should I know your work?"

He shook his head, with his own wistful smile. "No, I wouldn't really think so. Unless you have a predilection for lurid sex novels or corny spy thrillers and trashy magazines, and go in for used book stores and unimportant but hopeful little art galleries. No, not yet, at any rate. Some day, I hope. So do we all have our dreams." He glanced at his watch and quickly finished his drink. "Speaking of my wife, Ruth will think I've been shanghaied and bundled off to the China seas."

"I shouldn't have kept you," Linda pologized.

He smiled. "It's been my pleasure. Can I drop you off somewhere?"

She shook her head. "No thanks, John. Nobody around here really lives far enough to be dropped off anywhere." She held out her hand to him. "It's been very pleasant. I do hope we'll meet again."

The hand was cool and soft, her grip pleasantly firm. "I'm sure we shall. You must meet my wife," He laughed at the invitation. "That rather sounds like a line from a bad comedy, doesn't it? I do mean it, though. How about dinner some evening at the house of mystery? You and Sanders, if you like. Once we've settled and Ruth has mastered the complexities of an old-fashioned wood-burning stove. It's time you got to see the inside of the pirate's lair. Perhaps after dinner we can sound the walls and the flooring for interesting and promising hollow sounds."

"I'd like that very much."

She sat thoughtfully drawing on her cigarette as she watched him leave, his tall and slender form moving easily out of the bar with a grace that had nothing about it that was not masculine; a few seconds later, his car drove past in the direction of Fowles House.

Linda didn't really like very many people; she considered them too often dull, uninteresting, interferring, and false. Her life had not been a particularly happy one, and she had always been perhaps excessively wary and distrustful of others. That was what had made her tragically brief marriage to Richard so remarkable.

It had all begun as a frankly sexual liaison in those difficult and lonely weeks just after she had so suddenly lost both her parents, and had culminated in marriage only when she suddenly realized that she not only loved Richard but, which was more important and more unusual, she liked him as well.

Richard. Vibrant, dashing, warm, understanding, the only truly wonderful person she had ever known. For six months they had been unbelievably, excitingly happy, with a glowing joy whose remembrance would surely bring her considerable comfort through the remainder of her life. Not just yet, of course. The remembrance was still too sharp and painful. She would often lie alone in her bed and think of him, remembering his touch, his warmth, his smile, the wonderful awakening passion of their lovemaking, and her entire body would ache for him and her arms would reach out for a fantasy that had once been reality. She cried often in those lonely nights, her face buried in her pillow although there was no one to hear her, mourning the years of love that should have been theirs, and often she wondered if perhaps she had made a serious mistake in coming back here, where they had experienced their greatest moments of happiness.

She shook her head. No. That was wrong. Face the sorrow and get it over with, and then perhaps life could begin again. Vaguely, she wondered who had originated that old saw about getting right back on a horse once you've been thrown. It didn't apply only to riding. Life could throw you, too. The pain would fade in time, and only the gentle remembering would remain, and that was something she never wanted to lose. These were the only thoughts that could comfort her as she strolled alone at dawn on the deserted beach and stared across the sea to the distant horizon, where she always imagined she saw his face.

Paul was another of those very few people she both liked and trusted. He was good, kind, generous, anxious to please, eager to be liked. She was very fond of him, but not yet really certain in just what way.

Paul had been Richard's friend since childhood, and had been a bulwark of strength and understanding to her in those days when Richard lay in the hospital battling desperately and hopelessly against the terrible disease that was eating away his strength and his very life, reducing his powerful body to a trembling, pain-shattered shell. Paul had come to the city to be with her in those days, and it was he who had made all those difficult and painful arrangements for the funeral once Richard's laughing eyes had closed for the last time.

Of course, Linda had known all along that Paul didn't really need her in the office. It was just another way of coming to her rescue. That was like Paul. She realized, too, that he was in love with her, probably had been even while Richard himself was still alive. He wanted her; he made that sometimes rather painfully clear. As for herself, well, it was still soon to tell.

She thought John Kendall might easily be another person she could like; unusual for her to come to such a quick decision about anyone. There was something very comfortable about him; she sensed that even after their very brief, rather formal meeting this afternoon. Not particularly handsome, he was yet attractive in the way a young girl thinks her big brother is attractive. She wondered if he would object to her thinking of him in the rather unromantic way of an older brother; some men would consider it degrading to their sexuality. She didn't think John would really mind. Since Linda had no personal designs on him, she could hope he had a good, loving, loyal and competent wife, one who really understood and appreciated him; she felt John probably deserved that.

Frank removed John's empty glass and wiped at the wet rings on the bar. "Have another, Linda? On the house."

She was so deeply engrossed in her own thoughts, she failed to hear him until he repeated his offer; then she pushed her empty glass in his direction.

"Okay. I suppose so, Frank. Thanks. Paul should be along soon, but I think I have time."

He took her glass, again absently wiping the bar, and pointed his head towards the open door. "Who's the stranger?"

"John Kendall?" She had already ceased thinking of him as a stranger. "He and his wife have taken the Fowles House for a few months."

Frank's thick sun-whitened eyebrows raised, and he pursed his heavy lips, creating deep lines in his chin. "Old Fowles House? No one's lived in that old mausoleum for a lot more years than I can even 'member, 'n that's a helluva lot many more years 'n you'd want to admit to."

"It's a good house, and it's always been available," she said, somewhat defensively. "I guess nobody's ever been interested in it before."

Frank nodded his grizzled head. "Yeah. Real white elephant, that's for sure. Paul must be glad. Surprised anybody'd wanta live in the old place. Too damn big and old."

She snuffed out her cigarette as Frank prepared her drink; she immediately lighted another. She didn't generally smoke so heavily, but today she found herself feeling unusually nervous, without at all understanding the reason for it.

Linda found herself thinking about Fowles House. The old house was, indeed, always in the thoughts of the villagers, but no one ever spoke about it. The mere mention of Fowles House always stirred a sense of uneasiness in everyone. The villagers seemed embarrassed by the very presence of the great old mansion on the cliff-top two miles outside of town. Should it be casually mentioned by some curious stranger in town, the villagers would exchange glances of distaste and pointedly change the subject, as though the stranger had spoken of a shameful disease which no proper person would ever so much as mention. Peculiar, this evident uneasiness. Whatever it was that had happened at Fowles House had occurred two centuries in the past. Why should these events still cast so long a shadow?

Linda had no conception of what lay behind it all. She had tried to get Richard to talk about it, but he had been just as irritatingly evasive as everyone else, setting everything down to superstition and old wives' tales, but refusing to be more specific, maintaining it was just too ridiculous to be discussed. She had often wondered if his attitude was really that of the contemptuous disbeliever, or if he was a partner in the unwritten code of silence regarding the house.

She remembered one evening, as they strolled hand in hand along the beach with the dark gabled structure standing behind them like a Hallowe'en cutout against the clouded sky and she had again asked him about the stories connected with the abandoned structure. Oh, they really were nothing specific, Richard had again insisted. All old places have stories. Just vague and pointless tales, the kind of things that children tell each other at night when a house stands empty for too long, tales of hauntings and strange lights and mysterious sounds fall upon it like the dust of passing years. Nothing but local folklore. That was all Richard would say. When Linda probed for something more detailed, Richard merely laughed it off and, like everyone else, changed the subject, insisting on his total disbelief in the entire business.

Paul, too, was strangely reticent about the subject, although Linda sensed he knew more about the old house than Richard had. He would tell her only that Jonathan Fowles, the builder, had been a very nasty individual dealing in piracy and perhaps other highly disreputable pasttimes. When she pressed him for more, particularly for the reason why the house was still looked upon with almost superstitious fear, he became taciturn and actually unpleasant; these were the only times when he came close to losing his temper with her. It was all none of her business, he said. The whole thing was a lot of nonsense and he had no intention of wasting his time discussing it. Something happened to Paul whenever she mentioned Fowles House. His face hardened and became almost that of a stranger. She, too, began to avoid the subject.

Apparently Paul had said nothing to John Kendall about the past of the house and the villagers' code of silence regarding the long empty mansion. He was quite right, of course, in not doing so. They had agreed on that from the start, should anyone become interested in their books. They would freely discuss structure, plumbing, repairs, sea termites and anything else relative to the possibilities of the house as a place of residence, but there was no point in creating problems for everyone by mentioning unpleasant rumors that had become attached to the place over the years. They were nothing but idle gossip, utter nonsense. There was probably not a word of truth in them, whatever they were.

"Frank placed the fresh drink before her. "Well, guess it's time the old place was lived in again," he said. "Been empty too long. No reason to think ever'thing won't be all right."

No, Linda agreed. No reason at all. Was there?

She looked up when Paul entered, moving quickly to her and lightly kissing her on the cheek before he sat beside her. He brought with him that inevitable air of comfort and solidity on which she had come to depend; one could always count on Paul. He looked vital and handsome, very much at his ease, and well pleased with himself. He glanced at her full drink and smiled.

"I'll bet that's not the first one."

She shook her head. "You win. Mind?"

"No." The smile broadened; he had powerful, perfect teeth. "It might make you more receptive."

"You wouldn't want my receptivity to be based on the amount I drink, would you?"

"Sure!" he responded quite honestly. "On anything at all!" He turned to Frank. "Scotch, Frank." Turning again to Linda, he asked, "Go for a drive?"

She shook her head. "I don't think so, Paul; I've things to do."

"Dinner?"

She nodded. "If you like. Later."

"And later later?" He casually touched her leg with his knee; she looked at him with a reproaching eyebrow and moved her leg away, thinking again that Paul's sexualism had about it too much of the naughty schoolboy to be in any way offensive. "All right, all right," he said quickly, his good humor undamaged. "Forget it. Diner later and no later later, or no dinner."

She warmed under his infectious grin, and placed her hand on his; he quickly took hold of it. "You should know better by now."

"I know it. I guess I'm always hoping for a weak moment. Christ, don't you ever have them?" She smiled and said nothing; Paul looked at her more seriously. "You look sort of down, Linda. You've been thinking again."

"Not exactly. "I've been talking. Kendall just left."

"Kendall? Oh, him. Didn't take him long to find the place."

"How could he miss it?"

"What did he want?"

"What most people want when they come in here. A drink. He's a Scotch man, too."

"Doesn't care for cigars, either; he's got taste." Paul stared for a moment at the drink placed before him; he seemed suddenly less at his ease. "What did you talk about?"

"You can guess. The house."

There was a slight apparent tightening of his jaw. "He seems to like the place. His wife, too. I think it's some form of therapy for them to come here. You know, getting away from and all that sort of thing. They recently lost a child."

"Funny he didn't mention that. I wonder why."

"Not the sort of thing you talk about every chance you get," Paul suggested.

"You didn't tell him . . . anything?"

There are an almost unnoticeable pause. "What do you mean?"

"You know what I mean, Paul." She was becoming more serious. "I think I like him. I might even like his wife. What are they getting themselves into, Paul?"

"They're getting themselves into a very imposing and rather impressive house superbly situated on the top of a cliff with an excellent view of the sea. Just what our advertising has always promised, although nobody ever believed it before."

She made a gesture of impatience. "Please don't hedge with me, Paul. You know perfectly well what I'm talking about. Is it really being fair to them?"

"Oh, shit, Linda." He took a long sip of his drink. "Don't be so God-damned mysterious. What do you mean, fair?"

"Paul, we both know there's something . . . unusual . . . about that old house. I've been here long enough to see the way people look at it, when they can't ignore it altogether. Richard used to talk about rumors, gossip, but I never could find out exactly what it was all about. Richard either simply didn't know, or he just wouldn't tell me. You're no better. But shouldn't the Kendalls be told?"

"Told what?" Paul was becoming irritated, an unusual departure from his constant even personality, but the inevitable result of her probings into Fowles House. "Gossip and wild tales from the past? What good would it all do? Why bother them with that kind of nonsense?"

She frowned. "I don't know. Are we so certain it is all just nonsense?"

"We sure as hell aren't sure it's anything else."

"It's just that John . . ."

"John?"

"Oh, don't be silly, Paul. Why not? He seems like such a . . ."

"Please don't say *decent sort*, Linda."

She smiled. "I was going to, really; there's nothing wrong with that, is there? I just feel I wouldn't like anything . . . unpleasant . . . to happen to him there."

The ice tinkled against his glass when Paul raised it; that did not generally happen.

"There's no reason to believe that anything would happen . . . to him."

She immediately caught the slight pause in his voice, and the faintest stress on his last words. "To him? What does that mean? What about her?"

He shifted uncomfortably on his stool, and she suddenly noticed the perspiration on his forehead.

"Oh, come on, Linda, are we really supposed to believe in fairytales and ghost stories? I stopped that long ago, when I was still just a kid. You know the usual talk about living in modern times."

"The times are always modern for those who live in them."

"Do you really believe I would have closed the deal if I thought I was placing them in danger?" he asked, a bit peeved. "I hope I have a bit more integrity than that. Old, solitary houses always have strange stories connected with them; it's part of a house's aging process. But how seriously can you take them?"

"I have a feeling you take this one more seriously than you would care to admit." She smiled and took his hand again. "Oh, Paul, no, of course you wouldn't deliberately place anyone in danger, and I have no more faith in old wives tales than you have. But, somehow, I feel this isn't quite the same."

"Why?"

"Because I can see you are disturbed about this business, Paul, no matter how you try to hide it, and whether or not you believe these so-called tales. I know you well enough to see that. You're always uncomfortable when I mention Fowles House." He said nothing, but the grip on her hand tightened, and she felt the sudden moisture of his perspiration. "What is it, Paul. What is it about that old house?"

Paul looked at her, and his eyes were vague and distant, as though he were having trouble focusing in on her face. "I don't know, really. Women . . . die there."

CHAPTER FOUR

THE weather had continued to deteriorate during the short time John had engaged in conversation with Linda. As unusually early darkness was falling, and with it had come a light, uncomfortably chilly drizzle of rain, although the humidity had increased and the air had become sticky, heavy and silent. John opened the front of his shirt as he drove along, but the air remained still and warm despite the movement of the car, and only the occasional touch of lightly blown drizzle brought him brief moments of comfort.

John was feeling rather well-pleased with himself, and with the result of his brief visit to the village, particularly with the successful finalization of the rental of the old Fowles House. It was quite an expensive project, possibly a bit more expensive than they could really comfortably afford, but he was certain it would prove to be well worth the cost. New beginnings, after all, must always have their price.

He was also rather pleased with the brief, limited contacts he had made in the village. He could not, after all, put up a perfectly solid facade of indifference and unfriendliness, since he and Ruth would be living in the area for at least the next four months, and the necessities of life would naturally bring them into the village from time to time. It was possible they might, as some future period, want to break out of their self-imposed isolation for an evening or so on the town, and then it might be more pleasant to have . . . well, perhaps acquaintances would be a better word than friends . . . in the village. They might want to dine at the hotel, or perhaps go to the local cinema (regardless of the rather bland film fare). There didn't seem very much else to do here. In the meantime, the proper thing would be to remain somewhat aloof while not unfriendly in their contacts with the local population. It was unlikely that there were many in this small village who shared their own interests, and there would almost certainly be no basis for any really close relationships.

Sanders didn't seem at all a bad sort. Not overly sophisticated, perhaps, despite his transparent attempts at an atmosphere of big business, but a likeable chap, honest and straightforward, perhaps a bit over eager and inclined to reveal his youth and inexperience now and then. John sensed he could be depended upon in time of need. Ruth had seemed to have the same reaction towards him earlier that morning during their brief encounter when they had picked up the key to the house, and Ruth prided herself on the accuracy of her first impressions. He was certain they would get along.

Linda was both charming and friendly, possessing that touch of interest a writer finds in those who have obviously suffered tragedy and still bear its saddening marks. He did not even now understand the feminine mind and psychology well enough to hazzard a guess as to whether or not Linda and Ruth would take to each other . . . women were so totally unpredictable in their relations with each other . . . but he hoped they would, certain that Linda's appeal was not the kind that drew only men. He wondered if Linda were as yet in love with Paul, or if the unhappiness of her apparently very recent past still clouded her eyes to the interesting possibilities in that relationship. He would enjoy watching developments between them.

John smiled to himself. Time was indeed beginning to catch up with him, when he found himself thinking of watching the progress of other romances, rather than starting one of his own. Perhaps he was becoming something of a voyeur. Well, it would at least avoid any nasty personal complications. That sort of thing could well prove disastrous at this point in his marriage.

Despite his excellent spirits, John found the return journey to the house not nearly as pleasant as he had found the trip into the village. The slow, dampening drizzle and the rapid movement of the car still did little to ease the stifling humidity and its discomfort. The sea appeared darker, grayer, and there was an angriness in the way it hurled itself so violently onto the beach, tumbling with great spouts of dashing white spray, rolling hungrily over the exposed surface of the beach as though the long truce between sea and land had been broken at last and the ancient battle for supremacy had been resumed. He could no longer clearly discern the horizon, for the clouds had lowered and all about him had become a dirty slate gray, here and there slashed with a ribbon of billious yellow. The desolation of the sand dunes, the emptiness of the beach, the unbroken horizon, seemed somehow more depressing than before. The car obstinately sought and found every possible lump and irregularlity in the dirt road, and he cursed frequently at his rattling discomfort.

He glanced at his watch and felt the uneasy stirrings of guilt. It was considerably later than he had planned or expected. He had left Ruth alone for too long; that was both unfair and unwise. She had a tendency to become extremely nervous in a new place, particularly when left alone, and in her current state of mind that was not a good thing; her mind would be too filled with too many thoughts better forgotten. It was at such times that she suffered her bad nights, and that could be something of an omen on this first night in their new home. Perhaps she had managed to keep herself so busy with the cleaning that she hadn't really been aware of the aloneness, or of the passing of time. He was glad he would at least be back before it became really dark.

The old house finally loomed up before him, an almost ghostly white against the darkly clouded sky; the drizzle fell like a curtain of shimmering beads behind which the house waited for him, patient, tall and silent. Through a peculiar trick of the swiftly moving clouds, it momentarily seemed to him that he saw a tall dark figure, with blowing black skirts and wind-swept white hair, standing alone on the Widow's Walk, looking for a ghostly ship on the choppy seas. It would not really have surprised him to see such a spectre. Surely all Widow's Walks on all seacoasts of the world are haunted by the spirits of lonely, waiting women. He smiled at his own thoughts. What nonsense! He didn't believe in ghosts.

The stormy darkness had somehow changed the house. There was about the old structure almost a touch of ominous loneliness. He frowned. That was a peculiar pairing of words. Loneliness was often sad and frequently it was mournful. It could also be pleasant and soothing. Surely loneliness could become ominous only when connected with fear, and what was there to fear in this splendid old mansion on its rocky promontory by the sea? The vacant windows, with only darkness behind them, were like ebony walls concealing dark secrets of the past, and he wondered if the warm light of welcome had ever really gleamed through them. The gables seemed like angry fingers pointed defiantly towards the sky. Perched on the very edge of the cliff, the house seemed to float in space above the sea, part of a different, impenetrable and inexplicable world. Strange how different was this reaction to his first glimpse of the house. Atmosphere could do that, of course.

Ruth was seated on the top step of the veranda, sheltered from the drizzle by the overhanging eaves, her arms about her raised legs, her chin resting on her knees. Her attention seemed fixed on the dead tree, whose naked branches clashed like battling skeletal limbs in the light touch of an occasional breeze from the sea, gleaming slightly with the moisture of the rain. As John pulled up on the flat ground before the steps, Ruth's eyes followed him, but she made no other movement.

"Hi!" he called as he slammed shut the car door and quickly mounted the steps.

"Hi. Is it ours?" she asked, without raising her head.

"Every termite-riddled rafter of it," he assured her. "Every creaking timber and overstuffed chair. Every speck of dust. From the tip of the tallest gable to the bottom of the cellar. At least, for the next four months. Longer, if we should decide we simply can't be happy anywhere else."

He seated himself on the step beside her and put an arm about her shoulders, drawing her close to him, attempting to ignore that slight gesture of withdrawal that had lately become a habit with her. There seemed a strange rather was-like pallor in her face, and her eyes looked curiously distant and unfocused; he was again reminded of how thin and small a woman she was. He felt the protective instinct.

"Are you all right, dear?" he asked, unaccountably concerned.

She smiled, but her eyes still held just a ghostly touch of sadness; it was a sign she had probably been thinking of Elinor.

"Yes, of course I'm all right. I've just been sitting here, looking out to sea, daydreaming. Why does the sea make everyone a dreamer?"

"You'll catch cold out here," he cautioned her. "It's turning quite nasty. You aren't used to the sea air, you know; it can be pretty deceiving."

She shook her head, and he felt the damp fragrance of her hair. "Oh, no, no, I'm all right, really."

"I'm sorry I took so long," he apologized. "I stopped off for a drink, and got to talking with the secretary from the real estate office. I'm afraid I forgot to watch the time."

"Pretty?"

"The office, the bar or the secretary?"

"Any of them. All of them."

"Frankly, the secretary is the most attractive of the three."

"I don't remember seeing one this morning."

"She was out," he advised her. "Nice girl. She lost her husband recently, after a mariage of only six months."

"Sometimes it's a good thing when sorrow comes to the young," Ruth mused. "It prepares them for what's ahead. What did you two talk about?"

"Nothing very exciting. The house, mostly," he confessed. "I thought I might be able to learn something about it."

"Is there something to learn?" she asked after a moment.

Shrugging, he replied, "Oh, I don't know, really. Nothing, perhaps. But these old houses sometimes do have a story, a place in local history and legend. I'd like to know something more about this man Fowles himself. The writer in me, I guess."

"And what did you learn?"

"Nothing at all," John admitted. "Come to think of it, nobody seems to enjoy talking about the man or the house."

"Too bad. I hope the drinks were good."

"What can you do to Scotch?"

They were silent for several moments, seated warmly together, his arm protectingly about her, looking out to the empty sea. The pregnant clouds had steadily darkened and were now a dull black; they seemed to be lowering themselves, as though drawn by a powerful magnet beneath the sea. The wind was rising. The sea was whipped into whitecaps that were startlingly brilliant against the dark backdrop. The churning gray water hurled itself in angry frustration against the land, and the wind carried cold salty spray to their perspiring faces, refreshing them. A daring gull struggled momentarily against the sudden wind and then dropped from their sight over the rim of the cliff.

"Are we going to be happy here, John?" Ruth asked softly, her voice like a whisper in the wind.

She raised her face to him, and he saw the silent pleading in her eyes, the desperate need to be reassured, to find reason to believe, to hope. He pressed his lips to the chilled, spume-dampened forehead.

"Why shouldn't we be? We have each other, Ruth."

He felt warmed by the sudden glow of affection in her eyes. "I do love you, John."

"I know. And I love you."

Yet when his kiss became too intense, Ruth placed her hands on his chest and moved away from him; her eyes were bright and sharp again and the brief moment of sorrow . . . of shared hopes . . . of intimacy had passed.

"Do you realize how long it's been since we've eaten?" she exclaimed, brushing off his embrace and rising to her feet. "You must be famished!"

He twisted his face into a mock grimace. "And I thought we were going to live on love!" The light bantering tone served to disguise his disappointment at her withdrawal.

"Living on love may be all right for some people, but while love may fill the heart, it leaves the stomach empty. I didn't get very much cleaning done, I'm afraid, but at least we'll have a clean table to eat on. There is a grocery in town, I hope? I didn't notice this morning."

He rose from the steps, brushing from the rear of his trousers the sand that seemed to find its way everywhere. "As a matter of fact, there is a rather surprisingly well-stocked grocery store, complete with a funny bespectacled clerk in a white apron and two nosey old biddies just dying of curiosity to know who I am and what I'm doing here."

"Then you did manage to drop in at the grocer's between your visits to the village bars?"

"Yes, I did. And it was 'bar.' Singular."

"And girl, singular."

He nodded. "Girl, singular. It was one of my off days."

"What did you bring?"

He decended the steps and started towards the car. "Oh, all sorts of wonderful things, to paraphrase one Howard Carter. There are pheasants imprisoned under glass, and frogs legs without any frogs attached to them, and. . ."

"You brought hamburger and cold cuts," she interrupted.

He paused with his hand on the car door, ignoring the rain that was now beginning to fall more heavily, plastering his hair to his head and running driblets down the length of his nose. "What makes you say that?"

"That's all you ever bring," Ruth replied. "No matter where you are, or when, if I send you to the grocery, all you ever bring back with you in hamburger and cold cuts. You're like a little boy whose idea of the perfect meal is hot dogs and coke. You're totally devoid of all imagination when it comes to buying food. Either that, or you seem to think I'm incapable of preparing anything but hamburger; you've a very low opinion of my culinary talents."

"You warned me that the stove is an old one," he reminded her, reaching into the rear of the car for the packages, "and I was to bear that in mind."

"There's a specific difference between what is old and what is primitive!" She laughed at his now dripping, rather woebegone expression. "Oh, come on, don't just stand there and get wet. I'm starving, even if you're not."

The first meal they shared in their new home by the sea was by the flickering romantic lights of burning candles, which served to remind John that he had completely forgotten to do anything about having the electricity restored to the old house, for which he received another of those long-suffering, bad little boy looks from Ruth. Considering it incomprehensible that a house so situated would not have an emergency supply of candles on hand, they searched the kitchen and pantry, opening warped doors of ancient cupboards containing nothing but several decades of undisturbed dust, and rummaging through abandoned cabinets, until they found some old, yellowed tapers in a drawer of the kitchen table. There were several rather clumsy and amusing moments while they attempted to unravel the ancient mysteries of the uncooperative cooking range, but before long the hamburger patties were sizzling in their own juices, and the tangy aroma of fresh hot coffee and the pungent scent of burning wood (fortunately, a supply was on hand in the wood box beside the stove), odors and aromas for so many years absent from the old house, filled the kitchen with a decided air of hominess.

They sat facing each other at the uncovered wooden table, warm and comfortable in their own little circle of yellow light, with the wind now blowing gustily outside, like an orgre infuriated by its own loneliness, the rain tapping like a lost and hungry soul at the windows, their shadows dancing upon the walls and ceilings like insubstantial visitors from the forgotten past of the old house, while the memories of their own former, perhaps happier days surrounded them with their own particular warmth and sadness. The house had again a feeling of friendliness, as though enfolding them in a comfort that for too many lonely years had lain dormant. The city seemed far away, and they were in a world all their own, a world that promised them a wonderful new beginning.

Ruth reached out and touched John's hand, warmly running her thin fingers across the sparse dark hairs on its back. "It's almost like when we first met, isn't it, John? The candlelight, the supper, the romantic glow. . ."

"Not quite the same," John said with a smile, entwining his fingers with hers. "That night, we didn't have the rain beating at the windows and the wind trying to tear its way in and join in some of our comfort."

"It isn't very romantic to be exactly accurate," she insisted, placing his hand to her cheek.

"And it isn't very accurate to be too romantic," he quipped.

"Still, I'd like to think there will always be time for romance. . ."

That warm, now rare touch of intimacy lingered even after they had finished their sparse, makeshift dinner, when they decided to retire to the living room to sit together before another fire and strengthen those dreams on which they had both been building throughout that long and exciting day. Ruth stripped the dust cloth from the old red velvet sofa, in places worn thin by generation of sitters, while John struggled to kindle the decaying wood in the large fireplace. Both their attempts ended in total chaotic disaster. Ruth's activities succeeded merely in raising large clouds of ancient white dust that rose from the sheets like flocks of angry moths, while John managed only to fill the room with thick acrid smoke that caused them to flee, choking and laughing, from the house and once again out into the purer air of the veranda.

They sat for a time silently and comfortably on the topmost step, John leaning against the pillar with Ruth cradled in his arms, and they listened to the dying storm exhaust its final furies upon the indifferent and unconquerable sea. The rain was occasionally swept in upon them by the wind, but they found it cooling and refreshing, rather than discomforting. It was quite dark by this time, and they could see little beyond the immediate area of the veranda. The lone tree, so much lonelier in the empty darkness, had become part of the black fabric of the night, its branches like smears of ebony against black velvet. The sea had gathered the night about itself to conceal its ancient mysteries, and was hidden from their view, but they could still hear its steady thunder, a soothing natural symphony that swept their thoughts along a tide of happiness. A flickering beam of yellow light from a candle lighted on the table in the foyer streamed through the open doorway and deposited a pool of gold at their feet.

But it had been a long and very tiring day, and exhaustion soon touched them both. When Ruth had twice dozed off in John's arms, perhaps aided to sleep by the rhythmic rolling of the sea, they decided on an early retirement and, hopefully, an early rising to commence the numerous chores that awaited them. Ruth proudly pointed out that she, once again more alert than John to their most immediate requirements (she firmly refused to forget his failure about the lighting), had aired out the master bedroom and made it cozy and fit for human habitation.

They felt a peculiar sense of time misplacement as they undressed by the light of the candles and prepared for bed. Somehow they had become part of the history of the old house, and the modern world seemed distant in more than space. They were narrowly watched at their toilet by a glowering, bearded old seaman with piercing blue eyes who hung at the head of the giant fourpostered bed, and Ruth remarked that she actually felt uncomfortable under his stern gaze, while John, staring at the red-bearded face with the hawk nose and the livid facial scars of ancient battles, wondered if this could be the mysterious Captain Jonathan Fowles himself, sea captain and reputed pirate, staring angrily at them for invading the privacy of the house he had long ago constructed for himself. There seemed by now something strangely familiar in that face; John decided it was undoubtedly because there were so many similar faces hanging upon the walls of the house.

They crept into the bed that had been cold and empty

for so long, and lay for some moments in each other's arms under the light quilt, wondering at the stories of those who had lain there over the course of so many years. In a matter of moments, they were both sound asleep.

It must have been close to dawn when John awoke. For some moments, he lay motionless in the bed, his eyes staring up at the dark and unfamiliar ceiling, wondering at the total absence of city traffic sound beyond the windows, before at last he reached an awareness of his surroundings and remembered the events of the previous day.

Everything was perfectly still, with that peculiar silence that can bring a dull ringing to the ears. Only the gentle sounds of Ruth's regular breathing disturbed the quiet; he turned to look at her, but in the dark he could only discern the general outline of her form lying at his side. At least she was sleeping; the dreams had not yet come. He frowned. There was another sound lightly marring the silence. What was it? That rhythmic, rolling noise. Of course. The sea. They would have to accustom themselves to that. He wondered if it were possible to reach a point where you no longer heard it. He hoped not; he liked the sound.

He felt warm and sticky and sleep had temporarily gone from him. Careful not to awaken Ruth, he slipped quickly and quietly out of the bed, reaching to the bedside table for a cigarette, lighting it as he stepped rather gingerly out onto the little balcony overhanging the cliff.

It was a peculiar night. The storm had spent itself and retired to gloat over its temporary victories and lick its wounds while gathering force to resume the attack when the propitious moment arrived. The rain had stopped, and he could hear the dripping from the eaves. The wind had beaten itself to silence against the sturdy rocks. A thick fog had rolled in from the sea, enveloping the house in an opaque yellow-white envelope that John could almost reach out to touch. Below him he could hear the thunder of the waves crashing against the rocks at the base of the cliff. He bent over, tightly holding onto the cold metal railing, but he could distinguish nothing but the fog that surrounded everything. It was strange to hear the dull roar of the sea from behind a tenuous, swirling curtain his eyes could not pierce. The deep silence was somehow disturbing. He had a momentary fear that all the world was gone, and nothing was left but the sea, the fog, and the old house dangling above the bottomless pit of eternity.

He became gradually aware that the slight sounds in the room behind him had subtly altered. Ruth's gentle breathing was interrupted by low moans and sharp catches of breath and he could hear her stirring restlessly in the bed. The dreams had begun again, after all; he had hoped these new surroundings would hold them at bay. He felt perhaps he should end her discomfort, but disliked to awaken her; at least she was sleeping, and she had become too accustomed to wakeful nights. Perhaps the sea air would help her to sleep more peacefully in time.

It had been a full and exciting day. The city, with all its noises and irritations, seemed already prt of another world, not something they had left only two days ago, but something distant in both time and space. The yellow curtain of fog seemed to divide the two worlds.

He would, almost certainly, miss certain aspects of their city life, and there would undoubtedly be periods of crashing boredom here when he would wish himself back in the center of all that activity, but he still did not question the wisdom of this move they had made. Not yet, anyway. He could still manage to convince himself that it was good to be away from it all.

It was not the wisdom of the move that gave him this slight hesitation, but the ultimate success of what they had planned. He felt a deep need to convince himself that it was going to work. Why was there still that uncomfortable nagging doubt at the back of his mind? What was there to fear? The house was theirs now, and they were here alone, away from the well meaning but interfering friends and distractions. Was that it? Did he doubt their ability to form a new order all their own, excluding all externals, living with and for only each other? They had lived so long in that other world; had they waited too long to make the change? It constituted a complete about face in their entire manner of living. Perhaps it was too late. Perhaps they had already passed the stage where life was not enough when composed only of each other. Perhaps they were too old to start over, to try to recapture something that perhaps only youth can find.

The very suggestion seemed somehow treasonous. He loved his wife deeply, surely as much as he had in those first days of their marriage. The decline of physical intimacy in recent years, the fading of the first pinkish blush of romance, could not be attributed to any change in their feeling for each other. They had simply become too busy, so busy that they were unaware of the insidious decay that had entered their lives. He loved Ruth very much. Yes. Of course he did.

Why was it necessary to repeat that so constantly? Recent months, of course, had put a considerable strain on both of them. Ruth had become very difficult. Much affected by Elinor's death, she had sullenly withdrawn into herself, kept apart even from him. He had thought the greatest balm for her would be another child, but Ruth had recoiled at the very suggestion, turning on him as though he had suggested some obscene rite or blasphemous ceremony.

He tried to understand. Perhaps it was that Ruth feared another tragic loss as had come to them through Elinor's death. Nothing could bring their daughter back to them, and to Ruth another child would merely be a substitute intended to take Elinor's place; she would never be able to love another child. Only once did she let slip the suggestion that perhaps God, in removing Elinor, had indicated His decision that they were not to have any children.

Although they still shared the same bed, and John often felt a biting sexual need, Ruth now spurned all such overtures. The little affectionate gestures, such as holding of hands or sitting with his arm about her as they had that very evening on the veranda, were now rare and unusual instances. If he attempted to build on them to a mutual sexual desire, Ruth changed instantly and completely.

But surely this attitude would pass, in time. He would have to wait, somehow bridle his needs. He recoiled at the thought of being unfaithful to his wife. He was no prude, but the notion at this particular time was repugnant to him. His sexual needs must not be permitted to destroy the fragile threads of their marriage at a time when Ruth needed him more than ever. He owed that to her.

He frowned, again hearing the low sounds of Ruth's moans. He had better awaken her from the nightmare and attempt to comfort whatever new fears might have invaded the privacy of her dreams.

He would do his very best to make this work, for both of them. That was the only decision he could make.

As he flipped his cigarette into the solid yellow-white world beyond the balcony, John suddenly realized he was shivering.

Strange. It was a very warm night.

CHAPTER FIVE

DURING the days that so quickly followed one upon another, Ruth and John busied themselves with the considerable task of settling themselves into their new home by the sea and restoring the old house on the clifftop to an abode of the living after its many lonely years of dust-gathering abandonment. There was much to be done, for during its long years of emptiness there had been no attempt to keep the house in anything resembling a state of repair, but its isolation had at least prevented the visits of vandals and such who might have hastened the process of decay, and there were no really serious problems, aside from a loose board or shingle here and there, a leaking ceiling in one of the smaller second-floor bedrooms which they were not planning to use anyway, and a few broken panes of glass, and they soon found themselves enjoying all the work entailed in making the house again habitable.

They were, after all, working only for themselves, preparing for their own future happiness, whether for a period of four months or a longer time, and there was a simple joy in that knowledge. There seemed a new and exciting magic merely in being here together, and they felt like a young and slightly embarrassed couple just embarking on the intimate adventure of marriage, rather than an older man and woman whose lives had so recently been shadowed by tragedy, and who had come so dangerously close to losing each other.

Surely in all their years together, even in those gold-shadowed days of their first meeting, the world had never seemed to them quite so beautiful, so rich, so filled with glowing promise. They would often pause in their work just to look at each other and smile their new found confidence, or they would casually reach out to touch each other, and their fingers would be warm with love. The restless tide of the sea, endlessly casting its spume-whitened waves upon the long suffering sandy beach below the house, seemed to speak in hushed, perhaps reverent tones of their love as they cleaned, swept, dusted, washed, and generally put the house in order. Neither one would admit to the other that one of the driving forces behind this was the possibility that the house might one day be permanently theirs, but both often remembered there was that option to buy.

Ruth removed the yellowing dust covers from the furniture and stored them away in the vast cedar-smelling closet beneath the stairs, while secretly hoping they would not be used again. Most of the furniture was outmoded and badly worn, but already Ruth had earmarked certain pieces of undoubted antique charm which she would retain were the house to become theirs, while already picturing what would be replaced and how.

John grunted and swore under the unexpected weight of these furnishings as he moved the chairs and the sofas about from one position to another while Ruth attempted, with her sharply critical eye, to determine how they could be placed to best advantage. John was encouraged by this attention to detail, taking her insistence on proper placement as a sign that Ruth was preparing the rooms for viewing by future visitors.

They removed the grime of years from the tall windows and vigorously scrubbed the pantry to receive their supply of food; John wisely concealed from his wife the little family of mice he unearthed in one of the darker corners. The beauty of the old wood of the floors and doorjambs became clear with careful polishing. They aired out all the bedrooms, even those they did not at present intend to use, and placed clean, fresh sheets upon the beds, another indication which John silently took as a hopeful promise for the future. They explored the old house together, delighting in the airy rooms with their sweeping views of the sea, and admired the solid construction of a house so fully exposed to the elements which had nevertheless managed to withstand some two centuries of storm and wind and rain. Under John's practical eye and Ruth's artistic touch, the house once again became both attractive and pleasant, as it must have been in the earlier days.

It shortly began to feel like home. Ruth managed to master the intricacies of the old-fashioned wood-burning stove and even found herself enjoying the challenge of preparing food in the 'good old-fashioned way of our grandmothers', and proudly placing her culinary experiments on the table before her somewhat dubious and hesitant husband, who diplomatically announced himself thrilled and delighted with the results, whether truthfully or otherwise.

John accomplished whatever minor repairs were necessary about the house, such as tightening window frames, oiling squeaking doors, leveling warped flooring, and putting the various fireplaces in working order; any more involved and expensive repairs would have to be approved (and paid for) by the owners and there was, of course, no need for John and Ruth to become involved in such extensive matters until they determined whether or not they intended to make this house their own. There was actually little enough John could do; he had never been very successful at working with his hands, except when they were placed in position on the keys of a typewriter. The electricity was restored, the water turned on, and the high ceilinged rooms became warm with life and sunshine, as fresh sea air swept away the mouldy past, and life returned once again to a house that had been without it for too long.

And the more they saw of this new house, the more they came to love it . . . the often surprising little nooks and crannies with their startling views of the always empty sea, the portrait-lined corridors which were galleries of staring eyes and bearded chins (the portraits had been carefully dusted and cleaned, although John failed to see the necessity for this) . . . the wheezing grandfather's clock in the foyer which they had again started into motion but which boomed out its throaty announcements of the quarter hours just exactly two minutes earlier than it should, no matter how they tried to adjust it, the seaman's paraphernalia that seemed as much at home here as in some nautical museum, the Widow's Walk with its ghostly memories and superb panorama of the sea, the virgin white beaches, the just discernible roofs of the distant village. The foyer was returned to its early magnificence, and in the evenings the light glistened through the shimmering crystals and cast a warm glow upon the darkly burnished wood and the gracefully sweeping stairway.

They came to know something of the pride that must have moved Fowles to construct his eyrie on the very edge of the promontory overlooking the sea for which he obviously had felt a deep love, an emotion which Ruth illogically felt absolved him of many supposed wrongs.

Yet the house still told them remarkably little about Fowles himself, save for his love of the sea and his excellent taste. Although John was certain more than one of the sea captains portraits on the walls was that of Fowles himself, he could not determine which did actually represent the builder of the house, or what materials and furnishings had belonged to him and what to later inhabitants. So scanty was their knowledge of the history of the house that they were not even certain if it had been lived in after the death of Fowles himself, although Ruth sensed some of the furnishings were of a considerable older date than others.

John had always subscribed to the theory that you can tell much about the character of a man from the books he owns, but this theory was of little use in understanding the nature of Jonathan Fowles. Many of the mouldering old books in the library bore Fowles' inscription in a bold, oversized, scrawling, almost illegible hand, indicating a personality of dynamic, if erratic, powers. Although the majority of the volumes not surprisingly dealt with matters of the sea and seamanship, John was surprised by the number of books . . . some of them undoubted collector's items . . . concerned with various aspects of witchcraft and the supernatural. The *Malleus Maleficarum* Ruth had noticed on their first visit had in particular seen a considerable amount of handling. Why should the burly, brutal sea captain have possessed an interest in such subjects? The true nature of Fowles remained an enigma.

When their day's work was over and the soothing silence of night had fallen, Ruth and John slowly walked hand-in-hand on the damp, cool, hard packed sand, watching the graceful flight of the great gulls against the crimson of the setting sun as they dipped their large white wings close to the blue-green sea as though in obeisance to their royal master, tracing the erratic scurried movements of the tiny sand crabs as they burrowed into the smoothly wet surface of the beach at their approach, delighting in the counterfeit surge of the surf when they held to their ears twisted, convoluted, pink and white or pearl-gray seashells, examining the rather messy conformation of the soggy, lice-infested seaweed and the strange pattern of tunnel-like holes eaten into the salt-whitened driftwood by the constant movement of the sea and the strange pincered and toothed denizens of the deep. On rather rare occasions, the sun broke through the usual cloud covering to touch the water with a wand of fairy-gold.

Once darkness had settled upon the sea and the line of demarcation between sea and sky was concealed by the blackness of night, they sat before the crackling fire in the living room (for the nights had suddenly become chilly) and felt warm and satisfied in their reawakened love and in the peacefulness of their new mode of living.

And yet, despite this new found love and warmth between them, the barrier remained against the even closer intimacy that John came more and more to crave. If his embraces and kisses became too ardent, if his hands wandered too suggestively, Ruth quickly moved away with some lame excuse about work to be done, weariness, or the traditional headache. The new intimacy had become curiously asexual, like that between a brother and sister in Medieval romances, and Ruth shied like a startled fawn from the possibility of anything further. Often considerably aroused, John found it difficult to subdue his desire but, with rather remarkable restraint, he managed to control himself with the rather unsatisfactory understanding that the time was not yet:

They saw no one they were able to avoid. None of their erstwhile city friends knew where they were, and the house was superbly isolated from the village and from other lone cottages. There was an occasional fisherman on the beach, standing with the surf tugging at his great rubber boots while he tried to prove his superiority over the creatures who swam beneath the surface and could not resist the attraction of his lures, but they carefully avoided approaching close enough for conversation. The only mail that arrived came from the few who, of necessity, had been advised of their whereabouts: Ruth's gallery contacts, John's publishers, and John's grandmother. They received from Grandmother Ellen long and affectionate letters bearing various European postmarks, in which she did not attempt to conceal her curiosity about their current mode of life.

Paul Sanders dropped in two or three times during the first couple of weeks merely to check on conditions and make certain that his new tenants were comfortable and content, but pleasant though he invariably was, they never encouraged him to prolong his visits, and Paul himself apparently neither expected nor desired it.

John was often puzzled by these visits, for Paul seemed always strangely ill at ease in the house. He seemed to be looking for or expecting something, and he appeared intensely relieved when he failed to find it. There was about him an attitude of tense listening to the very silence of the old house, as though he were waiting for sounds other than those made by themselves, and his eyes narrowed whenever he approached the darker corners. The Paul they saw at the house—intense, alert, somber—was very different from the charming, gay and carefree Paul that John knew in the village.

Yet even more confusing were those times when Paul seemed so strangely familiar with the house, and at those times the difference in him became almost physical. He walked then through the house with an almost proprietary air, his hands clasped behind his back as though he were strolling the deck of a ship, commenting about the changes they had made, the alterations in rooms that Paul had previously admitted he had seldom seen.

It was during one of these visits, while Paul stood beneath the large portrait over the mantle in the living room, that John realized why these portraits had all seemed so familiar to him. Even without the beard, Paul bore a striking resemblance to the old Fowles of the portrait, and John recalled that Paul had been born and spent most of his life in the village. Ruth, rather surprisingly for one with so keen an eye, apparently did not notice this remarkable resemblance, and John did not draw it to her attention.

It was occasionally necessary for Ruth and John to make forays into the village for supplies, but such infrequent visits were made as quickly and briefly as possible, and they even enjoyed the parrying of searching questions from the incurably inquisitive shop keepers. The other villagers, although quite obviously intensely interested in the new arrivals, kept their distance and made no attempts at friendliness, looking at these strangers somewhat askance, as though they were suspected of having come from some strange and far distant world that did not belong in their peaceful, sane and simple little hamlet; they were often followed and rather morosely stared at by children hungrily sucking on their sticky lollipops. Their purchases were closely, if surreptitiously, examined in the peculiar hope that this might provide some clue to their characters and habits. Heads were turned and whispers followed them whenever they appeared on Main Street, but the villagers restricted their attempts at friendliness to a muttered *Good day* or *Nice morning* in passing, or a faint smile. Ruth credited this aloofness, welcome though it was, to the not unusual small town distrust of strangers, while John wondered if their residence at Fowles House might have something to do with it. At any rate, they were grateful for being left alone to do their shopping in peace and comparative solitude. They generally drove into the village in the very early morning, just after the shops had opened for the day, stopped only at those stores where they had specific business to contract, made their purchases very quickly (having determined before-hand exactly what was needed) and quickly returned home.

In view of Paul's apparent interest in and concern for them and his visits to Fowles House, John often felt it was rather rude of them not to drop in at the real estate office, but at the last moment he always decided against doing so, and Ruth never suggested it. Here, too, John felt the time was simply not yet ripe. Not just yet. Such calls would result in Paul's increasing the frequency and the duration of his visits to the house, and Linda would feel obligated to invite Ruth to those little teas or shopping sprees or whatever women delight in, and Ruth would find it increasingly more difficult to refuse. Their splendid isolation would vanish. No, it was too soon to risk it.

One morning, as they were driving to the stores, John spied the chic form of Linda walking briskly towards the office, but the secretary failed to notice him and, with a reaction for which he later felt a peculiar sense of guilt, John did not bring her to Ruth's attention.

And so the days passed quickly, marked by nothing but serenity and contentment. This wonderful new world was entirely their own, and they neither needed nor wanted anyone to share it with them. They were like growing children who have just discovered that the world of reality need not after all be totally devoid of a childlike wonder. They emphatically refused Paul's suggestion that they have a telephone installed in the house. They wanted to be alone.

John felt his confidence considerably increased. Ruth blossomed under the purification of the clear sea air, and the color began to return to her sadly pale and sunken cheeks. She began to laugh more often, and a true warmth returned to her voice. She slept much better now, and soon was almost completely free of nightmares. She appeared happier than she had been in far too long a time, and that brought John a measure of contentment which, at least to a certain extent, lessened the strains and the dissatisfactions that were already beginning to arise in him as a result of this sudden hermit-like existence.

For the dissatisfaction was beginning. Oh, he would not, or could not, admit that he was in any way really discontent. It was just that he did occasionally begin to feel, after a day of hard work about the house, that it would be nice to get out and go somewhere. The evenings were sometimes too silent; he found himself wondering what was going on at the places he had frequented in the city. He never mentioned this to Ruth.

Perhaps the concentration required by returning to his writing would put that to rest. John appropriated the old study, with its rows of leather-bound books, its now dusted globe, and its painfully polished and gleaming telescope, and soon the room was littered with discarded manuscript paper and filled with the rhythmic click-clack of his typewriter, which John hoped would not disturb the ghost of the old sea captain in the event Fowles disliked this intrusion into his old study. Ruth, rather outlandishly garbed in her many-colored smock and the floppy, wide-brimmed straw hat that she considered the only proper garb for an artist, took her easel and her paints to the bluff and attempted to transfer the ever changing shadings of the sea onto her canvas. Life seemed more normal with both of them back at work again, but both hoped the new surroundings would be conducive to a higher level of production than they had experienced before.

John was not surprised to note Ruth's strong aversion for the cellar . . . he was well aware of his wife's numerous little phobias . . . but he was amused to see how carefully she avoided even the area of the cellar door, frequently making a wide detour around the table in order to avoid approaching it.

"You're like a little child afraid of the bogey man," he chuckled as they sat late one morning over their breakfast table.

"Frankly, no one has ever really convinced me that there is no such thing as a bogey man, but the fact that I happen not to like the cellar doesn't necessarily mean I'm afraid of it," Ruth insisted. "It's fusty, dusty, and ugly. And a cellar is more of a man's world than a woman's, anyway. Men are always down there, hammering and banging and sawing away at something or other. I suppose it's something like a bar. Some place where a man can get alone to be with himself, or with others of his own kind, away from women, where he can talk dirty."

John smiled, pouring another dash of cream into his coffee. "How long since you've been to a bar?" he asked dryly. "That last stronghold of male chauvinism has long since tumbled to the insidious tunnelings of women's lib. We have no place any more where we can be by ourselves, except in a public men's room, and I suppose before long female determination and curiosity will bring that to an end as well. And as for getting together to talk dirty, nowadays women talk even dirtier than men."

Ruth looked at him over the rim of her cup, and it was obvious her mind was on more serious matters; he doubted she had heard much of what he had said. She flicked her eyes away when he looked at her, as though embarrassed at having been caught staring at him.

"Have you got into that little room yet?" she asked quietly.

"The room in the cellar?" John lowered his cup and pursed his lips in irritated puzzlement. "You know, it's the damnedest thing about that room. I just can't get the damn door open, no matter how I try. I've pushed it, pulled it, tugged at it, prodded it, pried it, but nothing works. It must have settled pretty good into the earth over the years. I think it's going to take some kind of blasting to move it."

"Why don't you just leave it?" she asked.

He smiled as though at a childishly naive remark. "Can you imagine a writer without a feeling for mystery? I can't see even the slightest reason for that room to be there in the first place. It does nothing but break up the spaciousness of the cellar, and why should anyone want to do that? If it were on the other side of the house, I might be able to get through the window, but perched as it is right at the very edge of the cliff, there isn't any way for me to get even near the window, unless I lower myself down on a rope or something from the story above, and I'm just not about to dangle my ass over so much empty space just to drop into the sea. I sure would like to know what's in that room, though."

"Nothing, from what little I could see through the opening." Ruth made the mark before realizing she would thus reveal a not previously mentioned interest in the room.

John looked up at her in surprise. "I didn't realize you were even aware of that slight opening. You never mentioned trying to look into the room."

She flushed slightly. "Well, after all, it's a natural reaction, isn't it? You see an opening, you try to look through it. Even a writer has nothing on a woman when it comes to sheer, brazen curiosity. I admit I did just try to peek in, but the opening isn't large enough to show anything. Oh, if there were actually something of use in the room, I could understand your interest, but obviously it's nothing more than a small, empty room, so why bother?"

"For the same reason I would climb a mountain, if I were ever inclined to be that physical," John suggested. "If something is there, you want to know why, and you don't want to be prevented from finding out by a stuck door." He shrugged. "Oh, well, I suppose I'll manage to get it open one of these days. It might make a good workshop."

"A workshop for what?"

He shrugged again. "Oh, you know. What men do in the cellar, when they aren't in a bar talking dirty. Machine work. Making things with the hands. Cabinets, chairs, stools, things like that. Be a good way to relax between chapters."

Laughter wrinkled the corners of her eyes. "And you really would make things in this workshop?"

"Of course. Why not? Chairs, tables . . ."

"We don't need any."

"That's not the point. We may some day. Can always use another chair. You can save a hell of a lot of money that way. With the proper equipment, you can make just about anything. The main purpose is just doing it. Best therapy in the world."

"Oh, John, I don't want to damage your inherent sense of masculinity, but you know you're just about the clumsiest man with his hands who was ever placed upon this green planet. You almost slice your finger off when you cut a loaf of bread or carve a roast. The only machine you're adept with is a typewriter, and you still can't manage very well with an electric."

"That's not very flattering," John complained.

"The only people who find it necessary to flatter men are old maids looking for prospective husbands. I've already got mine, so I don't have to concern myself with your ego any further, my dear. I've already landed you, and now you're stuck with me, even when I dare to tell the truth."

"Well, I guess I'll just have to learn to live with it," he smiled and, with his lips pursed for a kiss, leaned across the table toward her.

His smile quickly faded and he frowned when she evaded his kiss, as she still so carefully avoided all most intimate physical contact. So it had been since the very day of Elinor's death. This change of scene, the excitement of settling into an entirely new way of life, all this till had not changed that. Elinor was still there, the one shadow that still clouded their recently happier world.

After a moment, Ruth quickly finished her coffee and carried their few dishes to the sink. She hesitated a moment, looking at them as though they were something particularly obscene and loathsome.

"Oh, I think I'll just leave them for later." She stared at the dishes again, both accusatory and uncertain. "I suppose I really shouldn't, though. That could be a dangerous sign. I'm turning into a sloppy housewife with dirty dishes piled in the sink."

"A couple of coffee cups hardly qualify for dirty dishes piled in the sink," John mentioned.

She smiled brightly. "You've convinced me. I really do want to catch the light while it lasts; the clouds haven't been as thick these last days, and I should take advantage of it."

John looked at her for a moment, still smarting under the rebuff, trying to understand this still very attractive woman who had so completely lost all the sexual interest and curiosity she had once possessed. He sighed; writing about women had done nothing toward helping him to understand them. Well, he would have to go on waiting a little longer. How many times had he said that to himself?

"Don't forget your hat," he cautioned as she moved towards the veranda. "The weather's changing again, and it's going to be a bitch of a day. You don't have any protection at all out there, you know, and you always do burn like a protected virgin who's never been permitted out of doors." He touched a napkin to his lips and rose from the chair. "Well, with any luck at all, I should be able to finish another chapter today. Things are going pretty well here. I think better in this air."

But the expected chapter proved more difficult than John had anticipated, and he labored stubbornly and doggedly in his study all through that day, deeply immersed in the tangled complexities of a rather intricate plot that refused to move as he felt it should. Sheets of paper ended as snowballs in various parts of the room as they were angrily torn from the typewriter, crumbled and tossed aimlessly about the room, while the stack of completed pages on one side of his desk failed to increase appreciably in size. It became uncomfortably humid, and he removed his shirt and attempted to ignore the trickles of perspiration running down his bare chest as he pounded unsatisfactorily at one paragraph after another, pausing at times to pace the floor angrily, attempting to resolve his character difficulties in clouds of blue-white cigarette smoke.

He was startled when he heard the preliminary wheezing of the grandfather's clock in the foyer, and then the solemn, slightly off key striking of three sonorous bass notes; he had forgotten all about lunch and so, apparently, had Ruth. Wiping his chest with a coldly damp handkerchief, he rose from the desk and moved to the large open window beside the rows of books and looked out across the bluff toward the sea.

Ruth was in her accustomed spot very close to the cliff's edge, where she preferred to do her work, and a feeling of sudden warmth flooded through him at sight of her slender form, quickly followed by a rising of sexual desire that he attempted to subdue as quickly as it came. He had done well in subduing these emotions up to now, in spite of his growing need, and it would be best not to destroy that now. He knew Ruth was far too dear to him to jeopardize their future by forcing upon her intimacies for which she was presently not psychologically equipped.

He frowned, suddenly sensing something somewhat unusual in his wife's attitude. She was not seated on her little folding stool as usual, but standing rather stiffly beside her easel, one hand resting on a corner of the canvas, the other loosely dangling a paint brush at her side. She was not facing the sea, but staring intently at the seaward side of the house, as though watching something there. With some concern and a touch of irritation, John noticed that in spite of his warning, she had forgotten her floppy hat and was fully exposed to the hot sun. There was something disturbing in her stillness.

John stepped through the large open window, over the low sill and onto the veranda, calling to Ruth, who gave no sign of hearing him. Aware of a growing, inexplicable sense of uneasiness, he descended the steps and walked briskly toward her, surprised at the sudden intense heat of the afternoon. The air was very still, and the sky was white with heat, with a hazy halo ringing the sun. He tried to recall the mariner's superstition to determine whether a halo around the sun portended a storm; or was the moon the barometer? There were no ships on the shimmering horizon, and even the gulls seemed to have sought earlier shelter from the sun. He wondered when the early morning clouds had cleared and how long Ruth had been exposed to the sun.

"Ruth, honey, you shouldn't be out here without your hat," he chided as he approached the motionless figure. "I reminded you of that just this morning. You know how easily you burn, and you'll be up all night with the pain of it."

Ruth did not respond. She stared fixedly at the house, apparently totally unaware of her husband's approach. Perspiration gleamed on her forehead, and the brush trembled slightly in her hand; it had touched her smock with a smear of brilliant green. There was already an unpleasant pinkishness to the skin at the back of her neck. John took her by the shoulders and turned her to him.

"Ruth, are you all right?"

Slowly, almost dreamily, she turned and looked at him. Her eyes disturbed him; they seemed to have difficulty focusing in on his face. There was a vagueness about them, a swimming uncertainty, and the pupils seemed dilated, as the eyes of one who is drugged. There was a whiteness about the skin of her forehead, like the waxen sheen of polished imitation fruit, an almost phosphorescent glow that appeared strange and unnatural under the harsh touch of the golden sun beneath which she had been seated, totally without protection for so many hours.

Almost as though she were awakening from a long dream that had taken her to strange and far distant worlds, Ruth's vacant gaze slowly altered and the slightest touch of a smile parted her red lips.

"Oh, John! I'm terribly sorry, darling," she apologized. "I quite honestly didn't hear you. I must have been so absorbed in my work. Did you call me?"

"Are you all right, Ruth?" he repeated, staring closely at her, not liking that persistent vagueness of expression.

"Why, of course, John. Certainly, I'm just fine." Her voice, too, seemed not quite natural; her tone was dull and flat, lacking the usual lightness, and seemed to come to him with an extreme effort from some far distant place. "I'm sorry I didn't hear you, dear; I have been working very hard."

"You know you shouldn't work under a sun like this without your hat," he again cautioned her, and then felt foolish for chiding her like a little girl who has misbehaved. "I reminded you just before you came out here this morning, Ruth. You talked me into buying that hideous thing for you, and now I expect you to wear it."

She laughed lightly, somewhat embarrassed. "My hat? Of course! Why, if that isn't the strangest thing! I remember distinctly placing it on the table in the foyer just before going for my paints, so I wouldn't forget it. I thought surely I had it on! I am sorry, darling. Please don't scold me."

"And you've been working out here like this since breakfast," he continued in his naughty girl tone, "and here it is after three, and you completely forgot about lunch."

Mention of the time seemed to startle her. "Three o'clock? My goodness, is it really that late? Why, I had no idea. Oh, but then, you've had no lunch either, have you? Oh, I'm terribly sorry. I've been working. The sun came through the clouds and the light was so wonderful, I couldn't bring myself to stop."

He attempted to dismiss that sense of uneasiness that prevented him from taking her words with the same lightness of her tone. There was something just not right about her and her attitude. Perhaps it was the sun in his eyes that made it so difficult for him to see her face as clearly as he would have liked. It was as though a sparkling veil of fairy gossamer was concealing her features from him. He blinked his eyes, thinking to clarify the vision, but there was no change.

"Oh, lunch isn't that important," he calmed her. "I'm really not the least bit hungry; I've been working pretty hard myself."

"Neither am I," she confessed. "I never have much of an appetite in hot weather like this."

"Well, then, at least let me have a look at this masterpiece you've been creating under this boiling sun *sans* hat," he said in a somewhat forcibly lighter tone, stepping up to the canvas; Ruth moved aside, watching his expression.

John was startled by what he saw. To his surprise, Ruth had not been painting the sea, as he had assumed. It was the house that filled her large canvas, and although the sky that morning was clear with a blue-white haze of heat, it was as though a sudden darkness passed before his eyes when he looked at his wife's still largely unfinished work.

He immediately wondered why Ruth was so concerned about the proper lighting by which to do her work, for what she had painted was not the house as it now stood before them, but as it must have appeared in her imagination. Oh, yes, it was quite obviously the same house, but there was something different about it. It stood taller, much more gaunt, darker than the heavily clouded sky. It seemed different from the reality with a difference that was more easily sensed than actually determined.

He again thought of the word *ominous*. The house possessed a depressing air of emptiness, and its bare boards reminded him more of a skeleton than a house, a skeleton of clapboard wood and vacant memories. It seemed to have about it a cold touch of death and decay, as though it had been drained of all human contact, and only the bare whitened walls remained. The veranda was painted in deep purple shadow that appeared to spring from the ground itself and creep up over the walls of the house like an evil fungus that absorbed everything with which it came into contact. He narrowed his eyes and bent closer, trying to discern what appeared to be dimly, half-seen figures concealed in the darkness of the veranda, but the closer he looked, the more vague and indistinct they became, like those suspected forms that can be seen only out of the corner of the eye and disappear when looked at directly. The naked limbs of the dead tree beside the veranda had been extended with narrow, black brush strokes so that they almost seemed to embrace the house itself. The windows were more than ever like the empty eyes of the mindless, staring relentlessly and forever into nothing.

It was as though Ruth had painted the house through a confused overlap of time, both as it was now and how it must have been in its own distant past, distorted by the faulted mirror of two centuries. From where had come such a vision, he wondered? It was not in any aspect a pleasant painting. It was chilling, it was disturbing, it was almost frightening. But it was good, very good.

He bent closer again, narrowing his eyes against the deceptive glare of the hot sun on the shining wet oils. From the small, unseen cellar window on the seaward side of the house . . . the window of that still mysterious and unopened room . . . a bright splash of deep green fire seemed to flow directly towards the sea.

"Well, what do you think?" Ruth asked, her voice touched with that intense concern she always expressed in his personal opinion of her work. "Of course, it isn't nearly finished, and there has to be a considerable amount of touching up before I have it anywhere like the way I want it, but I do think it gives some slight idea of what I have in mind."

John stared silently for a moment at the mad swirls and sweepings of colors, the dark grays and blacks, the elongated windows, the touch of wildness that had never before appeared in Ruth's excellent, but rather subdued and orderly work. He shook his head slowly, trying to find the words.

"I'm not really sure it does," he replied. "It's . . . well, it's very strange, isn't it? Like nothing I've ever seen you do before. It's . . . dreary. Almost uncomfortable."

"You don't like it?" There was disappointment in her tone.

"I didn't say that," he added hastily; Ruth became very depressed at any adverse criticism from him of her work. He turned and smiled, trying to pass off lightly an extremely delicate moment. "Here all along I thought you were perched out here painting the sea."

"Yes. . . Yes. . . "she replied, her eyes vague again and her voice very soft, as though she were confused by her own thoughts. "Yes, that was the original idea, wasn't it? The play of light on the sea and on the soft underbelly of the clouds . . . That's what first struck me when I came here. But . . . I don't know . . . Strange. Something . . . I quite honestly don't know what, John. Suddenly, I felt myself drawn from the sea and toward the house. I just couldn't seem to help myself. I began to paint it. It's certainly nothing like my usual subjects, is it?"

He bent over the canvas again and pointed to the sticky fluid of brilliant green that flowered from the concealed cellar window. "And what is this . . . this green stuff?"

She was rather surprisingly embarrassed again, staring at the canvas, frowning. "That is rather peculiar, isn't it? Would you believe, John, I really don't have the slightest idea what that's supposed to be? I just seemed to see it that way. A . . . green . . . excrescence . . . sort of seeping from that cellar window, something from the house itself, from its very entrails, drawn to the sea in some strange way. Oh, I suppose it must have a meaning. It's got to, or it wouldn't belong, and I feel it does belong, as much as the gables and the veranda and the Widow's Walk; I can't see the house without it. After all, you know, I paint only what I see, whether it's really there for others or not. Perhaps when I've finished, I'll begin to understand all about...."

Suddenly she staggered slightly and John reached out quickly to put an arm about her, afraid she might fall. She sighed and ran a hand across her perspiring forehead.

"Are you all right?"

She hesitated a moment, then suddenly smiled and shook her head. "Why, yes. Yes, I really am. I'm fine. It was just for a moment." She looked up at him, and suddenly her eyes were clear again and the strange shadows he had sensed in her face were gone. She sighed and stretched, arching her back. "Oh, it really is murder to sit on that backless stool for so long. My muscles are terribly cramped."

"I keep telling you you should give yourself periods of rest," he reminded her, chiding again.

"Oh, yes, I know! I don't deny it. But when I'm working, I'm so completely unaware of the time and of my weariness. Well, I do believe I've had enough for today. The light has become rather hard on my eyes." She turned to him again suddenly, remembering, "And you haven't yet had your lunch!"

"Neither have you," he reminded her.

"It serves me right for being so neglectful," she responded. "There's no reason why you should suffer for it. I'm really not in the least hungry, anyway. But come on into the house, John, and I'll fix you something."

"Oh, no, don't bother about me," he said, feeling now that his earlier uneasiness had surely been only his imagination; Ruth seemed very much herself again. "I'd rather not bother now; might as well wait for dinner. I haven't had as good a day as you; I'm not at all satisfied with what I've done, and I hate to give up now. If I don't get this problem licked today, I'll have to face the same frustrations tomorrow, and that'll get me nowhere. If I eat something now, I'll just be sluggish the rest of the afternoon. I think I'll just work a bit longer."

"Well, I won't disturb you, then. I do believe I'll just take a little stroll along the beach. Ease my muscles."

"I'll go with you, if you like," he said, again immediately rising to the uneasiness of leaving her alone.

She laughed at his inconsistency. "And how will that help solve your little problems?"

He put his arm about her and was pleased that she did not, as always, immediately attempt to withdraw. "You're more important to me than any problem."

She quickly kissed his cheek, but then drew away before he could react. "It's all right, dear; don't be silly. You go back to work; I'll not be long."

"If you're certain . . ." he hesitated.

"Certain. I'd like to walk alone for a bit."

"You'll take your hat?"

She nodded emphatically. "The hat goes with me; you're not going to catch me on that twice in one day!"

CHAPTER SIX

RUTH walked slowly across the hard packed sand of the beach, her hands plunged as fists into the large pockets of her smock, the floppy brim of her hat shielding her face from the questing rays of the sun. Her feet left small indentations in the wet sand that quickly filled again with water, and it did not disturb her when a breaking wave shooshed further up onto the beach and curled around her feet. By now she scarcely heard the sounds of the surf, and the cawing of swooping gulls did not interrupt her reverie. She licked at the perspiration on her upper lip and tasted its saltiness.

She felt extremely tired, as she always did these days, and wondered again if her constant weariness was created by the unusual and excessive heat of the past few days and her too frequent long exposure to the sun's rays, or to the constant effort of the work she was doing. Although she had always been a hard, intense worker, she sensed there was nevertheless something unusual in the tremendous effort she was putting into her current canvas. It was as though she were driven by some inner compulsion to complete this painting as quickly as possible, as though time were short and she must take full advantage of every blessed moment.

That was foolish, of course. She lived now quietly, in surroundings she had always believed most conducive to achievement, there were no distractions whatever except the always present lure of the sea, she had no pressing duties save the minimal household responsibilities, and she was alone for most of the time, apart even from John, who was generally immersed in his own work in the study. These were all ideal working conditions. Why, then, this constant sense of pressing urgency?

Constantly sluggish and tired, she found her energy only when seated upon her folding stool with brush in hand. When not actually at work, she was restless and uneasy, feeling this constant call to the canvas, working herself daily to the point of physical and mental exhaustion, yet aware of this weariness only when she finally left her canvas and returned to the house, as though it were a punishment for leaving her work. It was uncomfortable to work at such a driving pace, and she sensed the constant pressure was not good for her, but there seemed nothing she could do. The canvas demanded completion and was impatient with any delays. And yet, she did not really mind, for she knew this canvas was good.

The exhaustion she felt at the end of each day should have helped her to sleep, but it did not. It was as though even during the hours of darkness her work called for her. She often lay awake for hours, staring up at the dark ceiling and listening to the thunder of the surf outside the window, her mind filled with thoughts of the next day's work, of new combinations of color, of a different brush stroke on the peaks of the gables, of a deeper shading on the veranda. The work was always with her.

And then, when she finally slipped into a sleep of sheer exhaustion, there were the dreams, strange dreams unlike any she had ever experienced before, dreams filled with the roar of the sea and with writhing, swimming forms moving silently through a green, wet darkness. She was herself always part of these dreams, one with the strangely convoluted shapes, moving freely among them through the sparkling green waters, and she felt then no fear, but rather a quite emarkable sense of freedom. The unknown forms that surrounded her did not touch her and she felt in them no menace; they moved with her, beside her, all around her, and the further they moved together through that bright green world, the greater became the sense of excitement. Somehow she knew she was not wandering idly and without purpose. Someone was waiting for her, and in the anticipation of their meeting she felt an almost unbearable ecstacy. Finally she would see before her a constantly darker world, as though the green waters had become filled with the shadowing ghosts of form, and before her was an ill-defined shape, a darker and more solid entity whose actual composition and appearance she could not pierce through the gathering green gloom. She knew the shape waited for her, that this was the entire purpose of her strange sea journey.

It was at this point she would awaken, and it was only then that fear arrived, and she would lie awake again and wonder and tremble and think perhaps she was losing her mind. The dream came every night and always ended with the the same awakening fear.

John knew nothing about all this. When she awoke from this ecstatically frightening dream in which she felt herself slipping helplessly into some shadowed liquid green void, she could not turn to him as she had in those past nightmares following the death of their daughter; somehow, she sensed there was no way he could comfort her now, no way he could share in these strange new dreams. He would not understand, yet she could not have said why this was so. Surprisingly, she found she did not even want his comforting. There was in her now a strange new need, and although she could not understand what that was, or from where it had come to her, she knew John could not fill it.

She paused and with the toe of her shoe turned over a

small sand crab, watching the convulsive movements of its many legs as it tried to right itself. She turned it rightside up again, and it scurried across the wet sand and lost itself in the surge of a breaking wave, becoming once again part of the teeming, hidden life of the sea. She climbed the sloping sand dune and seated herself on a scraggly tuft of grass. Removing her hat, she wiped her perspiring forehead with her handkerchief, unpleasantly aware of the tangy odor of her sweating armpit as she raised her arm over her head.

The day bore the oppressive silence of heat, and there was not the slightest breath of air to cool her. Gulls bobbed up and down in the waves near the shore, occasionally falling from her sight as though swallowed by the sea, and then rising again with the sea's regurgitation. She watched the stiff-legged birds scrambling upon the sand, pecking with long curved beaks at minute marine creatures, and again wondered what they were. The heat-shimmering line of the horizon was broken by a small black smudge that was probably a fishing smack from the village. She wondered about those on board, these men of the sea, about their families, their joys and sorrows, their forlorn hopes and shattered dreams. It was a game she and John had often played together, weaving stories and improbable fantasies about these men they would never see; it had always been fun.

They'd always had a great deal of fun, she and John, particularly in the earliest years of their marriage, when they still shared their thoughts, their dreams, and their ambitions. There had never been a moment of boredom between them, never a period of uncomfortable silence. Life was too interesting and the possibilities of discussion too varied.

Things were different now. When had it begun, the strangeness between them, the movement away from each other, the lack of sharing, the irritations, disagreements, unusual silences? Oh, there were still happy times, of course, good and warm times, perhaps even a little better than before because of their increased rarity. Had familiarity finally induced boredom? Coming here had been intended to change all that, new surroundings and removal of distractions had been meant to bring them together again, but it had not really done so. The first few days, during the excitement of a new time and a new world, it had been fun again, there had been a revived warmth between them, but then, all too soon, it was all the same again. Both she and John pretended this was not so, but they could not fool themselves, even while trying to fool each other. There were days when they met only over meals and when retiring, each spending their time in their own milieu, Ruth upon the bluff and John in his study. It was alarming how often John's occasional unexpected presence generally irritated her now, and she was happiest when alone at her work.

The thought startled her; she had never before made such an admission, even to herself. Did she then really no longer love her husband? An incurable romantic, she had always insisted love could not die, not under any circumstances, and she had clung to this schoolgirl belief even after the end of her first chaotic marriage, which obviously had been mere animal attraction, and not true love at all.

The truth was that her need for John was gone. Yes, she no longer needed that kind, gentle and thoughtful man she had once sworn to love throughout the remainder of her life. She seldom thought of him now when she was alone, certainly never while at work, and she was often surprised, when returning to the house at the end of the day, to realize that he was still there. She tried still to conceal this from him whenever she felt so inclined, yet she was now often cross with him, abrupt, uninterested in his needs and desires. To be completely truthful, she had to admit she had simple become indifferent to him. The most alarming aspect of it all was that she felt no sense of guilt. She had her work, and that was all that mattered now.

And yet, there were still those times when she found herself reaching out to him, with a sudden need that she thought had gone forever. These were the times when she stood in the gathered silence of Fowles House and felt the unknown past close in upon her, that sense of something hovering over the dark gables, that something that had for her moments of both ecstacy and terror. Then it was she went to John and placed her hand in his and felt the comfort of his nearness, and for a short time those fears melted into the background and she was content. But such times came now less and less frequently as she sought comfort only in her work, her aloneness, and her peculiar dreams.

Ruth turned her head and looked up the empty stretch of beach to the house, rising on the point of land jutting out into the sea, shimmering in the waves of heat. For several moments she stared as if mesmerized, and it seemed to her she saw vague, shapeless forms moving in the long shadows of the veranda, like the irritating, totally unplanned suggestion of movement on the veranda in her painting. In the distortion of the heat, the house seemed suddenly younger, newer, and again, as so often happened while she painted, she felt a sudden confusion between past and present. Light gleamed from the windows and an impatient dark form paced the Widow's Walk. The sounds of the surf grew louder in her ears, and then suddenly they seemed like screams of human agony, screams such as she sometimes imagined she heard within the house itself, and she gasped and threw her hands over her ears and closed her eyes.

The sound subsided and she opened her eyes and again looked at the house. It had all been only the heat. It was just an old house standing above the sea, the lights in the windows had been the sheen of the sun upon the glass, the figure on the Widow's Walk had been a swooping gull, and the only sounds she heard were the tidal rhythm of the surf and the calls of the feeding birds. She had exposed herself too long to the sun; it would have been wiser to go into the tall, cooler rooms of the house. John was there, and she suddenly felt one of those now rare moments of wanting to be with him.

Rising slowly from the dune upon which she had seated herself, brushing at the sand clinging to her clothing, Ruth started up the beach toward home. In the shimmering heat, the house waited for her.

It grew steadily more humid and uncomfortable as the afternoon lengthened into evening. Like the black sails of a phantom pirate vessel, dark clouds appeared quite suddenly on the hazy horizon, and crept slowly and inexorably towards the house across the smooth slate-like sea. Night fell earlier than usual, and it was by then almost suffocatingly hot. The dark sky was brightened by sheets of blinding yellow-white lightning, as though giant fireflies flitted back and forth across the night sky, and John was uncertain whether these frequent flashes were heat lightning or the harbingers of another storm, until the distant rumble of thunder answered his question.

John had soon enough abandoned his determination to resolve his particular plot dilemma before the end of the day, and had spent the remainder of the afternoon seated on the veranda, seeking comfort in one cold drink after another, thinking of nothing in particular as he stared at the panorama of the sea. When she returned from her brief walk on the beach, Ruth seemed unusually listless, saying very little, moving slowly, obviously almost overwhelmingly weary from her morning's work and her unwise over-exposure to the sun, while John himself felt totally drained of energy, as though the heat of the day had sucked it out of him. Even with all the windows opened, the house was like a furnace, and not a single breath of air moved down the portrait-lined corridors to provide the smallest measure of relief. He dabbed constantly at the perspiration that smeared his bare chest, and felt he was surrounded by the unpleasantly pungent aroma of his own sweat.

During their silent and unimaginative supper, Ruth seemed almost more uncomfortable than himself, yet John sensed there was more to her apparent uneasiness than merely the irritations of the weather. An unusual nervousness seemed to trouble her, and she constantly dropped things to the floor with a clumsiness that was very rare with her. Her eyes seemed constantly drawn to the closed door leading to the cellar, and John wondered if perhaps he had stressed too much the supposed mystery of that damned unentered room.

"It's certainly too God-damned hot for a fire tonight," he muttered as Ruth silently cleared the dishes from the table and, despite her earlier concern about sloppy housekeeping, merely piled them rather noisily in the sink. "How about just sitting on the veranda for a while? Or taking a walk, until the storm breaks? There should at least be some shadow of a breeze down on the beach, now that the sun has set."

Ruth hesitated at the sink and spoke without turning to him; her voice totally lacked color. "I don't think so, John. Not tonight. I've done enough beach strolling for one day. I'm really terribly tired. I didn't sleep very well last night, and now with this godawful heat. . ."

He looked at her, concerned again, still not liking the intense pallor of her complexion, particularly after a day spent in the burning touch of the sun. Her shoulders seemed to sag with weariness, and her movements were almost those of a sleepwalker; her hands seemed to be touched with nervous trembling.

"I hope you didn't get too much sun today," he commented.

Ruth slowly shook her head. "No, I don't believe so, John. The back of my neck is a little sore, but it's not too bad; I'll just put some salve on it. I'm over tired, that's all. The excitement of all this is beginning to catch up with me, I suppose, and I have been working very hard.

Please don't worry. I thought I'd just go to bed early tonight and get a good rest. You don't mind, do you?''

He rose from the table and approached her; when he slipped his arm about her waist, she moved slightly away from him and her body stiffened, but she meekly turned her cheek to his kiss; her flesh was cold and somehow wet, yet not with the saltiness of perspiration.

"Of course not." She wanted to be alone again, and he was still being understanding. "Do whatever you think best. Probably we've both been at it too hard these past few days, what with the house and all. What we really should do, you know, is take a hiatus. Maybe you'd like to go into town. They have a movie house there, you know. Everything nice and apple pie clean, of course, and I can't guarantee it's air conditioned, but it might be diverting for a change."

She turned, wiping a curl of hair from her forehead. "I don't really feel up to that. You go on with whatever you want to do, but I'm going to clean up and then go right to bed."

"Well, maybe I'll just take a little stroll along the beach before turning in," he mentioned. "Clear my mind of the cobwebs, if nothing else; still haven't straightened out that damned problem of mine. If you don't mind being alone for just a little while? I won't go far, maybe down to the lighthouse, and I won't be long; back before the storm breaks, of course."

She shook her head, smiling; she had never yet been alone at night in the house. "Of course not. Do as you like. Don't wake me when you come in; I'll probably be sleeping like a baby."

He paused on the veranda to light a cigarette. There was something almost eerie about the intense silence of the night, the almost total absence of sound. Not a hint of a breeze rattled the bare bony branches of the dead black tree. The sky was a billious mixture of black, yellow and purple. There were ever more frequent flashes of lightning and from the distance, across the glass-like sea itself, came a low rumble of what, in some more distant time, might have been the ominous rumble of a ship's cannon fire, but in these more peaceful days was only the dull bellowing of an approaching storm.

He slowly descended the wooden steps of the veranda and walked across the dry, hard packed earth to the edge of the cliff. The sea seemed to sense the approaching bad weather; away from the shore, the water was smooth and rolling in gentle swells, as though oil had been poured upon its surface, but at the base of the cliff the waters hurled themselves at the stubborn ebony rocks, the white spume shooting into the sea again, spent and exhausted. There was a deep swell, and it was difficult in the swiftly gathered darkness to distinguish the line of demarcation between horizon and sea, except when a flash of lightning revealed it to him. Flocks of gulls stood silently on the wet sand, staring out to sea like gatherings of people expecting disaster.

John glanced back at the house. How many fierce storms had it withstood over the years? How many, now long dead, had listened to the howling of the wind tearing angrily about the gables, the drumming of heavy rain on the rooftops and tall windows, the dripping from the eaves? How many weary, lonely women, with fear in their hearts, had braved the fury of the storm to stand alone upon the Widow's Walk in hopes of seeing something . . . anything . . . to calm their fears, their certainties that all was lost? Those days were long gone, merely another part of the cluttered memory of man, and now the house was silent and subdued, like a lively young girl who had slowly and almost unnoticeably slipped into a serene old age.

John could not see the bedroom window, which faced directly on the sea itself, where Ruth, in her strangely silent mood, was preparing for sleep, but a light still glowed in the living room, and it seemed like a beacon shining through the increasing darkness to guide him back home. He was still capable of feeling that way about the house.

Slowly, thoughtfully, he began to walk down the narrow weed-lined pathway that curved from the clifftop to the beach below, a quicker if somewhat more precipitous and difficult way of reaching the beach than by walking down the circuitous, rutted roadway. There was not the slightest improvement of the air down on the beach. The storm now appeared imminent, and he decided it would be unwise to walk too far from the house. The prospect of a drenching did not disturb him, particularly in such humid weather, and he always enjoyed the spectacle of a storm at sea, but it would not be wise to leave Ruth alone in that big empty house during the unsettling crashes of an electrical storm.

With his hands thrust into his trousers pockets, John strolled slowly to one of his favorite spots along the beach and seated himself on the warm sand with his back against a stunted tree, near a massive piece of twisted whitened driftwood that raised its shattered slivers against the sky like the contorted, pleading skeletal arms of the damned. He felt suddenly very tired, too weary to think clearly or to reason. The humidity of the evening seemed to close in on him. He drew slowly on his cigarette and stared out to the lightning-brightened sea.

He recalled the last time he had sat just this way, alone by the sea, his back against a tree, pondering his problems. Then the sky had been clear and the brilliant constellations took the shapes of southern skies. It was the night of his first meeting with Ruth. The problems had been different, then, selfish problems concerned only with his own dissatisfactions. The problems were more serious now, more baffling.

He thought briefly back over the years that had passed since that first night which had so radically changed his entire mode of living. Their marriage, their early happiness, Elinor, the agonies that had followed her death, and the strange distance that had since come between Ruth and himself.

But now here they were again by the sea that had first brought them together . . . a different sea, perhaps, but were not all seas of the world really but one? . . . where even before their marriage they had both been inclined to seek peace and resolution of their problems. While maintaining it was the need for work that had brought them here, they both knew that was only part of it; there was also the need to save their marriage. A home by the sea, away from all distractions, a chance to clear their minds and examine their hearts. It had been a wise move. It was going slowly, but time and the sea would clear their problems now. They should have done this long ago.

He cursed silently and tossed the cigarette away; it arched to the beach like a shooting star in a miniature world.

He was only fooling himself, and he knew it. Matters were not going nearly as well as he had hoped they would, and while he sat here, alone with the restless sea under the dark canopy of the approaching storm, there was no need to conceal the truth from himself.

The life they were now leading was, for people like themselves, totally artificial, something for which neither one of them was really suited. It was simply too late to alter so radically their way of living. They might love the house, love the sea, love just being together, but the truth was that they also loved and needed those other things . . . those supposedly vacuous, empty, meaningless things . . . that had been left behind in order to come here. Such a life as they now knew might be relaxing, envigorating for a short period of time, a breathing spell, perhaps, or an extended vacation, but it was a lie for either of them to pretend they could go on like this for an indefinite time. The truth was, they were city people, and nothing could change that.

John's primary fear now was that it might prove dangerous for Ruth to continue with this charade. Undoubtedly, she appeared now more content than at any time since Elinor's death. Her sorrowful withdrawal since that tragedy called for a period of peace and tranquility, and she had found a temporary asylum in Fowles House. But she must realize that this was only temporary, not a permanent solution to the problems of her withdrawal. Her state of mind was such that she might easily be seduced into believing this insubstantial, rather drab and isolated lifestyle could go on forever. The sorrow of their mutual loss was still being nursed too passionately, too self-pityingly to her breast, almost like a replacement for the little red mouth that had once nursed there. Perhaps the longer it was permitted to continue, the greater the danger became. She quite obviously had not felt any of those disturbing dissatisfactions that were already closing in on him and returning that sense of restlessness that he had come here to lose.

John sincerely tried to be totally unselfish in his process of reasoning, and to accept the bald truth. There could be many reasons for this new dissatisfaction . . . absence of other people, longing for the constant activity of the big city, all those little diversions he had thought he could do without . . . but there could be no question that the major portion of his dissatisfaction was due to the complete absence of any sexual contact between himself and his wife. The realization of this truth disturbed him, made him feel somehow immature and self-centered. Was sexual activity really that important? Apparently it was, for him, although he had always liked to consider himself above *that sort of thing*. His sexual appetites had always been very strong and easily satisfied, but he had experienced no release whatever since the death of their child, now almost six months in the past. The animal remains an essential part of man and, like all animals, becomes restive when not occasionally appeased. John could not doubt that this current existence would have been more of an idyll for him had a normal sexual experience been part of their lives.

The absense of sexual gratification appeared to have no effect whatever upon Ruth. John had always had the rather naive notion that women, although also possessed of that animal nature of man, could control themselves more easily. With Ruth, there were now other, more profound reasons for this control. Perhaps she feared another conception and another tragedy, and so preferred to remove all possibility of this from her life. One of those strange quirks of mind that can happen to people who have suffered some profound emotional shock. Fear had banished sexual appetite from Ruth, but not from himself.

John had tried to be patient. (Why did he praise himself so constantly on that point?) But how much longer could he continue with that patience and restraint? He loved Ruth as a man loves his wife, not as a sister or a platonic companion. In that crowded, busy world from which they had come, where temptation was as much and important a part of life as cocktail parties and restaurants, he had not always been faithful to Ruth but that, too, had changed with Elinor's death. Perhaps he felt a sense of loyalty to her now, or perhaps he was imposing a penance upon himself for not mourning his daughter's death as deeply as Ruth did. But how much longer could he wait? If it were not Ruth, then sooner or later it would have to be another woman. He didn't really want that.

The silence of the night was suddenly no longer so reassuring. It had become too quiet. Ominously so. There was that damned word again. Everything was somehow ominous these days. It reminded him too much of what he missed, of the noise, the confusion, the activity of the life they had voluntarily abandoned. The sea that he had always loved seemed no longer so restful. He was growing tired of it.

"Oh, Christ!" he moaned.

For John was not being completely truthful with himself even now. Ruth's behaviour was no longer connected strictly with the past. There was a new strangeness about her, a peculiar attitude that had appeared only since their arrival at Fowles House. She was now even more withdrawn, more isolated than before. There were long periods of silence between them now, and despite occasional moments of tenderness . . . more and more infrequent . . . John often had the uncomfortable feeling that his wife resented his presence. She worked much too hard, and there was about her expression a peculiar vagueness, an absent mindedness, as though she often simply did not realize where she was or what was going on about her.

It was the house, the damned house that was doing it, the house he tried so hard to convince himself he really loved. Ruth had become too immersed, almost as though the strange and still unknown story of Fowles House completely absorbed her. Be honest, John, he thought to himself. The problems now are greater than they were before. There's something . . . unhealthy about what was going on now.

He lighted another cigarette. The storm was coming closer, the thunder rumbling like the distressed digestion of a dispeptic giant. He had better start back. Problems could not be resolved simply by sitting on a quiet beach and mourning over them. Only the very young can find solutions in that way. What should he do, he wondered again? Wait and see? Bring it all out in the open and admit to Ruth the failure of their plan? That was admitting defeat.

John started at the unexpected sound of muffled laughter from just the othe side of the driftwood beside him; he had considered himself to be quite alone on the beach. He listened and heard it again, a light laugh, almost a giggle, that bore the unmistakeable note of pleasure. A woman's voice, and then the lower tone of a man; he could not make out any words. Again, laughter. It was a strange sound to hear in the intense stillness of that dark night. People from the village very seldom came up this far.

John raised himself slowly and quietly from the sand and walked the few steps to the salt-eaten barrier. There were a man and woman lying in the shelter of the driftwood, fully dressed in light beach clothing, but merged in a passionately clinging embrace. It had already become too dark to permit John to distinguish any features, and the couple were lying too close to the over-hanging driftwood to be fully outlined in the flashes of light in the sky. John felt a hot thrust of desire when he saw the man's hands wander freely and familiarly over the body of the woman whose mouth was pressed so tightly to his own. One of her hands moved across his taut buttocks, while the other was in his hair, holding him close to her, and her slight moans of pleasure as he pressed himself upon her seemed to become part of the sensuous murmur of the sea.

John turned quickly away, embarrassed at having been witness to an intimacy not intended to be seen by others. Desire. The thought was like a hot flame stirring his parched body. The desire that he must not be crude and brutal enough to express until his wife was ready to share and return it. How long must he wait?

He slipped quietly away from the driftwood that protected the two entwined lovers like a bedroom screen, thankful that the hard packed sand would cover any sounds he might make, and turned his way back to the cliff top. A sudden flash of lightning revealed a dark shape under the small clump of stunted trees at the edge of the beach. A parked car. It looked familiar; he had seen it somewhere before. His suspicion was confirmed in another flickering of lightning. It was Paul's car. The entwined figures on the beach, so immersed in their own passion that they were oblivious to the gathering storm, undoubtedly were Paul and Linda. Another step had been taken in that romance he had sensed on his first visit to the village. Linda had apparently finally made up her mind, at least to the extent of pleasure. Her own sorrow was fading. Perhaps Ruth's would also fade some day.

He quickly made his way up the trail and back towards the old house, clumsily stumbling on loose pebbles, his face flushed, his hands trembling, his breath drawn in hot, disturbed gasps, his vision blinded by the images of the couple on the beach. He cursed himself when he actually hesitated with thoughts of returning to the beach and concealing himself behind the driftwood to observe their action. He had never been a voyeur, and it had been a hell of a long time since masturbation had satisfied him.

The house was dark, save for the single glow of light in the living room, like a sleepless, unwinking eye of another world that watched the activities of mortals during the hours of night. A silence enfolded the house and the world. The lightning cast the sharp gables into black daggers surging upwards to stab the sky.

It would not be wise to go immediately into the house. This was no state of mind in which to enter a bedroom in which lay an attractive, although sleeping, wife. He would have a cigarette or two on the veranda, and would try not to think of those two down on the beach, to let the heat of his thoughts subside.

He tried to force himself to think of the complexities of his fictional characters, whose libidinous lives seemed suddenly vacant and unimportant. He tried to think of the further improvements still to be made on the house, which suddenly seemed unappealing. He tried to think of something, anything. . .

Two figures joined as one on the beach, their forms cast into moving, rhythmic shadows by the flashes of lightning. The moans of the woman, the pleasured sighs of the man. No, they were not proper thoughts. That way lay only danger. Paul and Linda. He was not surprised, not shocked. He had expected it, though perhaps not quite so soon. Why here, he wondered, down on the beach, just before the storm?

He straightened himself slightly at the silent question. Of course! He had been so stirred by sexual thoughts and erotic imaginings, the really important question had been completely driven from his mind.

Why were Paul and Linda there on the beach, so close to Fowles House? What were they doing there? Surely they had not driven all the way out here simply to commit the fornication they could much more easily and comfortably have done in town? Did they have to come this far for their love play? A certain amount of discretion was undoubtedly necessary in a small town like theirs, but why here? There were safely isolated beaches closer to the village, in either direction; they need not have come this far. And if this far, why not a bit further? Why so close to the house, where there was as much a possibility of being seen as Paul's being spotted by a nosey villager as he sneaked into Linda's apartment?

Something else had brought them here. The fornication had been a sudden and unplanned decision, not the primary purpose.

John recalled again Paul's constant uneasiness in and about the old house, his air of expectation and nervousness with which he walked about the rooms. He thought of something else that had previously no meaning for him: the unusual litter of cigarette butts on the beach in just about the spot where he had seen Paul engaged in dalliance with his secretary, a litter that indicated long periods of inactivity and . . . what was the word he wanted?

Observation. Paul and Linda had come to that spot to watch the house unseen. What were they looking for? What were they expecting? How often did John and

Ruth move within the house under the unsuspected watchful gaze of Paul Sanders?

John flicked his cigarette into the darkness and, uneasy, entered the house and mounted the steps to the bedroom where Ruth already lay in a deep, motionless sleep.

CHAPTER SEVEN

JOHN slept fitfully that night, tossing on twisted sheets clamily dampened by his own perspiration. The night air seemed filled with darkly shadowed dreams, and he was haunted by a suddenly new sense of uneasiness, by a dread uncertainty that seeped even into his slumber, a feeling that all was not quite as well in the old Fowles House as it would appear, that the gabled mansion perched on its stone eyrie by the sea was not quite the peaceful Paradise he and Ruth had hoped and intended it to be. In his fear-fevered dreams he saw enormous wooden ships with swollen black sails bearing remorselessly down upon the old house, and a heavily bearded sea captain with gold rings flashing in his ears standing upon the heaving deck, laughing, his sharp white teeth glowing through moist red lips, brandishing a sharply honed, wickedly gleaming sabre. He saw the green sea rise to mountainous heights, inching higher and higher upon the cliff that at last, exhausted by countless ages of battle against a stronger and more determined element, seemed to crumble under the cold touch of the salt-stained water until finally, with a triumphant roar, the sea swept over the cliff top itself like a quilted blanket of green and white and smashed down upon the house that fell into a mass of swirling, foam-covered rubble.

It was the first shattering explosion of the storm that finally awakened John from his tortured, watery dreams, and he welcomed the violent interruption. He lay on his back and closed his eyes against the dancing spots created by the constant flashing of lightning that brightened the room, and he listened to the peals of thunder that rolled over the house and caused its aged timbers to tremble with some vaguely remembered fear. The heavy rain seemed to hammer against the windows like angry fingers demanding entry into the warmth and comfort of the room. The wind whistled about the house and the window frames shuddered. It was still hot in the room, but the storm had somewhat eased the humidity. Through the open doors of the balcony, he could hear the angry muttering of the sea; he vaguely wondered if the rain had blown through the opening and stained the carpet, but felt too comfortable to get out of bed to see.

With one hand, John reached to the table beside the bed for a handkerchief to wipe the ever present perspiration from his chest, while his other hand went out to comfort Ruth, should the storm have awakened her as well. He was startled to feel the place beside him was empty. Sitting up in the bed, he saw, in another burst of illumination, that he was quite alone.

"Ruth!" he called. "Ruth, where are you?"

There was no response. He pressed the light switch, but the room remained in darkness brightened only by the shadow-tossing lightning; the storm had apparently affected the electricity. Slightly uneasy, John slid out of the bed and stepped into his slippers, calling again for his wife and still receiving no reply. He stood perfectly still for a moment, listening, but the house was silent; probably the stomach-rumbling of the thunder and the steady pouring and pounding of the rain would have drowned out any other sounds. Perhaps Ruth had merely gone into the bathroom; the day's over-exposure to the sun might finally have caused her some discomfort, and she might have become ill.

But the bathroom was empty, and there was no indication that Ruth had been there. He noticed then that Ruth's robe was still lying at the foot of the bed where she invariably placed it every night on retiring, and her slippers were still in their place, as always carefully set at just the exact angle so she could slip out of bed and right into them, without making contact with the cold, uncarpeted floor. Why would she have gone anywhere without them?

From the drawer of the night table, John took a flashlight kept there for just such power emergencies as this, and saw with gratification that it was in working order; why hadn't Ruth taken it, then, rather than risk wandering about the house in the dark? Casting the beam of light about the room showed him nothing; the room appeared to be normal, save for the fact that Ruth was simply not in it. The rain had, indeed, placed a dark stain upon the bit of carpeting just before the balcony, and John was foolishly reminded of carpet stains of blood in murder mysteries. He absently closed the open doors of the balcony and then stepped into the dark corridor.

"Ruth? Are you all right? Where are you?"

Aside from the outside sounds of the storm, the house seemed almost unnaturally quiet. He fancied he could hear the ticking of the grandfather's clock, mechanically passing its life away, and even the creaking of the old boards.

He felt a breath of colder air and noted, with some alarm, that it came from the stairway leading up to the Widow's Walk. Surely Ruth would not have ventured out there in such weather? The door leading to the platform was open and banging in the wind; heavy drops of rain were blown onto the stairway, and the carpet on the steps was saturated, squeeging when he stepped on them. Narrowing his eyes against the blowing rain, John peered out onto the lonely, haunted walk, but there was no sign of anyone. The night was exceptionally black and violent, and the sound of the invisible sea was a roar of anguished triumph and fury. A jagged fork of lightning, reminding him briefly of the branches of the dead tree beside the veranda, revealed the dark, storm-tossed horizon and a sky smothered by angry tumbling black clouds. The rain struck the platform with the force of hailstones. He closed the door and, wiping at the rain water that dripped into his eyes, descended the stairs.

It was only when he reached the bottom of the short flight and stood again opposite their open bedroom door that John noticed the wet naked footprints that told him Ruth had, indeed, been here. He followed the fading prints down the corridor and to the main stairway. What could possibly have drawn Ruth to the exposed Widow's Walk in the middle of the night, in such violent weather as this, and without either her robe or her slippers? And where was she now?

He stood at the railing above the foyer and cast the narrow beam of his light down over the stairway, past the dark porthole windows, the conch-bearing sea nymph on the newel post, over the polished floor of the foyer, the antlered hat rack, the umbrella stand and utility table covered with a lace cloth, the slowly ticking pendulum of the great clock; there was a startling flash of reflected light when the beam touched the mirror on the wall. There was no one there, although for just a moment he imagined movement in the lightning-cast shadow of one of his coats hanging near the door.

But Ruth had certainly gone down those stairs; the last of the damp prints could be seen on the top steps. John moved quickly down the stairs into the foyer, feeling the beginnings of fear.

Ruth would not wander alone in the darkness during so violent a storm; it was more like her to cower under the covers until the storm had passed, holding onto his hand with a tight, perspiring grip and gasping with fear at every crack of lightning.

The stolid furniture of the living room stood like

overstuffed ghosts in the flickering yellow flashes of lightning, and only the old spyglass stood silent guard in the empty study. As the beam of the flashlight touched the portraits on the walls, the old captains seemed to smile with some secret knowledge they dared him to discover for himself.

And still there was no sign of Ruth. Surely, with the thunder booming and the lightning flashing, she would not have ventured out onto the veranda, regardless of how badly she might feel the need for fresh air. And yet, there was no sign of her anywhere in the house and, despite all her natural inclinations to the contrary, there could be no question that she had dared the Widow's Walk. Could she be sleep walking? She had never done so before, but that did not mean it was impossible. It seemed the only way to answer the questions.

The door leading from the foyer to the veranda was still closed; apparently she had not gone that way. John had started towards the screen door leading from the kitchen out to the rear portion of the veranda, when he noticed that the door leading into the cellar stood open. He hesitated again. The cellar? Oh, no, certainly not. Ruth avoided even the proximity of the cellar door in the hours of daylight. He could conceive of nothing that would lure her down there on such a night.

But it seemed rather foolish for him to stand there, staring at that open door, and arguing with himself about what Ruth would or would not have done, when this entire peculiar incident was involved in would-not-have-dones that had been done. Ruth would not have risen from her bed during such a storm, but she had. She would not have ventured into a dark house without her robe and slippers, but she had. She would not have ventured onto the Widow's Walk at such a time, but she had. The cellar seemed the only remaining possibility; she was nowhere else to be found.

The house trembled as though it had been struck a physical blow by the cannon balls of thunder as John stepped onto the cellar stairs. Lightning flashed through the small windows, startling him and momentarily blinding him, causing him to drop the flashlight to the top step, where it promptly went out. He pressed his hand to his eyes and closed them until the dancing spots had faded, then bent to retrieve the light. Instead of the cold aluminum cylinder, his hand made unexpected contact with something soft, silky and feminine. He raised it to his face and recognized it in a lightning flash.

It was Ruth's nightgown.

As John rose from his stooped posture, with the nightgown clutched in his trembling hand, frightened now by the increasingly more mysterious train of events, he realized he was no longer in total darkness. He could, in fact, see quite well without the aid of the fallen flashlight. At first he ascribed the increased light to the storm, but the condition remained even after the brightness of the lightning flashes had passed. Nor was it quite an ordinary kind of light, the brilliant yellow-white of a lightning flash. The cellar seemed suffused with an intense greenish glow that apparently emanated from beyond the pot-bellied furnace. He sniffed; there was an uncomfortable stuffiness in the air, such as might be encountered when opening a room too long closed.

Slowly, with Ruth's nightgown dangling almost forgotten from his left hand and the now unnecessary flashlight held in his right, John started down the stairs, absurdly careful to make not the slightest sound, carefully testing each and every step before placing the full weight of his body upon it. The green glow seemed to grow more intense as he approached its source, and he suddenly became aware of the salty taste of perspiration on his upper lip; was it heat or fear? The house was very quiet, and even the noises of the storm were somewhat muted as the storm-light through the small windows cast his tall, distorted shadow on the bare cellar walls. It did not even occur to him now to call his wife's name. Why did he feel this sudden need for silence? Who was there to hear him? What did he expect to see?

Certainly not what he saw. As he slowly rounded the belly of the furnace, he found the door to the mysterious room stood wide open, and from it issued the strange green light. It seemed to pour through the open doorway, as the sea pours through a suddenly discovered channel in the land; for a moment, its brightness hurt his eyes.

The beating of his heart sounded in his ears even more loudly than the rolling peals of thunder as John stepped slowly into the room. He was immediately aware of the biting, piercing cold, such as he had experienced when, as a child, he had walked into an icehouse piled high with blocks of green-white ice. The walls, the floor, and the ceiling were all bathed in the brilliant green glow that seemed to pulsate with a life of its own; or was it merely the effect of the subdued lightning flashes that managed to filter through the very small window in the far wall and seemed to hurl the walls at each other? No, this was too brilliant. With an instinctive gesture, he suddenly lowered his head, and then wondered why; he'd had an overpowering feeling that something was passing over him. But here was nothing there.

And yet the room was not completely empty. There was a single object lying on the barren floor. It was Ruth. She lay completely naked on a small mound that rose in the exact center of the earthen floor of the room.

John quickly bent at his wife's side and raised her head. Ruth's eyes were closed, and she was breathing heavily, but his quick examination revealed no indication that she had been injured in any way. Her flesh was icily cold to the touch, and seemed tinged with that same green coloration that filled the room. Briskly rubbing her hands and holding her cold inert form next to his own warmer body, John tried to restore her to consciousness, but she did not respond.

The cold of the chamber seemed to have grown even more intense since John's entry, and it now reached a level that was almost unbearable; his visible breath touched the face of his unconscious wife as he bent over her. He would have to get her out of this ice chamber, upstairs into some warmth.

It was while he gathered Ruth's slight form into his arms to carry her back upstairs that the fear, forgotten in the confusion of this moment, arrived again, clutching at the very pit of his stomach as though a strong hand had grasped him there and was slowly squeezing pain into him, catching at his breath so he could feel himself tremble. He suddenly felt a certainty that he and Ruth were not alone in that small earthen chamber, that the room swarmed with . . . something, something both unknown and terrible. It seemed he could hear slithering sounds, harsh gasps and the clumsy movements of heavy bodies. And yet, he saw nothing. He and Ruth were unquestionably alone in that room, in that cellar, in that house. Weren't they?

And it was just at this same moment that he heard the sea. Not only the sea that had become a background for their every moment in this house, but all the seas of the world, suddenly rushing upon his hearing as though all the tides of earth were being poured into that one little chamber, drowning out the sounds of the storm, filling the vacuum of space with a tremendous, pounding roar that hammered against his eardrums and seemed to drive a burning wedge into his brain.

Quickly, holding Ruth's naked body tightly in his arms, John rushed from that hellish chamber and bounded up the stairs into the kitchen, pausing only long enough to kick the cellar door shut with his foot as he moved swiftly, not caring now how much noise he might make, through the dark corridor where the eyes of painted sea captains stared at him without wonder, as though the scene of a frightened man carrrying his wife's unconscious nude form held no surprise for them

158

any longer, on through the foyer and up the curving stairs two at a time to the bedroom, his way brightly lighted by the flashes of lightning that filled the house with wildly leaping shadow.

He carefully placed Ruth on the bed, then again pressed the light switch, hoping at least to relieve the nightmarish darkness of the room, but the power had not yet been restored. He propped the flashlight upon the bed table so that its beam fell upon Ruth, and the effect was chillingly like a white light touching a corpse. Flashes of lightning frequently outlined that naked form which, just a few hours earlier, would have aroused in him a strong sexual desire, the firm breasts and the slender line of thighs with their promise of imprisoning passion, thrown into deep shadow by the erratic light.

But those exposed charms had now no effect upon John. He was too confused and bewildered, too worried, too frightened to think now of his sexual needs. Almost without noticing Ruth's nudity, he drew a sheet over her, bringing it up close under her chin. She lay still and cold, her breathing heavy and labored. He bent over her, rubbing her hands for lack of anything else to do.

"Ruth!" he pleaded, his voice edged with hysteria. "Darling! Wake up, Ruth!"

For the first time, he regretted their decision to permit no telephones in the house, and their complete isolation from everyone and anyone who could now be of help to him. Perhaps Ruth needed a doctor. He could not leave her here alone while he fetched one. Could he put her in the car and drive into the village? The weather was too violent, and perhaps she should not even be moved. But what could he tell the village's sole doctor, assuming they were able to find him at home? That he had found his wife lying stark naked on the cold floor of the cellar during a violent storm? With the total absence of any physical injuries, what could the doctor diagnose or recommend? That it was Ruth's mind that was in danger? John had already begun to suspect that. The doctor was just as apt to decide that these *city folk* had involved themselves in some kind of wild orgy in which Ruth had been abused to the point of unconsciousness.

John quickly dampened a cloth in the bathroom and placed it over Ruth's forehead; she was not feverish, but again it was something to do. He stumbled as his foot caught in something lying on the floor; it was her nightgown, which he had unknowingly carried along with her. Should he attempt to put it on her? No, he was afraid of the movements that would involve; she was warm enough.

Ruth moved her head and moaned slightly. He held her close again, hoping the heat from his own perspiring body would stir a responding warmth in hers. The storm continued to rage almost as though howling with fury or triumph, but he was now scarcely aware of its sounds. The world was very different from what it had been just a few short hours earlier, and yet he could not determine how or why.

Slowly, then, so slowly that it was agony to watch it, the warmth at last began to return to Ruth's hands, and the waxen pallor faded from her face as her breathing grew somewhat less labored. After perhaps five very long minutes during which John continued to work over her with whatever actions came to mind, wondering if life would ever return to that cold, white face, she opened her eyes and looked at him.

The eyes were strange, unfocused, bewildered, as they had been on the bluff earlier that day. There was in her face not the slightest sign of recognition as she looked at her husband. John felt chilled; he had never before seen her look at him with such total indifference, as though he were an unimportant stranger she had never even seen before.

But then, again slowly, warmth began to return to her face, and she smiled slightly, tenderly placing one hand on his cheek in a gesture she had used all too seldom of late. Recognition returned, as though a veil had been withdrawn from before her eyes, and she could look again upon a more familiar world. Perhaps, rising out of her dream, she had failed to recognize him immediately in the insufficient light cast by the positioned torch.

"Why, John!" Her voice was strong and perfectly normal. "What's wrong? You look frightened to death!" She turned her head in the beam of light and squinted. "What's the matter with the lights?"

He looked at her for a moment, at a loss for words, confused by her apparent total unawareness of the situation, then quickly gathered her into his arms and held her close to him.

"It's nothing, darling. You cried out in your sleep, that's all. It must have been the storm; it's put the lights out. It upset me for a moment; you sounded so frightened. Go back to sleep, dear."

She leaned back on the pillow, absently running her hands over her body; an expression of surprise entered her face, and she quickly looked at her husband.

"But, John," she stammered. "John . . . I'm naked!"

He took her hand and patted it soothingly. "That's all right," he assured her. "It's a very humid night. You were probably only half awake when you took your gown off to be more comfortable."

"I don't remember that at all."

"Like I said, you were more than half asleep. It's quite all right, Ruth. Really it is."

She looked at him and, despite his fear and uncertainty, he felt a sudden hardness and displeasure when he saw the open suspicion in her eyes and the unasked question as to whether, in some way and without her knowledge, he had taken advantage of her nudity during her heavy sleep. He quickly dismissed the irritation; this was no time for anger.

"I was asleep, dear, and just now woke up when you cried out," he assured her, trusting she would understand his complete meaning. "You'd best just go back to sleep now. It's still very early."

He bent once again to kiss her and then, in the beam of the light, noticed a peculiar spot of bright green just below and behind her left ear, almost like a small growth of fungus, or a discoloration from a bruise. He casually ran his finger over the spot; it felt smooth and wet, although there was no apparent sign of any moisture, and it left no mark on his finger. It did not erase when he rubbed his finger over the spot. There was an unpleasant scaliness about it.

Her fears and uncertainties apparently put to rest by her state of only half-wakefulness, Ruth smiled at him again, yawned, and sank back onto the pillow. She was asleep almost immediately.

John sat beside her throughout the remainder of that long night, while the storm continued to rage and the waves dashed themselves senselessly against the sharp black rocks at the foot of the cliff atop which stood the lonely house that had suddenly been touched by fear.

CHAPTER EIGHT

SOME time shortly before dawn, with the sounds of the furious storm still drumming in his ears and his confusions of fear still lying upon him like a blanket of lead, John managed to fall into a fitfull, unsatisfying sleep that was peopled by strange colors and figures beyond description, swimming and drifting in a sea-green haze before his eyes.

When he awoke a second time, the morning was already quite well advanced, the storm had finally exhausted itself, and the bright sunshine touched the room with fool's gold. It looked like a good morning, he thought as he stretched his legs between the damp, rumpled sheets, a morning that promised real accomplishment. Perhaps he and Ruth could have lunch on the veranda today; there were so few really pleasantly sunny days like this, without either threatening clouds or burning heat. He was like a child awakening to the bright promise of a new morning, who has forgotten the dark shadows of the evening before.

But inevitably memory returned, and he suddenly recalled the inexplicable events of the terrible previous evening, and the golden morning became suddenly shadowed by an unknown fear. Startled, he saw that he was again alone in the room, but his concern subsided when he saw a small note propped up against the lamp on the bedside table; his flashlight beside it again reminded him of the strange night.

My, but you're a sleepyhead this morning! It's too glorious a day to waste any part of it in sleep, but if you want to be so unappreciative of this Gift of the Gods, go ahead! I've gone out to paint; one member of this family must justify his (or her, as the case may be) existence through achievement.

Your breakfast is on the table. Wave to me.

He left the bed and crossed to the window, wincing slightly as his warm bare foot stepped onto the cold wetness of the carpet, and out onto the balcony. Leaning on the railing, he inhaled the brisk sea air. The sky was, for once, beautifully clear and without clouds, and a refreshing breeze reached him from across the sea. The storm had left no reminders of its brief and violent visit, the humidity had broken, and the day was truly beautiful. The diamond-glint of the brilliant sun on the mirror-like waters below hurt his eyes. Could this calm, serene sea really have been touched with such fury last evening? Its anger was now forgotten; perhaps it and the storm had managed to reach a temporary truce. He could not easily believe in the events of last night on so lovely a morning. Had it perhaps been a nightmare? No, of course not.

He dressed quickly in light slacks and open sport shirt, then dashed down the stairs and right out onto the veranda. Ruth was seated on her little canvas stool before her easel, this time properly wearing both smock and broad-brimmed hat, facing the house; she had by now given up all pretense of interest in the sea, which had become so subsidiary to her main purpose. When she saw him standing on the veranda, she raised one arm and waved to him; he returned the greeting and attempted not to appear too eager as he crossed the slightly muddy earth to where she was seated.

"Just one moment, dear," she cautioned him as he approached, raising her free hand to hold him back as she bent over the canvas. "I just want to get this particular shading; it's been giving me trouble all morning."

John watched her closely as, with the tip of her pink tongue peeking from between her full red lips, Ruth ran the brush lightly over the canvas. She seemed somewhat paler than usual, yet there was a fresh beauty about her that he had never quite seen before or, perhaps, merely had never really noticed, and he suddenly realized again how deeply he loved her. Her hand was perfectly steady as she finished the stroke, then lowered the brush and turned to him with a warm and happy smile; he was somewhat startled by her uncharacteristic gesture of raising her face for him to kiss.

"How are you feeling this morning, dear?" he asked, trying to keep his voice casual.

She smiled again, and the sun seemed to dance in the golden flecks in her green eyes. "How should I feel? Isn't this simply a glorious morning?"

"You . . . well, you didn't sleep very well last night, you know," he reminded her, watching her face for any reaction.

But there was none; in fact, she even seemed mildly surprised at his word.

"Oh, didn't I? How very odd! I really don't recall. I thought I slept very well. I did have the strangest dreams, but I can't seem to remember any of them. It must have been the storm; I suppose I spent all night cowering under the sheets, as usual. I do feel just a bit tired this morning, but that's small discomfort for such a day." She spread her arms wide, as though opening them to embrace the morning, and breathed deeply. "Doesn't it make you burst with enthusiasm and ambition?"

He smiled, still confused, but greatly relieved to find Ruth in so happy and healthy a frame of mind; she seemed more like herself than she had in months. He turned to the canvas.

"Well, how's it coming? Have you done much this morning?"

"Oh, I've done a great deal while you were wasting your time in sleep and laziness," she assured him, enthusiasm still brightening her voice. "It really is coming splendidly. I think it's going to be the very best thing I've ever done, but then I always do think that, don't I?"

The painting seemed somehow darker, as though the tumbling gray clouds had thickened of their own accord since John had last looked at it, and when he saw the big gloomy house looming atop the starkly barren cliff top, he felt a sudden, inexplicable chill, a sense almost of staring into another, more mysterious and darker world. There was a stronger suggestion of half-seen figures lurking in the shadowed veranda, the merest hint of movement, but when he bent closer to the canvas, the suggestion faded. The green flow or seepage from the cellar window had instensified, almost like a nauseus green vomit spewed from the sick innards of the house. Ruth had now painted in a portion of the sea at the extreme left of her canvas; angrily dashing waves that hurled themselves suicidedly against the hard rocks and seemed to reach with long, skeletal foaming fingers for the house.

It was not a pleasant painting, and completely lacked the brightness and cheer that characterized Ruth's other work. It somehow spoke of death, decay, corruption, evil. He didn't like it, but there was about it a peculiar strength and force that made it the best work Ruth had ever done.

He was aware that Ruth was closely watching his face, and he tried to look as serious and contemplative as possible as he stared in some confusion at the canvas, pursing his lips, nodding, stepping back for supposed perspective, uttering *oh* and *ah* and *yes* as art experts do, while not in the least understanding what he saw, and evidently not fooling his wife at all, for Ruth laughed.

"Oh, don't try to impress me, John!" she urged. "You don't have to examine it so thoroughly, you know, just look at it. Please don't try to act like those terrible critics; I loathe them, and appreciate just a simple appraisal from someone who really knows nothing at all about art. Forgive me, dear, that isn't really meant the way it sounds. I realize this isn't ready to hang in the Louvre just yet."

"It's . . . very interesting," he said lamely.

His apparent confusion and lack of enthusiasm did nothing to dampen Ruth's surprisingly ebullient spirits.

"Oh, my, is it really as bad as all that? What could be more damning than to label a work of art as interesting?" She moved him aside and picked up her brush again. "Oh, John, I'm afraid your education in art has been sadly lacking. Well, anyway, I think it's really coming along, and I'm certain you'll approve once it's finished. I have a definite feeling about this one. It may be a whole new beginning for me, an entire new perspective. . ." She paused at these words, staring at the house, and her expression became intensely serious, as though she were trying to remember what the house had to say to her. Then she laughed again and turned back to him. "Now, you've wasted enough time for both of us, and you're interfering with the progress of genius. Your breakfast is on the table in the kitchen. You won't forget to pick up those paints for me?"

He turned; he had already started for the house. "Paints?"

She looked at him with a touch of exasperation, her brush held in mid-air. "Oh, John, of course you've forgotten! You're going into town today and you promised to check at the post office for those paints I ordered more than two weeks ago."

He hesitated for a moment, then walked toward the

edge of the cliff and stared down into the sea, not wanting her to see his concern. He didn't like the sea this morning, so smooth, so like glass, reflecting the brilliance of the sun and hurting his eyes. It seemed somehow secretive and dangerous. Could it mean yet another storm? Further down the coast, he could see the whiteness of the abandoned lighthouse. Was all this world in a process of decay?

"Yes, I'm afraid I really had forgotten." He looked again to Ruth, but she had returned to her painting and seemed almost unaware of him. He kicked a small stone over the edge of the cliff, but the jutting rim made it impossible for him to follow its descent into the maelstrom below. "Oh, maybe I'll let it go for another day or so; there's really no hurry."

"What on earth for?" she asked.

"Well. . . ." He turned again and looked back at the house. The windows were staring at him; perhaps they dared him to speak the truth. He knew he could not. "I think you're right. This looks like a wonderful day to get some work done, and I shouldn't pass up the chance."

The patently lame excuse brought another laugh from Ruth; surely she was happier this morning than she had been for some time, as though a long series of unused laughters were trying to escape from long imprisonment. Raising the hand that held the brush, she pushed the brim of her hat back and smiled at him.

"That's complete and utter nonsense, and you know it! This is an artist's day, and has nothing whatever to do with you. It's just not your kind of inspiration. Your weather is dark and cloudy, dreary and stormy. You like to hear the hammering rain on the windows, the growling of thunder in an angry sky, the crashing of the storm-strengthened waves on the beach. Your world is one of sound and motion. You don't need light and shade, hues and tints. You'll probably waste your entire day cooped up in that museum of a study, pacing back and forth, puffing one foul cigarette after another, swinging the spyglass in an interminable series of meaningless circles, and wishing you were out in the sun, and you'll end up by accomplishing nothing at all."

He concealed his irritation behind a smile. "Am I to consider myself chastised or educated?"

"Sometimes I think a little bit of both wouldn't hurt you," she replied. She set her brush down; a sudden breeze flapped the brim of her hat and she squinted at the sudden touch of sunlight. "John, you know perfectly well you have simply got to get that thingamajig to fix the drip in the bathroom sink before it drives us both out of our minds. I shouldn't be surprised if that weren't the entire cause of the poor sleep you said I had last night."

He returned to her and placed his hand on the top of the canvas; she moved it, commenting that he would clumsily smear the paint and undo all her work of the morning.

"Well, why don't you go with me, then?" he asked. "We could make a day of it, dinner and all. We haven't been out to dinner since we came here."

She gave his hand a light affectionate squeeze and released it, going back doggedly to her work. "And why should I abandon this glorious day after all the praise I've lavished on it? We didn't come out here to go to dinner, you know."

"We could have a picnic on the beach."

The thin thread of lines appearing between her eyes warned John that Ruth was becoming irritated. "John, what on earth is wrong with you this morning? I've got a marvelous creative urge and I'm not going to abandon it to spend the day on a damp beach covered with nasty little sand crabs."

"I . . . don't like to leave you alone," he confessed.

Her mouth became firmer. "Oh, for heaven's sake, don't treat me like a child. What could possibly happen to me here?"

Yes, what indeed, he seemed to hear from the surf below.

She sighed, lowered her brush again and turned to him with a more serious, slightly pleading face, but her eyes were touched with annoyance. "Really, dear, I do need those paints very badly, and they should be at the post office by now. I've been alone before, you know. There's no need to worry about me. I may have my hangups, but I'm not a child." She smiled rather impishly. "You can even stop off and have a drink; you might run into that charming little secretary again. I promise not to be jealous, provided you limit the matter to one drink . . . a short one." She pursed her lips. "Now please go, and don't waste any more of my time."

Realizing that further argument would only make her suspicious of his motives, John slowly walked back to the house. As he mounted the steps of the veranda, he noticed that the black limbs of the dead tree still gleamed with remnants of the night's rain; the wetness glistened under the light of the sun, and strangely made him think of black blood. He sniffed. There was a strange, unpleasant odor about the tree that he couldn't quite identify. He paused before entering the house and looked at Ruth, who had returned to work. She raised a hand to her ear and touched it carefully, tenderly, as though she had felt a sudden stab of pain. She looked so vulnerable a small figure outlined against the vastness of the empty sea.

John was not interested in breakfast this morning; there were far more important matters on his mind, which must be attended to while Ruth was busy on the bluff. He walked quickly through the portrait lined corridor, into the kitchen, and to the cellar door, his mind still completely concerned with the inexplicable events of the previous night.

He paused at the head of the stairs and looked down, not at all certain what he expected to see. There was nothing there. The cellar was empty, except for dust and whatever little creatures made their homes there. Bright sunshine streamed through the small dirt-encrusted windows, and motes of dust danced in the rays like the memories of long forgotten fantasies. There was complete silence. It was like staring into a barren world from which all vestige of life had been abruptly removed.

He slowly descended the steps, several of which sagged rather alarmingly under his weight, holding into the narrow railing and, for some absurd reason, as on the previous evening, walking carefully and silently, testing each step as though expecting the worn wood to split and precipitate him to the hard earthen floor. He knew the steps were sound, despite their excessive give, but old wood can be treacherous. There was a mustiness in the air, but it was his imagination that made it something strange.

He rounded the belly of the furnace and faced the room. The door still stood wide open, as he had left it on the evening before. He examined it closely, running his hands over it and testing its stolidity. It was old, marked and scarred by time, made probably of oak, criss-crossed with bars of badly rusted iron. All his efforts to move it since their arrival here had failed; he had not been able to budge it from its slightly ajar position. Now he could move it easily on its rusted and creaking hinges, and even its extreme weight presented no problem.

He stood back, staring at the door. Of course, there could be a totally logical explanation for all this. The little room was situated on the very edge of the cliff, and perhaps the storm had created a slight shifting of the earth, allowing the door to swing free at last. He made a mental note of this. Such earth shiftings might be serious and one day even bring the house crashing down into the sea. It was something a prospective buyer would have to bear in mind. He smiled grimly at the thought. It would not be his problem. Nothing could now induce him to make their stay here a permanent one.

He hesitated a moment before once again stepping into the room, feeling a strong aversion to entering that mysterious chamber again, but it was there he must search for some kind of answer to the peculiar events of last evening.

The room was completely empty, merely four bare walls, a hard earthen floor, a dark beamed ceiling, low enough for him to touch easily with his fingers without stretching on his toes. There was nothing at all remarkable about the room, save perhaps for the very fact of its emptiness. Why go to the trouble of creating this separate room and then leaving it empty? The walls were bare and unadorned, badly stained with the grime and dirt of years. The only distinguishable feature of the room was the slight mound-like rise of earth in the very center of the floor, on which Ruth had lain.

John squatted before the mound for a more minute examination. The dirt was hard packed and firm, almost like stone, and he determined the mound was almost certainly of artificial construction. It bore a slight polish, as though it had been frequently used for some purpose and been polished by constant rubbing.

It made absolutely no sense. The rest of the floor was perfectly level. Why break the symmetry in this way? This defect in an otherwise level floor could only be an inconvenience, something to be leveled or removed, rather than deliberately constructed. Why in the hell had Fowles constructed an empty chamber in the cellar and placed this mound of earth right in its center?

As John ran his fingers over the mound, he experienced a sense of wetness, and yet the earth was perfectly dry; it reminded him of the peculiar sensation when he had touched that strange green spot behind Ruth's ear. A sudden drowsiness came over him, and the mustiness of the room closed in about him. He quickly removed his hand from the mound, which he had been rubbing with an almost sexual pleasure, like those colored round eggs that some people like to fondle; the strange sensation passed.

He rose again, totally dissatisfied. The room was telling him absolutely nothing. He recalled the biting cold as he had bent over Ruth's supine form; his breath had crystalized in it. That, too, was gone. The room was a bit chillier than the rest of the cellar, but it was nothing like the almost unbearable frigid air of the previous night. Could the earthen floor have something to do with it? The small room was isolated from other parts of the cellar and with its compressed area might possibly retain its cold to a greater extent. His own fears might well have exaggerated that sense of cold. Had his breath moisture, then, also been imagination?

Then there was the matter of the emerald-green glow that had completely suffused the room when he had first entered it. There was now not even the slightest trace of it. Certainly it had been there; this could not have been entirely his imagination, for there would have been no reason for him to imagine that hue. Perhaps it was caused by some parasitic element in the earth, or something in the opaque glass of the window, something not as apparent in the light of day. The intensity of the glow might have been sharpened by the flashes of lightning.

He squatted uncomfortably before the single small window, a difficult task since the window was strangely placed with its base sash on a level with the floor itself. He could see nothing; the glass was not transparent. There would be nothing to see anyway, only the sea itself, and the empty horizon. The window was itself another ridiculous aspect of this curious room; it provided very little light, and its curious position made it absolutely useless for any other purpose.

If all these difficulties presented themselves in the physical aspect of the empty room, what could he possibly make of Ruth's presence here, totally naked, during the most violent hours of a furious storm?

The possibility of sleep walking again occurred to him. Ruth had never been subject to somnambulism but that in itself, of course, was no criterion; it could be another aspect of those psychological problems that had plagued her since Elinor's death. Somnambulists often do curious things. Ruth's intense dislike of the cellar might subconsciously have drawn her into it in her sleeping state. Once there, she had then innocently slipped to the floor to continue her disrupted sleep, totally unaware of her surroundings. That strange, almost trance-like nature of the sleep that had so concerned him might again have been his own fear-inspired imagination, or perhaps simply exhaustion from her over-exposure to the sun.

He shook his head, dissatisfied with this reasoning. Wasn't he attempting to explain away too much on the febrile grounds of fertile imagination? The difficulty he had encountered in bringing Ruth out of that sleep was not imagination. Did somnambulists sleep more deeply than others?

And what of her nudity? Artist though she was, Ruth was something of a prude and did not believe in unnecessary exposure of the human form. While fully appreciating the beauty of a shapely body, she had never painted it . . . actually, she had little talent in that direction, or in portraiture . . . and was not overly interested in such representation. She remained almost Puritanically shy and embarrassed in their own shared nudity. She had been quite furious when he had once half-jokingly suggested they view an X-rated movie.

John was hardly psychologist enough to understand any of the numerous possible explanations for Ruth's nudity last night. A natural reaction to the heat of the night? Then what about the extreme cold of the cellar room? (Again, unless he wanted to blame that on his imagination.) Many people . . . particularly the shy ones like Ruth . . . possessed a secret pleasure in nudity that they generally managed to control. (The generally prim and proper housewife who draws all the shades to do her housework in the nude, for example.) Could it possibly mean the reawakening of her dormant sexual drive? John shook his head. That thought obviously came from his own desires.

All of these were possible answers, logical within their own context, although none of them completely satisfying. Or they might be totally wrong and have no relevance whatever. He was neither a psychologist nor an expert on phenomena; not all writers could success-fully probe the human mind. He could only guess and hope those random guesses were somewhere near the truth.

As he prepared to leave the strange room, John's hand happened to touch the wall just beside the door, and his fingers encountered grooves that he had failed to notice through the heavy coating of dirt and grime that covered the walls. Curious, he looked more closely, running his fingers along the wall and tracing the course of dirt-concealed lines. They were obviously artificial. He had nothing with which to attempt to scrape away the covering, but his fingers traced strange, convoluted forms that had been deeply incised into the walls. He could make nothing of them. Strangely, they reminded him of the half-suggested figures on the veranda in Ruth's paintings. When clear of dirt, the walls of the chamber must have presented a curious tapestry of writhing movement.

John thoughtfully ascended the stairs into the kitchen. His breakfast . . . tomato juice, cold cereal, bread and jelly . . . was on the table, but aroused in him no sense of appetite. He prepared himself a cup of hot coffee and, still frowning, took it with him into the study, from where he could look out onto the bluff.

Ruth was still hard at work, obviously fallen into intense concentration; the shadow of her floppy hat brim concealed her face, but her hand moved decisively across the spread of canvas, without hesitation, as she often worked when the inspiration was upon her. A swooping gull was a brief white smear on the light blue tile of the sky. The sun had already dried the hard brown earth on the cliff top. The horizon was empty, the sea calm. It was going to be another hot day; the weather was so peculiar here. There was no one in sight but Ruth herself, seated at her canvas stool before the easel, a lone woman staring at a house that had concealed its own dark secrets for two centuries. John stood at the tall window, slowly sipping his coffee, almost absently watching his wife at work, wondering, puzzling.

There had to be answers somewhere. Things did not happen without a reason, a purpose, a cause as well as an effect, a catalyst. He glanced at the solid, comfortable study where Fowles had sat on dark nights two centuries ago, with its rows of books, its portraits, its marine mementos. Perhaps the answer was here, or somewhere else in the house. All old houses have their secrets, concealed in the most unlikely places, dropped haphazardly into nooks and crannies that are then forgotten and lost to memory until accidentally uncovered once again after many dust-covering years. Were there such places in this house? They had found none during their earlier explorations, but they had not been looking for anything of that sort. They might have passed by something that had then no meaning, but which now might help to resolve the problem. Perhaps Fowles had left some old records somewhere that would assist in clearing up the mystery of what had happened last evening. Where could he begin to look? The cellar was certainly empty and, strangely, the house had no attic. He would feel foolish walking through the rooms tapping the walls and the flooring for a hollow sound, like some amateur detective in a second-rate thriller. Besides, he had no idea what he would be looking for.

Fowles. John wondered about that man, certain that it

had all begun with him. What kind of man had he been, this brutal sea captain with so vile a reputation that nearly two centuries after his death people still did not care to discuss him? John looked at the painting on the opposite wall above the fireplace, which he assumed to be Fowles. A powerfully masculine man with a strong nose and full lips, a broad forehead and full brown whiskers with a reddish tinge. The eyes were disconcerting, a deep green, bearing a sardonic glint as though he had planned for John's problems and was now amusedly watching the result. John remembered something in Gogol about the mysterious portrait that looked with human eyes. Fowles must have been at best a frightening figure, and in a rage he must have been a terror. Not in any respect a comfortable man.

Another question troubled John, one enigma for which he could not begin to find an answer: that peculiar green coloring in Ruth's painting, at first seeping and then flowing from the cellar window, a brilliant sea-green shade exactly like the color that had suffused the cellar room last night. How could he explain this coincidence? It could not represent Ruth's subconscious remembrance of last evening, for although the canvas green was brighter this morning, he well remembered it had been there the very first time he had looked at the painting, before either he or she had found entry into the cellar room.

He now once and for all dismissed his imagination as the true culprit in this peculiar incident. No, it had actually happened, all of it. There was undoubtedly something very strange in old Fowles House. Something here had remained dormant for many years, revived by their own arrival. Why had the house stood empty for so long? Because others had encountered what he and Ruth had now found. But what was it? What was its origin? And, above all, what was its purpose?

He could not see that the strange event had affected Ruth in any way; she obviously had no recollection of the events in the cellar room, which perhaps confirmed their deeply traumatic nature. Perhaps he was making too much of the entire business . . . a curious incident, but not necessarily the portent of anything, or an indication of any serious problems facing them. Ruth had, for a brief time, acted irrationally, but it had passed and she apparently was none the worse for it. People sometimes did strange things. Perhaps the long dormant . . . aura, force, whatever it might be . . . had briefly been disturbed and put into motion by their arrival, as could happen in an old house, and had now become dormant again. Perhaps they had last night seen both the beginning and the end of it.

He saw Ruth pause in her work and again raise her hand to her left ear, at the same time turning her head and looking with a rather curious intensity at the dead tree near the veranda.

No, it was not over. It had not passed them by untouched. John remembered the peculiar green spot behind Ruth's ear.

CHAPTER NINE

IT was already approaching noon, and beginning to grow considerably more humid and uncomfortable when John started for the village. Ruth was still at her accustomed place near the edge of the bluff, a rather pathetically small and vulnerable figure seated on her small canvas stool in the midst of that splendid empty panorama of sea and sky, deeply engaged in the work that was her entire purpose in life. When John called his goodbye from the veranda just before stepping into the car, she paused only long enough to raise one small white hand before returning to her work, touching her brush to the canvas while intently scrutinizing the seaward side of the house. Again, John felt that powerful protective instinct towards her. They'd had their problems, but he still loved her deeply. There would have to be some way out of this new dilemma.

The unusual intensity of Ruth's preoccupation was somehow disturbing. Always an extremely introspective worker with little time or patience with distractions, Ruth had at no other time in his recollection seemed so completely absorbed in her work. Painting was her entire life, and she was an accomplished artist who showed considerable more promise for the future, but she generally worked in spasmodic, uneven spurts of activity, insisting painting was something that must come of itself; it could not be forced. There had been many times while at work on a project when she had gone for days and even for weeks without so much as touching her brush to the canvas. This complete and total absorption was unusual and disconcerting, lasting as it had now for an unprecedented number of days. Could it really be good for her? It would of course keep her mind off other problems and worries, but it still smacked of unhealthiness. John hoped she would at least stop work and return to the shelter of the house later during the afternoon, when the heat might become too intense. He again disliked leaving her alone; he would try not to be away for too long.

John found little pleasure in the brief trip on this day; his mind was too filled with the curious questions that had so suddenly arisen to shadow their somewhat artificial happiness in their new home. The brightness of the sun on the calm surface of the now placid sea irritated him, even with the shielding of dark glasses, and the steady roar of the surf interfered with his process of thought. He found little beauty in the scenery that surrounded him, in what had never before failed to fill him with a wonderful sense of serenity, in the purity of the beach lined with deep green scrub and spotted with relics of other times, the white puffs of well-washed clouds like cauliflower blossoms now drifting across the empty turquoise sky, and the peaceful aspect of the swelling green sea flecked with foam. He could not dismiss his fears by viewing the seascape. The loneliness, the complete yellow-white barrenness of the land seemed symptomatic of the aridity of his own life.

For he now knew that the events of last evening had abruptly and permanently changed the course of their lives. Fear had entered his mind and could not be dismissed. There was no point in attempting to evade the truth, in trying to find hopeless alternatives that would fit more comfortably with his own desires. Realities would have to be confronted, even though the incident itself remained totally inexplicable.

Ruth had been drawn into a cellar she feared during the night of a violent electrical storm and there she had lain herself, stark naked, on the icily cold earthen floor of a room whose massively heavy door had successfully defied his most determined efforts to open. There were the basic and unvarnished facts of last evening's incident.

The explanations were not nearly that simple. None of this had been the result of his own over-active imagination. That had merely been a form of fright-created wishful thinking. All of it had really happened, he could not understand why. It could not be shunted aside and ignored.

There was something very wrong about Fowles House, the great, rambling, Widow-Walked, gabled house by the sea, something unnatural and perhaps something horrible.

Why did he still hesitate to apply the most obvious word? Supernatural.

He shook his head, still refusing to accept this explanation. We do not believe such things in modern times. Surely we know all there is to know. What had Ruth said about the times in which you live always being considered modern times? The reign of Tutankhamon was once considered modern times, the time of the priests in the temple of Baal in Babylon had once been modern. Was man as arrogant then as he is now? Wisdom will truly be ours when we have the wisdom to realize how much wisdom we lack.

The strangeness of Fowles House could not be something new. He and Ruth had not brought it with them. It had been here, perhaps, for two centuries, festering, waiting, even during the long years when the house had stood empty and abandoned. Surely, then, someone must have noticed or experienced something strange in or about the house over the years.

The car rounded a curve and he saw before him the strangely convoluted piece of whitened driftwood behind which he had no unexpectedly and disturbingly spied upon Paul and Linda in the first stages of their passionate love-making; he determinedly forced his mind from the rousing mental images brought to it by remembrance of their tightly joined bodies on the warm sand. He was again certain that Paul, and possibly Linda as well, had often watched the house, looking and waiting . . . for what? Why was Paul always so uneasy when he visited them? Why had he never brought Linda with him?

Paul must surely know more about the old house than he was telling, and perhaps it was now time that he told more. John would not struggle alone with this problem while there was someone who might be in a position to answer his questions.

John entered the village and felt a touch of irritation at its constant somnambulistic appearance. It never looked any different from one visit to the next . . . the same sleeping main street, the same shipmasts bobbing up and down at the decaying wharfs, like knitting needles being pushed in and out of a skein of blue-brown wool, the same totally uninteresting people patrionizing the same dull shops with their ordinary wares unimaginatively displayed. The grocer was in front of his store again, at his everlasting task of arranging and rearranging a display of red apples that always ended in the same standard triangular form. Was this all that comprised his life? Did he have dreams of artistic achievement with his little apples? The bearded keeper of the fishing tackle shop next door to the grocer was sound asleep as always, his burly form resting comfortably in an arm chair tilted back on two legs and resting against the window of his shop, his hands folded over his ample belly, totally indifferent to the non-existent pressures of his business. Two old gossips, dressed in proper but inexpensive print dresses, walked primly down the walk and threw sharply disapproving glances at a remarkably full-breasted young blonde girl who went bouncing by in a brash, bright manner they had never known even in their youngest days.

John sighed with boredom. How could people permit themselves to spend their lives merely on the fringes of existence? He felt like shouting to them about a great big world out there that was swiftly passing them by. It was no wonder Ruth had indicated no desire to enter into the social swim of the village, such as it was; he and she had very little in common with these undoubtedly good but boring people.

He sighed again. At least they were safe, free from those fears and uncertainties that constantly filled their more active and worldly counterparts. They were content with what they had, not constantly striving for more that was beyond their reach, living their lives in reasonable ease and comfort, wending their colorless ways to the grave. Who was he to say they were wrong?

Or perhaps this was all just a blind, a cover, a false facade revealing a much more ominous and terrible truth. Perhaps the entire village knew of the strange events at Fowles House, knew the truth about what occurred there in the darkest of nights. Perhaps there was some insidious conspiracy in which the entire village played a part, perhaps these simple people stared at John not merely out of curiosity, but watching him and waiting, aware of what was to come. Perhaps all the village knew the truth about Fowles House, and remained silent.

The village was too small to boast of a post office building of its own, nor did it provide any form of mail delivery. Those with such needs stopped at the brass-grilled cage in one corner of the lobby of the hotel, in which stood the village postmaster, a pompous, prematurely balding youngish man who took his position of officialdom with an extremely serious mien. He wore a green visor to shield his spectacled eyes from the dim lighting of the lobby, wide rubber bands on his upper arms to raise his sleeves out of any possible soiling from the inky materials of his trade, and wore his rimless glasses low on his nose, enabling him to peer over them at those who stepped up to his cage and demanded the important services he offered.

The postmaster happened to be an extremely suspicious man. He knew it was part of human nature to extract from government agencies all that could possibly be secured, whether by legal means or not. But as long as he represented this particular branch of the government, no one was going to put anything over on him. A villager who came for his mail, which was carefully sorted into rows of pigeon-holes against the wall, was very closely examined by the postmaster, who had probably known the inquirer through most of his life, before the letters addressed to him were slid below the grill. Letters being mailed were carefully weighed on a small scale kept nearby for that purpose, and the postage required was reported in stern, no nonsense tones. One does not fool around with a government agency.

The postmaster neither particularly liked nor fully trusted John Kendall, with an attitude typical of small towners to folk from the big city. When mail arrived for the new inhabitants of Fowles House, it was closely examined before being placed in its proper slot. Of course, he would never dream of actually tampering with the mails, but on occasions when he was certain not to be observed, he would raise the envelope to the light and attempt to make out what it contained, but always without success; these city correspondents were clever enough to fold their letters with the print inward, somewhat suspicious in itself. He wondered just what kind of mail these newcomers received from the city, and his curiosity was converted into deep suspicions of mysterious plots of various kinds whenever that mail happened to include a large package which might, after all, conceal just about anything.

This particular morning the postmaster handed just

such an ominous package to John, opening the brass grill with the little key that never let his person, passing it through with narrowed, suspicious eyes that were intended to convey to John the message that he might be able to fool the rest of the village, but never the government appointed local postmaster. Slowly reclosing the brass grill that set him off from the rest of the world, the postmaster watched narrowly as John took the package and his other mail to the table before the windows.

Most of the mail was quickly discarded into the circular wire basket under the table. There were several highly misleading colorful circulars insisting he would remain abysmally ignorant of world and national affairs unless he subscribed immediately to a certain magazine, or be unaware of the current literary gems if he did not become a member of a certain book club that offered a variety of luridly pseudo-sexual novels intended primarily to tittilate the fancies of love-starved suburban housewives who lacked the imagination, appeal or courage to become involved in their own extramarital adventures to brighten their drab lives. Again, John wondered at the mystical talents of such organizations that invariably managed to track him down no matter how desperately he attempted to conceal his traces. There were three letters from readers, forwarded by his publishers, which he placed in his pocket for future reading and answering, and a rather strong letter from the publishers themselves, expressing their keen disappointment over the unexpectedly long delay in the completion of his promised new work, demanding at least one more chapter during the coming week. At this point, John was not particularly concerned about their displeasures or demands. Aside from the package of paints, there was no mail for Ruth.

The surprise was the yellow Transatlantic cable from his Grandmother in Vienna, simply stating:

ARRIVING SUNDAY 18TH. IT HAS BEEN TOO LONG. ANXIOUS TO SEE YOU. LOVE TO RUTH.

John raised his head, gazing absently into the street, curious about this terse wire. Aside from his publishers and Ruth's gallery contacts, Grandmother Ellen was the only person who had been informed of their move from the city. What could possibly be bringing her here from Vienna at this time, and apparently in something of a hurry? Grandmother Ellen belonged in the glittering cities of the world; this was hardly the place for her. She demanded comfort and elegance, the best appointed hotels, fashionable society and a great deal of attention. An old mansion set above the sea near a dull provincial village would scarcely interest her. Her previous letter of some two weeks earlier had made no mention even of the possibility of such a sudden and unexpected visit.

He absently tapped the cable against his hand as he pictured again that small, white-haired lady who had been so important a part of his childhood. The image she presented of physical weakness was highly deceptive, for in that small frame was an iron will that would brook no nonsense in or from anyone, as always quickly apparent to those who served her in any way. Ellen Pirenne demanded perfection in herself and in those about her and had no patience with human failings of any kind. Now well into her seventies, she still spent all of her time traveling about the world, studying interesting places and meeting interesting people. She felt an insatiable thirst for life and refused to permit her advancing years to stay her course. She was interested in everything.

Including, John quietly told himself, the unusual, the unknown and the supernatural. She was unshakeable in her firm belief that she had once seen the ghost of Catherine Howard in the Queen's Gallery at Hampton Court, and claimed a certain measure of clairvoyance. Was it mere coincidence that was bringing her to Fowles

House just at the time when John had felt the first chilling touch of the supernormal?

"Why, Mr. Kendall, what a rare pleasure to see you in town!"

Startled by this unexpected interruption, John quickly gathered his thoughts together and turned at the sound of the pleasant, slightly familiar feminine voice. He smiled at the perky, pretty face of Paul Sanders' secretary. Why did he also feel a sudden flush of embarrassment?

"I thought it was going to be John from now on."

"If it isn't naturally so, the fault is your own," Linda responded. "It's been so long since I've seen you, I feel we've become strangers again."

"That would be my misfortune," John smiled. "I haven't that many friends here, you know; I can't spare a single one of them. But I have dropped in to see Paul several times; you always managed to be somewhere else."

"Not intentionally, I assure you. I'll have to spend less time out of the office, won't I? But what brings you to our fair but dull village today? Nothing wrong with your private little world on the cliff, I hope?"

"Only if you consider a leaky faucet trouble," he explained after a moment's hesitation. "For the past few nights, Ruth and I have been subjected to a form of Chinese torture by drops of water that explode with atomic fury just as we're about to drop off to sleep. I came into town to buy a washer and pick up our mail." He indicated the parcel at his side, as he slipped his grandmother's cable into his breast pocket. "And if you want to make your postmaster happy, look askance at the package."

She smiled, and a deep dimple creased one smooth white cheek. "Look askance? I didn't know anyone used that word any longer. Why should I look askance, pray?"

"He suspects a nihilist bomb or some such thing."

"Who would want to blow up this magnificent little burg?"

John shrugged. "Perhaps your postmaster has a dark secret of his own and suspects he has enemies. Can't trust these men who peer over their glasses, rather than through them; it's always a disguise. Maybe there's some highly secret undercover project going on somewhere under the sand dunes, or there's a concealed UFO base somewhere that only he knows about."

"And is it? A bomb, I mean?"

He shook his head. "Sorry. After all that buildup, it's only paints for my wife."

"And how is your wife?"

Again, he paused for a moment. "I left her happily at work in her favorite spot on the bluff; I doubt she even realized I'm gone. She's enjoying herself tremendously; this kind of life appeals very strongly to her."

"And to you?" There was a touch of rare mischievousness in her glance.

"Of course," he responded, perhaps a bit too enthusiastically. "Else I wouldn't be here, would I?"

Her glance now held a touch of doubt. She was clever, this one.

"But how have you been?" he asked, anxious to escape her rather disturbing scrutiny.

"Just fine, thank you," she responded. "Still waiting for that long-promised invitation to explore the mysterious inners of Fowles House."

"I assure you, that invitation hasn't been forgotten," he advised her, adding with more assurance than he felt, "and it should be coming along very soon now, I promise you. I think we're really beginning to settle in, and before long those mysterious doors will be opened. I'm rather surprised you've never come out with Paul."

"So am I, frankly," she admitted. "He's never asked me. Gentlemen in this town seem rather lax in that respect."

John had a sudden thought and touched the envelope in his pocket. "As a matter of fact, I've just learned that my grandmother will be visiting us very soon. I'm certain she'll expect something of a dinner party in her honor, and I'd like to have both you and Paul. You'd like her; she's a loveable old lady with a sometimes acid tongue and an always warm heart."

"That would be very nice," Linda commented. "Things have been rather dull around here lately."

He silently chided himself for the ungentlemanliness of the sudden vision of Linda and Paul on the beach. Dullness was sometimes merely a matter of personal opinion.

"Actually. . ." he began. "Well, I was hoping to see Paul today."

She shook her head. "Sorry, John, but you're out of luck there. Paul isn't here just now. He left only this morning for the city. A death in the family. He'll probably be gone for at least the better part of the week."

"I'm sorry to hear that," John hesitated; this upset his plans.

"Is there something I can do for you?" she asked. She looked more closely at him. "You seem a bit upset, John. Is it something about the house?"

"Well, in a sense. . ."

She smiled encouragingly, adopting some of her professional polish. "I'm still chief clerk and bottle washer of the firm. Perhaps I can help you."

John hesitated again. "I don't know. . ." It would be so much easier to talk to Paul, yet Linda might also have some information that would be of help. "Are you going back to the office now?"

She shook her head; the light glinted on the small golden earrings in the shape of half moons. "Not just yet, although I can, if you like. Actually, I was planning on lunch."

"Alone?"

"I told you things have been rather dull lately."

"Would you have lunch with me, please?"

"Of course!" She laughed. "I'm not supposed to appear so eager, am I? It's the best offer I've had in a long time. If you can really spare the time?"

"Time is the one thing I seem to have plenty of since I came here!" He was still concerned about Ruth, and anxious to return to her, but it was important to learn whatever he could about the house.

Aware of the close scrutiny of the postmaster as they headed for the restaurant door at the far side of the lobby, John pointedly carried the package of paints between himself and Linda, and within several moments they were comfortably seated in a quiet corner of the *Whaler's Rest*, sipping martinis that were large and contained far too much vermouth, with slices of lemon that half filled the glasses. John ordered a roast beef for both of them. Linda eased the twist of lemon from her glass and nibbled at it as she closely looked at John.

"There really is something troubling you, John," she said quite seriously.

He raised an eyebrow. "How do you know that?"

She shrugged. "Oh, I can tell. Your eyebrows are closer together than the last time I saw you. That means you've been doing a lot of frowning lately, and that indicates worry."

He laughed, but the sound was hollow and lacked the true lilt of pleasure. "You can come to a decision like that just by looking at my eyebrows? That's a new one; I'll have to remember it."

"It doesn't work on just anyone," she cautioned. "Only on the sensitives. What is it, John? Can I help?"

Again, he hesitated, thinking that his life had become full of these hesitations. He liked Linda, and he trusted her, but how much could he tell her? He would have felt much easier talking to Paul.

"Is it this something you wanted to see Paul about?" she asked. "I really know almost as much about the business as he does, you know, although you could never get him to admit it." A sudden thought came to her. "Or is it one of those things . . . well, those men things that you don't talk to women about?"

He smiled and shook his head, displeased by the heavy sweetness of vermouth as he sipped his drink. "I've scarcely been here long enough to get myself involved . . . in anything like that. No, to tell you the truth, I'm just a bit curious."

He looked directly at her, anxious to catch any passing emotion that might be reflected in her face. He was again disturbed by a brief mental flash that showed two figures lying on the beach. Why couldn't he get that out of his mind? He didn't want to miss this opportunity of getting some answers. Undoubtedly she would soon learn anything he might say to Paul, anyway.

"For one thing, I'd like to know why Paul has been watching the house."

Her face betrayed nothing. In the brief but heavy pause that followed his words, her features remained perfectly immobile, almost as though she had not heard him, and this told him what he wanted to know. If she had not been aware of Paul's activities, something would surely have shown in her face. She discarded the lemon and tasted her drink, looking at him over the rim of the glass.

"Has he?"

"You know he has. . . You were with him last night."

She arched her eyebrows, but made no comment.

"I'm not trying to embarrass you. . ."

"Don't worry. I don't embarrass easily."

". . .but I must know."

She took a cigarette from her bag, and he lighted it for her with a book of matches from the table.

"What is there to know, John?"

"That's what I'd like you to tell me. I've been curious for some time about signs on the beach . . . paced footsteps, too many cigarette stubs . . . that indicate someone was spending a considerable amount of time there, in a position where he could watch the house without being seen. It was only last night it occurred to me that it might be Paul, there to . . . observe."

"He hasn't really been spying on you, you know."

"I've never really thought that," he agreed. "But he has been watching."

She shrugged. "I don't see that there should be any great mystery about it. It's natural he should be concerned about those who rent our properties. Paul happens to be an extremely conscientious person; he feels a certain responsibility."

"When he spends hours each night watching a certain house, it does seem that he's carrying that sense of responsibility a little too far. Does he show the same motherly concern for all his tenants?"

"No," she admitted. "Not all." She was beginning to sound evasive.

"Only for those who rent Fowles House?"

She smiled and attempted to inject a touch of lightness into their conversation. "But you forget, John, we've never rented Fowles House before. You and your wife are the first to live in the place for I don't know how many years. It's a very important and valuable property, and Paul is naturally concerned that all should go well with you there. There's the matter of possible future sale, too, you know. He's still hoping you might make your stay a permanent one."

They fell silent as the waiter delivered their orders. Somehow, John felt little sense of appetite. He waited until the waiter was out of earshot before turning again to his charming companion.

"Linda, I want to know about that house." He raised his hand to stop her interruption. "All there is to know about it. I mean it."

Finally impressed by his obvious serious attitude, Linda looked at him with a touch of alarm shadowing her eyes. "Is there something wrong there?"

He still could not bring himself to speak of the peculiar events of the previous evening. He would have to learn more first, before he could broach so strange a topic to someone who might not understand. It was possible some information about the house would provide him with a simple explanation for what had occurred, and then his fear and his uneasiness would all seem rather foolish.

"That's what I'd like to know," he replied. "Linda, I'll admit there is something . . . well, something uncomfortable about that house, and I have a feeling that you . . . or at least Paul . . . wouldn't be too surprised to hear that. I haven't been blind to Paul's expective, uneasy attitude whenever he's visited us. He looks, and he waits. What for? He's never really at ease there. I think he's afraid of the house. And so are you."

"You forget. I've never been there."

"You don't need an invitation, Linda. You could come with Paul at any time, whether he asked you or not, either as chief clerk and bottle washer or just as a friend. You've as much right as he does. I've often wondered about that."

She said nothing, avoiding his eyes.

"It really is quite a wonderful house," John continued. "It's firm, solidly built, comfortable, and it has the most magnificent view for miles around. The rooms are large and airy, and it has that wonderful freshness that you find only in old buildings by the sea. But when the wind blows, the old house creaks, and it's like the past moaning through the timbers, and then I think the house shakes not from the touch of the wind, not from the sudden harshness of cold, but from fear."

"Fear of what?"

"I don't know that," John confessed. "There are many different kinds of fear, aren't there? But I sense something happened in that house, perhaps many years ago, and the aura of it is still there."

"That surely can be said of many houses," Linda

commented.

"But of some more than others. That's really why I came into town today, why I'm so anxious to see Paul. I'm sure he can tell me something."

Linda picked at her food, showing as little interest as he. "I don't know, John."

"I suppose what I really want to know is if the fear of that past poses a danger for the present."

Linda didn't answer immediately, and a rather uncomfortable silence fell between them. John watched her very closely. He had finally managed to make her understand the intense seriousness of his words, and of his questions. She was somewhat paler than when they had entered the restaurant; perhaps she sensed even more in his words than he cared to put there. She placed a cut of roast beef into her mouth and began to chew slowly, but obviously with little relish. Almost the entire restaurant seemed to join in the sudden silence, as though all were waiting to hear Linda's next words. A low, subdued murmur of conversation came from one of the nearby tables; it was the only sound in the room.

Then the bartender clumsily knocked some glasses together and the jarring seemed to draw Linda from her trance. She looked at John, and her eyes were serious.

"John, I can see you're upset. Tell me. Has something happened?"

He still could not bring himself to give words to what was uppermost in his mind. "My wife. . ."

Linda looked up sharply, suddenly intensely interested. "Yes? What about your wife?"

"She's . . . not very comfortable in the house any longer. Oh, she's fine when she's out there on the bluff, painting away; she forgets everything when she's working. But she sleeps very badly, and her appetite has fallen off. Ruth is a very highly sensitive woman, Linda, and she . . . well, somehow she feels things. Some people do, you know, in old houses." He sighed. "I might as well be honest with you. Things aren't going as well as I had hoped they would, and I feel, somehow, there's something about the house that's responsible."

The food was growing cold by this time, but neither of them seemed to notice. John reached out and took Linda's hand.

"Linda, is there something about that house that I should know? Tell me, please."

Linda returned the pressure of his hand and smiled, a warm and comforting smile of friendship and honesty which still, to him, seemed to conceal something.

"I quite honestly don't know what there is to tell you, John, or if there really is anything for that matter. Of course, it's a very old house and, as you've said, sometimes with old houses . . . Oh, it isn't that there's really anything wrong with the house itself, of course not. I don't believe anything can be *wrong* with a house, unless we're talking about structural defects that imagination so easily can turn into inexplicable phenomena. Superstition will fasten legend to an old and empty house, and people like to talk. Legends fall upon an old house like the dust of passing years. An aging timber creaks, and there are whispers of spirits walking in the night; a shutter flaps in the wind, and people talk of ghosts seeking revenge."

"And what about the legends of this particular house?"

"I honestly don't know much about them. Paul never likes to discuss it with me."

"And doesn't that seem rather strange?"

She shrugged her shoulders, pushing her dish aside and leaning her elbows on the table; she had now fully entered into the seriousness of the conversation.

"I've never really thought so. Paul is an intensely moral guy, John, as I'm sure you realize. He has always had something of a personal interst in Fowles House, and also something of an internal struggle. I don't really know why. When you indicated your decision to rent, we both agreed merely to let matters take their course and not stir up all sorts of unanswerable questions by mentioning ridiculous legends that no one believes anyway. But I do believe Paul has always felt a certain sense of guilt about concealing anything from you, even something as simple and meaningless as *old wives tales*. Of course, you are right about his watching the house. He's often spent long periods on the beach, when the uneasiness he feels becomes particularly strong. He was always confident that he would never be seen; his ego will be damaged to learn he hasn't been completely successful in the role of Sherlock Holmes. It's not that he was there out of any expectation of danger or misfortune, or anything of that sort, but merely from a sense of responsibility. I've gone with him now and then just to keep him company. Going out there, watching, the whole business seemed to soothe his conscience, although I don't know why it's necessary."

"Linda, have you ever seen a portrait of Fowles, or any members of that family?"

She shook her head. "No. I don't believe there are any about."

"Well, there are a good number of them in the house," he advised her. "I can't be certain which are Fowles himself, and which are just other members of his family, but they all bear a resemblance to each other. And Paul resembles them all."

She looked at him, startled. "You mean you think Paul is a Fowles himself?"

"The resemblance is unmistakeable. He's certainly connected with the family in some way."

She thought for a moment. "He's never mentioned it. I really know nothing about his background, except that he was born and raised here." She frowned. "He always seems very strange . . . disturbed . . . whenever someone mentions Fowles. He doesn't like to talk about him, or even hear about him. His face becomes . . . dark."

"He may not be too proud of the connection," John

suggested. "You know, it's possible that he doesn't even know about it himself, but he may suspect something and it makes him uneasy."

The waiter approached them, surprised at their total lack of interest in their food; John gestured to have it removed, and ordered two coffees.

"And what about those legends? You still haven't told me anything."

Linda paused, thinking. It had grown darker in the room as sudden clouds covered the sun. Several more guests had taken their places at the tables and the bar, and the room began to hum with conversation.

"As I've said, I really don't know about the legends, John. I suppose it sounds strange, but I know very little about the house. You know how it is . . . you hear there are *stories*, and you get into the habit of them yourself, even without actually knowing about them. When someone mentions Fowles House, people nod and give the impression that they know a great deal more than they care to tell, when actually all they know are the vague rumors about *something strange*. People like to think they're part of a mystery. Over two hundred years, truth can become distorted and even forgotten, lost under a tissue of confusion. It's so long since anyone has really talked about the place, I believe most people really know as little as I do. All I know is the house does have a rather violent history, going back to old Fowles himself."

"Tell me about Fowles. What kind of man was he?" He smiled slightly. "Provided you know anything about him."

"Something," she admitted. "He at least was a real figure. Strange, brutal, violent, certainly not very likeable from what I've heard." She crushed her cigarette in the glass ashtray that bore the figure of a whale. "Like the house, he's somewhat shrouded in his own legends, and that makes it very difficult to get at the truth. He was a sea captain, of course, and a brutal

197

master. It seems he first made his fortune in the slave trade and practiced it with all the horrors connected with it; they say on more than one occasion he threw his cargo overboard when threatened with search and seizure. Then he went into outright piracy. He delighted in torture, both of men and women, plank-walking, live burial, all that sort of thing. Any woman who fell into his hands suffered the usual fate worse than death, and I guess a lot of other terrible things as well. He went from piracy into the even dirtier business of wrecking ships right here on the coast. You know, the false lights, plundering of deliberately wrecked ships. Fowles was feared and detested, and the house was shunned even in his day. The sense of evil that surrounded the place when he lived in it has never completely dissipated; most people still won't go near the place. The whole business is just made for strange stories, gossip and legend."

"How did Fowles die?"

She shook her head. "I don't know. Violently, I suppose. I can't imagine it any other way."

Linda fell silent. A woman at a nearby table laughed, and the sound seemed to contain the tinkling of icicles. John pictured Fowles as he was in several portraits of the old house, and could well believe the aura of brutality that surrounded his name. Yet, it still just didn't seem enough.

"No, there has to be more, Linda," he objected. "How long ago was that . . . two hundred years or so? What happened to the house after his death?"

She hesitated. "It became what I suppose people would call a hard luck house. There were a lot of rumors and unpleasantnesses and coincidences that don't really add up to anything at all, but helped to build up the legend of mystery. Fowles's heirs were never happy in the place. They seemed a rather unfortunate family to begin with, the kind that brings disaster with them no matter where they go."

"What do you mean?"

She thought for a moment, frowning. "Let me see if I can get this straight. There are no dates in it at all, and some of the stories get all mixed up with the various descendants of the old pirate, and the times may be wrong. After the death of Fowles, the house fell to a nephew or a niece, I don't remember which. Fowles himself had never married . . . that's not surprising, is it? . . . and he had no more direct heirs. His descendants continued to live in the house for nearly a century after his death, but it was never a happy place. . . May I have another drink?"

"Oh, I'm sorry. Of course."

John signaled for the waiter and ordered two more martinis, extra dry this time. Linda had become suddenly intensely nervous, and when the drinks arrived, she took somewhat too large a sip, resulting in a fit of coughing. She sipped some water and sank back, sighing and wiping the cough-tears from her eyes.

"I'm sorry."

"All right now?"

She nodded.

"You said it was never a happy house. Why not?"

"There were a series of unfortunate accidents." She paused only for a moment. "To women, in particular."

He suddenly felt he was coming closer to what he wanted to know. "And what about the women?"

Her smile was strained and unnatural, her attitude that of a person who wants people to understand she doesn't really believe what she is about to say, but finds it necessary to conceal her own uncertainty in an off-handed manner.

"That's where the coincidences come in. The women who made their home there after the captain's death . . . mostly relatives by marriage, I believe . . . suffered rather tragic fates. I'm not certain of the number actually involved, but from what I understand at least two women went mad and had to be confined. Another fell to her death from the Widow's Walk during a particularly violent storm, and the last woman to live there, just about a hundred years ago, committed suicide."

"Why?"

"Oh, I don't know. She was probably as mad as the others. Madness did seem to run in the Fowles family. Understandably, I should say."

"But what about the legends?"

She gestured emptily with her hands. "That's it. That's all I know. Honestly. Just that this is a particularly unfortunate house for women to live in. Not particularly harrowing, is it? It seems to me what happened to the various women was pretty much their own doing. But again, you know how superstitious minds elaborate the smallest story. A few unfortunate incidents, and a house becomes *strange*.

"Strange? You mean the house is haunted?"

"You should know that better than I. Haven't even been in the place, remember. Any specters on the stairway? Any moans or sighs or rattling of chains in the dead of night?" She smiled again, apparently very much relieved by having freed her own mind of the perhaps unsuspected burden of shared guilt. "Any bloody phantoms in the cellar?"

He had been staring thoughtfully ahead, but turned sharply at these last words. "Why do you say that? What about the cellar?"

"Isn't a ghost supposed to haunt the scene of its death? The suicide occurred in the cellar."

He felt a sudden tightness in his chest, and the golden glow of sunshine was suddenly tinged with a touch of sea-green.

"Tell me about it."

She sipped her drink, again gathering her thoughts. "It's not a very pleasant story. Apparently the young woman, bride of the then owner of the house, found her way down into the cellar during the night of a tremendous storm; you know how often we have them here. No one knows why. She was a rather meek, kittenish little thing, afraid of her own shadow. She may have been frightened by the storm and wandered about the still unfamiliar house and into the cellar, God knows why. She stripped herself naked and drove a butcher knife into her abdomen. They found her there, cold and stiff, the following morning. No one has ever been able to determine just why she did it. Mad, I would think."

He hesitated before asking the next obvious question, knowing it would have to be asked, yet fearing her answer. The palms of his hands were wet.

"Just where in the cellar did this happen? Do you know?"

She thought for a moment. "Of course, I've never been in the house. Is there a small, empty chamber somewhere in the cellar, with a bare earthen floor?"

A quick mental image came to John of Ruth's naked body lying on the small mound of earth in an empty chamber that glowed with a brilliant green light.

"Yes. Yes, there is such a room. . ."

CHAPTER TEN

RUTH was scarcely aware of being alone once John had left for the village and their small red car had disappeared in its swirling yellow cloud of dust down the narrow, bumpy dirt road. She remained seated on her small canvas folding stool, carefully moving the stiff bristles of her brush across the smooth wet surface of the painting, moving her head from side to side and carefully examining the various perspectives. It didn't at all trouble her now to be left alone. It was sometimes necessary for artistic concentration not to be bothered by the frequently disturbing presence of others. Dear and sweet though John tried to be, even he could often be a considerable distraction at times, with his constant well-meaning attentions and concerns. Surely God must have been alone when he created the world.

It was another extremely quiet day, as most days here were silent, with that particular hushed somnambulance that is part of such humid, lazy afternoons in late summer or early autumn, when people find it difficult to bestir themselves into activity. A gull occasionally swooped low over the cliff with a startling cawing sound, which alone disturbed the sleepy stillness; its broad white wings provided the only brief spot of shade on the sunbaked prominence, although clouds were now beginning to raise themselves on the horizon, as though from a deep sleep. The sky itself had been turned almost white with heat, all color having been sucked out of it, and with the sun directly overhead, the house cast no shadows upon the barren yellow cliff-top. The sun was a brilliant, shimmering orb . . . she was reminded of Lovecraft's oft-repeated description of a painted wafer . . . but Ruth refused to alter her appreciation of color by donning her dark glasses, preferring to squint and narrow her field of observation to falsifying what she was seeing by the use of tinted glass. The broad floppy brim of her straw hat . . . it was the same one John had purchased for her in the islands that summer of their first meeting . . . pulled low over her eyes, would have to serve as enough protection from the glare. Facing the house, her back was almost completely to the sea, so she was not bothered by the intense sheen of sunlight on the smooth water surface.

The intensity of her concentration also helped her to avoid dangerously unhappy thoughts that still occasionally came to her, and this had provided her with the most important anesthetic during the past few weeks, that period in which, wherever she turned, she still seemed always to see the bright image of little Elinor, standing with her arms longingly outstretched to her, smiling, her blue eyes dancing with the joy of living.

Ruth had never been particularly interested in the cult of motherhood, and the awe that surrounded pregnancy and birth seemed to her more than a little foolish. She felt enough fulfillment as a woman in her work. Her own unexpected motherhood had only slightly changed these views. It was the unexpected, sudden loss of Elinor that sharply brought home to her the wonders of having given birth to someone who was her own, part of her self. But the realization came too late, and perhaps it was that which was responsible for her personal distress and bitterness. Work made things somehow easier, although even now Elinor's face sometimes seemed to come between the brush and the canvas.

Ruth was too intelligent a woman to succeed in completely blinding herself to what she was doing, and she often wondered how long matters could continue in this way. She had placed herself in a dream world where she could escape the harsh realities that had intruded themselves into her generally placid life. But this could not alter anything that had happened. Was she being selfish, childish, perhaps even a bit psychotic? Others had suffered equal and even greater tragedy and managed to rise above it. Surely she possessed the strength and the character to do the same.

This new life of theirs, this intense absorption in her work, all of it was merely another part of her self-constructed crutch, a portion of that covering shield behind which she could conceal her own nagging uncertainties concerning both her private life and her artistic capabilities, both of which had stumbled to an alarming stalemate at the time of her daughter's death. This change of life, this isolated existence in the lonely old house by the sea, had been her own idea, although she had carefully permitted John to assume the credit for it. We simply had to get away, she insisted to herself. We had to examine and find ourselves.

But was that really the truth, all the truth? Perhaps she was simply afraid of going on as they were. A moral and professional precipice seemed to yawn at her feet, and this was at least one method of pulling herself back from the dangerous brink. Perhaps she failed to notice there was another precipice just behind her. One or the other would sooner or later have to be bridged, or she would spend the remainder of her life in the narrow, barren world between them.

Was she merely using her daughter's death as an excuse to escape her own inadequacies?

There was considerable danger in what she was doing, and she was well aware of it. She had immersed herself in a totally false existence, one in which she really did not and could not belong, any more than could John. It held back the dread realities. For a time, at least. But how long could she permit it to do so? How much longer would it be before she completely lost all touch with that reality which, unpleasant though it might be at times, must provide the basis for any truly meaningful and useful life? She was an adult, mature woman. She was no meandering Alice in Wonderland, and she must not permit herself to become completely lost in the comforting and benumbing world of self-imposed fantasy.

Ruth pulled a large white handkerchief from the wide pocket of her paint-daubed smock and ran it wearily over her forehead. The heat seemed to be increasing. Perhaps she had better stop work for a time. She looked again at the house, boldly outlined against the heat-washed white sky, and at the broad swirls of color on her canvas. She was working well today. Perhaps just a bit longer.

It was obvious to Ruth that John was not really happy here. He tried to pretend, realizing how much this meant to her, but she knew him well enough to look through that pose.

Certainly all had been fine during the beginning of their stay. It had been fun during those earlier days before the novelty and the excitement of their new surroundings had begun to wear thin. He would say nothing now, of course, but the signs of his growing restlessness were already apparent. His eyes had lost their lively sparkle when he stared out at the vast and empty panorama of sea and sky at their very doorstep; he even moved about the house in a totally different way, his fingers no longer touching the walls and the maritime momentoes with quite the interest of those first days. He was bored, and becoming steadily more so. Where would it lead him? How long could she keep him here? He had his own ambitions, desires, talents.

She was really not being fair to him. She was thinking only of herself.

Ruth frowned, lowering the brim of her hat just a trifle, realizing she was again attempting to escape reality. John's basic restlessness could be somewhat relieved through work, as was hers, but that was not quite enough for him; he needed more. She could make him happier here, had she the unselfish desire to do so. Ruth fully realized her husband's sexual need, and there were times when she longed to ease him, when she recalled the earlier days of their passion, his lean hard body against hers, the words of love whispered in the silent hours of darkness. John was possessed of powerful sexual appetites, which had somewhat startled her after their marriage, and she was now doing nothing to slake them. But she could not. No, no, she could not go through that again, not yet, not now. Perhaps soon. Perhaps never. Their sexual intimacy had resulted in the birth of a lovely little girl who had died because of their own personal shortcomings and failures as parents. She could not risk that again. A person can fail only so often before failure becomes a way of life.

Ruth sighed and placed her brush in its rack on the easel. No, it was becoming too humid and uncomfortable to permit her to continue. The work she could do under such circumstances would be forced and not really acceptable; in all probability, it would all have to be redone in the morning. It was still early afternoon. There was no reason why she should not take a brief hiatus during these hottest hours of the day; it would become cooler towards evening, and perhaps she could spend another hour or two at work at that time before the light failed.

She examined the canvas for a moment, and was both pleased and confused by what she saw. Her color sense seemed to have improved considerably, perhaps sharpened by the brightness of the sea world in which she now lived. The large canvas was a swirling mass of shades she had never before dared to use. It was so completely unlike anything she had ever painted before; dark, brooding, mysterious for all its color. Her previous work had always spoken of light and beauty, of the sea and the sky, brilliant with color and the excitement of creation. She had come here to paint the sea, and instead had produced this rather strange portrait of the house as an introspective study of her own confused emotions.

Strangely, she did not particularly like this painting, but she was well aware that it was an interesting work; it could provide an important step in her sagging career. She would have a success to counter her recent professional and personal failures. Perhaps then life could really begin once again. There was so much she just could not understand about this particular canvas; it sometimes almost frightened her. It was as though her hand moved the brush with a volition all its own. What was that peculiar green flow issuing from the seaward side of the house, those darkly suggested hints of peculiar shadows in the purple swirl of the veranda? Well, as long as it was good. . .

Ruth rose from the stool and, feeling a sudden flood of intense weariness, placed her hands at the small of her back and arched her body outward, feeling the release of strained and tired muscles. She had again worked too hard and too long, too intensely. It was part of her current pattern, to work herself each day almost to the point of exhaustion. It numbed her mind, prevented intrusion of unwelcome thoughts.

She plunged her hands into the deep pockets of her smock and walked slowly to the very edge of the cliff, kicking idly at the harsh tufts of yellowed grass, staring disinterestedly out to the empty horizon. They seldom saw ships going by here. She missed that. It only sharpened the sense of loneliness beyond what she was really willing to accept. Sadness marked a perpetually empty sea; it seemed too much like an empty world, like that prehistoric time when gigantic forms moved beneath the turbulent waters and no print of animal or man yet marred the surface of the land.

There were other aspects of life here that occasionally disturbed her now, incidents that she found difficult to understand, little fears and uneasinesses that came to her suddenly and without any apparent reason. She was gratefully free now of those agonizing dreams about Elinor, but other and stranger night fantasies had taken their place, dreams in which she was constantly caught in a world of swirling green sea populated by ill-defined shapes that had no meaning for her. Was it the influence of the atmosphere, of the constant rhythmic tidal sounds that filled the air?

Other matters were even more alarming. Often she would not remember events for hours at a time, and then would suddenly find herself standing silently in the foyer or at the head of the cellar steps without any recollection of how she had got there, or why. There were times when she could scarcely bear the presence of her own husband, when she looked upon John, this man with whom she had shared the most important years of her life, as a total stranger, an alien, an interloper who did not belong in her present world. Such strange attitudes were brief, but it was disturbing that they seemed to come now more and more frequently. At such times, it seemed to her that everything that did not belong to the house and the sea had no place here, only she herself really belonging. It was an uncomfortable feeling, particularly when she could not understand the reason for it.

The sound of the surf drew Ruth's attention from the face of the cliff, over the rugged, scarred, pock-marked precipice to the sharp gleaming black rocks below. Here there was never either peace or quiet. Here the fierce battle between the sea and the land was waged without cease. For countless ages, the waters of the ocean had battered against these same sharp rocks, slowly eroding them, wearing them steadily down, patiently working for the inevitable day when the cliff itself would slip into their wet, hungry embrace. Again and again, the waves dashed themselves against the pointed black granite, and again and again they were repulsed in an angry swirl of tossing white foam. The impatience of the waves was feigned. They could wait. Time was on their side. There had been ages when all the planet was theirs. So it would be again, in time. The land could not forever hold out against them.

The spume-covered rocks gleamed wetly in the sun, and the light of it momentarily dazzled her eyes. She closed them for a moment, feeling suddenly extremely tired, but quickly opened them again, startled when she felt herself in danger of losing her balance. She swayed for a moment, and reached out her hand to support herself, but there was nothing for her to grasp. She had never before suffered from vertigo. She raised her head again, and the horizon became a shimmering haze of white-blue-green in which it was impossible to separate the sea from the sky. The sun seemed to divide itself into two great haloed balls of burning fire casting sharp daggers of pain into her eyes. She experienced a sudden difficulty in breathing, and the roar of the breakers seemed to swell in her ears, becoming louder, heavier, more insistent, almost like shouting voices calling in some prehistoric language she could not understand. If only she could have a breath of coolness.

Ruth stepped quickly back from the edge, of the cliff, suddenly terrified by visions of herself tumbling over and over into the waiting maelstrom of churning foam. It was the heat, of course. John would be justifiably displeased that she had exposed herself for so long. The work would have to wait. She would go inside, perhaps have a cup of coffee, or just sit on the shaded veranda with a book until the sun dropped a little lower, allowing the first cooling touch of approaching evening. By that time, John would surely be back and they could have dinner. She looked towards the vacant yellow-brown road, stretching like a soiled ribbon towards the village. Was it a sign, she wondered? She suddenly no longer wanted to be alone, and would have been pleased to spot an approaching car on the roadway.

Ruth walked slowly back to the house, her hands still thrust deeply into her wide pockets. She felt strangely light headed, almost faint. The heat again. Or perhaps she'd not had enough of a breakfast, just toast and coffee; she'd been too anxious to get to work in the brilliance of a wonderfully clear morning. John said she hadn't slept very well, even though she couldn't recall any periods of wakefulness. Perhaps all the excitement was catching up with her at last.

She paused and looked again at the great house that had now become so central a part of her life and art. It seemed somehow taller than it really was, thrusting arrogantly against the pale sky. A trick of perspective, no doubt, since there were no other structures by which to measure it. Its rusted gables, urged on by the life-giving touch of the sun, stretched themselves up to reach the sky itself. An invisible cloud of sadness seemed to hover about the vacant Widow's Walk, and she idly wondered about the women who had held vigil there over so many years. It was a strange house, certainly. What joys and sorrows had it known? Two centuries is a long time.

Another wave of faintness came over her as she crossed the hard brown earth towards the veranda, and she paused in her step, quickly placing her hand to her forehead, swaying slightly and feeling a rush of nausea to her mouth. It passed as quickly as it had come, and she opened her eyes again, frowning with alarm, perspiration again beading her forehead. The great solid structure of the house seemed to swim before her eyes. She felt a great desire for its cooling shade.

As she reached the steps of the veranda, she paused again and glanced at the naked tree that seemed to reach its skeletal arms with a mute plea not to be forgotten. She wondered again why the tree had been planted just there; it was too close to the house and would surely have grown better several yards further away. Perhaps it had been intended to provide shade for the veranda; a shame it couldn't do that now. She shrugged. The tree was dead, anyway.

Almost unaware of her movements, as though the heat had stricken her with a form of somnambulism, Ruth turned and walked slowly towards the dead tree, examining the dark tracery of its black limbs against the pale blue-white sky. It should really come down. It certainly provided not a spot of shade, and its stark bleakness marred the purity and beauty of the view. Yet, aside from its leaflessness, it really seemed healthy enough. There was no sign of blight or disease on the blackened trunk, yet it had obviously been long dead. She wondered what had killed it. Something internal not evident to the eye? She knew nothing of such things.

Reaching out her right hand, Ruth lightly touched the bark and then, with a gasp of surprise, quickly withdrew the hand. The bark felt like stone, or petrified wood, with an almost painful clammy coldness, and there was a seeping sliminess in the touch. She brought her hand to her smock to wipe away the excrescence, but found there was none; her hand was dry and unstained. Looking more closely to the bark itself, she could find no indication of sap or seepage on the black trunk. No, of course not; there couldn't be. The tree was dead.

An unexpected breeze must have at long last found its way up to the sun-baked platform, for the dead branches above her slowly began to move slightly, soundlessly. They were like famine-thinned Negroid limbs raised in a rhythmic African cadence, back and forth, back and forth, yet making not the slightest sound, not touching each other, simply moving as though at some unspoken command. She was surprised that she felt none of that breeze that was so silently stirring the ebony branches.

211

A small cloud passed briefly over the sun, and the area under the tree took on the blackness of the shadows cast upon it. The sudden darkness seemed unnaturally intense, and Ruth felt a sharp chill that was not connected with a drop in the temperature. A peculiar odor struck her nostrils. Acrid and unpleasant. She had smelled something like it somewhere. It filled the air, almost chokingly heavy, and she suddenly became aware of a dull and heavy pounding in her head. She slowly moved from the tree, her eyes hypnotically drawn to the sinuous movement of the branches, and as she moved back, the odor receded. Suddenly she identified the choking stench. Brimstone.

Suffocated by the heat, her mind too weary even for thought, Ruth slowly made her way to the steps of the veranda, stumbling clumsily over the uneven earth, her eyes still drawn to the curious tree. What kind of tree was it? She had never seen one like it before.

She suddenly wondered then why she had connected the strange odor with brimstone. She had meant sulphur, of course. What was the difference between brimstone and sulphur? Sulphur came from a struck match, and brimstone came from the Bible and the rantings of hell-frightened evangelists.

There was still not the slightest breeze on the veranda, yet those dead branches continued to move slowly, sinuously, like twisting black serpents. There seemed something not quite natural in the movement of branches unaccompanied by the sibilant rustling of leaves; the clatter of bare winter branches had always made her think of the rustling of dried bones. But these ebony branches made no sound whatever. As she stared at them through the shimmering haze of heat, they looked more than ever like long thin arms, and there was a mysterious invitation in their shadowed movements.

Ruth swayed slightly and grasped one of the veranda posts. She again felt unwell. It was the heat, she once again reassured herself, only the heat. She looked at the open door leading into the house, and felt an urge to go inside. There was something she had to do in the house. She shook her head. No. Was there, really, something she had forgotten? At least, perhaps it would be a bit cooler inside.

She entered the silent foyer, slowly, almost carefully, as though she half expected to see someone or something there. She still seemed to feel the remorseless sun beating fiercely down on her. The atmosphere in the foyer was musty and heavy. It seemed to weigh down upon her like a smothering blanket.

The house was as silent as the rest of the world, even the rhythmic ticking of the grandfather's clock seemed to come to her almost hesitantly, as though it were afraid to disturb the sepulchral stillness, and the sound was strangely muted, like the buried ticking of a clock through a covering of cotton. Her eyes moved restlessly about the foyer. The portraits, the newel light, the table, the mirror, the hat rack, all were the same, as they had been through all the silent and lonely years before she and John had come here, when the house had stood alone on this cliff top and all the memories of the past slumbered. The carpeted stairs rose like a frozen cascade to the deeper silences of the upper floors, speckled like a series of spotlights by the sun rays sliding through the portholes of the windows. The doors to the living room and study stood open and both rooms, embracing their mementoes of the long-distant past, reminded silent in reminiscence. The burnished floor of the foyer seemed to glow with an inner fire.

She was alone, yet the silent house spoke to Ruth of a presence, of someone she could not see. Was there a shadow moving slowly down the stairs, or standing in the open doorway of the study? No. Surely she was quite alone. But perhaps not. Perhaps John had come back and, somehow, she had failed to note his arrival.

"John. . . John. . ."

Her voice sounded hollow in that large and empty house. There was no response. Was there no sound left in all the world? A sudden coldness came upon her and she shivered, while her face remained bathed in heated perspiration. Something was wrong. The world was not as it should be. She stepped into the study.

"John. . . John. . ."

The room spoke of her absent husband. The typewriter was uncovered on the desk, with a sheet of white paper curled around the black roller; he had a habit of impatiently breaking off with his paper still in the machine. The spyglass pointed to the empty horizon; was it still moving slightly from the interrupted touch of some invisible hand? Beyond the window, the great orb of the sun glinted like flashes of lightning on the vacant molten sea. The unfathomable eyes of Captain Fowles watched her from the far wall; they had been painted with that Satanic ability that caused them to follow the movements of anyone in the room. It was disturbing that most of the portraits in the house had that same talent. She smelled the mustiness of the old books. The room was filled with *Presence*; the captain peering at the horizon through his spyglass, John pounding at the typewriter. Yet the room was empty.

Back in the foyer, Ruth listened for another moment in the leaden silence, a silence that was not yet complete stillness. She seemed to hear little sounds . . . rustlings . . . movements . . . as though from memories somewhere within her own mind, as though all other sounds than these miniscule noises had been drawn from the world. The clock began to chime, its great booming tone echoing in the well of the staircase, but Ruth was totally unaware of its strokes.

A peculiar confusion filled her mind. She tried to grasp her vague thoughts, but they eluded her. Something had surely brought her in here. It was not the desire for coolness, for the heat was as enervating here as it was outside on the bluff. She had again a sense, a dull reminder like something her mind had tossed aside and left only an incomplete forgetfulness of the event, that there was something here that she had to do. Someone was expecting her, waiting for her, wasn't that it? But who could that possibly be? Had she forgotten something in her irritatingly increasing absent-mindedness? Had she a visitor? Was there someone in the house she should be attending to? Surely she could not forget something as important as that. Besides, who could it be? They had no friends here.

It was so difficult to remember things in this sweltering heat. Ruth opened her mouth and gasped for a breath of cooler air, as she felt perspiration streaming down her face. Why had it become so close in the foyer? With all the doors and windows open, there should be something of a breeze, a touch of cross ventilation.

Ruth took a step towards the stairs, and staggered again; she would have fallen had she not managed to reach out and grasp the newel post. She clung to it for a moment, aware of a weakness in her legs. She glanced up the stairway. Perhaps she should lie down for a while. She'd obviously had a touch of the sun, and a brief rest would be good for her. But the stairs seemed to shimmer and waver before her eyes, the colored strips of carpet twisting and writhing like some fabriced serpent, and it seemed to her that the stairs reached upward to a distant shadowed darkness whose summit she could barely see.

She turned with a sudden touch of fear and gazed about the foyer. The dark numbers on the face of the clock seemed to dance like motes of dust torn from a shadow, rising and falling before her blurred eyes like silent figures in a ballet of time, and the brass pendulum swung remorselessly back and forth like the dread scythe of Father Time. She knew she lacked the strength to climb those stairs.

Her eyes moved to the corridor running beyond the stairway, leading through the house to the kitchen. A cup of good strong black coffee should help to restore her mysteriously dissipated energies and sharpen her dulled mind. All of this was really quite ridiculous. She had never felt like this before, and she was not going to let it get the better of her.

Moving slowly and almost dreamily, as though every step were a painful effort, Ruth walked through the darkly shadowed corridor to the kitchen. A brilliant burst of sunshine struck her as she entered the back room of the house; she had left both front and rear doors open in hopes of stirring a breeze that would cool off the house a bit, but it had had little effect.

The kitchen seemed filled with dark shadows despite the strong sunlight, and Ruth imagined unseen movements in the darker corners. She heard the irritating dripping of water in the sink and automatically turned the tap tighter; the sound stopped. The room fell into total silence. She had a sense of the walls closing in upon her, and as they came closer her breathing became more strained, with a fierce burning in her chest. Leaning with her back against the sink, she began to tremble with ridiculous fear. She needed air, a breath of coolness, something to raise the smothering blanket of heat that pressed down so heavily upon her mind.

Her eyes fell upon the closed door to the cellar.

With an almost trance-like slowness, Ruth approached the door. The cellar was the part of the rambling old mansion that Ruth liked the least and she had not, at least to her recollection, been down there since the first uncomfortable day in her fruitless search for a broom.

But weren't cellars generally somewhat cooler than the rest of the house? They were part of the earth, shielded by the mass of the house itself from the bombardment of the sun's rays. She felt herself burning with the heat. If she could have just a few brief moments of coolness so she could breathe again and soothe the confusion in her mind, perhaps she could shake off this strangeness that had fallen upon her and straighten out her jumbled thoughts. This antipathy towards the cellar was childish, anyway. Surely she could tolerate the cellar for just a few moments on a day like this.

Besides, she had to . . . what?

The smooth enamel knob of the door was refreshingly cool in her hand and awakened a memory of touch that she could not fully recall, as well as promising a temporary relief from her discomfort; she felt an urge to drop to her knees and press the smooth cooling knob over her flushed face, but the sudden desire to descend into the greater coolness of the cellar itself was stronger. The door opened easily and for a moment she stood holding the knob, still enjoying its coolness, looking down into the dark cellar world that made her think of black pits and the mysterious, frightening world of unexplored underground caverns. The cellar was down there with all its dust, its little crawling things, its darkness, its sense of loneliness. Its cooler air.

And something else as well. Yes, of course. There was something else for her in the cellar, although she irritatingly could not recall just what it was. She felt a sharp flood of desire, a need, a hunger. There was something for her in this dark, cool cellar that she wanted more than she had ever wanted anything in her life. Of course. This was why she had come into the house. Not for the shade or the coolness, but for . . . for the something down here in the cellar. How foolish of her to have forgotten.

She quickly stepped back. What strange kind of thoughts were these? What was she thinking? None of this made any sense. The cellar. . .

The top step creaked slightly when she stepped out on it. Her eyes were wide and she was scarcely aware of her own movements as she very slowly descended the steps one by one, like a small child in terror of falling places both little feet firmly on each step before descending to the next one. She thought she heard a slight scurrying sound beneath the steps, but found herself strangely indifferent to the once terrifying possibility that a rat or some such repulsive creature was moving through the gathered dust at her approach.

When she reached the bottom of the stairs, Ruth stood for some seconds with her hand still touching the rough wooden railing, looking about herself. She could still hear the sea, now distant and remote, but there was no other sound. The dust lay everywhere like gray reminders of the passage of time.

She felt confused by her presence here. One part of her recalled the strange fear she had always known of cellars, while another part seemed to whisper that here she would find peace, pleasure, and contentment. Her steps left blurred, confused traces in the dust that she failed to notice was already disturbed by footprints that were not only those of John's heavier step, possible reminders of a terrible evening of which she now possessed no recollection whatever. Something did seem strangely familiar about the place. She had of course been here once before, but the vague remembrance was something quite different, as though this were a place she really knew quite well.

When she rounded the belly of the furnace, she was surprised to see that the heavy door to the little room stood open. When had that happened? John had said nothing about his success in moving the door from its frozen position. Strange that he hadn't told her; they had again been discussing it just the other morning.

A peculiar greenish glow seemed to emanate from the little room, and her mind became sharpened by a touch of cold. She hesitated, looking about her at the bare, dust-streaked walls, the coated pipes, the dangling cobwebs, staring as though only now suddenly aware of her surroundings.

What on earth was she doing down here, she suddenly

wondered. She whimpered with a slight reminder of fear and looked about as though expecting something to drop upon her from the low ceiling. She tossed her head, trying to clear her mind of thoughts that did not belong there, and seemed to battle for control of her badly confused reasoning. There was a choking mustiness in the air despite the coolness, and the tall shadows in the corners seemed to move silently toward her. What was she doing in this place? She never went into the cellar. Perhaps it was John? Was he down here? Had she seen him come down and followed him? Funny, she couldn't remember at all.

"John!" she called. "John!" Her voice sounded strange, flat and muted, as if it, too, had been swallowed by the hungry dust. "Are you down here, John?" she pleaded, becoming frightened. "John! Please answer me!"

There was no response. She heard nothing but the distant sound of the sea. She placed a hand to her warm forehead, looking about the barren and completely empty cellar. She could almost touch the silence that surrounded her, could almost see and reach out to it, but she could also see that there was no one else here. She knew she was alone in the house. John had not yet returned. She remembered that now. Surely he would be back soon. . . .

Ruth turned again and faced the open doorway. Had the green glow become suddenly more intense, as though the sun had issued from behind a dark cloud and was beaming its rays through a heavy green veil? The light was somehow soothing, comfortable, the rich emerald shade of the deep sea; it did not hurt her eyes as did the brilliant yellow rays of the sun. It was cool. Refreshing.

Then her face was touched by a welcome breath of sharply cold air from the room itself. She looked through the doorway. The room was empty, green and cold, like the sea. Surely there could be nothing to fear here. Her fingers touched the sudden coldness on her cheek and she sighed with comfort. After the heat outside, it was so wonderfully cool. . . .

Two steps took her across the threshold and into the small barren earthen chamber, and with those two steps suddenly all Ruth's fears, uncertainties and bewilderments faded. As her foot touched the earthen base of the room, a sudden strength seemed to surge through her, as though rising from the ground itself and sweeping through her body. The place was no longer strange. She was comfortable here. She belonged here. She felt at home.

The room was almost icily cold, and the sudden crispness of the air raised her mind from the stultifying dullness impressed there by the heavy heat outside. She walked slowly about the bare room, running her hands along the hard earthen walls, her fingers unconsciously searching out the ruts of indentations that had been covered by time, as though she knew they would be there. The dull thunder of the tumbling sea was strong in her ears, and the rhythmical tidal movements were reflected in the graceful, almost flowing steps with which she moved about the room. She felt lighter, younger, cleansed of all her problems as she brushed her hair loosely back from her head and kicked the shoes from her feet. A slight smile curved her lips, and her eyes glowed with a touch of the green light that suffused the chamber. She felt more slender, infinitely more desirable than ever before in her life. Her hands ran sensuously over her form, and she enjoyed the warmth of her own smooth flesh.

Ruth turned from the walls and stopped before the small earthen mound in the center of the floor. Her eyes narrowed as she looked at it, and flecks of green danced in their centers. The mound seemed to tell her something, seemed familiar to her, stirring in her mind long forgotten memories that had nothing to do with her own past. Her body began to move from side to side, slowly and sinuously, like the movements of the naked branches of the dead tree under the caress of a breeze no one else could feel. She closed her eyes, and her breath came slowly from slightly parted green-tinged lips.

With a slight graceful movement, she settled to her knees before the mound and her long artist's fingers carressingly ran across its smooth, almost glass-like surface. The earth was very cold and felt damp, yet there was no sign of wetness. She felt the contact surge through her body, and her breath quickened. The sound of the sea filled the room, and the walls seemed to glow with a green vibrancy of their own.

Ruth settled slowly upon the mound, smoothing its hardness with her hands. She moaned slightly, a moan of ecstacy rather than fear. She felt herself surrounded by a world of exquisite emerald, and the more she soothed the surface of the mound, the more she bathed in the rich green glow, the more she felt like a nereid of mythology exulting in the touch of the waters that gave her life. Her limbs twitched, and the low muttering sounded like the sighs of a woman experiencing unparalleled sexual ecstacy.

She no longer felt herself to be alone. She could see nothing, only the time-dusted barrenness of the four green earthen walls, but she could sense the presence of . . . others. The room swarmed with unseen movement. She placed her face to the rounded earth, resting her cheek against its smooth coldness, and all around her were swirls and mists of life. She felt herself descending into the depths of the ever friendly sea, and all around her swarmed the myriads of life that populate all the vast unknown oceans of the world.

CHAPTER ELEVEN

THE following days continued oppressively hot and uncomfortably humid as the early autumn heat wave gave no indication of easing. The sun, which during the first weeks of their time of their residence at Fowles House had been almost constantly obscured by scudding gray clouds and was so seldom seen, now burned fiercely in a milky white sky of choking heat, turning the strangely quiescent waters of the sea into a dazzling, blinding mirror that made seeing difficult, and created painful red rims around John's eyes. There was not the slightest movement of air, and even breathing became a strain. The house, although its large windows were all thrown wide, retained its suffocating heat even after the sun had finally lowered its flaming rim behind the empty horizon, creating uncomfortable sleepless nights in twisted, perspiration-soaked sheets.

An intense stillness seemed to have fallen over all the world, broken only by the lonely cries of the wheeling gulls and the constant, monotonous rhythm of the sea. They saw no one. The deserted sands of the beach, which the sun had painted heavily with the brush of its golden rays, glowed with the sparkle of fool's gold, and the distant horizon shimmered like the torturous imagined waves of a swimming mirage to the parched desert traveler. The dust lay thick and undisturbed on the abandoned ribbon of roadway and the few clumps of tough green shrubbery on the cliff top withered and turned yellow with thirst, and the black branches of the dead tree seemed raised in mute supplication to the sun for some small measure of relief. John had the feeling that Nature was holding its breath for . . . what?

John found it impossible to concentrate on his work in such hot weather, even after he had moved his typewriter out onto the veranda in the quite futile hope of catching an errant breeze that never came. His brain was numb, his fingers moved so clumsily over the keys that each day resulted in hours of totally wasted effort. He could not bring himself to the slightest concern over the fictitious trials and tribulations of the rather insipid characters he had created, and the entire scheme of this supposedly brilliant novel of his now suddenly appeared to him trivial, banal and a total waste of his time and talent. He sat for long hours staring at the blank white paper in his typewriter, sipping too many iced drinks that refreshed him too little. No thoughts would come, and the paper curled unused about the platent until, still white and empty, it had to be replaced with a fresh sheet.

He braved the touch of the sun and stood at the edge of the cliff, staring vacantly down into the seething, tumbling, crashing mass at the base of the rocks, but the chaos there only reminded him of the tumbling confusion within his own mind. He strolled along the deserted beach, kicking aimlessly at the scurrying little sand crabs and tracing in the wet sand runic figures that were quickly destroyed by the hungry, hissing sweep of the sea, but the serenity of his surroundings seemed a mockery of his own troubles.

For it was not only the heat that kept John from his work; it was rather the constantly growing turmoil in his mind. Although the sun blazed so pitilessly from a clear, cloud-free sky from which all the gentle color had faded, a darkness hovered about Fowles House, as though a great mass of cloud, long concealed behind the shimmering facade of the distant horizon, had now raised itself and was spreading slowly above the barren cliff top, enfolding the house in its smothering darkness and casting a shadow upon their lives, a shadow that filled John with an inexplicable fear that he could not even begin to understand. He stood often staring at the gaunt, silent house, wondering what mysterious past events still hovered there, what fears and sorrows had echoed within its walls that still seemed a part of the atmosphere, and the shushing sound of the sea was like a hammer of fear pounding at his tired brain.

Happiness had flown from this wonderful new home where they had so excitedly looked forward to a renewal of earlier happier days, as though lifted on the wings of one of the many great white gulls that endlessly wheeled, swooped and circled about them, and a strange uneasiness had taken its place. He could find neither joy nor peace in standing on the veranda at dusk to watch the huge burnished shield of the sun turn the sky to red-streaked gold and touch the sea with its mysterious fire. The constant thunder of the surf no longer soothed him, and he had long since tired of the touch of salt in the air.

There was no accounting for it, but that feeling of dread was there, gnawing like an ever growing cancer, robbing him of his rest and his concentration, making serious work impossible, converting his once busy days into long and empty hours of worrisome pacing and . . . waiting.

It had begun with that lunch with Linda, when he had been told the vague and still unclear tales and legends of the women who had met such strange fates in the old house, and the growth of the even stronger tales that surrounded them. Meaningless and confused as they were, they had been shadowed enough to start the fear that had now become a permanent part of his life.

No. No, that wasn't quite right. It had begun before that fatal luncheon, on the evening before, the moment he had lifted the naked body of his unconscious (a better word, that, than asleep) wife from the cold barren earth floor of the little green-glowing room in the cellar. He had tried to dismiss the entire incident, tried to bar it from his mind, but he could no longer do so. Linda's stories . . . and he believed, despite their irritating vagueness, that she was now honestly concealing from him nothing further that she herself knew . . . had confirmed the belief that there was something wrong with the house.

But again he was wrong. He shared Linda's belief that there was no such thing as a house with an aura of *wrongness* about it. It was people who brought disaster. A house was after all only an inanimate structure; it had neither heart nor soul nor feelings. But Fowles House had stood for more than two centuries, and during that time it could not have escaped the occasional stigma of tragedy. Yes, tragic things had undoubtedly happened here, but that was not the fault of the house, but rather an indication of the basic instability of the Fowles family. What then could it have to do with them?

There was absolutely nothing wrong with the house itself, and this applied as well to the empty cellar and the rather curious and useless chamber beside the furnace. Following his conversation with Linda, John had again carefully examined the entire house, from top to bottom, while Ruth was at work on the bluff, looking for anything that might have a bearing on the curious situation that had arisen. But there was nothing. No secret passageways, no sliding panels, no concealed rooms, no mysterious documents. There was only a considerable amount of dust and moldering, meaningless remains and reminders of the past. Fowles House remained simply an old house where several unfortunate incidents had occurred.

The cellar was no different from any other part of the house, John constantly assured himself. If that particular room was colder than the rest of the cellar, that was due to its composition and its exposed position on the very edge of the cliff. The green glow came from a pigment in the glass of the single small window, occasionally brightened by the natural movement of the sun. It was all quite simple, logical and obvious.

The only truly disturbing and inexplicable element was Ruth's curious action, and there was the basis for his concern. While he dismissed the notion of a *haunted* house he was willing, within reason, to accept the possibility of a particularly sensitive person sensing and sharing the aura of the past. It seemed a contradiction of terms. If a house could not be evil, how could it possess an aura of evil? The past everywhere was dead the moment it became the past, and could live again only between the pages of a historical narrative. Yet this seemed the only possible solution to Ruth's behaviour. Could he accept so much and no more?

At any rate, no amount of reasoning could alter the fact that the house was not the paradise they had hoped it would be. It was too silent, too brooding, too isolated. It seemed to enfold the mysterious events of the past and hide them from outside eyes. The rooms were not as comfortable as they appeared. Despite the lofty ceilings, they retained too much of the day's heat, and they too often echoed with unpleasant sounds. A heavy weight seemed to press upon the gables and the walk where widows were born. He felt it, sensed it, as he stood in the silent living room. Was the house listening, waiting? Sleeping? Dead? Laughter could never belong here. It was the air that was haunted, not the house.

Yet strangely enough, Ruth seemed suddenly happier here than ever in those first exciting days of mutual discovery. Upon his return from the luncheon with Linda, John had found his wife seated quite passively and comfortably on the veranda, reading a book and sipping an iced drink. The sun was beginning to set . . . he had stayed away much longer than he had planned . . . and the tall house seemed bathed in a golden glow stained with deep scarlet; the black branches of the dead tree were moving slightly against a crimson background, apparently stirred again in that curious way by a current that could be felt only in the upper air. The scene was so peaceful and idyllic, John felt his undefined fears to be somewhat foolish.

"Well, I'm glad to see you got yourself out of that sun," he commented as he mounted the steps towards Ruth, wiping his perspiring face with his handkerchief.

Ruth smiled, a cool and completely relaxed grin. "Give me a little credit for a certain amount of plain ordinary sense, will you? You make me feel like a child going to school in a heavy rainstorm who has to be reminded to wear rubbers. Even I can realize when it's just too hot to work, so I came here to relax a bit. It's really quite comfortable here now, and the view is so marvelous. But I didn't expect you back quite so soon."

"So soon?" he repeated. "I've been feeling guilty all the way home. I hadn't intended to stay away so long."

She looked at him with a sudden archness. "Did you meet your little secretary friend?"

"As a matter of fact, we had lunch together at the hotel," John admitted, seating himself on the top step. "I ran into her at the post office, and she seemed rather lonely. Paul's out of town. Death in the family."

"I wondered why we hadn't seen him lately."

"Then you don't mind?"

She sipped her drink. "Of course not. How is Girl Friday?"

"Fine. You really must meet her soon; I'm certain you'd get on very well together. I've promised we would have both her and Paul out here for dinner sometime soon. She's never been in the house. It wouldn't hurt, just once, would it?"

Ruth's eyes had wandered to the sea, and there seemed a curious luminescence in the red-tinged shadow cast on her face by the brim of her floppy hat.

"Of course not. Whenever you like. Paul's a nice young man. The house could use some people in it, I suppose. Did you bring my paints?"

John nodded. "They're in the car."

"Anything else in the mail?"

"Some of the usual advertising," he replied. "Nothing interesting. And, oh yes, there was a note from Grandmother Ellen." He looked at her closely. "She's on her way here. She wants no nonsense about it."

Her face told him nothing. "Well, that will be nice for you, won't it?" He was surprised by the total indifference in her voice. Ruth had always been very fond of his grandmother.

John wiped his face again. "It's so God-damned hot! I should think it's past time for this weather to break."

She was again staring vacantly out to sea. One hand rested in her lap and the fingers of the other hand gently, almost sensuously, rubbed up and down on the frosted glass it held.

"The sea looks so much more inviting in weather like this, doesn't it?" she asked. "How wonderful it must be to plunge beneath the waves, to feel its cold wetness all around you as you go down deeper and deeper, away from the blinding golden light of the sun, into a world of rich, soothing emerald green, a world of rest and silence, filled with myriad forms of friendly life. . ." She turned again, smiling. "Wouldn't you like a cold drink, John? I've already mixed one for you and left it in the so-called refrigerator so the melting ice wouldn't dilute it more than you like."

"Fine. Good idea." As he rose to his feet, he noted the green silk scarf that Ruth had wound about her neck; it seemed to cast a greenish reflection on the under part of her chin, like the buttercups that children held under their chins to determine whether or not they liked butter. "What the hell is that for? Aren't you hot enough as it is?"

With a gesture of guilt, Ruth quickly placed a hand on the green fabric. "I'm just protecting my throat," she explained. "It got a bit of a burn this morning. I didn't realize the brim of the hat wasn't shading it, and it was too exposed. It's all right, John; I just don't want any more sun on it, that's all. Go and get your drink."

As he had expected, the house was hot and stuffy, and he grumbled to think of another evening tossing without proper sleep. At least their city apartment had air-conditioning; hadn't they ever heard of such a thing out here?

He paused in the foyer, listening to the silence. He felt strangely ill at ease. Was it just the heat? There seemed a heaviness . . . Strange how his spirits sagged the moment he entered the foyer. Perhaps the place was really getting him down.

He found the drink in the old-fashioned icebox that Ruth sarcastically referred to as a refrigerator; it was made just the way he liked it. He took a long, deliciously cold sip, feeling the sharp liquid bite its way down his throat.

It was then that he noticed the door to the cellar stood ajar. He'd not been down there for several days. He had abandoned his earlier plans of turning the cellar room into his private workshop. Aside from his readily admitted clumsiness, he simply would not have the time to make such a project worthwhile. Besides, although he had as yet said nothing to Ruth about it, he had by now also completely abandoned any possibility of becoming the new, permanent owner of Fowles House. There was now nothing to draw him into the empty cellar.

Curious, he placed his glass upon the table and, opening the door, stepped out onto the platform. Nothing had changed. The cellar was as silent and empty as before.

But in the dust on the floor, leading towards the little room on the other side of the furnace, he could see footprints that he knew were not his own.

CHAPTER TWELVE

JOHN was later to remember those pleasant moments on the veranda in the early part of that evening as the last moments of closeness between himself and his wife, for matters were never quite the same after that day, and slowly the disturbing changes appeared to shadow their formerly happy lives in the great old Fowles House, like the first unnoticed wisps of cloud heralding the darkening of a clear summer sky just before agreat storm. The house became strange to John, almost an alien world in which he now could find neither rest nor comfort. He strolled through the large, sea-framed rooms with their heavily over stuffed furniture, their dour portraits of bearded sea captains, their dust-covered maritime equipment and pieces of discolored brass, and he wondered that he had ever been drawn to this musty old museum. It was dark and dreary, too reminiscent of the unlightened period long past and hopefully forgotten, and he came to resent the heavy-lidded painted eyes that followed him with silent recrimination from one room to the next.

Everything about the old place suddenly displeased him. He tired of the constant, monotonous roar of the surf on the rocks below the cliff, and reacted with automatic gestures of irritation when a gull wheeled too close to his head. The empty beach, with its flotsam-like memories of long vanished worlds and seaweed like the torn train from a mermaid's wedding gown, depressed him, and he no longer found any beauty in the blue-white panorama of the distant always empty horizon. He became ever more restless, longing for the more active and interesting life they had left behind them, bored with the silence and the loneliness, frightened by an inescapable sense of something . . . a waiting . . . a terrible sense of expectancy. The view of the sea and sky from the veranda reminded him only of the sudden emptiness of his own life.

And he could no longer ignore the fact that a strangeness had come over Ruth. She seemed to withdraw into herself, and more and more John felt himself completely isolated and alone. She became unusually silent, immersed in her own thoughts which for the first time in their lives together she refused to share with him, talking only when he first spoke to her, and then but briefly and uninterestedly, as though she talked to a child whose problems were really no concern of her own. She spent longer and longer periods silently seated on the veranda, simply staring out to sea, her eyes following the erratic flights of the gulls. Often she would move her chair to the far end of the veranda and stare instead at the dead tree, watching the spidery tracery of the naked limbs against the sky, seeming to listen to the unheard sounds of·their ghostly movement in the unfelt breezes that always seemed to move through the topmost branches.

Despite the heat, Ruth still spent the greater part of even the hottest afternoons on the bluff with her paints, clad in her paint-daubed smock and floppy straw hat, completely oblivious to the intense humidity that lingered day after day and made work impossible for John. She even claimed not to feel the heat at all, insisting that her loose-hanging smock protected her from it. She worked furiously, constantly, without ceasing, but now refused to permit John to watch her progress, rather reluctantly promising only to permit him to see and comment upon the finished project.

Somewhat miffed by her cold attitude, John began to avoid her painting area, sitting in the shade of the veranda and thoughtfully watching her at work, wishing he could himself turn to such steady and unrelenting accomplishment. Ruth was drawn again and again to the edge of the cliff, staring with an almost hypnotic intensity down into the churning, tumbling, crashing surf. In spite of the amount of time she spent under the hot sun, her peculiar pallor seemed to increase with each day. Her eyes were strangely empty, her movements, save when at work on her canvas, slow and listless. The green scarf was at all times about her throat.

Any hopes John may have nurtured of a gradually renewed sexual intimacy in the fresh, clear-aired comforts of their new home quickly were dispelled. Ruth seemed actually to consider abhorent even the most casual physical contact. She drew her face away from his kisses with no attempt to conceal her revulsion. One evening she removed her things from the master bedroom to a smaller room at the end of the upstairs corridor, near the stairway leading to the Widow's Walk, explaining they would sleep more comfortably apart in the intense heat, that same heat she often claimed did not trouble her.

From the night John saw those unexpected footprints in the dust of the cellar floor, all close contact between him and Ruth seemed to come to an abrupt end, as though he were being punished for making the unexpected discovery. They spoke to each other seldom and spent most of their time apart, not even getting together for their meals.

On the morning following that incident, remembering her tacit and unexpected acceptance to the suggestion on the evening before, John again raised the question of inviting Paul and Linda for dinner, but Ruth had changed her mind.

"We came here to get away from that sort of thing," she reminded him in a firm, no-nonsense tone.

John tried to smile, surprised by this about-face. "Yes, but there's surely no need to cut ourselves off so completely," he mentioned. "They have been very good to us, Ruth, and I think it would be a nice gesture to invite them here."

"I haven't the time for nice gestures," she responded in a cold tone. "I've work to do. I can't spare time for anything else, particularly for inviting dinner guests."

"That's nonsense, Ruth," he insisted. "You don't work in the evenings. I have promised them, you know."

"I wasn't part of your promise," she said indifferently. "I'm the one who would have to do all the work."

"Not necessarily. We could probably have the dinner catered for us by the hotel restaurant in town."

"Then take them to dinner there; I don't care what you do."

And she would hear no more of it.

Ruth became just as uninterested as the time came closer for the arrival of Grandmother Ellen, whose departure from Vienna had been postponed for several days due to a slight indisposition. They had not seen her since just shortly after Elinor's death, and her warm sympathy had done much to help them through those trying days. Ruth had been very grateful then, drawn closer than ever to this wonderful old woman. Now she showed no interest.

"I suppose we can't keep her from coming," she admitted, "but I'll depend on you to keep her amused, and to see that the visit is a short one."

So had their lives changed in just a matter of days. Often in the earliest part of the evening, when John stood on the bluff, he would see Ruth, still and motionless, standing on the Widow's Walk, staring with a fixed intensity towards the horizon, like those long dead women of the past centuries watching for their men to return from distant parts.

Ruth's attitude about the house had also undergone something of an alteration. Her liking had now become an absolute passion, and she would listen to no talk of the approaching time when they would leave the bluff and return to the city. She became possessive of the house, as though it were her own property, as though she had constructed it with her own hands. She abruptly rejected any suggestion that they should now spend some time in the village, get away for an occasional evening and enjoy a movie or a dinner at the hotel. Ruth was not interested in leaving the house for even the shortest time, even refusing to join John now in the necessary shopping forays. The matter of purchasing food no longer interested her, nor its preparation; their meals became ordinary and uninteresting, composed of dishes quickly prepared, and before long each was preparing only for him or herself. John could do as he pleased. Ruth made this very clear to him. She had here found the only home she ever wanted, and he had become of very little importance to her. She now used no pretense in making it evident she even resented his own presence there.

Most surprising of all was the change in Ruth's attitude toward the cellar. In a total reversal of her earlier feelings, she now no longer insisted that the door to the cellar be kept closed at all times. The undisguised antipathy for the cellar had vanished, and she no longer avoided passing the frequently open door.

One afternoon, following the usual uncomfortably silent cold luncheon which, for a change, they shared together, Ruth failed to appear on the cliff to resume her work, as was her invariable custom. John, who had long since abandoned all pretense of work, seated himself in his usual shaded spot on the veranda with a book and a cold drink, and was surprised, some twenty minutes or so later, to note that Ruth's canvas stool was still empty. He looked for her in the house, but she was neither in the living room nor in the upstairs bedroom; he even checked the Widow's Walk without success. He was beginning to feel concern when he noted that the cellar door stood wide open. Puzzled, he silently descended the rickety wooden stairs.

The large main chamber of the cellar was silent and empty. The musty silence disturbed him. He thought again that Ruth was right. There is a strangeness about cellars, as though this portion of a house preserved the memories of the joys and sorrows of the upper floors, concealing them from the eyes of those who might not understand. He was about to return to the kitchen when he noticed the touch of green beyond the furnace. Uneasily recalling the last time he had seen that peculiar green glow, John approached the small room.

Ruth stood on the small mound of earth, staring trance-like at the opaque window overlooking the sea. Unlike her earlier mysterious visit to the chamber, she was now completely clothed. She apparently had been preparing herself for work on the bluff when something had drawn her down here; the smeared daubs of paint on her smock looked in the green light like something of a surrealist's nightmare. There was a peculiar tautness in the way she held her slender figure, with her hands almost rigidly at her sides, her head lowered stiffly so her eyes could fasten upon the low window. The sun was already quite low on the horizon, for the room was fled with that emerald light that John had convinced himself was the result of the sun's last rays filtering through the pigment of the glass. John stepped into the room and felt the sudden sharp cold.

"Ruth. . ."

She whirled about in an almost violent motion that seemed to convert the daubs of her smock into writhing serpents, and he was startled by the vague, far-distant look in her face.

"Ruth, are you all right?"

The vagueness was quickly replaced by an expression of intense irritation; her body became less tense, and she stepped from the mound and faced her husband. It was evident she was not pleased to see him.

"What are you doing here?" she asked in a harsh voice of undisguised hostility.

He tried to smile. "I was looking for you, dear. When you didn't come outside, I was concerned, and I couldn't find you upstairs." He looked about the harshly barren room. "I certainly never expected to find you down here."

Her gaze softened somewhat as she followed his eyes about the room, like someone proud of a dear possession. "Why not? It's the coolest place in the house. It's . . . comfortable here."

"Well, it certainly is cooler," John admitted, and shivered slightly. "It's even cold. But there's nothing down here, Ruth, and you and cellars. . ."

"What about me and cellars?"

"Why . . . you've never cared for them, you know," he commented, trying to keep from his tone the sudden sense of concern and bewilderment.

"That doesn't mean I can't come down here when I choose," she insisted irrationally, in the tone of a child discovered in a forbidden place. She turned to him again, and her face seemed different, almost alien, too harsh and unfriendly to be the still lovely face of the woman with whom he had shared so much of his life. Have you become so insensitive to all feelings other than your own?" Her voice was rising almost to the pitch of hysteria; her face was twisted with anger. "How tired I grow of your constant meaningless haggling, the watching, the spying. . ."

"Oh, come now, Ruth, I haven't been spying, and you know it!" He tried not to permit his voice to adopt the same sharp edge that had so altered her own. "If I seem to be watching you sometimes, it's simply because I'm concerned . . .

"There's nothing to be concerned about!" she flashed back at him. "I simply want to be left alone! Is that so difficult to understand? Why don't you go and sit on your veranda and leave me alone?"

She turned her back on him and, again adopting that peculiar rigid posture he had noticed upon his entry into the room, stared once more at the small green window. What was she looking for? What did she see there? What drew her eyes back again to the strangely greenish opaque glass which could not even give her a glimpse of the sea whose sound seemed so loud in that room? She had forgotten he was there. He looked at her for a moment, and then slowly backed out of the room.

The cellar seemed darker than ever as he made his way to the stairs, his vision impeded by the curious green flashes dancing before his eyes. He slowly climbed the stairs to the kitchen, pausing at the topmost step to glance behind him. The cellar had become an ominous place. Too dark and too quiet. From beside the furnace came that strange shading of green. He entered the kitchen, closing the door softly behind him, leaving the cellar to the darkness, the dust of the past, and the rigid presence of his strange wife.

There was no further pretense between John and Ruth after that. Ruth openly resented John's very presence in the house. She grew increasingly surly and unpleasant, highly irritable and impossible to please. They began to quarrel more frequently, and unexpectedly harsh words passed between them. The house became a place of gloom and strain. They no longer sat in warm companionship on the veranda, nor strolled hand-in-hand like lovers along the peacefully empty beach in that golden twilight when the fading rays of the sun restored to the world that serenity which mankind has so often destroyed. The warmth, the closeness of those first happy days was gone, and John despaired of ever finding them again. His loneliness became more and more intense as he permitted Ruth to remain in that strange, sudden, self-imposed isolation, permitted it simply because he did not know what else to do.

Ruth now never made further mention of Elinor. It was as though she had forgotten their little daughter had ever existed. John had at first taken this as a hopeful indication that she was, at long last, beginning to recover from their mutual tragedy, but there was something strange in the fact that not once now did Elinor's name cross her lips; the change was too abrupt and too complete. He would much have preferred to see the sorrowful, teary attitude replaced by a calmer, more reasonable and sensible discussion of their daughter's tragically brief life, gentle reminiscences and appreciation of the memories of the happy days they had known with their lovely little girl, rather than this total exclusion of someone who had once been of such importance to them both. Had Ruth really managed to block Elinor so completely from her mind and heart? That would be even more alarming than the earlier constant, gloomy, tearful self-recriminating mentions of their daughter. If Ruth had so suddenly closed her mind to such an important segment of their past, it might be an indication of a new and more serious mental ailment. There must always be mourning for one who has gone; complete forgetfulness was as irrational as over-indulgence in sorrow.

John now began to look impatiently for the impending arrival of his grandmother. Even in his childhood, he had always turned to Grandmother Ellen with his problems and, somehow, in some miraculous way, she had always managed to find the solution, to resolve the difficulties, to sooth the hurts. He was again like a child turning to that single source of strength. Somehow, he would have to hold on until her arrival. Grandmother Ellen would have the answer. No one else could help him now.

If only they had never found this old house; that was where the problem lay. It was as though the sharp salted air that permeated the old wooden boards had created *a strange sea change* in his wife, or perhaps in him, or perhaps even in both of them. They had become strangers again, and an air of growing antipathy amounting almost to open hostility was rising between them.

He could blame only himself, for the suggestion had originally been his. The change in their way of life had placed them in a false world in which their tragedy seemed so unreal that it had become misplaced in their recollection. That was not the proper way to forget. They should have remained in the city and, somehow, worked out their problems, resolved them where they had originated. Flight to totally different surroundings had warped their perspective. It would be best for both of them to return to where they belonged.

John again broached the subject over breakfast on the morning before his grandmother was scheduled to arrive. Both had slept rather later than usual after another uncomfortably sticky and humid night and had unexpectedly entered the kitchen for their breakfast at the same time, something that had become increasingly rare. Ruth's movements were slow and listless as she mechanically prepared their usual sparse breakfast, with little waste of words, and John already felt the day's perspiration running down his back.

It was while they were seated over their second cups of coffee that John carefully raised the question of their future.

"Grandmother Ellen will be here tomorrow," he said casually. "I don't suppose she'll be staying very long; this isn't exactly her kind of place. Why don't you arrange to go back with her?"

Ruth's cup clattered noisily as she placed it heavily in its saucer, and a bit of the black liquid spilled over its lip. "Why on earth should I do that?"

He turned to face her and tried to smile; her face was wan and drawn, her hair uncharacteristically untidy. "Our rental will be over soon now, you know," he reminded her. "There's no reason for you to get involved in all the business of closing up. I can do that myself, and you can go back to the city and reopen the apartment. Traveling with grandmother would be more pleasant for you; you should have a good deal to talk about."

Ruth looked at him for a moment, and there was a touch of mockery in her eyes. She again sipped her coffee and said nothing, as though dismissing the subject without further word or comment.

"We can't stay here forever, you know," he added, attempting and failing to make it sound something like a joke.

"And why not?" she asked. Her voice was harsh and heavy with loss of sleep. "The house is for sale, and we have an option to buy it. You remember that, surely."

He hesitated, frowning. This was going to be difficult, but it was best to have it all out now. "Yes, of course I remember that, but I don't think it would be a good idea. We've been away from the city for too long. We're losing all contact with our friends, not to mention our professional connections."

"We don't need one or the other," she interrupted harshly. "We don't need anything that we don't have right here."

Uneasy, irritated by such difficulty in speaking with his own wife, John began to trace lines in the white tablecloth with the tines of his fork.

"That isn't true, Ruth, and you know it as well as I. We're not natural born recluses. We've tried it, we've had our time in the sun, but now I think it's . . . well, it's time to go. We've been here quite long enough."

Ruth placed both hands on the table and rose to her feet; her chair scraped as she pushed it behind her. "And just what is that supposed to mean?"

"I don't think this place is good for us," he said quite frankly. "It's had a bad effect on both of us. I think we've been here long enough and now we should go back."

She stared at him, and he felt uncomfortable under the openly sarcastic expression in her eyes; they seemed to be more deeply shadowed than he had noticed before. She said nothing for a moment, merely staring at him, and then a slow, unpleasant smile crossed her face as she began to gather the dishes from the table and place them in the sink.

"Well, I'm not leaving. This place has been good for my work. That's why we came here in the first place, isn't it? I know you haven't been very successful in your own attempts, but I have. I'm achieving something important here, and I'm not going to give it all up simply because you happen to be bored. If you think you can conceal your own failures by attempting to destroy what I. . ."

He rose angrily, interrupting her. "That's a hell of a thing to say! You know it isn't true!"

Ruth said nothing as she placed the last cup into the sink . . . she always left them for later in the day now . . . wiped her hands on a towel, and then moved with an almost impertinent slowness to the door leading out to the back, pausing to smile at him in a cold way that sent a sudden chill rippling down his spine.

"I'm staying, John. Go, if you like. It doesn't matter to me in the least what you do. I don't need you any longer. I don't need anyone. I've found what I want here, and what happens to you or to anyone else in the world doesn't mean a damn to me."

The screened door slammed loudly behind her, leaving John standing alone in the gray, dreary kitchen with its hanging pots and pans and already wilting flowers, his face white with shock and anger. She had never before spoken quite so harshly, voicing the attitudes and feelings he had begun to suspect.

And he suddenly realized she had spoken only the

truth. Ruth no longer cared for him. That was the basis of all his doubt and confusion, the sensed feeling of total rejection by his wife. She no longer needed nor wanted him.

In a childish bit of hurt fury, John swept the small vase of flowers from the table to the floor; the vase broke and the damaged flowers lay like small bent corpses in a pool of water.

John stormed from the house and out to the veranda. He was not surprised to see Ruth already seated on her folding stool, painting as though nothing had happened between them. He paused for a moment, feeling again that familiar tug of love for the small figure outlined against the blue-white horizon. What could he say to her now? How could he force her to understand what was happening between them?

Why should he bother? She had surely made it amply clear that she no longer cared.

John cleared the veranda steps in one movement and stepped into the car. Without bothering to look again to the bluff, he started at high speed down the dirt road and toward the village.

CHAPTER THIRTEEN

JOHN'S trips into the village, which had formerly been primarily matters of only necessity, had become increasingly more frequent since the unfortunate alteration in his relationship with his wife. More and more often, he found himself in desperate need of a release, a temporary escape, somewhere that give him an opportunity to get away from the constant air of dreariness and gloom and that indefinable menace that had descended upon the old house and seemed to pervade its every room, and his own irritating inability to apply himself to the work he felt he must do, an inability which he quite unabashedly ascribed not to lack of ability, but to the detestable weather and the unhappiness of his present circumstances.

Where formerly he had disliked leaving Ruth alone, John now felt not the slightest hesitation about leaving the house for any length of time. Ruth no longer feared being alone, and John often traveled into town where the villagers, dull and uninteresting though they might be, at least managed to make him feel a little less alone. He found himself almost pathetically grateful for a smiled hello, or simply for the wave of a hand. Once he was bored enough to drop into the local cinema . . . a small house smelling of stale buttered popcorn, its walls marked with childish graffiti and juvenile obscenities, and its auditorium filled with noisy children who spent the time chasing each other up and down the aisles and had no interest in events on the screen . . . but quickly fled from the meaningless pap that here passed as entertainment.

He was beginning again, almost without realizing it, to drink considerably more than was now his custom or than was good for him, and had become quite a familiar figure at the *Whaler's Rest*, having his own stool at the far corner of the bar. More than once, he had returned to the house a bit the worse for drink, but Ruth had never seemed to notice . . . or, more likely, simply did not care. On two occasions, he had lunched with Linda, during which time, as though by some silent mutual agreement, neither one even mentioned the curious shadows that hovered above the gables of Fowles House, or the vague stories that had composed their conversation during their first luncheon. Paul still had not returned from the city, where he had become enmeshed in the tangled legalities of a complicated estate involved in the unexpected death of an encouragingly wealthy close relative.

The village shared in the general discomfort caused by the unusually extended spell of hot weather that had settled upon the coastal region. As John topped the small rise and saw the slumberous little town beneath him, there were few enough indications of life; the inhabitants found it more comfortable to remain indoors with the windows closed and the shades drawn in an attempt to keep out the suffocating heat. As with most seaside towns that hesitate to hinder their supposedly inspiring view of the romantic blue horizon, the village had too few large trees along its streets to provide a touch of much needed shade and coolness during the hot days of summer; the streets, spotted with yellow beach sand, gleamed under the sun like hot yellow ribbons, and the drabness of the wooden buildings was accentuated by the brilliant golden light that baked them. The little fishing vessels bobbed like bathtub toys lazily up and down at their deserted wharfs. The polished brass weather-vane atop the church steeple, with *Moby Dick* gayly flicking his tail at the world, cast light daggars into his eyes as John slowly guided his car down the barren strip of Main Street.

There was little sign of activity on the street: several irrepressible boys in bathing trunks whose violent play could not be interrupted by the vagaries of the weather . . . two little girls in sunsuits playing mama with their dolls on a heat-yellowed lawn . . . a small, unhappy and extremely uncomfortable shaggy dog pattering down the street with its dripping purple tongue dangling from its mouth . . . several drowsy shopkeepers seated before their open but empty stores complaining to each other about the heat and what it was doing to business, while lazily wafting the hot, motionless air with bamboo fans colored by shopping slogans of local merchants. John licked his lips and decided there was nothing he needed just now more desperately than a good, stiff, cooling drink. He drew up before the *Whaler's Rest* and quickly entered the cooling darkness of the bar.

There were several casually dressed patrons perched on the tall plastic red-topped stools and in the booths along the wall, despite the still rather early hour, engaged in quiet conversation or merely staring morosely into their glasses with the hypnotic expression of the frequent bar drinker who hopes one day to discover the solution to all of his problems in the iced liquid. John paid no attention to any of them as he seated himself on his customary stool, aside from an automatic slight dipping of his head to one or two who had become nodding acquaintances; he really knew none of them save by sight, for relations with the reticent and suspicious villagers had not yet gone beyond this stage, and it was just as well, for in his particularly unsettled state of mind, he was not interested in engaging any of them in their dull, insipid, unimaginative form of conversation. Two young girls at the bar, dressed in extremely brief shorts and very tight halters, their hair hanging in loose cascades over bare shoulders and their faces over-painted, looked up as he passed them, but seeing his obvious indifference to their well-exposed charms, returned to their quiet banal talk.

Bartender Frank approached him with a rocks glass in his hand; his breath, as always, held that slightly pungent sweet aroma which indicated he had been wiling away the slower hours of the long business day by an occasional raising of the bottle.

"Afternoon, Mr. Kendall," he greeted. "Good to see ya. Scotch on the rocks?"

John nodded rather absently. "Yes, please, Frank."

After a quick invigorating sip of the drink, John lighted a cigarette, leaned his folded arms on the scarred wooden railing of the bar, and desperately tried to force himself to relax. Slowly, his tensions began to release themselves, his jaw became looser, the tight knot in his stomach unraveled, and a certain calmness returned.

He had come to like it here at the *Whaler's Rest*, with its subdued lighting, its somewhat romantic reminders of the lost era of the great whaling vessels, the oh-so-welcome low murmurs of quiet conversation; it was pleasant, friendly and comfortable, if not exactly up to the more elegant and polished cocktail lounges to which he was accustomed. How different was the atmosphere here from the gloomy and suffocating silence of the old house by the sea, a morgue-like stillness broken only by that goddamned constant thundering of the sea at the base of the cliff, the ear-splitting shrieking of the ever-wheeling, shit-dropping seagulls, and the discordant sounds of his and Ruth's voices now raised in constant argument.

Yes. Oh, yes, he told himself with a vigorous nodding of his head that caused his neighbor to look at him with slight amusement. He'd had quite enough of the damned old house on the cliff, of the perpetually empty horizon and the dreary loneliness. The shade of old pirate Fowles and his peculiar family were welcome to it; for all of him, they might rattle about the vast empty rooms undisturbed until the house finally crumbled into the sea where it belonged. If Ruth wanted to stay . . . well, then, let her stay. He was returning to the city where he belonged, to the bright lights, the theatres, the bars and restaurants, to the conversation of people who at least had an interest in what went on about them. There's a whole exciting world out there, Johnny-boy, and it's leaving you far behind. Better get with it before it's too late.

It was a startling and unexpected thought, this decision to return. He paused, blowing a trail of blue-white smoke from between his lips and watching it curl and twist as though it might resolve itself into the towering of a wish-granting genie. Was he really so readily confessing the total collapse of his marriage? He shook his head. Surely a marriage doesn't end that quickly, that unexpectedly.

But this was really neither quick nor unexpected. The deterioration had begun several years ago, been temporarily halted by the birth of their daughter, renewed after Elinor's death, and accelerated by the foolishness of imprisoning themselves alone together in that house.

That made it all seem very compact and simple, but even now he refused to accept it. There was much more to this than these bald facts. There were emotions involved, there were the years of happiness that they had known together; all this could not be that easily dismissed. It was true that they were going through a difficult time just now, still touched by the trauma of Elinor's death, but John still nursed the hope that it would pass in time and their normal relationship would resume. Despite Ruth's harsh words, they loved and needed each other as when they had first met. Perhaps it was simply the surroundings that had done such incalculable harm. Their problems should have been resolved where they had occurred. Surely Ruth would still come to her senses, given time. She would have enough of all this before long, particularly if left alone. Perhaps that was the answer, after all. Leave her alone for a while, and she would realize what had happened between them. The love she still bore him, whether or not she was willing to admit it, would bring her to her senses. Wouldn't it?

There was no evading the fact that Ruth had been severely and strangely affected by too long a stay at that house, stuck away up there on the bare cliff like some aged recluse, without ever coming down into the village to mix with people, save for the more and more infrequent, extremely brief and hurried shopping expeditions which she had lately left entirely to John. Gloom begets gloom. He should have been much more firm with her and insisted that she occasionally come into the village for a drink or a movie or a dinner, or just for a quiet arm-in-arm walk along Main Street, anything to bring her into contact with people again, rather than permit her to continue nursing her sick grief in the isolated old mansion.

He reached for a bowl of salted peanuts and unthinkingly began to shovel them into his mouth, ignoring those that fell onto the bar while sipping again at his refreshing drink.

He could not quite escape the feeling that perhaps at least some of the fault was his own. Perhaps his attitude towards Ruth's emotional problems had been mistaken. Had he perhaps been playing at psychiatry himself? Perhaps he had catered too much to her sorrow, emphasized it, even glamorized it. The simple truth was that Ruth rather enjoyed being the sorrowful central figure of a poignant tragedy. Oh, her grief was certainly authentic enough, but grief can become almost as pleasurable as joy. That grief had now lasted too long; it had become her crutch and her shield against the world, and the old house had become part of it.

But how do you forbid a mother from mourning for her only child? Yet he, too, had mourned, and his grief had not become such a sickness with him. Of course, a mother's grief, he supposed, was different. As she was more personally involved in the process of birth, perhaps she more deeply feels the sense of loss.

What Ruth actually needed, of course, was psychiatric help, but he knew she would never agree to that, to the admission that she had a problem so badly in need of professional counseling.

John shook his head again, drawing almost angrily on his cigarette. Perhaps he had not done all tha should or could have been done, but he refused to accept the full responsibility for what had happened to his wife. He loved her, he cared for her and, right or wrong, he had done his best. The fault was surely not his alone.

He ordered another drink.

The bar became quieter and emptier as the afternoon progressed, and the good people of the village returned to their homes, or went about their business, while John remained firmly entrenched on his stool, attempting to forget these problems in the tart taste of his drink. The two young girls, still giggling at their own secret imaginings and tossing coyly inviting glances in his direction, left the bar together, having totally failed in their campaign and not even gaining a free drink. The grocer from across the square came in for a quick beer to relieve his heat-induced thirst, still wearing his long white apron and eyeing the entrance to his deserted store through the window while he raised the bottle to his lips. There was the sound of screeching brakes as a car stopped short to avoid hitting a dog ambling indifferently across the street, and the startlingly sharp sound reminded John again of that day, of Elinor, of Ruth.

John sensed he had already been too long at the bar.

He'd had too many cigarettes, clearly evidenced in the overflowing ashtray before him, and too many drinks, indicated by the sopping wetness of his portion of the bar and the increasingly more frequent visits to the men's room. He really should go . . . he hesitated to apply the term *home* to the place on the cliff. Back to the house. Ruth would be wondering what had become of him.

No. He quickly corrected himself, with an irritated toss of his head. That wasn't true. Ruth would not be wondering about him at all. She probably was not even fully aware that he was gone. There was no reason for him to hasten back to that great solitary old house with the dead tree and the moribund atmosphere. He was not going to bury himself there as Ruth had done. Life was not yet over for him. There was still too much enjoyment available, too much pleasure, comfort and companionship. He refused to permit the shadow of that goddamned house to hover over the rest of his life.

Having won this rather halfhearted battle with his conscience, John had just ordered still another Scotch when Linda suddenly entered the bar, a pleasant and wholesome figure dressed in white, for a moment rather fetchingly outlined against the light of the open doorway. She saw John immediately and, smiling broadly and warmly, approached him.

"Why, hello there, John!" The sound of her voice was something of a tonic, instantly raising his badly sunken spirits. "How nice to see you! I had no idea you expected to be in town today, or I wouldn't have gone to lunch by myself!"

He smiled, hoping he didn't give the appearance of having spent the entire afternoon ensconced at the bar just where she had found him, and slipped slowly and carefully from the stool, taking her cool, slender hand in his own.

"Well, the loss is my own. It's nice to see you, too,

Linda. I really hadn't expected to be here myself. How are you?"

"Just fine," she responded. He caught a slight whiff of that delicate perfume that had so pleased him on his first visit to her office. "No, please don't get up." He seated himself again; the stool rocked slightly, didn't it? "Mind if I join you? I've had a rather hectic day, and I could use a bit of relaxation."

"I'd be disappointed if you didn't join me," John assured her, wondering if she noticed that his speech was just a bit thick and somewhat slurred. "Wouldn't you be more comfortable in a booth?"

She shook her head, raising herself to the stool next to him; he couldn't decide if his sudden flush came from drink, or from the quite accidental contact with her shapely leg.

"It gives a woman an added sense of equality once in a while to plant herself on a barstool with a man."

The remainder of that afternoon passed more quickly in Linda's pleasant and cheerful company. She was bright, perky and interesting. John found himself more and more enjoying being with her, and whenever he was struck by a momentary recurring sense of guilt or uneasiness, for being where he was, he compared Linda with Ruth, her bright cheerfulness with his wife's current gloom, her warm friendliness with Ruth's bitter hostility, and her infectious good nature with Ruth's strangely bitter present attitude. Surely he had every right to enjoy himself after what he had been through. Ruth no longer needed him; she had her own sick fantasies to keep her company.

Linda's sharp eye had immediately detected the uneasiness and unhappiness in John's attitude, and Frank had confirmed with a slight nod of his head and widened eyes her suspicion that he had been drinking heavily. She was concerned, but not surprised, for she had noted John's increasing strangeness in their recent meetings. Things were not going well with him. She did not feel justified in attempting to uncover the cause for his nervousness, for the darkness about his eyes and the slight trembling of his hands; he would tell her if he wanted to. She could, however, attempt to ease and soothe him by giving him the little time in which to forget whatever troubles plagued him. She liked John and for some reason she felt sorry for him. She would give what help she could.

They had several more drinks, and suddenly the entire world began to look rosier to John and more filled with promise than it had been for the past several days. Perhaps matters weren't after all as bad as they appeared. That old business about hope being where there is life? Even a bad day is a good day as long as you are alive to see it. So he and Ruth had had a quarrel! Was that so unusual between married people?

He found himself laughing a good deal, and it was good to realize he still knew how to do that. The towering house on the cliff with its huge rooms haunted by the unseen specters of the pirate captain, its shadowed veranda with dried leaves forever rustling in every slight breeze, its dead and blackened tree like an ever present reminder of mortality, and its cold cellar chamber with its peculiar green light, all slipped from his awareness, and it was as though the painful days had never been.

This could well be Ruth here at his side, he thought, Ruth as she had been much too long ago, filled with the pleasure of life and love that she had, somehow, lost somewhere along the way. His mind traveled fuzzily into the past, and he seemed to see her before him as she had been . . . standing on the beach of their Carribean isle with the palm trees swaying under the clear blue sky, the gentle lapping of the waters on the smooth white beach . . . outlined against the scarred columns of the Parthenon with the clear Attic sky behind her . . . strolling with her arm in his along the *Champs-*

Elysees, raising her head to the scent of the fresh, pure air under the yellow-green trees . . . the happy days, the warming memories, the companionship and the love . . .

He shook his head, trying to bring himself back to reality. That was all too long ago now. A different time and a different life. He had to remind himself that this woman seated beside him was not Ruth. He was seated here with another woman, while Ruth . . . a so different Ruth from the one of these memories . . . was back at the unfriendly old house, alone, listening to the thunder of the hungry sea, part of a vastly different world from that day they had known together, part of the past that the house enfolded in its harsh gables and salt-whitened old boards. No, this was someone and somewhere else.

This was Linda at his side. It was somehow ludicrously difficult to keep the two women apart in his mind. He had had so many drinks and the room, again filled with noisy people and blue-white cigarette smoke curling like a sinuous interior fog, suddenly seemed stuffy and uncomfortably hot. He felt the trickle of perspiration down his chest and glanced down to his shirt front to see if there was a wet stain, and then couldn't remember if there was or not. His eyes become overly sensitive to the lights, and he winced and closed them for a moment, feeling the world suddenly somewhat unsteady and confused. He was aware of a tremendous pressure on his bladder, and of the warm and inviting smile of the lovely young woman seated beside him, this Ruth who yet was not Ruth. . .

And then, quite suddenly, and he could never afterward remember just how it had happened, it was all gone, the noise, the smoke, the people. It had all faded, and now it was dark and silent and there was no one about them, and he and Linda were alone in a room whose only light came from the white moon sending its questing rays through the bedroom window, and his arms were about Linda and his hungry lips were pressed tightly to hers, feeling their almost velvety smoothness. He could sense in her a hunger as great as his own, as she brought her body against him and he felt the firmness of her breasts against his chest. She moaned slightly as she ran her fingers up over his back and into his hair.

"John. . . John. . ." she sighed, as if the words could only with difficulty pass through the lips pressed to his cheek, his throat, his open mouth.

John moved back, and his eager fingers fumbled with the buttons on her blouse. She pushed his hand away and opened them for him, exposing her full breasts, firm and trembling with the same desire that had so aroused him. He placed his hands upon them, and she moved closer to him again, her mouth open, the breath of desire touching his flushed face. He moved her towards the bed, and she sank onto its whiteness, and her eyes seemed to sparkle like two rays of desire as she watched him quickly remove his clothing and approach the bed where she waited for him. . . .

CHAPTER FOURTEEN

IT seemed that at last the unusually long spell of sultry, uncomfortably hot and humid weather was about to break. As he lay on his back in the bed beside Linda, his body still wet with the heat and the exciting frenzy of their startlingly passionate love making, John watched the leaping, contorted shadows cast upon the white ceiling like figures in a nightmarish ballet pantomine, as jagged forks of yellow lightning rent the velvet fabric of the dark starless sky and illuminated the empty horizon beyond the open window. They reminded him, briefly . . . as everything reminded him in these darkly shadowed days . . . of the impenetrable darkness that surrounded Fowles House, of the mysterious reachings, the unseen presence of some unknown violent past, the ominous atmosphere so heavily pregnant with suspected menace, and of the intangible elements that had destroyed the happiness he and Ruth had initially known in the old house.

The storm had not yet arrived . . . the sound of thunder was still low on the horizon, like the uneasy rumblings within the vast stomach of a dispeptic sleeping giant . . . but he could already hear the rising of the wind, and the low moaning of its passage through the narrowly constricting space between the old wooden buildings of the sleeping village. The storm would follow closely behind, and then after too many weary days of baking heat and choking dust, the rain would bring with it a cleansing and refreshing to the village, washing away the heat-engendered discomfort like the needle-spray of a cold shower wipes away the grime and perspiration from a tired body.

The rain would fall, too, upon the hard yellow packed earth of the barren cliff top on which the house stood like a perpetual sentry of gloom, its drops pockmarking the ever thirsty, arid soil, and on the sharp rusted gables of Fowles House and upon the vacant platform of the Widow's Walk where on windy dark nights you might perhaps hear the sibilant swishing of ghostly skirts, but it could never wash away the buried past and the unpleasant memories that for so many long empty years had darkened those long vacant windows that stared so emptily out to sea.

It was late now, and he could only hear the gentle sobbing of the lonely wind, as though the entire world, exhausted at last by its battle with the remorseless heat, had finally fallen into a dreamless sleep. A lonely, perhaps hungry dog bayed at the lightning, imagining it to be spear-hurled rays of the moon. He heard the soft, shallow sound of Linda's easy breathing, but in the darkness he could not determine whether she slept or, like himself, lay with open eyes creating dancing figures upon the ceiling.

He was not particularly surprised that he experienced not even the slightest semblance of shame or guilt for what had now happened between himself and Linda. He was not a prude, but neither did he advocate sexual promiscuity, particularly in the married. He had been unfaithful to Ruth on several occasions in the past, and always there had followed that small nagging uneasiness, that vaguely disconcerting sense that he had given to someone else something that was no longer his to give. It had never, of course, prevented a recurrence of the event at the proper time and under suitable circumstances, but that same feeling of guilt and dishonesty, like a hammering hangover following a drinking binge or a gut-twisting stomachache after incautious overeating, had always made it seem quite all right again. He knew he was doing wrong according to the perhaps somewhat narrow mores of the day. This did not prevent him from doing it, or enjoying what he was doing, but his conscience was always somewhat salved by the sense of admitted guilt. The sharp pricks of guilt are a punishment . . . the least painful and most bearable of punishments, of course . . . for infidelity. It would be somehow shameless and uncivilized to be unfaithful and, while still deeply relishing the physical action, not feel the least bit uneasy about it all. That was probably what a sin would be, if he believed in such things.

But this, somehow, was different. He was surprised that it had happened at all. He had certainly not been looking for it or expecting it, and he was quite certain Linda felt the same way. It had just happened. It was a natural effect. Both he and Linda were depressed by their own measures of unhappiness and loneliness: John by his sudden inexplicable problems with Ruth, and Linda by the sudden return of her widowed loneliness, occasioned by Paul's prolonged absence. They had met at the most propitious time for what had happened. Why should they feel guilt? Linda had no specific ties with Paul, and Ruth would surely not care, had she known. In the past, she had frequently been pained by his little infidelities, more as a matter of personal pride than an actual sense of grievance. This was different. How long had Ruth been aware of John's growing sexual needs and simply ignored them, not caring where it might lead him? Ruth would not care about this at all, and therefore there was no need for a sense of guilt.

This rather elaborate self-justification made John feel better, and he relaxed again, the leapings of the ceilings having become a child's shadow play.

Linda's warm hand reached out to his perspiration dampened bare chest, and he took it in ihs own. It was a small, narrow hand, somehow as fragile as the finest piece of bone china. It felt so different from that so casual contact they had made when she had first entered the *Whaler's Rest* earlier that afternoon. Of course, matters had changed since then. Then it had been just the hand of another woman. Now it was a more familiar hand. It made a difference.

"You really should be going, John." The soft voice sounded somehow lost and lonely in that dark room; it unpleasantly reminded him that he had strayed from his world into hers. "It must be very late."

"Yes, I suppose I should," he agreed rather reluctantly, stretching his legs on the rumpled sheet and tightening his hold on her hand. "There's a storm coming, too. Well, it should break the heat. It'll be good to feel cool again."

She moved closer to him, and her bare leg brushed suggestively against him. He felt relaxed and comfortable, but the warm physical contact created no sudden reawakening of desire. He knew she had not moved against him for that purpose. What had happened, had happened, and they were both somehow better for it, but now it was over. These were those few warmly comfortable moments of relaxed intimacy remaining to them before the world broke in on them again and all this would come to an end.

"Paul will be back soon now. Tomorrow. Perhaps even tonight."

"You've missed him, haven't you?"

She sighed heavily, and in a coloring of lightning, he could see the gentle outline of her breasts. He reached out his hand and gently stroked them.

"He's always been very comfortable to be near," she replied. "Paul is . . . kind, understanding, good. Yes, comfortable is the best word. I don't mean that in the patronizing sense; he's much too sincere for that." There was just the briefest pause before she added. "He's asked me to marry him."

"I'm not surprised. I only wonder he hasn't done it before now. Or has he?"

"Oh, yes," she replied. "Many times, in fact. But casually, half-jokingly. Almost in passing, although I always felt there was a more serious undercurrent somewhere behind it all. But this time he does really mean it. I'm supposed to give him my answer when he gets back."

They fell silent, but the silence between them was in no sense an awkward one. Everything was all right. There would be no problems between them because of what had happened this night. It had been a casual thing that would not happen for them again. They both knew that, too. It had brought them release and enjoyment when they were both so badly needed, but this would be the end of it. It was not the beginning of an affair. It was something to be remembered with fondness, but it had created no embarrassing, restricting bonds between them. They would be able to meet in the future, anywhere, without that touch of embarrassment that was often the result of intimacy. They could go on being friends, without the often difficult confusion of being something more and yet something less.

"And you will marry him?"

In the darkness, she shook her head, and several strands of her silken hair brushed lightly across his face; he again caught the whiff of her perfume.

"No. I don't believe I will."

He was surprised by her response, and raising hmself up on one elbow, looked into the darkness where her face lay; he could see the slight glitter of her eyes.

"You won't? I'm sure Paul will be expecting quite a different answer. He'll be quite surprised . . . and disappointed."

She sighed again. "Have you a cigarette somewhere, John?"

"Yes."

He rose from the bed and, with the aid of the flashes of lightning that seemed to hurl dark, misshapen forms in his path, crossed the unfamiliar room to where his jacket was rather carelessly and hurriedly flung over a chair; he found himself absurdly embarrassed by his nakedness. The cigarettes were, of course, in the very last pocket he examined . . . he was briefly reminded of the business with the house key on the first visit to Fowles House . . . and he was glad Linda could not witness the foolish, futile fumbling. He returned to the bed and gave her a cigarette; the flame of the match played on the surge of her breasts and deepened the shadows between them, also emphasizing his own nudity. He felt a momentary rekindling of desire, but it faded as he returned to the bed. He lighted a cigarette for himself, and they lay close together again, as though the greater intimacy of their joined naked bodies was already something from the distant past.

"I'm very fond of Paul, of course," Linda admitted in a thoughtful tone. "I'm deeply devoted to him, and I'll always be grateful to him. I suppose I do love him, in a very special way. I hate that trite kind of phrase, don't you? I should have added *reserved for people like Paul.* I don't know how I could have survived these last lonely months without Paul at my side. But now that need is over. I can stand on my own two feet again, without help, without a crutch of any kind. I have my strength back, after the long post-operative illness of having lost my husband."

"You mean you don't need him any longer?" John asked, and then immediately felt ashamed for the callousness of the asking. "No. I'm sorry. I didn't really mean that the way it sounded. I think I really do understand."

"I honestly did believe, at one time, that I could be happy here with Paul," Linda continued, as though he hadn't interrupted her thoughts. "I certainly hoped I could. But I was wrong, and I'd be a fool to pretend otherwise. Oh, of course, he would do everything in his power to make me happy; he always has. But it would be unwise, for both of us. Once a patient has recovered from her illness, she's got to leave the rest home and reenter the mainstream of her own life. I really don't at all belong in a peaceful little seaside village like this."

"Too many memories?"

He felt her shake her head again. "No, I'm not afraid of memories. It's just not the place for me, that's all. Any more than it is for you, John. I could never be really content and happy here, not on a permanent basis, not with anyone. And Paul deserves much more than one of those I'm-so-terribly-grateful marriages. I'm not tossing him aside; I could never do that to Paul. I'm thinking of him as much as I am of myself."

"I'm afraid it's going to be rather hard on Paul, nevertheless, isn't it?"

"Yes, I suppose it will be, and I'm genuinely sorry for that." The glow of her cigarette lightened her face for a moment, and the shadows upon it stressed her remark of sadness. "It's another trite phrase to say he'll get over it in time, but he will, of course. After all, it's not as though I were turning him down for another man; at least his ego won't be damaged to that extent." The words sounded peculiar under the present intimate circumstances. "Paul will always be someone very special to me, and I'll always care very deeply about what happens to him. But I'll no longer really be part of it. I'm sure he'll manage to find someone more amenable to the kind of life he wants to lead here in this small seaside village that means so much to him, away from the murderous pressures that we in the city have all about us. I'm sure he'll be happy; I hope so."

"You make him sound like a paragon of all the virtues."

He was surprised that she hesitated before speaking again. "That's not exactly true, either," she then said

softly. "He's good, kind, gentle, and considerate, and yet
. . . I don't know. There's something. . . Sometimes I
sense a strange hidden darkness in him, another side
that he seldom lets me see, that perhaps he doesn't even
realize exists. He has dark moods, sudden depressions,
and then he seems like an entirely different person,
times when I feel more comfortable away from him.
Then I realize that even Paul has his troubles, but he
conceals them, even from me."

"And what of you?" John asked. "What will you do?"

There was another pause. "Go back to the city. There
will be no problems. I used to have a good position with
an advertising agency, and I'm sure I can go back to
that. Pick up again as though these last months had
never been."

John drew on his cigarette and winced as a bit of hot
ash fell on his bare chest; he brushed it away irritably.
"Are you going to tell Paul about this?"

"About us, you mean?" She shook her head again. "I
don't believe so. I would have to, of course, if I were
going to accept his offer of marriage, that would be the
only fair thing to do, but now it isn't necessary. What I
do is really no longer his concern, is it? He'd understand, of course. He always does."

He laughed slightly at the sudden slight touch of
disapproval in her voice. "You'd much rather have him
beat the shit out of me, wouldn't you, if he found out?"

Her voice attempted to match his lightness, but not
too successfully. "A woman would always prefer such a
reaction, I suppose. It makes her feel much more
valuable, much more wanted. I think secretly we all
somewhat regret that you men don't fight duels over us
any longer; it was a marvelous tradition, with the
ground mist at dawn, the silent trees, the somber figures
facing each other with raised pistols or, better still,
drawn swords, all in the name of love. Or passion. I don't
suppose many of us were really worth it all." She sighed
again. Our liberation has had its price. But, no, I won't

tell Paul anything about this. He'd always have a slightly regretful feeling that this had something to do with my decision about not marrying him." He could feel her turning towards him. "And it doesn't, of course. Nothing whatever. I had made my decision before tonight. You do realize that?"

"Yes," he said, and believed her.

They fell silent again. His fingers ran lightly over her thigh, and she lay without moving, enjoying his touch, but not inviting more, accepting it as his right. The lightning flashes became more frequent now, and the giant below the horizon stirred restless in his uncomfortable sleep, for the thunder was growing louder and clearer. The wind still had a mournful sound, as if it were seeking a long lost love, as though it felt unwanted and unneeded. John could understand such a feeling.

"And what about you, John?" she asked after a moment. "What will happen to you now?"

He hesitated, still strangely unwilling to speak of the fears and problems that so constantly occupied his mind. "Oh, I don't know, Linda. What should happen to me?"

"Oh, John, anyone can see you aren't very happy here. It's obvious matters haven't gone as well for you at Fowles House as you probably hoped they would. It hasn't been quite the seaside paradise you expected, has it?" She paused for a moment. "I never did get that invitation to see the inside of the old house. Perhaps I'll take a look after you're gone. If I'm still here. I've never even met your wife. Now I never will, of course. You asked me about Paul. What about Ruth, John? Will you tell her about this?"

He spoke without hesitation. "I don't know. Some day, I suppose. Those things have a habit of revealing themselves, sooner or later. She'll probably realize it even without my saying a word." He paused. "It's not the first time, of course."

"Will she care?"

"That's a strange question."

"Will she?"

Why pretend? He shook his head. "No. Not in the least. She would have once, but not now. I think that part of our marriage is over . . . if not all of it."

"What's happened, John?" Her voice was honestly concerned, rather than merely curious; she cared now, if not before. "Or would you rather not say?"

He reached over to the bedside table where he had noticed an ashtray, and carefully snuffed out his cigarette, slightly burning his fingers in the process.

"I really don't know," he confessed, still propped up on one elbow and looking at the shadow of her face. "Lots of things. Nothing at all. I can't say. Oh, yes, of course there is something wrong. Something has happened between us. That's all I can tell you, because that's really all I know. I'm not being devious. I can't figure it out, any of it. I've been trying to understand it, to know where it all began and how and why and where it's heading, but I can't."

"But what is it, John?" she asked, trying to understand and wanting to help.

"Ruth has changed. Changed so radically that I scarcely seem to know her. She's a totally different person. Her behaviour is . . . peculiar. She often walks about the house as though she's in a trance, as though her thoughts have gone to a distant place and a distant time. She spends most of her time out on the bluff, very hard at work, and she has little time or patience with me. I seem to be only an encumbrance to her. We scarcely speak now, except to quarrel. She often behaves in ways that I simply can't understand."

"In what ways, John?"

He had a quick mental image of Ruth's naked body resting upon the mound of earth in the cellar room, and for a moment felt an urge to describe to Linda this most baffling of incidents. He could not. Still he could not.

"It's hard to explain," he said instead. "Our marriage

was in trouble some years back, until the death of our daughter. That brought us back together again for a time, at least. Now even that is . . . well, gone again. Ruth is different. She prefers to be alone, she seems to have little feeling for me. Contempt, perhaps, but that's all. I honestly don't know what it is."

"She's had a geat sorrow, John," Linda reminded him.

"Yes. So have I. The loss was mine as well as hers."

"It's different for a woman."

"Everything's different for a woman, isn't it?"

"You've got to try to understand."

His slight laughter carried a brittle age. "Oh, Christ, Linda, that's all I've been doing through all these months. Understand! Hell, sometimes a man needs some understanding, too. If a woman really wants equality, let her act it, emotionally as well as in other ways."

"John. . ." Her tone was slightly accusing.

Again, he softened his words. "I know. That's a bit too harsh. It's just that . . . well, I simply don't know how to handle this any longer. I'm certain she was improving, coming more to grips with herself. The first few weeks in the house, she was almost like her old self again, gay and warm, almost happy." He shook his head as though trying to escape the memory. "I hoped she was finally beginning to snap out of it, that things would finally once again be what they were. She didn't seem to brood as much, or constantly talk about Elinor, as though the accident hadn't happened at all. But now, it's worse than ever, but in a different way. Now she mentions Elinor not at all. It's as though she has entered a totally different world, or become an entirely different woman, with a different past that has nothing whatever to do with me. Sometimes I feel she scarcely remembers who I am."

"Perhaps she needs more help than you can give her."

"Naturally I've thought of psychiatry, but it would be no use. Ruth would never agree. She still has that strange sense of guilt admitting to mental problems. I thought people were over that by now."

Linda hesitated for a moment, and then spoke very softly, as though uncertain of her words. "Perhaps it's the house, John.

John once would have responded instantly and negatively to such a comment; now he hesitated. Perhaps the past months had changed him more than he realized.

"No," he said, shaking his head. "No, Linda, I still won't believe in such nonsense as a troubled house. We're intelligent people."

"Truly intelligent people will admit that they might be wrong," Linda mentioned. "Is it that we are really intelligent or just smugly narrow-minded? Many highly educated people do believe in such things, you know. Perhaps atmospheres do linger, where they have been powerful enough."

"And because some obviously mentally disturbed women have been unhappy in that house and met rather unfortunate ends, Ruth should become a total stranger to her husband? No, I simply can't go along with that, Linda. It's just another form of nonsense left over from the misunderstood shadows of man's days as a dweller in caves. Like the ogres and dragons in fairy tales or the stories of saints and bloody martyrs."

"Yet martyrs did exist, and perhaps the tales of dragons are a racial inheritance of a time too distant for us to remember."

He again shook his head in the darkness. "I can't deny there is something strange about the house, something uncomfortable, even ominous, but I can't bring myself to believe that this could have such an effect on Ruth or anyone else. Lingering atmosphere? Perhaps. You can sense it in many historic places, but perhaps that arises from your own mind, from your knowledge of what has occurred there. Certainly there are people supposedly sensitive to . . . what shall I call it . . . an aura? Ruth has never been one of them, and we don't even really know what happened in Fowles House over the years to create such an aura, if anything really did, and as for Ruth herself, she knows absolutely nothing about any of it, so why should it affect her in this way?''

"We're not talking about sympathetic magic," Linda reminded him. "I don't agree that such feelings arise only from our own knowledge. An atmosphere needn't necessarily be known and recognized to have its influence upon a stranger."

"You didn't feel that way the last time we discussed the subject," he reminded her.

"I know. Perhaps I can admit I may have been wrong. John, why don't you just take her away?''

"I've thought of it. I'm sure it would help to get her away. I've even mentioned it to her. The lease hasn't much longer to go, and of course I have no intention of buying the house. But Ruth refuses to leave. She won't even discuss the possibility of leaving. For some reason, she's become very strongly attached to the house. I wouldn't be at all surprised if she tried to buy it for herself.''

"But if she leaves you, John. . ."

"If. That's the big word there, Linda. I'm not at all sure she does."

"I don't believe love can die that easily," she responded firmly, "regardless of the influences and pressures brought against it. Or am I just being romantic?''

"I suppose you are. There's really nothing wrong with that. I imagine I'm something of a romantic myself. I battle against change, particularly in the people who are close and dear to me. We think they'll always be with us, as we've known them. The loss of Elinor was the first major change against which I was so utterly helpless, and once something like that happens, you doubt your ability to do anything about other changes. I hoped bringing Ruth here would help her, but it hasn't. The situation has become more than a little frightening. Yet, is running away from it really any kind of answer? I would always be afraid it would happen again. My confidence in my ability to control my own life has been badly shaken."

"But then what will you do, John?"

"I don't know," he admitted. "My grandmother is arriving here tomorrow. She's a marvelous old woman, perhaps a little strange in her outmoded ways, but sharp and perceptive. She's always had a very ungrandmotherly interest in curious things of this sort, claims to have second sight, ESP, that sort of thing. Her greatest pride is that she has seen the haunting at Hampton Court, or claims to have at any rate, and her greatest disappointment is that she's never sen a UFO; she believes in them implicitly. I've always laughed at her ideas, in a good-natured way, of course. Now I'm not so sure. Ruth has always been extremely fond of her. It may do some good to have her here for a few days."

"And if it doesn't?"

"Then I don't know."

Linda moved closer to him, resting her head on his shoulder, and he placed a comforting arm about her. They lay there for several moments, like long time lovers now content merely in the nearness of each other, not requiring the exhausting mechanics of physical love to prove their mutual devotion.

"Poor John," she murmured, and he felt the touch of her soft breath on his bare shoulder. "Surely it will come right for you, one of these days. I hope so."

"When shall I see you again?" he asked, lightly pressing his lips to her warm, smooth cheek.

She shook her head, while withdrawing slightly from him. "I don't believe you will, John. What good would it do either of us? We mustn't permit this to develop into something we can't control. It's so much better . . . I'll be leaving very soon now, I think. There's nothing to keep me here any longer, and the sooner I leave the better. Don't you agree?"

John nodded, knowing there was no need for further

words. She was right, of course. He had made the suggestion merely because it seemed the proper and chivalrous thing to say. They had served each other's needs, and now it was best that they go their separate ways. They would both remember, and the remembrance would bring them comfort in future lonely days and leave no trace of bitterness that would inevitably follow the ultimate dissolution of a longer, more intangling relationship. People should love either very briefly or permanently, or not at all. A love that withers with boredom and disinterest is an injustice to itself. At any rate, there was here surely no question of love. They were both being quite superbly sensible. Or was civilized the more acurate term?

He eased his slightly cramped arm from about her shoulders and swung his legs over the side of the bed, sitting for a moment, knowing he shouldn't delay his departure, yet a bit uneasy about the moment.

"I suppose it's best for me to be going now," he confessed. "Whether Ruth wants me there or not, I'm always a little uneasy when she's left alone in that house for too long. So many things could happen." It suddenly struck him as ridiculous that he should be speaking of his wife at a time like this. "And there is a storm coming, too."

He dressed quickly, without turning on the light, and while he clumsily fumbled into his clothing Linda lay quietly in the bed, watching the movements of his shadowed form, looking at his smooth, strong body in the flashes of lightning that were like lantern-slide views of her own past. She lit a second cigarette and tried to subdue the feeling of . . . disappointment? Relief? Sorrow? Regret for something that might have been but now could never be?

John was pleased Linda made no move to turn on the light. He felt strange about this parting, somewhat guilty, and more unhappy than he would have expected. There was no reason for it, he again told himself. They had both known what they were doing, they had both agreed to the impossibility of a continuing relationship. Hell, how many times in his life had he played out just exactly this same scene? It had never bothered him before. Yet, he was glad he could not see Linda's face.

He finished dressing and stood awkwardly in the center of the room, at a loss what to say. Perhaps nothing at all would be best. Just open the door and walk out, and that would be that. The only difference between this night and the last rather sordid escapade in a rather dingy city apartment was that he wouldn't slip a twenty dollar bill to the dresser on the way out. No. That wasn't really the only difference.

He walked to the door and hesitated with his hand on the knob. Linda slipped quietly from the bed and came to him.

"Goodbye, John."

She placed the tips of her fingers to his cheek and then moved them to his lips, almost carressingly, as though wanting to remember their touch. He released the doorknob and gathered her supple naked body into his arms and, for a brief moment, held her close against him, smelling the warm, sweet fragrance of her flesh, feeling the brush of her moist lips against his cheek, the soft pressure of her breasts against his chest. For a moment desire returned, strong, almost overpowering. But no. It was too late now.

"Take care, John. Take care."

He quickly, lightly, kissed her on the lips, and he knew there was no need for words between them. This was done now, over. He opened the door and stepped into the empty corridor; she instantly closed the door behind him, softly but firmly, and he knew she would not open it to him again. He heard the click of the lock, and it was like the turning off of a certain part of his life.

He stood for a moment in the dimly lighted hallway with its brown carpet, faded geometric wallpaper, and frozen green-leaved potted plants, wondering at the salty taste on his lips, refusing to accept the possibility of Linda's tears. The chapter was closed and he mustn't think of it any longer. He walked briskly down the corridor without looking back at the closed door.

John was surprised by the intensity of the darkness when he stepped through the doorway of the small building where Linda lived. There was nowhere the slightest sound or sign of life or movement. The sky was leaden, a solid black canopy drawn to conceal the sins of the world, and although he knew the bay was just at the end of the street, he could see only the impenetrable wall of darkness. It was was though someone had cut off the rest of the world. He was almost blinded by a sudden intensely brilliant sheet of lightning that showed him the dark, sleeping buildings across the way and the descent of the narrow street to the wharfs. The wind had risen, moaning with lonely fury as it swept up the street, blowing the hair about his head.

He paused for a moment on the dark sidewalk, somewhat refreshed by the touch of the strong breeze that was a further promise of the coming storm. His head had cleared, although he was aware of a dull throbbing at the very base of his skull, probably the precursor of a good-sized headache, the natural and justified result of more drinks than he could clearly remember. Indeed, much of the evening was already becoming rather distressingly vague in his mind. Probably it was just as well.

He found the darkness confusing, and for a moment was not certain of his exact whereabouts. He had never bothered much to explore the dull and uninteresting little village, seldom wandering from Main Street itself in to the brief and drab little side streets, and in the storm-deepened darkness he did not immediately recognize his surroundings, until he saw the darker hulk of the hotel looming against the night sky. He glanced at the single street lamp near the corner and, to his surprise, noted his small car parked on the opposite side of the street. He had no recollection of having driven it there. Perhaps Linda had done the driving; he doubted that he had been in any condition to do so, and wondered wryly how he had been able to participate in any of the more intimate acts that had followed.

He stepped into the car and paused to light a cigarette. His mouth was painfully dry, with the uncomfortable stuffiness of cotton, and his stomach felt squeamish. His eyes fell on the illuminated face of the clock set in the dashboard and he noticed it was not yet quite midnight; he had thought it much later. This rip-roaring town really retired early, he thought.

He started the car and turned off the side road and into Main Street, driving slowly, unconsciously looking for some sign of life, merely to remind him he was not the only person in the village. There were few lights to be seen. The local desire for retirement at an early hour had been sharpened by the threat of the approaching storm which had driven even the few night owls to the security of their homes. The hotel was silent, with light streaming through its open doors, and there was light in the *Whaler's Rest*, with the faint sound of music issuing from its open entry, from which a yellow bar of illumination sliced into the darkness. A night lamp glowed in the rear of the grocery store, and the ranks of stacked canned goods stood like metallic sentinels in the half-darkness. A tangled mass of rope and tackle had turned the shadowed fishing-gear shop into a nightmarish web of giant spiders.

He was further surprised when he saw a light burning in the Sanders Real Estate office, and then recognized Paul's car parked directly before the door; he remembered Linda's comment that Paul was expected back in town either tomorrow or sometime this evening. Linda would have her difficult moments in the morning, when Paul called upon her to give an answer to his proposal of marriage. It would be hard on him. Poor Paul. He was a nice guy.

John slowed the car. He was still convinced that Paul had the answers to some very important questions, and he had been wanting for some time to confront him in hopes of securing a resolution of the problems that now confronted Ruth and himself. He drew the car up before the office and came to a stop, drawing heavily on his cigarette as he stared at the light glowing dimly through the office window. Linda's office was in darkness brightened only by the flow of light streaming through the open connecting door to Paul's inner office.

Frightened by the rapid deterioration of their life at Fowles House, John had anxiously awaited Paul's return, determined finally to learn the truth, but now again he hesitated and could not quite understand why. Perhaps he was fearful of hearing what Paul might have to tell him, somehow sensing that his life and Ruth's might never be the same again, clinging like a child to the vain hope that matters might yet straighten themselves out without further revelations that could only increase his fear. Ignore what you don't want to see, and it may go away. Ruth would sooner or later get over her current strangeness, they would return to the city, pick up their normal existence, in time, forget what had happened here.

That was ridiculous, of course. It was clear that Ruth was getting worse rather than better. If he learned the truth, he might in some way manage to stop what was happening, to bring Ruth back to her senses and return sanity to their marriage. It was possible there lay great danger in every hour of delay.

John grasped the handle of the car door, then released it again, shaking his head. No. This still was not the time. Perhaps tomorrow; things had gone this far, and surely one more day's delay would not make that much difference. Paul had just returned. It was late and Ruth was waiting for him at Fowles House, surrounded by the mystery that had become so terrible a part of their lives. Waiting? Well, perhaps not. But she had been alone for too long in that strangely violent and indifferent mood in which he had left her. He felt concern for the first time that evening. He could not, at this late hour, burst in upon Paul who had possibly returned only moments before, and pour out his somewhat hysterical tale like a frightened schoolboy. His mind was now too confused, still considerably dulled by his over indulgence in liquor and the exhaustion of his long needed sexual escapade. He would have to wait until he was calmer, when he could sit down with Paul and discuss the entire matter sensibly and rationally and come to a definite determination of what was to be done.

And there was Grandmother Ellen, who would be arriving now very shortly, perhaps as early as tomorrow. Since receiving word of her pending visit, John had clung to the febrile possibility that his wise old grandmother might be of some help to him in this terrible quandry in which he now found himself. This was not merely a reversion to the days of his childhood, when his grandmother had seemed able to resolve any and all his little problems. Ellen Perrine had always been fascinated by the unusual, the unexplained. the macabre, and in her travels about the world she had seen and encountered much that would have baffled others. Indominable, insatiably curious, totally without superstitious fear, she had eagerly sought out such experiences, and they had brought her an insight and a wisdom not possessed by many. What would she make of the strange events here at Fowles House? Wait and see what that canny old woman would have to say.

John would not admit even to himself that he could not now, in this silent darkness, face Paul when he had just come from the bed of the woman Paul hoped to marry.

John tossed his cigarette through the open window, started up the car again, and drove swiftly down the deserted Main Street towards the greater darkness of Fowles House.

CHAPTER FIFTEEN

PAUL watched John's car move away, and stared for a moment longer into the again empty village square, at the vacant park benches where during the day housewives sat and discussed their meaningless lives and childish gossip, at the bulk of the town hall with its broken tower clock whose face could not be seen since its illumination had also long since failed and apparently no one was interested enough about time to repair it, at the gleam of light from the lobby of the hotel. Lightning flashed and the whale immolated atop the church spire seemed to flick its tail in defiance. A dark figure stepped from the entry of the hotel bar and, staggering slightly, headed away from the square. That would be Hank Burrows; every little village has its town drunk.

Paul sighed and wondered how he could have spent all of his life in this narrow and constricting world, filled with uninteresting people with whom he had nothing whatever in common, bound to each other only through common need and the inherited fear of loneliness and death. He sipped again the drink he held in his hand and closed his eyes, wanting if only for a moment to blot out the drabness of his life.

The sound of the approaching car had taken Paul from his inner office into Linda's anteroom. He had known it would be John; it could be no one else at this hour. Standing in the shadows at the window, he had then watched the car pull to a stop and seen John's brief period of indecision, wondering if he would dare come into the office, and not surprised that he lacked the courage to do so.

The hum of the car's motor faded in the distance and was lost; the usual evening silence of the village returned, seeming somehow even more intense than before. Paul turned from the window and, himself a trifle unsteady, returned to his own office. Most of the room was in deep shadow. The three-way lamp on his large desk had been lighted to its lowest level and cast but little reflection about the room, throwing its pool of light upon the cleared surface of the desk. Beside the aluminum decanter on its tray on the corner of the desk was an open bottle of Scotch; newly opened just that evening, it was already almost half empty. Paul had been drinking heavily since his return, and as he stepped into his office, the light for a moment seemed to swim before his eyes. He walked over to the windows, cursing as he struck his leg against the jutting edge of the oversized desk, and stood staring out across the harbor, its emptiness fitfully lighted by the constantly more frequent flashes of lightning.

He wondered what he would have said to John had he stepped out of his car and entered the office. Why, hello John, nice to see you. I hope you had a pleasant evening? Perhaps he would have simply ignored the entire matter, but that would have been both difficult and unmanly. He pictured John now, driving perhaps blissfully through the darkness along the beach, fresh from his conquest of the woman he, Paul, had intended to marry.

Surely it would not have surprised either John or Linda that Paul's first thought upon returning to the village after his extended absence would have been to see Linda. He had driven with mounting excitement towards her apartment, longing to see her once again, to feel her warmth, to see her smile. It had been difficult, these past few weeks, without her.

He had almost brought his car to a stop when he noticed John's vehicle parked just across the street. There could be no doubting its ownership; the unimaginative villagers did not go in for cars of so bright a hue. It was no indictment of either John or Linda that, somehow, Paul did not for a moment doubt the meaning of its presence there; after all, they were none of them children any longer. Conquering an almost irresistible impulse to burst in upon them, he had continued on past the building and returned to his office. He had sat there now for almost two hours, drinking, imagining the activities of his two friends, trying to sort out the sudden confusion that filled his mind.

What was he to do now? Should he be noble and make no mention of his knowledge, pretend to Linda that he was totally unaware of what had happened during his absence, assuming of course that Linda herself would make no mention of it? Could a man behave in such a way and still retain his self-respect? He did not doubt his continuing love for Linda, but he strongly doubted his ability to conceal from her his bitter disappointment and disillusionment. This would be forever a silent barrier between them, like hidden shoals and rocks at the entrance of an inviting harbor.

And what of John Kendall, this man he had befriended and who had now so basely betrayed him, who had taken advantage of his absence to take away from him what he treasured most?

With an angry gesture, Paul drained his drink and made his way uncertainly to the bottle on the desk. Although he poured with intense concentration, somewhat hazily noting the level of the liquid, his hand seemed to tremble slightly, and a bit of the whiskey poured over the glass and onto the tray. He drank quickly and filled the glass again. The light on the desk flickered for a moment as a heavy roll of thunder caused the pictures on the wall to tremble as in an earthquake.

For some seconds, Paul stood beside the desk, wavering slightly, resting his left hand on its surface to provide a support; a sudden spasm caught his right hand and some of the whiskey splashed onto the smooth top of the desk. He closed his eyes and moaned slightly, reeling as he felt the whirling vortex of the world about him. John and Linda. Linda and John. He seemed to see their faces before him, laughing at him, mocking him, he saw their embrace, their kiss, the joining of their naked bodies. . .

He hurled his glass across the room; it struck the wall with a loud crash, spraying whiskey over the framed portraits of local rentable properties, then fell heavily and unbroken to the carpet. Wringing his hands in impotent and impatient anger, Paul began to pace the small open area before the desk, walking up and down, back and forth, four steps either way. His pace slowly became heavier and more determined, that of an older and larger man, totally without the natural effortless grace of his regular step, and in the erratic lighting of the small room he was like a fretful captain pacing the bridge of his storm-battered vessel.

He fell heavily against the desk and the light flickered again as he poured liquor into the second glass, quickly drank it down, and immediately poured another.

The sudden haziness continued in his mind, the strange sense of disorientation, as it had with such disturbing frequency during the past few weeks, during those moments of stress and anger, when he seemed to lose awareness of himself, when all the world became strange and alien. He looked with widened eyes at the surroundings that had suddenly become totally unfamiliar to him, raising his glance for the tangled tracery of rigging, listening for the pistol-like flapping of the canvas and the shushing of the boiling waters against wooden walls. Where was he? What was this strange place?

He staggered to the window and in the lightning he saw the harbor now crowded with mighty wooden vessels moving boldly through the heaving seas, their decks streaming with cascades of white water, torn canvas flapping like a bird's broken wings. The scent of the sea came to him, sharp and bracing. He was back in his own world, back where he belonged.

A strange strength and sense of power flooded through him. The weakness was gone. He was a man, and he would act like a man, generous with his friends and ruthless with his enemies. Yes, he had enemies, but he well knew how to deal with them. The sea was a harsh teacher, and its lessons are not easily forgotten. Many men had opposed him, and their fleshless bones now whitened on small uncharted islands or served as havens for the crawling crustaceans on the bottom of the sea. Yes, he knew how to deal with his enemies.

A dazzling burst of lightning whitened the entire sky, followed by a peal of thunder as deafening as the great guns of Waterloo. The light on the desk flickered once, twice, then went out, plunging the room into darkness. Again and again, lightning outlined the firm figure standing before the window, his stance firm and decisive as he raised his glass and drank again. He laughed. His voice carried a note of triumph.

In the strong profile, the cruel mouth and hard eyes, John Kendall would have recognized little of his betrayed friend Paul Sanders, but he would have been strongly reminded of the strange staring faces that seemed to watch his every movement in the corridors and the rooms of Fowles House.

CHAPTER SIXTEEN

DURING the next few days, a cloud of darkness seemed to hover over the pointed glabes of Fowles House and seep slowly down towards the village itself. The air remained almost unbearably hot and humid, and the sky seemed permanently covered with thick gray clouds that tumbled over each other in some heavenly contest for supremacy, their dark swollen bodies rolling and touched with streaks of livid purple. The sun never showed itself, and the world appeared as it must have been during the antediluvian days when the planet was wrapped in an all-encompassing blanket of cloud. Both day and night, the coast was struck by frequent electrical storms, brief in duration but of unusual severity, in which the blinding crackling bolts of lightning seemed tossed at the helpless village by the hand of an angry god. The streets streamed constantly with rain water, the square with its flowers drooping from rain saturation was deserted and forlorn, and the heavy rain beat a relentlessly monotonous tattoo upon the house tops that often made normal conversation difficult.

The villagers grumbled with irritation and discontent. Never had the season been so dark, so dreary, so violent. The village was bypassed by the usual trickle of tourists and travelers . . . a trickle at any rate becoming smaller with every year . . . and business suffered. Tempers were short, faces long and unsmiling. Rain-imprisoned children wore on the taut nerves of their weary parents and the fishing vessels strained restlessly at the hawsers that bound them to their wharves. Most commercial activity, save for essential trade at the grocer and the pharmacy came to a complete stop. The single motion picture house presented an additional showing each day, for the cinema is a good place to forget what one wants to forget, as is a bar; the *Whaler's Rest* was doing the best business in town.

Paul spent those dreary days alone in his office, with nothing to do, pacing the floor, drinking too heavily, staring morosely through the window at the rain-pocked gray waters of the harbor, struggling with his own fears as the violence of the weather mirrored the growing uncertainty within his own mind. The confusion of his thoughts frightened him. Often he was totally unaware of his surroundings or his time. As he listened to the pounding of the rain and stared vacantly at the weather-bound harbor, strange thoughts and images entered his mind, thoughts that should not and could not have belonged to him, thoughts of older and darker times, visions of the sea like memories of something he could never have personally experienced. His imagination was filled with billowing canvas and crashing breakers, and often there was a darkness and a bloodiness suggested in these thoughts that snapped him back to reality and left him trembling and perspiring with fear. He thought he might be losing his reason. These terrible memories belonged to someone else. How had he come upon them?

The sensation was not entirely new. Throughout his life, even as a child, he had experienced these peculiar lapses of memory, these shadowy incursions into his mind of memories that did not belong to him. He had thought it was something that occasionally happened to everyone, as someone who is born with color blindness assumes everyone suffers from the same affliction. These strange thoughts would come to him at any time, without warning, and he would briefly suffer from a unnerving disassociation from his surroundings. Companions would then look at him with a touch of fear, for it seemed to them he had suddenly become a stranger. The strangeness passed for a time during his period of military service, but had appeared again on his return to the village.

During the past year or two, the lapses of identification had become more frequent, lasting for longer periods. He seemed to move between two different world and two different times, and more and more he found difficulty in understanding to which world he truly belonged. Now, suddenly, it was growing steadily worse, and the fear of madness haunted him.

Never had he felt so completely alone, and the aloneness served to heighten the fears of his thoughts and dreams. Even Linda could provide no comfort. He saw her only once, the morning after his return, when she had entered the office to find him gaunt, dissheveled and bleary-eyed from drink and lack of sleep. He stared at her silently, his eyes strangely unfocused and reddened as she told him, as gently and kindly as she could, that she felt their marriage would be a very serious mistake for both of them, that she was leaving the village and returning to the city to take up her life again where she had left it upon her husband's death. He listened to her concerned words of gratitude and affection, slumped in his chair and occasionally raising a glass to his lips, increasing her discomfort and embarrassment with the strange silence of his stare. When Linda had finished her carefully prearranged speech, the silence fell between them, marked only by the ever present and constant drumming of the rain. She looked at him for a moment, and he returned the stare without a word. She turned and left the office, knowing she would not return.

Paul remained seated and watched her leave, silently closing the door behind her. For a brief moment, he felt the emptiness of his loss. He had loved Linda since the day Harry had first brought her to the village, watched his friend's happiness with an aching jealousy he had desperately attempted to conceal. With Harry's death, he had felt a rush of hope that now he might have his chance. He had kept Linda near him, had surrounded her with attention and love, certain that one day she would be his.

But now it was all over, and he knew why. Not a word had been said about John Kendall, yet Paul knew it was he, this stranger with a wife of his own, who had destroyed their chance of happiness.

The sorrow faded. Paul's lips became harshly severe lines and he tightened his grip on the glass when he thought of Kendall. His eyes became darkly shadowed with hatred of this man who had betrayed him, and once again his mind became filled with visions of revenge. Only the weak could forget what had been done to him, and Paul knew suddenly he was no longer weak, but overpoweringly strong, a master of men. There would be a way.

And suddenly he thought of Ruth, the wife of his betrayer, and a strange, chill smile crossed his severe face.

The rain-thrummed silence was shattered by the jangling of the phone. The sound startled Paul, and he stared at the dark instrument. It seemed a noise unknown to him, one that did not belong to his life or time. It rang again, and Paul closed his eyes, as though this would shut out the noise. Reality returned at once, and he opened his eyes again, as though hearing the ring of the phone for the first time. Who could it be? He was in no mood for idle conversation. He let it ring once, then twice more, and then raised the receiver from its cradle.

"Hello," he said softly.

"Paul. It's John Kendall."

Kendall. Paul tightened his grip on the phone. "Yes?"

"I'm calling from the hotel, Paul," John said. "I'd like to see you I . . . wasn't certain you were back."

No, of course he wasn't. "I'm afraid I can't see you just now, John." The voice was flat, emotionless; on the other end of the line, John scarcely recognized it. "I have a geat deal to do; I was away longer than I had expected."

"Yes, of course," John agreed after a moment, puzzled by the touch of unfriendliness in the tone. "Well, look, Paul, my grandmother is arriving this Saturday, and we'd like to have a little dinner for her at the house on Sunday evening. We'd be very pleased if you would come. I know it's very short notice. . ."

Dinner at Fowles House. "All right, John," Paul responded, still in the same toneless voice. "I'd be glad to."

"Fine. Will you bring Linda?"

There was only the slightest hesitation. "I think you had better ask her yourself."

So Linda had given Paul her answer, John thought; that would explain his tone. "Well, all right. See you then."

Paul slowly replaced the receiver and leaned back in his chair. He pictured Fowles House rising against the dark sky, its gables, its shadowed Widow's Walk, its strange aura of the past. That was the proper place for him. He felt suddenly anxious to be there, to walk its high-ceilinged rooms and be surrounded by mementoes of the past. What past? Why did he feel he belonged there?

And suddenly he had a vision of Ruth. Kendall's woman. Strange that he should see her thus, lying naked upon barren ground. Strange, too, that he should immediately recognize her surroundings. He had never been in the cellar of the old house.

Linda politely but firmly rejected John's invitation to

the dinner for his grandmother, and she knew John was not surprised. He had surely called merely out of courtesy. They had agreed they would not see each other again. He had neither spoken nor even hinted at what had happened between them, but surely it was in his mind as much as it was in hers. To see each other again would only weaken her resolve for what had to be done. Someday, perhaps, they could meet again, but not yet.

She stood at the window, smoking heavily, staring out into the gray day. The clouds had lowered and the heavy rain had, for the moment, changed to a light, dreary drizzle; she could only vaguely see the harbor.

She thought of Paul and realized, again, that somehow he knew what had happened between herself and John; only this could have caused his unspeaking reaction to her refusal of marriage. It was not impossible that he might have seen John leaving her building, and it would not have taken much imagination to guess at the truth. She was genuinely sorry for that. The incident with John had really had nothing to do with her decision, but Paul would now never believe that. It would have made his rejection somewhat easier to bear if he had not known.

Linda again felt a surge of affection and concern for Paul. He had looked so haggard, so worn; he was not accustomed to such heavy drinking. But there was something else, something even more disturbing, something almost frightening. That strange look in his face, the dullness of his eyes as he sat so silently staring at her while she told him of her plans. The eyes were different, and it was not only drink that was responsible. She had felt suddenly uncomfortable in his presence, as though something had changed him. The warmth and friendliness were gone. There seemed no love in him. He had suddenly become a total stranger, someone she did not know and did not want to know. There was a quiet, ominous wildness about him, an aura of brutality that she had never before seen there. It frightened her.

She sighed and crushed out her cigarette. It no longer

mattered. On Sunday she would leave this village and never return. The memories would go with her. Perhaps some day times would be happy again.

In those days, Ruth seemed to have lost all track of time. Every day seemed like every other day, and yet different from any days she had ever known. The weather prevented her from continuing with her work on the cliff top, but she was content to remain in the house, wandering in a dreamlike trance through the dark corridors and the lofty, sea-filled rooms, her hands touching like a caress all the momentoes of another age. She seemed more at home here than anywhere else she had ever been. The aura of the past soothed her; she felt at one with the house and with all in it. She stared at the portraits on the walls, those severe and almost brutal faces, and she felt they were friends she had once lost and now found again. She knew she was waiting for something, but what that something was she could not understand. At times she became impatient, but always that impatience was soothed by the knowledge that the time would come, and soon. She need only wait.

There were still moments of confusion, brief periods of terrible fear, when she again became briefly aware of herself and of the strange new world into which she had somehow drifted. Then the house itself became a strange and alien place, and at the back of her mind was the terror of something unknown and unseen, something evil and deadly. Then she looked at John, the husband once dearly loved who had become only an irritating stranger to her, and he could see the fear shadowed in her eyes. In those ever rarer moments, she would cling to him, and he felt the trembling of her slight, slender form. He tried to soothe her, but she would not be soothed, for the fear then was too great.

But always it would pass, almost as quickly as it had come, and Ruth was again the cold, aloof, indifferent woman who had neither need for nor patience with the man she had married. She would laugh then at her own foolish fears, calling them the lingering nightmares of a lost childhood. She would refuse even to discuss leaving Fowles House, now or at any other time, and John's insistence would make her angry and brutal. This was her home. This was where she belonged. Her destiny waited for her here, and she would never leave.

John was confused by Ruth's attitude towards his grandmother's pending visit. At first, she had seemed somewhat resentful of this unasked and unexpected intrusion into her own private world, then merely indifferent, but gradually her attitude had changed and apparently she came not only to accept the idea but to look forward to it. It was Ruth herself who had suggested the dinner on Sunday evening, her first attempt at socializing since their arrival at Fowles House.

"Why shouldn't we have a dinner party?" she asked in response to John's expression of gratification. "I've always liked Grandmother Ellen, and we should make something of a fuss over her when she's coming all this way just to see us. Besides, women have always been welcome in this house. They have a special place here."

And, somehow, there was a tone in her voice that chilled him.

John's fear had grown into a choking panic that seized him every moment of both day and night. He knew something was terribly wrong, that something incomprehensible had entered their lives and would not easily leave it again. He watched the changes in Ruth's expressions and mannerisms, and realized this woman he had loved through the years had indeed become a total stranger to him. She walked slowly and silently about the house in the rain-filled darkness of those days, her wide eyes consuming everything like someone who, returning to a childhood home after too long an absence, must hungrily reacquaint herself with everything she had once known. She drifted like a wraith through the rooms, always with that green scarf peculiarly wrapped about her neck, not even seeing him or being aware of his presence. When he spoke to her at such times, she either did not answer or perhaps simply did not hear him. She seemed to have slipped into another world, or another time. On the infrequent occasions when she did speak to John, her words were strange and senseless, like the meanderings of the mindless, wild and senseless fantasies of the swirling green depths of the sea, of the cool comforting darkness of the wet abyss, and of something for which she waited confidently, something that would bring a new rich meaning into her life.

When he questioned her about the ever present green scarf, Ruth abruptly brushed aside his comment with the remark that she found it comfortable.

But still, though very rarely now, there were those brief times when that coldly hostile face would suddenly change, as though an emotionless mask had fallen to reveal the true features that lay behind it and then, for just a few moments, Ruth would be Ruth again, that lovely and charming companion whom John had first met years ago in the beauty of a tropical night, and with whom he had hoped to spend the remaining years of his life, the young girl filled with the vitality and curiosity of life, who laughed freely and easily, who clung to him for the love she had always needed. For just a few moments, then, he would hold her close again, sensing the fear that filled her and which had to be stilled.

And then he would feel her stiffen and slowly draw away again. The mask returned and there was cold hostility in her eyes. She moved away from him and seemed to forget the few moments of weakness and fear, to be ashamed of them. She became again the woman he had never known.

John lay sleepless at night, alone in that great bed where once the evil Captain Fowles had slept, and he stared up at the shadowed ceiling and wondered why this had happened to them, why their life together had become so disrupted, when and how it had all begun, and how it was to end. Terror filled him as he listened to the silence of that big house, broken only by the distant thunder of the waves lashing the defenseless beach, and the frequent patter and pounding of the rain. He would think back over their years together, Ruth's almost childish happiness in the beauties of Paris, her joy in the musical aura of Vienna, her artist's ecstacy in the honey-columned world of ancient Greece; he remembered the first happy years of their marriage, the warmth of their love, their need for each other, the all too brief joy with little Elinor, and he would turn his face to the pillow so that Ruth, sleeping her own strange dreams in the next room, would not hear his sobs of sorrow and loneliness.

It would not, it could not, last much longer. John sensed that. Something was now approaching that would bring this all to an end, and he both wondered and feared what that end might be, and in the darkness he reached out for the hope that the twice-delayed arrival of Allen Pirenne might somehow serve to avert the darkness that hovered above them.

CHAPTER SEVENTEEN

TRAVELING a considerable distance by public vehicle of any kind was a totally new and not particularly pleasant experience for Ellen Pirenne. Fastidious almost to the point of fanaticism, she found the close proximity of others, particularly total strangers, both uncomfortable and often quite distasteful. To one accustomed throughout her life to travel by strictly first-class accomodation, to the use of private cabins and sleek limousines, the more public means of transportation were something of which she had very little knowledge and which therefore came to her as something of a startling revelation, one that did not particularly please her.

Ellen had at first completely refused to believe the statement that a public bus was the only means by which she could hope to reach that ridiculous little fishing village where her grandson and his wife were spending their rather juvenile and self-pitying period of total withdrawal from the rest of the world. There was no airport anywhere near the town, and the closest railroad station would deposit her an appalling three hours (by road) distant from the village. She quite naturally assumed there would at least be a limousine service linking the village with that town where the railroad ended, and she inquired about such a service before boarding the ugly black train with its dust-streaked windows.

"Oh, no, ma'am," the railroad porter told her. "Don't zackly know what you mean by a lim'zene service, but ain't no cars going back and forth like in the city."

"Well, then, a taxi," Ellen suggested. "If the town has a railway station, surely it has a taxi service."

"Oh, sure thing." The porter hooked his fingers in the gold watch chain that crossed his ample waistline like a caravan of camels crossing a desert. "They got a real good taxi service right there at the end of the line. Two cars, one of 'em almost brand new. Gonna get a third one, too, real soon now. Kept up good, too. Clean, good shape. But Frank, he needs both them cars right there in town for his own regular customers. Ain't about to be interested in takin' one of 'em out of town on a six-hour round trip."

Well, after all, Ellen certainly expected to pay for any such service, and pay well, too, but the answer remained a very firm and unshaking negative. You want to go from one town to the other, the only way was by public bus, 'less, of course, you got a car of your own, which Ellen did not have any longer.

It was really quite outlandish and unbelievable, a tremendous irritation and a sign of primitivism that Ellen had thought had long since vanished from the American scene, even in such out-of-the-way spots as this, and for the first time she regretted having two years before finally disposed of her own limousine and chauffeur as unnecessary extravagances, considering the really excellent limousine service available in such cities as London, Paris and Vienna, where she so comfortably spent most of her time, and also in view of the really appalling inflation that was taking so much of the true comfort out of life. Who could have imagined at that time that she would one day be forced to travel along a dusty, deserted seaside road leading to a small fishing village that few people even suspected existed?

Indeed, she would even at this point have abandoned the entire project had it not been for her urgent desire to see her grandson, and her genuine concern about his current way of life. She had not seen John since the death of little Elinor, that sweetly adorable little great-grandchild whom Ellen still missed more than she could say, and she had grown steadily more concerned about him; that concern had finally induced her to change her plans to attend the Langelenie Festival in Copenhagen and to chance the rigors of a visit to the rugged seacoast of New England where John and Ruth presently made their home.

The trip on the train was from the start not a very pleasant indication of what was to come. There were no first-class coaches, and she was forced to tolerate screaming little children with chocolate-smeared mouths running unsteadily up and down the swaying aisle, and with food peddlars constantly urging her to buy a bar of melting candy or a dry sandwich wrapped in dusty looking plastic bags. She sighed as she thought of the comfortable, civilized, semi-private first-class coaches on the express trains that ran between the capitals of Europe.

As she finally stepped from the train, tightly holding onto her one large suitcase since she had seen no one she felt could be really trusted with it, Ellen found that even the weather was going to add to the unpleasantness of the trip. It was insufferably hot, the sky was thickly covered with tumbling gray-black clouds, and a light saturating rain was already falling; there was a faint distant flash of lightning, followed by a low mutter of thunder, like a low growl of warning about an approaching storm. She walked with her firm, determined step to the ticket window and demanded of the rather seedy looking man behind the grill the exact and precise spot where this bus was loading that would take her on the interminable trip to her grandson, and the exact moment of its departure.

The ticket seller looked with some surprise, and perhaps with a bit of amusement, at the small but quite proper and firm-lipped old lady grimly grasping her single suitcase, rather incongruously in this heat, clad in a high-necked black dress with white frills upon the collar and the long sleeves, her tiny hands encased in white gloves and a pillbox of a hat perched squarely atop her beautiful white hair. (The toque hat was designed after those worn by that dear departed Queen Mary, to whom Ellen had once been presented at a simply marvelous lawn party at Buckingham Palace shortly before the old queen's unfortunate demise; it was one of her most treasured memories.)

"Bus loads right 'round the corner over there, lady," the railroad man informed her, removing a toothpick from his mouth and pointing with it just past the unpainted depot building.

"Thank you, my good man," Ellen replied with just the proper tone of hauteur considering his position. "And just at what time does it depart?"

The man grinned and scratched the top of his head, further mussing his already uncombed scrabble of red hair. "Well, now, a bit hard to say about that. Depends on when Jim . . . that's the driver . . . has enough people on board to make the trip worthwhile. Any time 'tween now an' half an hour from now, I guess."

The bus was something that might still be seen in some of the old Hollywood films (in the days when the cinema was still worth going to; Ellen had not now seen one for many years, they were so filled with filth and ear-shattering noise, and all those dear stars were long gone), when traveling cross-country by bus strangely seemed the romantic thing to do. It was large, square and bulky, its dirty yellow body perched high on large wheels encrusted with dried mud, its small windows thickly covered with grime. The interior smelled strongly of petrol and other less easily identifiable odors, and the seats were hard, narrow and most uncomfortable; Ellen almost expected to see Gable and Colbert sleeping on each other's shoulders on the rear porch.

A large, hairy, sweating man wearing a badly stained undershirt (once no doubt white, but now gray and smudged with remnants of past greasy meals) and a several days stubble of reddish beard came to her rescue and easily hoisted her suitcase to the sagging overhead rack, and Ellen, after carefully brushing the lumpy cushion with her handkerchief, took her seat beside the window and prepared to suffer through the next undoubtedly unpleasant three hours.

The bus did not fill completely, but there was a rather bewildering array of people such as Ellen had never come into contact with in all her days, and she stared at them with some amazement and not a bit of uneasiness.

There were several overly-enthusiastic young couples who leapt into the bus like Crusaders attacking an infidel fortress. All were most improperly attired for travel. The girls were far too scantily clad in halters tight enough to over-emphasize their nubile charms and amazingly brief shorts of yellow, pink and white. They were followed by rather uncouth young men with wild hair worn too long to be attractive, big, brawny and deeply tanned, clad in chest-revealing T-shirts and clinging faded dungarees. All were chewing gum with an almost fanatical frenzy, and Ellen winced at their squealing, almost hysterical laughter as they ran heavily down the aisle, causing the bus to rock from side to side, and threw themselves onto the rear seats where their little pettings and explorations would not be so easily observed.

Several weary, rather tawdry-looking housewives wheezed aboard, grumbling about the height of the step as they were forced to maneuver with arms laden with badly wrapped packaged parcels that swayed dangerously from side to side; they were undoubtedly returning, tired and worn, to their simple homes after a shopping spree in the more varied shops of this larger town. They sat through most of the trip blowing strands of mousy-colored hair from their faces, wiping at dripping perspiration, constantly dropping their parcels into the aisle, and attempting to cool themselves by flapping the blouses of their cheap print dresses.

A scrawny teen-aged youth, with long blond hair dangling untidily over his shoulders, his strong bronzed hairless chest revealed by his open shirt, took a rear seat and immediately polluted the air with outrageous noise from a huge, glistening, black-and-chrome transistor radio, and a massive blue-black Negro, perspiration gleaming on his bulging muscles, commandered a double block of seats, spread himself comfortably, and went promptly to sleep. A slatternly young girl with eyes blackened by heavy mascara and a crimson slash for a mouth and bouncing breasts overflowing with milk, carrying a small baby, took a seat behind the driver and carried on a running conversation with him throughout the trip. The driver was a totally indifferent young man, quite attractive in a rather common sort of way, with a cap perched on the back of his sandy hair and jaws moving constantly to masticate the huge wad of gum in his mouth; Ellen was surprised that, despite the cap which served as a badge of office, he wore no uniform.

They sat in the sweltering heat for almost a quarter of an hour before the driver paid any attention to the complaining hoots and cat-calls of his passengers and they finally started on their way with a maximum of smoky explosions, grindings, sudden stops and startling lurches forward. They made a side-tossing circle around the depot, paused momentarily at the entrance to the highway, then lurched into the roadway and moved swiftly and uncomfortably in a cloud of their own dust down the broad dirt roadway stretching beside the sea. A slight mist of rain swept in upon Ellen through the narrow opening of her window; when her own efforts to close the stubborn window failed, her baggage raising companion again came to her rescue, leaning over her and inundating her with an overpowering odor of pungent perspiration while he tugged and hammered the window until it was finally closed.

Ellen sighed and closed her eyes, leaning her head against the hard back of her seat, after covering its suspicious darkness (no doubt created by the grease of many resting heads) with her handkerchief (which would certainly have to be destroyed upon completion of the journey.)

She was not very pleased with her present situation. Who would have imagined that she, Ellen Pirenne, at the age of seventy-five years (this she would admit only to herself, of course) would be subjected to this absolutely incredible mode of transportation? She sniffed as the whiff of cheap cigarette smoke passed her, and she was already beginning to develop a severe headache from the tangled jangle of supposed music endlessly and loudly blasted from the radio behind her, with no consideration whatever for the other passengers. The baby in front began to scream with sharp cries that shot like daggers of sound into her head. There were angry comments from several of her fellow travelers who apparently were more willing to endure the noise from the radio than that of a fellow human being in obvious discomfort; recalling accounts of bus travel in Mexico and such places, Ellen would not have been too surprised if the young mother had given the screaming infant her breast right then and there. An unpleasant, tangy odor of perspiration (even now, Ellen could not bring herself even to think of the ugly word *sweat*) soon began to permeate the vehicle with its windows closed against the rain. The conversations about her became a meaningless drone punctuated now and then by the hysterical giggles of the amorous-minded young girls.

The horizon to which they were headed was ominously black and the rain began to fall more heavily. She saw little in the harshly barren landscape, the arid shoreline, and the tumbling gray sea to interest her. A wasp flew in through one of the slightly opened upper windows, and the young girls screamed with delighted fear while their brave male companions flapped handkerchiefs until the harried insect made its escape through another window.

The seat beside Ellen remained fortunately vacant. She had firmly placed her handbag on the adjoining seat in hopes that this would guarantee her at least a small measure of privacy, not realizing that her *grand dame* appearance and aloofness were quite enough to hold the other passengers at bay. At the beginning of the journey, several of the passengers looked at her with amused smiles and made sniggering whispered comments, but interest in this prim and proper old woman, dressed in an outmoded style seldom seen in these parts, quickly faded and the passengers concentrated on muddling their own thoughts, staring vacantly out of the windows, or sleeping with their heads lolling on the back of their seats.

Only her love for John could have brought Ellen to such a pass. John was her only surviving relation, and he was very dear to her. She had a great many friends, of course, in all parts of the country as well as in most of the capitals and resorts of Europe, but her grandson was someone very special to her. She had carefully watched over him through the passing years, intensely proud of his writing talents while still certain he was capable of far more than he had as yet accomplished.

Ellen had always liked Ruth as well. She was a sensible, pretty, intelligent and quite talented young girl with whom she had always got along extremely well. Marriage had been good for John (with the passing of the years, she had been afraid he might remain a bachelor), and his choice of a wife had been a rather surprisingly excellent one, considering that he really knew rather pitifully little about the feminine sex, like most men. Ellen had not been blind to the strains apparent in their marriage in recent years, and these signs of deterioration had saddened her. The death of Elinor came as much of a blow to her as to the parents themselves, and she had feared more than ever for the marriage.

Yet she had not at all approved their decision to leave the city and immure themselves out here in this lonely wilderness, away from all those friends who might have helped them through a particularly difficult and agonizing time. What had caused them to do this, she wondered again? Was it merely self-pity or was there perhaps in them both a touch of self-guilt? This business of taking the time to *find themselves* was simple nonsense, another result of all this business about psychiatry and self-identification; you were what you were, and you did what you had to do, and that's all there was to it.

Ellen had disapproved even more about this move when she learned they were staying at Fowles House.

Ellen Perinne came from an old, almost aristocratic French family which had not taken enthusiastically to her marriage with the American banker Martin Kendall, despite his considerable wealth and prominent social position. But she had been remarkably happy through more than thirty years of marriage. Now that he was gone, and their two children as well, there was only John left to her. She clung more closely to him with the passing of the years.

She realized the family had come to view her as something of an eccentric. Oh, there was no doubt that she was loved by the members of her family, and by her many friends after they were gone, but she knew they were amused by her attitudes and her habits. She was constantly twitted about what they considered her outmoded fashion of dress, but this did not bother her. She was an old woman, and she dressed only to please herself, in the solid style of a happier time; surely she was not expected to adopt the garish, almost indecent fashions of the day. She liked to think she always brought with her a comfortable touch of a much more sensible era.

The family had also always laughed at Ellen's claims of super-sensitivity in matters dealing with the paranormal. No one today really believed in such things as ghosts, hauntings, auras, or anything smacking of the supernatural, they insisted, except for some whose sorrows or loneliness or greed or sense of guilt had driven them into the frequently questionable clutches of mediums, fortune tellers and other quacks who made their living by battening on the gullible and superstitious. Extra sensory perception had a certain respect and acceptance since it bore the slight touch of scientific rationale and happened to be the *in* thing at the moment, but they scoffed at Ellen's claims of actual belief in all such phenomena. She saw the way they looked at each other whenever she described (as she perhaps did too often) her wonderful experience at Hampton Court, that thrilling sight of the lost and moaning Cahterine Howard walking slowly, dreamily, along the richly tapestried corridor and down the broad sweeping staircase, lamenting her tragic (and, at least in the minds of some) unjustified fate. They insisted it was simply her over-active imagination, that aspect of family character which she had passed along to John, who had fortunately managed to channel it into more remunerative channels.

But Ellen knew better and remained totally un-convinced by all of their belitting arguments. The experience at Hampton Court was only one of many such instances in which she had sensed the presence of the unknown, and no one could convince her of their unreality, despite all their senseless chatter about hyper-thyroids, fevers, heat strokes and other sorts of nonsense. There were too many places in the world where the aura of the past became almost visible to those capable of lightly touching the world beyond that seen by others. She had too closely felt the chill of the violent sadness in the private apartments of the Empress Elizabeth in the Hofburg. Twice, aside from the marvelous experience with the discarded wife of Henry VIII, she had seen specters in the haunted mansions of England. She knew full well that strong emotions can and often do linger long after those who originated them have gone, the emotions of fear and sorrow, of love and tragedy, of longing and loneliness.

Above all, Ellen found it impossible to understand why people whose religious faith taught the unquestioned existence of life after death should so vigorously refuse the acceptance of specters from that other world to which all would one day be called. What could be more logical than that such specters could, on occasion, manage to cross the tenuous line of division between the two worlds? Their very existence, mournful though it might be, should provide comforting and indisputable proof that death was not really the end.

Such experiences never frightened Ellen, as they generally did others. Indeed, she often sought them out in her travels, going considerable distances out of her way to check personally on strange tales, although despite numerous hours spent wandering aimlessly and hopefully through the silently haunted gardens of Versailles, she was unable to duplicate the thrilling experience of the two English spinsters. Most specters she found rather pitiful beings, bemoaning an unhappy life, expiating a hideous crime, expressing longing for those left behind.

Yet she was stll wise enough to realize that if there are such forces that are either harmless or even beneficent, there might also be forces of great evil, both malevolent and dangerous. *Evil* has an even greater strength of survival than good.

It was just such forces that she feared in that Fowles House were John and Ruth had now taken residence. She vaguely recalled the name when John first mentioned the house in one of his letters, but for a time she could not recall just in what connection the name had meaning for her; it had undoubtedly occurred in some of her wide readings.

Then she had again come across the name of Fowles in a rather obscure and quite forgotten book on the supernatural. The extreme vagueness of the comment, merely mentioning Fowles as a pirate and slave trader believed to have dabbled in some particularly terrible form of the Black Arts, irritated her, but fortunately the appendix indicated other works in which further information might be obtained.

She sought out these books in some of the dustier shelves of the British Museum and other libraries and read them avidly. Still they told her surprisingly little, too often skirting the main issues and merely hinting at matters that were not fully revealed, but she did not at all like what she read, and the more deeply she delved into the matter, the more uneasy she became. That Fowles House was a place of extreme ill repute was quite apparent, but what most disturbed her were the implications of forces even more dreadful than appeared in the grizzly story of a particularly evil man who, through his own misdeeds, had come to a most unpleasant end. All the accounts, distressingly, lacked specifics, but she sensed that the ghastly tale of the life and death of Captain Jonathan Fowles did not by any means tell all there was to be told.

The accounts were quite candid enough in speaking of the incredibly evil character of Fowles himself, and as Ellen sat back with her eyes closed, somewhat lulled by the rapid movement of the coach, she pictured again that brutal face as she had seen it in a drawing in one of the books, the coldly brutal eyes, the hawk-like nose, the lips as thin and white as the firm lines of evil, the bearded jaw, square and totally devoid of any indication of emotion but harsh brutality. She had wondered then what horrors those cold eyes might have seen before they were closed in death. She lightly ran her lace handkerchief across her perspiring face and thought again of the strange story she would have to tell her grandson.

There was no indication of just where Johathan Fowles originally came from, or of his family background, but apparently the family had its roots in some small English seacoast village. Fowles had appeared on the American coast in the middle of the Seventeenth Century, a tall and powerful bearded man with a voice like thunder and a temper that could bring fear to the heart of the most dauntless. He was physically possessed of tremendous strength and power; he could easily bend a poker in half. He was already captain of his own vessel at this time, although still apparently a comparatively young man; the name of the vessel had apparently long been forgotten. The village to which Ellen was now headed became his home and his base of operations, no one knew why; perhaps merely because of its isolation, which would be to him a considerable asset, particularly when he abandoned the more acceptable forms of trade and began dealing with the more lucrative business of shipping slaves.

The accounts became chillingly graphic in their descriptions of Fowles's participation in this most nefarious of all forms of trade upon the sea. His massive figured loomed black against the scarlet dancing background of burning African villages, and he answered with bitter laughter the screams of terrified natives as they were brutally crowded into the barracoons to await shipment across the great sea to a world and life that held unknown fears and sorrows; those natives who resisted too stubbornly were merely tossed back into the flames of their own grass huts. It is an interesting point that Fowles did not share the view generally held in these times that these dark moaning forms were something less than human; to consider them on a level of the ape would have negated the pleasure Fowles found in brutalizing and torturing them. There is little excitement in the screams and the agonized cries of an animal; only the screams of man could bring rich satisfaction to his own black soul. The manacled natives were stacked like cordons of firewood into the sweating, stinking holds of his ship for transport to the open markets of the New World. Much of the cargo did not survive these terrible voyages, but expecting this, the brutal captain overloaded his holds so that it was a wonder that any of the frightened, home-sick blacks arrived alive in the New World. There had to be an excess of human cargo to provide diversion for his men and himself on the long, tedious, monotonous voyage between two worlds. There were tales told of Fowles that even in those brutal days people found difficult to believe . . . the way he permitted his men to inflict unbelievable torture on ailing slaves merely for their own amusement (the slave was going to die anyway), the many times he cast his human, screaming cargo overboard into the sea, heavily weighted by their chains to sink promptly beneath the surface, rather than risk capture and exposure by searching government ships. His ships became floating charnel houses, filled with the screams of the horrified and dripping with the rich red blood of the black victims.

And while enjoying it all, Fowles managed to amass great wealth through this inhuman trade, yet he was never quite satisfied, for above all in life he craved wealth and power. When the pressures against the slave trade made the risk too great, Fowles freely moved into piracy, and his name soon became the most feared on the coast. His brutality became legend even in his own lifetime during an age which was generally indifferent to human sufferings. Not even children were spared the terror of stepping from a narrow wooden plank into the churning sea. Fowles was particularly brutal in his treatment of women, most of whom he laughingly turned over to the far from tender mercies of his savage crew.

The logical next step was for him to turn to wrecking, one of the most infamous of all crimes of the sea. It was a familiar story of the time . . . the false lights on a dark and lonely shore, the wrecked ship torn to pieces on the jagged rocks, and then the ruthless plunder of the cargo. Fowles and his men soon became adept at the art.

There was now no one who could stop him, or who even dared to try. His wealth increased beyond all measure. Scarcely a ship passed that stretch of coast without falling into his greedy, bloody hands. Whatever Fowles wanted, he managed to gather unto himself. There was safety for no one.

Fowles erected his great house on the jutting promontory overlooking the scenes of his greatest wrecking triumphs. He stored his great wealth there, and few people dared even to approach the lonely eyrie. It was reported that terrible and unspeakable things happened in that house, and often on dark silent nights, when even the frigtened moon concealed her face behind the scudding clouds, the quiet air would be torn by the terrified screams of women, survivors of wrecked ships, subjected to unimaginable tortures and obscenities. Sometimes Fowles's own laughter rang out sharp and clear even above their cries, ringing like an evil tocsin across the salt-scented air. Villagers at a safe distance could sometimes see his tall dark form impatiently pacing the Widow's Walk of his house, staring out to the churning sea for his next victim.

The villagers remained silent about all this, accepting the presence of Fowles and his crew, for they were permitted, in some small measure, to share in the plunder Fowles brought ashore, and the weak can be as greedy for gain as the strong. But before long, even they began to know the touch of fear. Fowles was too successful. There seemed to be something not quite natural about his power and wealth, something perhaps unholy, something almost supernatural. He was too successful, and the successful are always envied.

If you want to find an answer, you will find one, logical or not. You can invent one, if you have to. To the villagers, there was only one obvious solution to Fowles's continued prosperity, his immunity against justice. It was soon generally believed that the evil captain had sold his soul to the *Satan of the Sea.*

Ellen frowned and waved her hand as a curl of smoke drifted past her. This would be, perhaps, the most difficult part of her story to make John believe, for it was both the most terrible and the most irrational, something that the cold light of modern reason would undoubtedly make him instantly reject.

She would have to remind him of the strange time in which all of this took place, one of the darkest ages of civilized man, darker by far than that earlier period so smugly and inaccurately referred to as the Dark Ages. Man's mind was slowly awakening to the possibilities of life about him, but true knowledge had not yet come to him and he saw life as a mass of confusion as through a dark mirror, with little understanding. It was a time of witchcraft and sorcery, of possessed children, of burnings at the stake, accusations without basis springing from hatred, fear, envy, when man's obsession with religion and his fear of death turned into a horrible cancerous sickness. The world lived under an oppressive cloud of superstition, surrounded by demons and devils anxious to seize the unwary soul and carry it down to the fires of hell. That tenuous entity called the soul, which death-terrified man had convinced himself would survive his own physical destruction, became man's most precious commodity, and to Satan the most desirable. It could be used as a bargaining power between Satan and those mercenary men to whom worldly wealth and power were more desirable than an uncertain heavenly eternity. Anyone who lived as

Fowles did, with his unsavory reputation and his unexplained wealth, was ripe for accusations of sorcery and communion with Satan.

Those who lived by the sea had their own particular devils. An old legend, its origin lost in the mists of time, stated that there were actually two Satans, twin brothers fallen from heaven, who ruled in hell together. But they were a very jealous, envious and constantly quarrelsome pair, each attempting to surpass the other in the practice of evil and the gathering of lost souls. They one day quarreled fiercely over a particularly desirable black soul; some said it was that of Emperor Caligula himself. Their quarrel erupted into open warfare, in which the supporters of one bloodily and brutally slaughtered the followers of the other. The world itself trembled during the course of their titanic battles; earthquakes tore the earth asunder, burning lava exploded from the craters of long dormant volcanos, entire civilizations were destroyed, the turbulent, hissing sea rose and covered much of the land.

After many years, which were but a fleeting moment in the long history of heaven and hell, the terrible wars ended, with both sides totally exhausted by the conflict, but one brother emerged somewhat stronger than the other. Strangely enough, the victor revealed himself as unusually magnanimous under the circumstances; it was said he enjoyed the prospect of future battles between himself and his brother, with all their resultant carnage to the despised human race. Rather than humiliating or destroying the vanquished twin as he might easily have done, he gave his defeated brother a hell of his own . . . the sea. They entered into a pact which has been observed to this very day. All souls lost at sea were to become the unquestioned property of the vanquished Satan, while the stronger brother took the larger number of evil souls of those who perished on land. Their continued animosity is still expressed in the warfare to which the human race is so sadly susceptible, which is merely the continued flare-ups of the hatred that still exists between the Satanic brothers, and their striving for the souls of the lost, both upon land and sea.

The two Satans were possessed of tremendous powers with which to entice their own coteries of followers. To the supporters and abettors of the more powerful were opened all the riches of the earth, the buried treasures of ancient times, the secrets of lost worlds, unlimited power over the minds of their fellow men; we have seen in our own time what dangers that presents. *The Satan of the Sea* offered to those who would worship him all the darkest mysteries of the deepest caverns of the sea, the wealth of treasures lost in sunken ships along the Spanish Main and the China and Indian seas, the silver of the New World and the jewels of the Rajahs, and also the knowledge and control of the winds and tides, the power to seize all ships and make them their own.

Fowles, who had spent all of his life by and upon the sea, could not resist this lure, andhe entered freely into a pact with the *Sea Satan*. He secured all the wealth and power he desired, while the Satan obtained a valuable black soul which his brother would have been very pleased to claim as his own.

Fowles thus created his own world of incredible evil and darkness, obeying always the obscene commands of his new master, thrilling to the lust for evil. His wealth increased beyond all measure. Without ever again leaving his house on the cliff, he secured from the sea all he desired or needed, and much more. He controlled the winds and the tides about the cliff and no ships could safely pass by. On the clearest of nights, the sea would suddenly rise and not the most skillful hands could prevent a ship from dashing itself upon the sharp black rocks. But when the villagers arrived, they would find nothing, not a single sign, not a board or a spar or a square inch of canvas, not the slightest suggestion of what had been there, no wreckage, no bodies and, above all, no plunder. All had disappeared into the mysterious maw of Fowles House, and none was ever seen again.

For in his greed, in his insatiable hunger for treasure and power, Fowles at last made his fatal mistake. He became too greedy, leaving nothing for the natural greed of others. He no longer saw need to placate the villagers by permitting them to share in his booty. The power was his and his alone, and no one would dare oppose him. He refused to permit the people of the village any further part in his good fortune. All was for him; they were to have nothing, not a single gem or piece of cloth. The villagers became envious of his constantly increased store of wealth as their own prosperity declined. Hard times came to the village, and all knew only too well who was responsible.

It is quite likely their final determination to put an end to the captain and his evil world resulted more from their badly injured sense of greed than from a sense of righteousness, but they told themselves at last that Fowles must be destroyed for having brought Satan to their shores. One evening, they decided they'd had just about enough.

A particularly valuable ship, reputedly laden with an almost incalculable treasure, was to sail past their part of the coast, and the hungry villagers licked their dried, thirsting lips at the thought of the great wealth that could be theirs. It was a night with a calm sea, but that particular misfortune had never troubled them before. It was the dark of the moon, with no natural light to reveal their perfidy. A series of false lights carefully placed to bring the ship in too close to the dangerous reef, the extinguishing of the single guiding beam of the lighthouse, that was all that was needed. They knew their job all too well; they had done it often enough. This time they were determined to foil Fowles at his own game.

But still they failed. They waited, concealed behind the dunes, heavily armed to overcome any possible resistance from chance survivors, but there was no sign of the ship, not a single gleam of a white sail or a mast light, not even the leather-creaking sound of the rigging. They waited throughout the long, silent night, but in vain. The ship had simply disappeared. They knew where. With the aid of his evil master, Fowles had again gathered all that treasure to himself.

This was too much. Fowles had at last gone too far. The villagers determined to rid themselves of the captain and the malignant influence that surrounded him. In a sudden fit of long-forgotten righteousness, they determined at one stroke to serve the interests of God and also to restore their own nefarious trade.

Carrying torches and whatever crude weapons they could find, the people of the village . . . men, women and children alike . . . stormed the house on the bluff as the terrified villagers might at a later time have surrounded the house of Frankenstein. . . .

Ellen had fallen into an uncomfortable doze, her mind filled with terrible images from the days of Captain Jonathan Fowles, her head constantly sliding across the stained hard-leather rear of her seat to strike rather painfully against the window, and she was now awakened with a sudden start by a tremendous blast of thunder. She quickly opened her eyes, momentarily confused by her strange surroundings, and peered through the rain-streaming window at what appeared a totally alien world.

The stormy gray sea tossed its white-foamed breakers upon the hard barren yellow sand of the beach, and the dark sky was torn by frequent forks of jagged lightning; thunder rolled ceaselessly, as though old Rip's transported ghostly Bhurgers were again at their endless game of nine-pins. The driver was bent with narrowed eyes over his steering wheel, chewing nervously as he peered closely through the windshield that was only ineffectually cleared of rain by the scraping, stuttering rubber wipers. The mother seated behind him was angrily bouncing her wailing infant, the radio was still screaming, and from behind Ellen came the loud rasp of snoring. She shifted herself uncomfortably to ease a cramped shoulder, and stared unseeing into the pelting rain and the gray tumbling clouds as she again returned her thoughts to the infamous Jonathan Fowles.

It was just at this most interesting point in the story of the brutal captain, with the villagers converging in righteous fury upon the house on the cliff, that most accounts Ellen found came to a sudden and inexplicable end. There were darkly shadowed suggestions of some unspeakable horrors found in the great house Fowles had built for himself, but nowhere was Ellen able to uncover a specific reference to what was actually seen there. Even Fowles's own end was shrouded in mystery, the clearest reference being that of an old and dusty tome that merely remarked Fowles came at last to a *particularly hideous end at the hands of those he had raised against him*. Ellen had an uncomfortable feeling that those concerned with the Fowles story shied away from too close a revelation of the events of that terrible night, as though mere mention of it might prove dangerous.

Thus it was that while Ellen had read enough to be greatly disturbed by the story of Fowles, she was even more disturbed by what remained unsaid. How had the evil captain perished? Why did all accounts of his life seem to end just short of its termination? There are, after all, no horrors that can not be described. Such writers, and their readers, glory in the most blood-thirsty of descriptions. This silence bothered her.

Of one thing Ellen felt certain. Fowles had brought a great and terrible evil to that house of his on the cliff overlooking the sea, and Ellen was certain it could not have been easily dispelled. Could an aura of his monumental evil still linger about the house he had created? She began to fear that the peculiar silence with which the end of Fowles was surrounded might, in some uknown way, pose a threat to her grandson and his wife.

She had tried to dismiss the matter from her mind, but it was not an easy thing to do, and it was in Vienna that she finally made her decision. After a most delightful evening of Strauss at the *Theatre an der Wien*, followed by a delicious but quite outrageously calloric *torte* at Sacher's, Ellen had returned to her suite at the Imperial Hotel and later awakened from a ghastly nightmare of which she could later remember nothing but swirling masses menacingly moving through a sea of turgid green. She had tried to convince herself that the rich *torte* was responsible for the dream, but the touch of fear remained, and she could not doubt that in some way the dream, with its basis in the sea, had been intended as a warning of some danger that threatened John whose increasingly sparse and unsatisfying letters in past weeks had been marked by a false cheerfulness which she could see through very easily.

Ellen was in the habit of taking such dreams quite seriously, for on more than one occasion they had proved portents of danger and disaster to those near to her. Without hesitation, she had wired John about her intended visit, and now here she was, bouncing along this abominable road during a violent storm in an uncomfortable public vehicle filled with the most out-rageously common and ordinary people. John would undoubtedly think her foolish, but there was nothing else she could do. It was more foolish, and far more dangerous, to disregard the warnings of danger. She had not been able to lose that sudden touch of fear that had come to her that night in Vienna. Twice her departure had been delayed, once by a brief illness and then by a bungling airline agent, and she could only hope the delay in her arrival would not prove serious.

The trip began to seem interminable. The rain continued to hammer thunderously on the roof of the bus, streaming down the windows so that it was impossible to see if there were anything to be seen, and with all the windows now closed against the rain (which nevertheless managed to seep through loosened frames so that several passengers were required to change their seats), the odor of the bus was badly sharpened. Ellen winced at the scent of urine as the young mother spread her infant on the seat beside her and changed a wet diaper. The noise of the never silent radio competed with the unpleasant sounds of those who had managed to fall into an uneasy sleep.

There was still an hour of travel ahead of them. Ellen again attempted to divorce herself from this unwelcome world by closing her eyes, but just as she slipped into an uncomfortable doze, she seemed to see again that evil man who had built the cliff house where John and Ruth now lived.

CHAPTER EIGHTEEN

ELLEN next awoke when the bus came to an abrupt stop that brought her up sharply against the back of the seat before her. She straightened her hat, winced at a crick in her neck, and peered narrowly through the streaming window. They had stopped in a small and incredibly drab little square whose unattractive buildings were all centered about a lifeless little park with sadly dripping trees and gleamingly wet benches, before a large building whose sign announced it to be a hotel, one very much different from the hotels to which Ellen was accustomed. It was still raining heavily, and Ellen was unpleasantly reminded of the dreary gatherings at rainy open grave sites when she saw the people standing under their black umbrellas before the entrance to the hotel, which was apparently the single stop made by the bus in this village. Her dampened spirits soared immediately when she saw John standing among them, peering anxiously from under his own umbrella, the one bright and cheering sight in those rather doleful and unimpressive surroundings. Ellen waved broadly to her grandson, but he was apparently unable to see her through the rain cascading down the window.

Even before the bus had come to a stop, the teen-agers, still screaming with hysterical laughter and unquenchable high spirits, dashed down the aisle of the bus and, not at all discomforted by the heavy fall of rain, jumped to the sidewalk the moment the door was swung open. The housewives, muttering their own imprecations against the weather, clumsily gathered their parcels together and waited impatiently on the bus step until their husbands, as dull and unimaginative as themselves, offered the shelter of their umbrellas, and then they walked off together, unsmiling and unspeaking, back to their private little worlds. Ellen suffered a last irritating blast of cacophonous noise as the youth with his radio still blaring full volume passed her and stepped from the bus.

Ellen painfully eased her cramped and stiffened frame from the seat and stood on her toes as she reached for her suitcase. A pungent aroma told her who stood behind her even before she heard his flat voice.

"No, now, little lady, you jist let me do that there little thing fer ya!" There was a chuckle and a whiff of heavy tobacco. "You ain't hardly tall enough nur strong enough t' handle that all by yerself."

She stood back with a polite, somewhat condescending smile, hoping she was not too obviously attempting to avoid personal close contact, as her suitcase was lowered from the rack.

"That's very kind of you," she muttered somewhat uneasily, wondering if that was the correct phrase to use to such a man and if he expected a small renumeration for his unrequested but appreciated services.

The bristles of the unshaven cheeks bunched up in a slight smile that might have been rather pleasant save for the soggy unlighted cigar stump that was tightly clamped between the yellowed teeth; Ellen felt a sudden touch of nausea.

"Nothin' at all," he assured her. "Ain't nothin' at all for me, little lady." He stooped and peered through the rain-beaded window. "Mighty wet out there, little lady.

Why don't you jist wait right here an' I'll see if I kin get us an umbrella."

"Oh, no," Ellen responded quickly and with some relief. "No need for that, I assure you. My grandson is out there waiting for me, with an umbrella." She hesitated a moment, then thought it only courteous to add, "Perhaps you'd care to share it with us, at least to the hotel entrance."

The nauseating breath of stale tobacco touched her face again as the man laughed in reply. "Hell, little lady, I don't mind no rain! Makes me grow!" The big man almost choked on his own laughter, moving the wet cigar stub from one side of his mouth to the other, and then swung the suitcase before him into the aisle. "Now, you jist go right on ahead of me an' wait until that there grandson of yours comes to you with that there umbrella. Can't get that pretty little hat wet, nosiree!"

Ellen made her way down the aisle, nodded a farewell to the driver who took her ticket with an automatic gesture while still staring at the breasty young girls who had already left the bus. Pausing for a moment on the step, Ellen waved to John, who saw her immediately and rushed to the door, smiling broadly.

"Hello, John darling!" she cried.

John looked into that sweetly remembered face, saw again the great warmth in the twinkling gray eyes, and felt suddenly that surely all must now once again be right with the world.

"Hello, Gram!" he greeted, feeling like a small boy as he titled back the umbrella to look into her gentle face. "Where's your luggage?"

Ellen indicated the waiting fellow traveler standing just behind her. "I've only brought the one piece, dear, and this gentleman was kind enough to take care of it for me."

John smiled and nodded at the stranger, whom he vaguely recalled having on occasion seen on the streets of the village; he reached behind Ellen for the suitcase.

"Thank you very much. It was very kind of you."

"No trouble, tall," the man assured him, munching on the end of his cigar as he handed the suitcase to John. "Always like to help out a little lady." He turned to Ellen and stuck out a hairy hand; fearful that her white glove might forever retain marks of the contact, Ellen reluctantly took the hand in her own, which was almost totally lost in the great paw. "Have a nice stay fer yerself, lady."

John grinned at her poorly-concealed discomfort as Ellen replied. "Thank you. Thank you very much. You've been most kind."

The man walked indifferently off into the rain while John, holding the suitcase in his free hand, carefully guided Ellen under the umbrella, holding it in such a way that his own left side became streaked with rain water, and for several seconds the thunder of the rain on the umbrella made further conversation impossible as they walked quickly through the rain and up the steps to the hotel entrance. In the shelter of the doorway, as John lowered the umbrella and held the dripping instrument safely away from him, Ellen brushed off her dress and sighed with relief.

"Oh, my, but I am glad that's over! What a terrible, tiresome trip! How people can travel in such a way, I'll certainly never be able to understand! Just dreadful! Dreadful! And the people, with their odors, their noises, their . . . their sweat! Oh, my dear John!"

John laughed at her unaccustomed use of the over-descriptive term, and bent to kiss her cheek. "At least you managed to find one helpful friend," he commented.

She nodded with some satisfaction. "Yes, oh yes. He was really extremely kind and most helpful. I must admit that, although he could have been . . . well, just a bit tidier, you know? I wonder, John, do you suppose I should have tipped him a little something? That kind always like a . . . a beer or something, don't they?"

"I'm quite certain he didn't expect a thing," John assured her. "He was just trying to be kind; most people enjoy helping others."

"I suppose there is some truth in that," she agreed. "Still, I shouldn't really care to make a habit of that kind of travel."

"You should have let me drive out to pick you up, as I wanted to," John commented. "It would have been much more pleasant for you."

Ellen firmly shook her head. "No, no, no. There's no need to put you to all that trouble. It's bad enough having me drop in on you like this. It's over now, thank goodness. Well, it was an experience! Perhaps I'll allow you to drive me on the way back."

"You mustn't talk about leaving when you've just arrived," John complained. "And why only the one suitcase?"

"Oh, I can't stay long, John," she replied, "and since I was by myself and had no conception of conditions, I felt it best to travel as light as possible. Good thing, too!"

"I was hoping you would stay with us for a while," he said with a sharp sense of disappointment.

"Oh, no. I really have only a few days. I'm due in London on the 27th, and if I miss her charity party, Lady Masters will never forgive me. You know how really difficult she can be when she has a mind!"

John again picked up the suitcase and peered into the rain-drenched square. The bus at this moment gave another explosion and moved on out of sight, heading back to its place of origin; most of those waiting at the hotel entrance had already gone their ways.

"My car is just around the corner," John mentioned, "but perhaps you'd like a good cup of hot coffee before we start off. You must be very tired, and perhaps the rain will let up a bit by then."

Ellen nodded. "Yes, by all means. But I'm afraid I'll require something just a bit stronger than coffee, my dear; I'm chilled to the bone. That is, if you're certain we have the time. Won't Ruth worry if we're late?"

She did not miss the surprisingly harsh tone in her grandson's voice when he replied. "Oh, don't concern yourself about that. Ruth isn't likely to worry."

Several moments later they were comfortably seated opposite each other in a quiet and comfortable booth before a window in the hotel restaurant, before them each a cup of coffee and a glass of brandy which Ellen declared, considering all the circumstances, was really quite acceptable, although certainly not at all up to her usual standards. The room was warm with the presence of diners, and the soft hum of their conversation, and through the window they could see the continuing stream of rain that had already created minor rivers running along the curbstones. Now and then someone dashed past the window, clad in a bright yellow slicker with a hat to match, but for the most part the village square had been abandoned to the elements. The room was shadowed by the darkness of the day and the approach of evening, and John felt a welcome, long missing sense of cozziness.

He looked fondly at the small, dignified woman seated across from him, and for the first time in several weeks, he felt a sense of comfort and well being. It was foolish of him to think so, but again he felt as when a child, that somehow all would be right as long as Grandmother Ellen was here.

She looked remarkably well for her age, he thought, and if there were signs of fatigue in her light gray eyes, that could easily be attributed to her having spent three uncomfortable hours in the bus, something of an ordeal even for those much younger and less accustomed to greater comfort. That small face with the high aristocratic cheekbones (remarkably unlined for one of her years), the sharply piercing eyes that never missed anything that went on about her, the rosebud mouth so easily pursed in disapproval or opened in laughter, the carefully coiffured snow-white hair of which she was so proud, with the inevitable toque hat perched at the very top, the almost regal carriage, all seemed as they had been through John's long knowledge of her.

His grandmother would have stood out in any crowd, but her style of dress made her even more noticeable. Ellen never dressed casually, no matter what the circumstances, and she felt dark shades most suitable for one of her years; she was not at all unaware of the dramatic effect created by a black dress and her white hair. Although her style may have been somewhat outmoded, her wardrobe was both elegant and expensive. About her throat she always wore a single strand of exquisite pearls, with a matching pair of pearls in her pierced ears. She always wore white gloves out-of-doors, even in morning hours, which had now been removed and rested beside her on the table; her fingers glittered with expensive rings. There was about her a deliciously gentle fragrance; her perfume was a special blend prepared for her at a small shop on the *Rue de Rivoli* in Paris.

She had always been just this way . . . lovely, dignified, somehow ageless, like the shadow of a different, more reasonable time, possessing the comfortable assurance of the past. She sat now bolt upright, her head held high, never permitting the slightest slump of her aristocratic figure, neat, tidy, fastidious. People often thought her something of a snob, the kind of wealthy person so constantly mocked and ridiculed by film makers preparing banal entertainment for their more plebian audiences, but there was nowhere a warmer, kinder woman, clearly attested by her many anonymous charities. It was wonderful to have her here.

Ellen was not quite as pleased by what she saw. This was the same, handsome, considerate grandson who had been the very center of her life for the past twenty years, but even her love could not blind her to the startling alterations in his appearance. John was much too thin, thinner than she had ever seen him before. There was the unmistakable mark of strain in his face, thin lines at the corners of his full mouth, and she did not like the constant nervous movement of his eyes, nor the dark shadows beneath them. She noticed that his long, slender fingers were heavily yellowed by tobacco stains.

She reached out a bone-china thin hand marked with faint light blue veins and took his hand in hers.

John grasped the hand in his, surprised at its firmness, and smiled. "It's always good to be with you," he responded. "It seems such a long time! But you're looking simply marvelous!"

"Oh, but I am!" she assured him. "I'm really feeling quite remarkably well. Oh, I admit, I have a slight touch of rheumatism now and again, but nothing to be concerned about." She shook her head sadly. "Poor Empress Elizabeth suffered from rheumatism far more severely than I do, and if she could be so brave, there's no reason why I shouldn't be the same."

He smiled at the typical royal reference with which she constantly sprinkled her conversation, always giving the impression that she was on the most intimate terms with even long departed figures of Europe's great families; what in others might have been irritating in her was simply endearing.

"And how was Vienna this summer?" he asked.

She smiled with obvious gratification, clasping her hands together in a gesture of intense pleasure. "But Vienna never changes, my boy, regardless of what horrid modern influences are brought to bear. The trees along the Ring were more beautiful than ever this year. Ah, *Wien bleibt Wien!* I do believe that when my traveling days are over, I just might decide to spend my last days in Vienna.

He smiled again. "That won't be for a good many years to come! Hard to think of you settling down anywhere."

She sighed slightly and shook her head. "Oh, I don't know about that, John. I tire much more easily now, and

I've become quite as irritable as an old maiden aunt. Too much has changed; Europe simply is not what it used to be. Paris tires me with its arrogance . . . justified or not . . . and in London even members of the royal family seem to have lost their sense of propriety. Rome is constantly in political turmoil, and one never does feel quite at ease in Berlin, with that horrid wall staring you in the face at practically every turning; we really should force them to take it down, you know; we really should. The Riviera is filled with tourists with outlandish clothes and worse manners, and as for Spain . . . oh, my dear, it's quite impossible; nothing but Americans. There are too many people able to travel to Europe today; it has spoiled everything. Only Vienna remains the same, calm and beautiful, filled with music and a rich sense of the past." She glanced out of the window as lightning again brightened the sky. "Still, at least all these places still have something to offer. How anyone could possibly be content to be buried in a godforsaken place like this. . ."

"Oh, there are compensations," John assured her. "There's considerable peace and quite here."

Ellen snorted slightly, in a most undignified manner. "Yes, I can well believe that, my dear! Peace and quite indeed! We'll have more than enough of that when we're in our graves; we don't need it now."

"It's really unfortunate the weather is so bad," he added, as a gust of wind cast hammering raindrops at their window. "We haven't seen the sun for the past week. The place really has quite a bit of charm all its own, and there's really a fine view of the sea. . ."

"I'm certain the view of the sea is much more beautiful at Cannes," Ellen interrupted, "or in the Greek isles. There's too much an air of untamed violence about the sea here; most unsettling. When you speak of the beauties of the sea, you really can speak only of the Mediterranean."

She looked about her at those seated at surrounding

tables, pleasant if ordinary people enjoying themselves with what passed here for a night on the town. Most were casually dressed, the men with open throated sport shirts, the women in slacks and either blouses or halters. He could see her making visual comparisons with the dining rooms at the Imperial or the Kempinski.

"I don't suppose there is much cultural or social activity here, is there?" she asked somewhat dryly.

John found himself smiling again; he was feeling so much more at ease. "Well, no, I'm afraid not. Not what you're accustomed to, at any rate. They have a big fireworks display on the Fourth of July, with a band concert in the square, and the church has an occasional tea. . ."

She waved her hand and the rings sparkled on her fingers. "Oh, my dear boy, please spare me! Fireworks and teas! How perfectly dreadful! How ever can you bear it?"

They looked at each other and suddenly burst into laughter at their light badinage; John hadn't laughed in weeks. He again took hold of her hand and held it tightly in his.

"Oh, Gram, you never change, do you?"

She squeezed his hand. "Would you want me to, dear?"

"Not on a bet!" he assured her.

Her eyes became suddenly serious. "But you have changed, John. I can't say this place has done you very much good. You really don't look at all well. You're much too thin, there are shadows around your eyes, and you look as though you hadn't slept in weeks."

He released her hand and looked away, suddenly uneasy; the present had again forced itself upon him. "Well, I've been working very hard," he said somewhat lamely.

"Nonsense!" It was the familiar voice that had chided him as a youngster. "You've always worked very hard;

it's never made you look like this before. I know what it is. You've got to get back to the city, where at least there are things to keep a man alive, things much more interesting and exciting than band concerts and holiday fireworks." He turned his head away and her voice became harsher again. "Don't you try to evade me, my boy! I know you too well for that!"

A brief silence fell upon them, and they listened to the low murmur of quiet conversation, the clatter of dishes, and the droning of the rain. John recalled an equally uncomfortable luncheon in this same room with Linda, how long ago? Matters had changed since then, and certainly not for the better. He felt a curious catch in his throat when he thought of Linda; what was she doing now? A waiter passed close by their booth, precariously and professionally balancing on one hand a large tray filled with dishes. A car drove swiftly through the village square, sending cascades of water up from either side. A small slicker-covered boy leaped nimbly out of the way; his lips moved in a very un-small boy curse.

John turned to his grandmother and asked quite bluntly, "What is it that brought you here?"

"You, of course!" she replied lightly and perhaps just a bit too quickly, as though waiting for the question. "Certainly nothing else could bring me here. I wanted to see you, John. It's been much too long, you know. I realized you weren't about to come to Vienna just to visit me, so. . ."

"And now who's being evasive?" he asked. "You didn't fly from Vienna at the peak of the season and spend three hours in a very uncomfortable bus just because you wanted to see me, particularly when you knew I expect to be back in New York before too long and you could well have waited. I know you just as well as you know me. . ."

She paused a moment, then placed her handbag on the table, opened the clasp and fumbled in it for a moment before closing it again, with an expression of irritation.

"How foolish of me! I've left all my cigarettes in my suitcase. Have you one for me, dear?"

John reached into his pocket and extended his cigarettes. Ellen, who had always been a heavy smoker disdainful of medical reports, took one while looking somewhat askance at the somewhat crumpled package. John smiled in spite of himself.

"I'm afraid they aren't quite what you're accustomed to," he apologized as he flicked the lighter for her. "Your brand isn't easily come by in these parts."

He could see those sharp bright eyes watching him through the slight veil of blue-white smoke. "And how is Ruth?" The tone was somehow not as light and purely conversational as it should have been for such a question.

"She's . . . all right."

"More evasion, John? Ruth is never just *all right*, and you know it. She does everything by superlatives, both good and bad, and that includes the state of her health. She is either actually glowing with health, or there's something wrong with her."

John sipped from his brandy again and lighted a cigarette for himself before answering, feeling curiously uneasy. He had been waiting for this moment, for the chance to speak with his wise old grandmother about the problems and the uncertainties that now filled his life, but now he wondered what to say. It all seemed somehow foolish at this moment. How could he put his fear into words, even before one he knew would try to understand, when he himself was at a total loss to gather any meaning from recent events?

"I'm afraid you'll find Ruth . . . well, considerably changed," he said hesitantly.

"Changed in what way?"

He shrugged. "I really don't even know how to tell you that. You'll see for yourself, soon enough. She's different, strange, withdrawn, interested now in nothing but her work."

"Painting has always been Ruth's primary interest in life," Ellen reminded him, "even before you were first married. You've always known that, John."

"Yes, of course. But this is different. She's become totally absorbed, more so than I've ever seen anyone before."

"And how is her work?"

He wasn't quite certain of the words to use. "It's really very good, but totally unlike anything she has ever done before. Perhaps she'll let you see the canvas; she keeps it away from me now. Good though it is, I don't like it. It's morbid, dreary, haunting. But she seems to resent every moment spent away from her paints. She simply has no time for anyone or anything else. Not even for me."

"It sounds like you've been quarreling."

He hesitated. "Well, you might as well know it. We quarrel constantly. We're like total strangers who for some reason are living under the same roof. I irritate her simply by being here. She much prefers to be alone, spending most of her time on the bluff before the house, painting for hours at a time. She's moody, irritable, difficult. I think she sleeps very badly."

"You think?"

He really hadn't intended to tell her this, either. "We sleep in separate bedrooms. Ruth says it's the heat and she sleeps better alone, but I think she just wants to be away from me. Sometimes I hear her moaning in the night, tossing, as though she's having bad dreams."

"Her dreams have been haunted since you lost Elinor."

He shook his head. "No, this is entirely different; it has nothing to do with Elinor or, for that matter, with anything else I know about." The words came with difficulty. "She seems to have completely forgotten

Elinor; she never even mentions her name any longer. She seems to have forced from her mind everything that happened in our lives before we came here."

"Perhaps that's the answer," Ellen offered. "Perhaps Ruth has finally found that defensive shield to shut out a particularly unhappy time in her past."

"I don't think so," John objected, thoughtfully. "If that is the case, the shield is more dangerous than the unhappy memories." He fumbled for words. "Ruth's entire world is here now, right where she is, as though she'd never had a life before coming here. She's become part of the old house and refuses even to discuss returning to the city. She wants simply to stay right here, even if it's without me. She's even said she doesn't really care what I do; I simply don't matter to her any longer. I have no further place in her life." His voice dropped. "I don't know. She's become a total stranger to me."

Ellen was silent for a moment, and in those sharp blue-gray eyes John could almost see the process of thought. There was a sudden crackling of lightning that threw the room into blinding light, immediately followed by a heavy roll of thunder; a woman at a nearby table squealed with sudden fright and then laughed at her own reaction.

"John, Ruth was crushed by Elinor's death," Ellen said, groping for a solution. "Oh, I see more than you realize, my boy. She felt a sense of guilt about what happened, as though some of it at least was her fault, as though she was being punished for some sort of failure in her role as a mother. You would know more about that than I would. I still think it's possible there may be a connection. A total reversal of thought and habit may have been her only way to cover her sorrow and her guilt, wise or not. Perhaps this attitude of hers now is merely a defensive one, an attempt to force all that guilt and sadness from her mind, to replace it with something else, real or not, even if Ruth herself may not be aware of it. She may still be suffering from something of a trauma. . ."

John decisively shook his head. "No. I'm sorry, but I think you're wrong, Grandmother. I thought so at first, too, but not any longer. I'm quite serious when I say none of this has anything whatever to do with Elinor or, as far as I can see, with anything that involves the two of us." He frowned and continued after a moment. "It's the house that has done this, some how, some way. Ruth has developed a . . . a positive mania about the place. She's become part of it, as much a part as the dried land on which it stands and the empty seascape that surrounds it. She won't leave the house for a moment, not even to come here into town. When the weather keeps her from the bluff, she just wanders about the house, through the rooms, drifting like some memory of the past, touching things as though she were remembering them. There's something . . . eerie . . . about it all."

"That may be," Ellen admitted, "but not necessarily either alarming or dangerous. I still may be right, to an extent; Ruth may consider the house a refuge from the rest of the world, and that's why she refuses to leave it."

"I think it's more than that," John said stubbornly. "There's something about this place . . ."

"Very possibly there is," Ellen admitted. "We all react in different ways to different surroundings. Ruth is an artist, and an extremely sensitive woman. It perhaps isn't so unusual that she should feel a . . . a rapport in an old house with a history of its own."

"There's . . . there's something else . . ."

And then at last it all came out in a rush of words impossible to stop, and for the first time John fully cleared his mind of the frightening burden it had carried all these weeks. He told his grandmother everything, about finding Ruth lying naked on the cold cellar floor, about the increasing violence of their arguments, about the growing strangeness of Ruth's moods and her apparent withdrawal from their life together, her peculiar and constantly deepening dissociation from the present. He poured out all his uncertainties, his confusions and his fears. He forgot where they were, became totally oblivious to all those about him, to the pounding rain on the window and the increasing blackness of the sky, and his mind returned to that strange house on the cliff and the darkly ominous atmosphere that had hovered over him and Ruth since their arrival.

Ellen listened closely, intently, slowly sipping her brandy and drawing delicately on her cigarettes, watching her grandson with eyes that never for a moment wavered from his face, as though the expressions she saw there were more important than the strange words he said. She sensed the near hysteria in his tone, noticed the sudden trembling of his hands, and knew that John was really terribly frightened and confused by confrontation with something he could not even begin to understand.

And as Ellen listened, the fear that had for the past weeks filled John with foreboding touched her as well, for she realized at once that this was not just another strange tale constructed out of imagination and mis-understanding, but something very real and very ter-rible. She knew her grandson and his wife were faced with something incomprehensively strange, something deadly which they were not at all equipped to handle. She realized she was fully justified in her suspicions that had brought her to this little seacoast village, that something of the terrible past still lingered in the dark atmosphere of Fowles House.

The room became darker as the storm brought an early nightfall, and small candles in ruby-red glass containers were placed on each table, but their crimson light did little to dispel the greater unseen darkness that settled upon them as John continued with his strange story. Moving shadows were cast upon the room, and

Ellen wondered at the source of them all. She gazed out into the deserted, rain-drenched square and wondered again at the terrible sequence of events that had occurred in this quiet spot two centuries earlier.

When John had finished his disturbing account of the events and the situation at Fowles House, they both remained silent for several moments. The ashtray before them was overflowing with gray residue and crushed cigarette butts, even though the waiter had twice emptied it. John was perspiring heavily, despite the fact that the room was not particularly warm; Ellen indeed felt something of a chill, but did not attempt to define its cause. The little fishing village had suddenly become a terrible place. Did the people here not sense the iced chill of the past that lay about their simple little homes?

John looked at her and there were haunted shadows in his eyes lighted by the red glow of the table lamp.

"That's all of it," he said with something of a sigh. "That's all there is. I don't know what it means, or if it means anything at all. I've tried to tell myself most of it is just my own imagination, but I know that isn't true. I only know something strange and . . . and somehow terrible . . . has happened to Ruth since we moved into that old house, and I quite honestly don't know how to cope with it. I want to help her, but I don't know what against, and she doesn't seem to want my help. I think perhaps Ruth doesn't even realize what has been happening."

"Who else have you told this to?" Ellen asked.

John shook his head. "No one else. Oh, I've tried to; I've wanted to. No, more than that, I've needed to. I thought someone here, in the village, might be able to help me, tell me something that would give me the glimmering of understanding. But I couldn't. I tried talking to Paul Sanders, who rented the place to us . . . you'll meet him at dinner tomorrow . . . and to his assistant, Linda, but I just couldn't bring myself to tell them everything. It all seemed so deadly and yet, somehow, so foolish."

Ellen stared through the window as a miserably wet, bedraggled cur moved slowly across the square, heedless to the rain, its tail dangling as though from weariness. She spoke to John without turning.

"John, just what do you know about the house?"

"Fowles House?" He paused to gather his thoughts, then shrugged. "Not very much, to tell the truth. It's really a fine house, very well constructed, perfectly situated; it could be very comfortable, I think. I know it's had a very unpleasant history and, at least in the minds of some, it has a bad reputation, the kind of thing that ends in all sorts of wild stories and local myths. I know this Fowles character was some very special kind of bastard, dealing in the slave trade and piracy and God know what else, and he was feared and hated by just about everyone. I've never been able to learn more than that. I'm not on really friendly terms with any of the villagers, and they don't like to talk about him; actually, I doubt that they really know very much themselves, just keeping alive old tales that become vaguer with the passing of the years. Maybe they like to retain a touch of local color and mystery. Paul either doesn't know or, for some reason of his own, won't tell me." He looked at her again. "Is there more to know?"

Ellen turned back to him, nodding slowly. "A great deal. You know only the barest skeleton of the story, John. It's not particularly pleasant."

Her words surprised him. "How do you know this? Why should you be interested in the events in a small fishing village like this?"

"I'm interested in everything that concerns you, my dear boy," Ellen assured him. "I became concerned when you first mentioned the name of Fowles in your letters, and I looked into the matter."

"But why would you know anything about a rather obscure sea captain who's been dead for two centuries?"

"Fowles is not as obscure as you think," she replied, "and you forget my interest in the . . . let's call it the unusual. I remembered having come across the name somewhere, in some unpleasant connection. I have access to sources and information that most others do not have. There are books in the British Museum, in the *Bibliotech* of Paris that speak quite graphically about this sea captain of yours."

"But that's incredible!" John remarked. "What possible interest could others have in him, whatever he was? I'd never even heard of the man before I came here."

Ellen shook her head. "He may be a generally obscure figure today, but he was much more widely known in his own time. And there was more, much more, involved than a simple story of piracy in a blood thirsty age. Your Captain Fowles was in his own time a notorious man. Infamous probably would be a better word. His reputation was by no means confined to this little village."

Quietly, then, Ellen told her grandson all she knew about the monstrous Captain Fowles, of his days of piracy and slave trading, of his career as a wrecker, of the tremendous wealth he accumulated for himself in some way no one could quite understand, of the terrible stories and legends that surrounded his name, and of the lingering mystery of his death. Not for a moment did she take her eyes away from John's face, and he listened in something of a trance while that softly gentle voice recounted the terrible tales from a distant past of two centuries ago. About them, the storm continued with unabated fury, the now dark sky torn constantly by crackling lightning and the very walls of the hotel shuddered under the impact of cannonades of rolling thunder. At times the rain fell so heavily that it was impossible to see across the square, and John felt had he been able to peer then through the heavy curtain of rain he might have seen that the entire village had changed, reverted to a past that had now for him become dark and filled with evil.

It was a long story Ellen had to tell, and before she had finished deep night had fallen and the restaurant was empty save for themselves. Waiters and busboys were clearing away the tables, the bartender was cleaning his glasses, and their own waiter was watching them with considerable irritation, waiting for signs of their departure, though neither one noticed him, for Ellen's words had plunged them into a more distant time.

When she had finally finished, John sat thoughtfully, gnawing his lower lip, wondering what to say, finding it difficult to bring himself back to the world he knew.

"*Satan of the Sea?*" he mused. "That's something I've never heard before."

"Most people have not," Ellen agreed. "It's a very strange legend, or superstition if you prefer, and old one, peculiar to those whose lives were spent, and lost, at sea. I believe . . . I hope . . . it has long since vanished from the mind of man; its a particularly unwholesome thought. But it has left its mark, and I know of no one so closely associated with it as Fowles himself."

"You mean to tell me that people actually believed in this . . . this Devil, whatever he was, that people actually worshipped him? But that's utter nonsense!"

"What is and what is not nonsense, John?" she asked, musingly. "We today consider nonsense the worship of Amon-Ra, and yet he was adored for a longer period of religious history than our own Christ. When you think of the countless prayers devoutly offered to the ancient gods for hundreds, even for thousands of years, it is perhaps dangerous to think they were all wasted and for nought. Stand at night in the ruins of the temple of

Amon at Karnak, and you will feel yourself still surrounded by the prayers of many centuries ago. I wonder if any god . . . or devil . . . ever worshipped did not really exist as long as his worship continued."

"Then you believe there really could have been such a . . . such a . . . what shall I call it . . ."

"Faith? Belief? Undoubtedly there was. If there can be one Devil, why not two? There have been multitudes of gods. At any rate John, you don't have to believe something to become frightened by it, and you don't have to accept belief in order for it to become dangerous. Superstition or not, such matters can become extremely perilous when people begin to fear it. And the people of this village at that time both believed and feared."

"But even if all of this is true," John insisted, "I still don't see what it all has to do with Ruth, or with myself. Admittedly, this Fowles appears to have been a spectacularly evil man, greedy for power and wealth, concerned only with his own comforts and totally without a conscience, but what's so unusual about that? That was quite a brutal time, and I'm certain there were many others like him, and there certainly are enough legends about men selling themselves to Satan, whatever you want to call him. Besides, this all happened two centuries ago. What could it possibly have to do with us today?"

"Is the past ever really past, John?" Ellen asked quietly. "Aren't we all, every one of us, composed of the elements of the past as well as of the present? Each generation does not start life afresh, without assimilating some of the experiences and understandings of all the generations that came before."

John shook his head. "We're talking from different tangents now. Of course the knowledge of mankind is gathered from events of the past as well as the present, but you're speaking of elements that are not natural, that have long since been discarded as useless ignorance and superstition. They have nothing to do with the gathering of knowledge and the progress of the human race."

"It may have more to do with it that we realize," Ellen insisted. "John, do you think anything man does is ever done without purpose, or is ever really forgotten? Racial memories remain with us all, even though buried in our subconscious. We are the accumulation of evil as well as of good."

"And what has all this to do with Fowles House?"

"If the memory of good can survive, so perhaps may the memory of evil," Ellen replied, "and particularly an evil as great as that committed by our good Captain Fowles."

"I don't believe in haunted houses," John insisted. "That's a bit of childish nonsense that has no place in our world of today, except as Hallowe'en stories. We have seen no dark shadows on the stairway, no ghosts in white sheets running about the bluff; there have been no things going bump in the night, no dragging of chains and mournful wails."

"The fact that we personally may not believe in something does not necessarily mean it doesn't exist," Ellen said firmly. "There are many who do not accept the belief in any kind of God, but that does not negate his existence for those who do believe. Those of us who . . . yes, like myself, dear John . . . have seen strange things are not moved by your refusal of acceptance. We know there are such things, and you cannot convince us otherwise. There are many kinds of hauntings, John, and the most terrible and the most dangerous is the haunting of the mind."

He found the words difficult to say. "You mean Ruth is being . . . haunted?"

"In some ways, yes."

John lighted another cigarette. "Setting aside the fact that Ruth is an intelligent woman completely free of superstitious fear, I can to a point accept the power of suggestion. Voodoo dolls and all that sort of thing. I know they work. But it can't apply here. Ruth knows nothing about Fowles."

"You needn't be aware of something to be affected by it."

"Little though it is, I've known more about Fowles than Ruth does," he reminded her. "Why haven't I been affected?"

Ellen shrugged her shoulders. "I don't know. Your mind perhaps is not as receptive as hers."

John started to speak again, then stopped, at a loss for words. The waiter pointedly approached them and again emptied the ashtray, lingering for a moment in hopes they would give him some sign of their departure; when they did not, he returned, glowering at the bartender, to his place against the wall.

John sighed and shook his head. "I can't understand it," he complained. "It just doesn't make sense to me. Why should Ruth feel things this way?"

"I don't know," Ellen confessed. "There is still too much about all of this that I simply can't understand. There are too many missing pieces. I only know there is something exceptionally evil in that house, a lingering foul aura from the past, and from what you tell me, I think that evil has in some way attached itself to Ruth. I can't begin to guess at its cause, its reason, or its final effect."

"Must there be one . . . either reason or final effect?"

"Everything in life has a purpose, even death. Whatever it is that hovers over Fowles House is there for a reason." Frowning, Ellen toyed for a moment with her cup, half-filled with coffee that had long since gone cold. "There are too many aspects of the story that disturb me, particularly the inconclusive conclusion, if I can put it that way."

"You mean the death of Fowles?"

"Why do all the accounts end at the same time in the story?" she wondered, "Just at the point when the villagers are converging upon the house? Writers of the time delighted in gruesome descriptions of the horrors of the Inquisition and the witch trials, they relished in tales of burnings and torn limbs and tortures of every kind. Why have they not, not a single one of them that I have found, recounted what the villagers found in that house and what was finally done to Fowles?"

"Perhaps they didn't know," John suggested.

Ellen shook her head again. "No. That's unlikely. If they knew so much of the story, they surely knew the rest of it."

"Then why?"

"I don't know. I just don't know. Perhaps they felt it was too terrible to be believed." A brilliant flash of lightning cast tall shadows on the walls. "Perhaps if I knew the rest of the story, I might understand better." She absently drummed her fingers on the table and spoke almost to herself. "And where is the catalyst?"

"The catalyst?" John echoed.

"The driving force that has revived all of this after so many long years."

"Wouldn't that be Ruth?"

The white head moved in an uncertain denial. "No, I don't believe so. Ruth is the recipient of the force, not its originator. I don't believe her presence alone could have precipitated this. There is some other . . . influence . . . involved." She put out her cigarette, sending some of the ash unto the white tablecloth, and took a firm grip on her handbag. "Call the waiter, John. We must go."

"Go?" He seemed confused.

"Yes," Ellen firmly replied. "It's getting late, and Ruth is alone in the house."

"Ruth has been alone many times before," he pointed out in a rather grim tone. "She much prefers it that way."

"Her constant desire to be alone may be the most ominous fact of all," Ellen insisted.

John looked at her for a moment. "Then you really think Ruth is in danger?"

There could be no further evasion. Ellen looked at him quite frankly, and the fear was apparent in her face and in her eyes; the fingers holding her handbag had become white with the pressure of her grasp.

"Yes, John. I think Ruth is in terrible danger," she confirmed in a soft, emotionless tone that was somehow more frightening than anything she had yet said.

The lights suddenly flickered and went out, plunging the room into crimson shadow from the few candles remaining on the tables. It was but the darkness of seconds, and when the lights flashed on again, John signaled for the waiter who, relieved by their apparent departure, rushed over to them with the check.

CHAPTER NINETEEN

THAT was an exceptionally dark and lonely trip to the house on that strangest and most terrible of all evenings, and John drove very swiftly, almost with a wild recklessness, hearing always his grandmother's ominous last words, suddenly overwhelmingly anxious to return to the old house and to his wife.

Surely he had never seen a night quite so dark; it was something like being smothered in thick masses of blackest velvet. He could scarcely see the road before him, as though even the roadway had been swallowed by the dark void; the twin narrow slashing beams of his yellow headlights, themselves almost defeated by the cancerous blackness, showed him only the dreary yellow of the dirt road directly before him, and the sparse, spiney, somehow alien vegetations on either side. It was like moving through a world that had been instantly frozen in a lost moment of time. The wind whistled through the windows of the car that had been slightly opened, for it was oppressively hot, and tossed his hair about his head, as though it were trying to overturn the small beattle-like vehicle and make them a part of the silent darkness of the night. There was an occasional flash of lightning that starkly revealed the barren, hostile surroundings, like the dark and angular shadows of a surrealistic cinema set, and he could see the heavy darkness of the vast mysterious world of water to his left and that thin line, like the firm whitened lips of an embittered spinster, that separated the black sea from the even blacker sky. The sounds of the surf battled for preeminence with the steadily increasing moan of the wind and the deep growling of the thunder.

Ellen sat silently at his side, tightly grasping the handbag on her lap, a small yet stolid figure who seemed to be both out of place and time, staring ahead, firmly upright and unbending, looking neither to left nor right, saying not a word after the exhaustion of her long narrative in the restaurant, scarcely noticing the wind that came to them through the open windows, salted by the slight touch of spray from the storm-tossed surf. In that erratic yellow light her eyes seemed to gleam like tiny pinpoints of fear.

Ellen had not said a word since they had left the finally empty restaurant, seized by a fear neither was able or willing to express, crouching under the umbrella as they rushed through the wind-whipped rain, splashing unheedful through puddles and evading miniature brooks. John had tossed the suitcase into the rear of the car and they had started off quickly through the silent, dripping village, its streets empty and abandoned like those of a ghost town. An occasional light gleamed ineffectually through the falling rain, as though bravely attempting to defeat the elements, and John wondered if there had been nights like this in the distant past when the villagers had cowered with fear in the uncertain protection of their homes.

They left the village behind them and started swiftly along the shore road to the house on the cliff. As he drove, John occasionally cast a quick glance at his grandmother seated at his side, so immobile, like carved white marble, the strong profile etched by lightning, firmly gripping her purse as though desperately needing to hold onto something. There was a clamp of fear in the pit of John's stomach, such as he had not felt since, as a small child, he had feared the discovery of some infraction of the family rules.

Now the fears had become all too real; the dark dreams had at last become a living nightmare. He needed only the fear-frozen white face of his grandmother to tell him that. Grandmother Ellen knew about such things.

That ride through the stormy darkness seemed interminable, and the roaring of the wind and the growling of the thunder were like angry howls from another world, a world that perhaps was attempting to force its power on the living. The rain pounded upon the roof of the car and made it difficult for John to see his way through the streaming windshield. They rocked back and forth on the rutted roadway, but still Ellen made no sound, staring straight ahead at the blackness, and John wondered what thoughts were going through her mind, what terrible thoughts.

They passed the abandoned lighthouse, rising like a ghostly white specter from the evil past, and John imagined he could almost see the crouched concealed forms of the wreckers gathered about its base, their faces alight with hunger for plunder. Everything tonight seemed to speak of the past, and he would not have been surprised to see, in a flash of flickering lightning, a wounded sailing vessel with broken rigging and tattered canvas in its death throes upon the black-salted rocks reaching out to sea. The air seemed to swarm with demons.

They zoomed quickly up the rise to the bluff and came at last in sight of the old house. Ellen moved then for the first time, as she placed a hand on John's arm.

"Stop, John," she ordered harshly. "Stop here for a moment."

John brought the car to an abrupt stop just at the beginning of the curvature of the road as it looped before the veranda and went on to rejoin the descent again, and they sat silent for a moment, hearing but not listening to the storm.

Ellen looked closely at the large house looming so darkly against the blacker darkness of the stormy sky, like a blot of midnight ink against black velvet, and the house seemed to leap at them like some giant wingless creature when lightning brightened the scene with the sudden flash of a lantern slide. The house stood somewhat taller than she had expected, rising to its pointed gables that streamed now with the rain water like cascades of silver hair. Beyond the darkness of the broad veranda, she sensed that the windows were vacant eyes returning her curious stare; through them, no light showed. An angular, naked tree stood like a black exclamation point at one side of the veranda. The silence seemed to surround the house with a darkness greater and more ominous than that of the night itself.

She had wondered what would be her first feeling upon seeing this house about which she had read and wondered so much during the past several weeks. Would it be fear, uneasiness? Would she feel a chill of evil, sense the aura of terrible things that had happened here? She strangely felt none of these things. As she gazed up to the rain-swept vacant Widow's Walk, she was aware of a sense of deep sorrow. There had been evil here, but there had been great sadness as well, yet strangely that sadness did not come from the Widow's Walk, for on that flat expanse facing the sea she seemed to sense only the dark form of Captain Fowles himself, and there had been no sadness in his dark vigils. No, she felt the sadness had a deeper origin. It seemed to come from the land itself, from this unfortunate land that had been chosen as the site of horrors still unknown.

Ellen sighed, almost with a touch of disappointment; perhaps she had expected something more dramatic. This was simply a large old house standing alone on a bluff above the lonely sea, isolated from the passage of time itself. It would probably be quite an attractive house in the purer light of day.

"Go on, John," she said softly.

He pulled up before the veranda and stepped out of the car, instantly drenched by the falling curtain of rain before he was able to raise the umbrella, which had a somewhat stubborn catch. He then ran quickly around the front of the car and opened the passenger's door, carefully sheilding his grandmother against the rain as they mounted the worn wooden stairs. Ellen paused for a moment on the veranda, frowning as she glanced at the dark empty expanse and the few always present dead leaves; no lights shone from the interior of the house. She stepped to the railing and looked curiously at the dead tree, its forlorn naked branches dripping rain like white blood. She sniffed the air.

"Sulphur," she muttered. "Strange."

They entered the foyer and as John closed the heavy door behind them, shutting out the rain and the swirling darkness, Ellen with interest examined the entry, the darkly burnished wood, the ticking grandfather's clock, the shadowed well of the graceful staircase. The rooms opening upon the foyer were in darkness brightened only by brief flashes of lightning flickering through their open doors; the only illumination in the foyer itself came from the lighted newel lamp at the foot of the stairs and the lightning through the porthole windows lining the stairway. The house was completely silent, as though it were empty save for the memories of a terrible haunted past. The foyer felt somewhat colder than it should have been, but while she wondered at this unusual chill, Ellen still felt no particular aura in the attractive entry, no sense of the unknown or expected.

"I don't know why the house is so dark," John muttered with some irritation as he placed the wet umbrella in the stand near the door. Raising his voice, he called, "Ruth! Ruth! Where are you?"

His voice, amplified by their surroundings, echoed hollowly through the vast empty chambers, drifting up the stairway that seemed to writhe in the erratic light through the windows, floating down the corridor lined with the hostile faces from the past, seeping through the rooms of the house to lose itself at last in the mysterious chamber in the cellar. Startled by the echoing sound, Ellen lightly raised a hand and then placed it on John's arm as though for support; he could feel it tremble slightly.

"She must be upstairs," he commented. "She probably didn't hear us pull up." He raised his voice again. "Ruth! It's John! Grandmother Ellen is here. Ruth, where are you?"

The voice was strangely soft and distant, unexpected as it drifted down to them from above, like a reawakened voice from the past.

"I'm right here, John. I can hear. There's no need to shout."

In the often blinding flashes of lightning from the round windows, they saw Ruth standing at the head of the stairs, one hand just resting lightly on the carved bannister. She wore a flowing, diaphanous sea-green silken gown, and had they not heard her voice they might easily have taken her for a restless specter chained to the old house by some tragedy of earlier years.

John pressed the switch beside the door, and the great chandelier exploded into prisms of colored light, casting daggers about the foyer and dimming the light of the storm. Momentarily blinded by the sudden brilliant illumination, John briefly closed his eyes and then looked up to where Ruth stood quite motionless, gazing down at them, a slight smile on her face, and then she began to move slowly down the stairs, and John caught his breath, for he had never seen her move with such effortless grace, the gown trailing behind her, her head held high, the crystaline colors flashing in her hair. He thought she had never been more beautiful.

Ellen watched Ruth closely, narrowing her eyes

against the sudden light, as John took a step towards his wife. Ruth's smile broadened as she neared them, and she extended her hands towards the grandmother.

"Grandmother Ellen! How very nice to see you again!"

John had been concerned about this moment of meeting. It was difficult to forecast Ruth's moods, and he feared she might greet his grandmother with the same hostility she expressed to all that interrupted her new isolated way of life. But there was a surprising warmth of welcome in her deep, soothing voice, and John thought that Ruth suddenly seemed more herself than she had been in weeks. The woman who had so confused and worried him with her recent attitudes had suddenly become the charming hostess greeting a sincerely welcome guest, like a *grand dame* of the past might have welcomed visitors to her manor by the sea.

Ellen peered closely at Ruth as her grandson's wife approached them down the broad sweep of the stairway, and she was also struck by Ruth's unusual beauty. Ruth seemed to possess a radiance and sensuality that Ellen had never before seen in her. The body outlined by the sheer silken gown was supply curved and ripe, the breasts surprisingly full. Ellen was startled to note the dark nipples through the cloth of the gown; she had never known Ruth to dress in so obviously sexual a manner. Were it not for her poise and grand air, there might have been something almost wanton in her appearance, but it would have been an unconscious wantonness, like the natural sensuality of an ancient fertility goddess. Her skin seemed as white as alabaster, or like the salted driftwood tossed aside by the sea. Ruth seemed somehow much younger than when Ellen had seen her last, but she remembered that at that time she had been bent and temporarily aged by the sorrow of her daughter's death.

Yet there was as well something undeniably strange and disconcerting about Ruth's beauty now. Despite her smile, her face was like that of a stranger, a white mask, unlined, almost waxen, unstained by make up of any kind. Her thick chestnut hair hung as a loose frame about the pale features. The cheekbones seemed higher than Ellen remembered them to be, and the eyes darker and somehow more alert with, nevertheless, a curious vagueness of expression, almost as though Ruth were looking above and beyond them into another world, while still bound to this one. Ellen wondered why, in this oppressively muggy weather and despite the lightness of her garb, Ruth wore a green silk scarf closely wound about her throat.

John was right, Ellen decided. Ruth had indeed changed considerably, but not at all in the way John had implied. She had expected to see a drawn, thin, nervous woman with the shadowed eyes of the haunted, but she saw instead a woman who seemed radiant, composed, serene, as though imbued with some unknown secret of a new life. There was decidedly something uncomfortable about her. She seemed to have a beauty that did not belong to her, that had come to her from somewhere else outside of herself.

Ellen stepped out to meet Ruth at the foot of the stairs, and the two women embraced briefly. There was a surprising strength in Ruth's arms, and Ellen was briefly startled by the coldness of the cheek pressed to her own.

"Hello, Ruth, my dear!" Ellen greeted, attempting to keep the sense of uneasiness from her voice. "Oh, but you're looking quite remarkably well!"

"Why yes, of course," Ruth replied, and her cold lips touched Ellen's cheek; they seemed uncomfortably wet. "I'm always well, now." She drew back and looked with a peculiar intensity into Ellen's face; Ellen had never noticed the deep green of Ellen's eyes, green and in constant motion as though swirling with vitality. "Welcome to this house, Grandmother Ellen." The words seemed curiously proprietary, as though Ruth were introducing Ellen into a new world that belonged to herself alone.

"I'm sorry we're so late, Ruth," John apologized. "We stopped at the hotel for some coffee, and got to talking. I'm afraid we quite forgot the time."

Ruth turned to him with the first smile she had given her husband in some weeks; was there just a slight trace of mockery in the movement of her red unpainted lips?

"Why, that's quite all right, John." Her voice was languid and devoid of emotion. "I really didn't expect you much earlier. To tell the truth, I'd already gone to bed. I've developed a really dreadful headache."

"Oh, but then we shouldn't have disturbed you, my dear," Ellen said quickly.

"I'm certain it will pass," Ruth remarked with a slight smile. "It must be the heat."

"Nonsense," Ellen said firmly, casting at John a glance that enjoined his silence. "There is nothing better for a headache than rest, and nothing worse than rest that has been disturbed. Now, you go right on back to bed, my dear; we'll have plenty of time to talk in the morning."

Ruth protested feebly, but her voice lacked conviction. "But that is hardly the proper way to greet a welcome guest. . ."

Ellen tossed John a look asking for his assistance, and he at once understood her desire to have Ruth leave them alone.

"I think Grandmother Ellen is quite right, Ruth," he said. "It really is very late, and I'm sure Grandmother and I have already done enough talking for one day. She's had a very tiring trip. You go on back upstairs, dear. I'll make Grandmother Ellen comfortable and show her to her room. We'll want you bright and chipper tomorrow, you know; you'll have a great deal to talk about, and then there's the dinner tomorrow evening. We'll want our first social function to go well, won't we?"

Ruth hesitated a moment longer, but her weariness suddenly became more evident, and a peculiar change came over her. Her figure sagged slightly, lines of strain appeared on her face as she ran her hand lightly over her forehead and down to the green cloth that circled her throat; she held her hand there as though seeking strength from its touch, and for a moment her eyes wandered vaguely about as though she were not quite certain of her surroundings.

"Well, perhaps you are right after all," she commented, and her voice had again become strangely weak and distant. "I do feel rather peculiar this evening. Perhaps it would be best for me to rest." She turned again to Ellen and then frowned slightly, as though having difficulty in gathering her thoughts. "If you're sure you don't mind?"

"Not at all, my dear," Ellen assured her soothingly, staring intently at the face that seemed to have become distorted by an invisible veil. "I'll be asleep before long myself. Oh, tomorrow I must tell you all about the perfectly dreadful trip I've had! A bus ride! Just imagine!"

Surprisingly, Ruth turned her cheek for John's kiss, then lightly brushed Ellen's cheek. She staggered, and John put out a hand as though expecting her to fall, then lowered it when she turned away from them.

"Very well, then, I'll see you in the morning." Ruth started up the stairs again, then paused and turned back to Ellen. "I'm glad you've come, Grandmother Ellen. Women have always had a very special welcome in this house, you know." Her voice was strong, yet still distant, not like hers at all.

Ruth started again up the stairs, but her earlier grace and lightness of movement had suddenly disappeared, and she walked very slowly, heavily, almost like a sleepwalker, leaning on the balustrade and almost painfully moving up step by step. In those few seconds she had somehow become older, more distant and withdrawn, anxious to be away from them. She paused at one of the porthole windows as lightning outlined her profile and a heavy peal of thunder rocked the house. She spoke with her face turned to the window, and John for one uncomfortable moment felt he was watching an actress making a dramatic exit.

"You know, you mustn't be afraid of the violence of the night, Grandmother Ellen," she said in a soft, soothing voice, as though she were placating a child's fears. "It will pass, once the sea has had a chance to express its fury."

Frowning at these strange words, John turned to Ellen, who again placed a silencing finger to her lips. Ruth slowly turned again and continued on up the stairs, a small green drifting figure that seemed to have stepped from some more distant time. At the top of the stairs she paused and looked down at them, and lightning cast dancing green shadows upon her pale face. She turned and disappeared from their view; they heard the closing of the bedroom door.

Ellen quickly turned to her grandson, deep concern in her face. "Yes, you are right, John," she said. "Ruth has changed. I don't understand how or why, but she is greatly changed."

John stared at her for a moment, his confusion growing; he had somehow not expected these words. "But she seems more like herself this evening than she has been in weeks," he insisted. "She's a little tired, that's all. . ."

Ellen shook her head. "No, John, no. She is different, far more different than you know. There is a strangeness about her that I don't understand. Didn't you notice how suddenly she altered? It was as though she had somehow found the strength and the will to welcome me, and then had no more, as if the effort drained that strength out of her. Her strength seems to come . . . oh, I don't know . . . not from within, somehow, but from somewhere. . . That expressionless face, the vague voice, almost as though she were in some kind of

trance. . . . Oh, John, I don't like it. I don't like it one bit!"
She paused and looked confusedly about, as though
searching about the old house for an answer. Then she
drew herself together and turned once again more
briskly to John. "I wanted her to go upstairs so I could
see the house. Now, quickly, show me to that room in the
cellar."

She held tightly onto John's hand as he guided her
through the dark narrow corridor leading to the
kitchen; she nervously averted her gaze from the
shadowed portraits lining the walls, yet she seemed to
sense implacably hostile eyes staring at her. They
moved through the dark kitchen and stepped carefully
onto the platform of the cellar stairs. John turned on the
light.

In its faint dusty glow, Ellen stared down into the
empty mustiness, glancing over the asbestos-covered
pipes, the accumulated litter of bygone ages. The dim
light cast huge shadows upon the barren walls. The
silence seemed more intense here, the sounds of the
storm muted. There was almost an air of peace about
the cellar, a serenity, a sense of slumbering, as though
this cellar were completely apart from the house and
separate from all that occurred in the regions above it,
and yet for the first time since actually entering the
house, Ellen had a distinct feeling of uneasiness. It was
almost as though by stepping onto the platform she had
entered the past, or a different world. She sensed that
there was here a force gathering itself for some dreadful
purpose.

Peering closely about her, stooping slightly, she
asked, "And where is the room?"

John indicated the dark squat form of the pot-bellied
furnace. "Over there at the far wall, just beyond the
furnace."

"I see. Turn the light off, John."

"What?"

Ellen gestured impatiently towards the light switch.

"Turn off the light. Do as I say!"

The cellar was momentarily plunged into total darkness, and then they could see the pale green glow emanating from beyond the furnace, a pale incadescence that spread its eerie light in only the one small corner of the cellar.

"That's the glow you spoke of?" Ellen asked.

"Yes," John replied. "But it was much brighter then."

"Green has always been the color of evil," Ellen muttered, almost to herself. "I've often thought it comes from the green of the Garden of Eden, where *Evil* first entered the world. And, of course, it's also the color of the sea." She took John's hand. "Come on down with me. No, don't turn the light on. The lightning will help us."

"Are you certain you want to go down there?" John asked somewhat hesitantly.

"No. I don't want to at all," Ellen admitted with a slight shake of her head. "It frightens me more than anything else I've ever done. But we must go down. I don't know what happened in that room or why, but there's no doubt that it's the center of these strange events you've told me about. Perhaps it will tell me something."

Clasping hands, they carefully made their way down the sagging stairs and across the bare floor towards the furnace; lightning flashing through the small dirty windows hurled their shadows ahead of them, as though the shadows were more anxious than they to reach their destination. The green glow seemed to brighten as they approached, as though it, too, were lighting their way, and the closer they came to that mysterious room, the more did Ellen feel the cold clutch of fear.

The door of the little room stood wide open, and the small chamber was suffused with the bright green color of a clear, deep sea. Ellen hesitated for a moment, one hand to her breast as though trying to gather her courage, and then, with an obvious effort, she stepped into the room.

She gasped at the sudden touch of cold, an almost cutting iciness that made her breath apparent in little white crystals from her mouth. At the same moment, she felt a terrible oppressiveness, as though a great weight were being pressed against her mind. She looked about her at the harsh barren walls, and the fear grew in her face as the terrible aura of the room touched her.

"Oh, dear God, what an evil place this is!" she gasped.

"What is it?" John asked, standing behind her, feeling nothing but the intense cold.

"I don't know," Ellen replied, glancing again about the small room. "I can only feel the evil, seeping from the walls and the floor itself, a greater evil than I have sensed before, anywhere." She turned to him, her face agonized by fear. "Oh, John, terrible things have happened in this room, and the memory of them has survived so that I can almost feel them, almost see them hovering about us!" She clasped her white-gloved hands together and again looked about the room. "It's as though these walls drip with blood!"

John took hold of her arm. "Come. Let's get out of here."

Ellen shook her head and her voice trembled slightly. "No, no, not yet. There is more. . ." She looked at last upon the central mound upon which Ruth had lain herself in that terrible evening when it had all begun. "And is that where you found her?"

"Yes," John confirmed. "She was lying directly on the mound, the roundness arching her back. And she was naked."

"Was it as cold as this?"

He nodded. "She didn't even seem to feel it."

"What could have brought her down here?" Ellen wondered.

She moved slowly towards the mound, her piercing eyes fixed to the polished concave surface. Her walk seemed curiously stilted, almost as though something within herself tried to hold her back. As she approached the center of the room, she slowly removed the glove from her right hand. Standing before the mound, she paused for a moment, staring down, and then, with some difficulty, dropped slowly to one knee; John felt an almost irresistable urge to laugh hysterically at the incongruity of her slight, elegant, smartly clad figure kneeling on the bare earth before the irregularity in the cellar floor.

Ellen reached her hand out to the mound, then quickly pulled it back. She glanced up with a startled expression and waved her hand above her head, as though brushing aside something that had touched her, then reached out again and placed the hand upon the hard earth.

The earth was smooth and somehow comforting, and she ran her hand back and forth over its surface; there seemed a wetness in the contact, yet her hand remained dry. She closed her eyes, and suddenly her mind was filled with strange images, of rolling green seas in which drifted large dark forms she could not recognize. She began to moan slightly, and her body moved ever so slowly from side to side as her hand continued to caress the polished mound. Her face became pale, and tiny beads of perspiration appeared on her forehead. and attitude, John took hold of his grandmother's shoulders.

"Grandmother!" he called, as though summoning her. "What is it? What are you doing?"

His abrupt movement and call awakened Ellen from her near trance and removed her hand from the mound. Startled, she looked up at John; a momentary vagueness in her eyes vanished quickly when she looked into his face. She held her hands out to him.

"Help me up, John!" she ordered in a voice that trembled. "Help me up, quickly!"

He lifted her to her feet and she stood for a moment, leaning heavily against him, her wide eyes again running over the empty room.

"We must get out of here!" she said softly, her voice

taut with fear. "This is a terrible place. Take me upstairs to my room. Close the door of this room as tightly as you can. Let whatever is in here be kept behind that door!"

CHAPTER TWENTY

IN the darkest hours of that strangest of nights, the evil that had for two centuries surrounded Fowles House found its last strength and spread about the surrounding countryside like a poisonous miasma that destroyed all it touched.

The storm exhausted itself in senseless fury and then slowly abated during the last few silent hours before daylight. The crashing of thunder sounded like the distant growling of wearied cannon, and the lightning descended below the horizon, its weakening flashes like the sporadic breathing of a dying man. The rain eased until it became but a light shower, as though the dark clouds were being squeezed of their final drops of moisture. For some moments, the clouds parted like the separation of gossamer veils and the moon showed her white face, but before long the sky was again a covering of slate gray; more rain was coming. The silence of the night was broken by constant drippings and gurglings as the rain trickled from soaked surfaces.

There was scarcely a sound in the village. The earlier rain had kept everyone indoors, and now it was too late and still too wet and threatening to venture from the comforts of a warm home. No lights shone, as though the rain had extinguished them all. The square was empty, the lonely benches gleaming with rain water, and the battered flowers still drooped from the cruel onslaught of the storm. Perhaps the village was silent because it sensed the presence of evil.

Linda nervously paced the floor of her dark room, smoking constantly, twisting her hands in fear and confusion; the dark violence mirrored the chaos within her own mind. The darkness seemed to glow with Paul's eyes, bearing an expression that could have nothing to do with the kindly Paul she had known, and she seemed to hear his voice . . . his voice, yet surely too harsh and bitter to be his voice, repeating those terrible things he had told her.

It had been an impulsive decision on her part, to see Paul once more before morning, when she would at last leave this little village once and for all. She had not planned to see him again; surely all had been said that could be said. But she was concerned about his peculiar attitude since his return, and suddenly realized she could not leave him without in at least some measure setting her own mind at rest. Paul had been good to her when she needed him most, she had surely loved him in her own way, and she could not abandon him to false thoughts that could only increase the sorrow and the bitterness of her rejection. She had to be certain he fully understood the reasons for her leaving.

But he had refused to listen to her. They had stood facing each other in that office where once they had worked together in such close harmony, and he had poured out upon her a torrent of invective in incredibly foul terms she had never before heard him use, vile accusations that Paul surely knew could never have been true. She had recoiled from his vicious attack, her face pale and her eyes wide with disbelief, incapable through sheer startled horror of defending herself. She could make little sense of much that he said, his sarcastic contempt for her, his bitter denunciation of John Kendall, his veiled threats towards Ruth, the wife of the man he felt had betrayed him. He spoke of revenge, and of power, and of a deep secret knowledge, and the words that came from his mouth sounded like sheer gibberish.

She had stared at him in horrified fascination, certain he had lost his mind. This was Paul, yet surely it was not Paul, for the Paul she had known was totally incapable of such bitter, obscene fury. As she watched him, even his appearance seemed to change; fury made him taller, more powerful, and that handsome, always pleasant face became so twisted with hatred and anger that she could scarcely recognize him.

And yet even in the midst of this vile, vicious tirade, there had been flashes of the old, gentle Paul, brief moments when the fury had faded, and Paul's face had returned to her, looking at her with those warmly gentle eyes, as though begging her forgiveness for what he could not avoid saying, and then there was in that face the expression of a lost and frightened little boy. Linda had suddenly remembered, then, John's comments of the strange alterations and attitudes and even appearance of Ruth. Why this peculiar similarity?

Then Paul, at the height of his rage, had revealed to her the true horrors of Fowles House what had happened there, those horrors of which he had before seemed totally ignorant, and there had tumbled from his foaming lips the most terrible filth and unimaginable horrors she had ever heard or even imagined. She had felt an urge to vomit before the dreadful degradation of Captain Jonathan Fowles that was now revealed to her for the first time, and at last, gathering all her fear-frozen resources, with a slight cry she had staggered from the office, Paul's harsh voice calling obscenely after her, and somehow made her way back to her home.

Linda lighted another cigarette before the other had been quite consumed, and continued her nervous pacing. She had been doing this now for some hours, torn between fear, doubt, indecision and the greatest terror she had ever experienced. How much of what she had heard was true? Had Paul indeed gone mad? How could she help him? What could she do? She thought of Paul as she had known him these past years, so kind and always considerate through his unexpressed love for her, and saw again that gentle face and her heart cried out at what strange thing had happened to him.

She crossed to the window and stared out into the darkness. Nothing could be seen, but she knew Fowles House stood out there beyond the dark, a tall and lonely house surrounded by the implacable hatred of centuries, and again she cried out, this time with fear as she realized the horrors that awaited those within that house if Paul's mad story could possibly be true.

Paul sat slumped in the large leather chair in his office, his eyes glazed as they stared at the darkness of the harbor, seeing there things he could not have seen . .

wooden vessels with billowing sails, tall masts reaching to the clouded sky . . . and hearing things he could not have heard . . . the creak of rigging and the spanking of canvas. Sweat beaded his face and glistened in the several days growth of beard that sharpened his resemblance to the dusty old portraits hanging on the walls of Fowles House. His hands grasped the arms of the chair with a tightness that turned the knuckles white. An occasional moan of agony and fear escaped from between his dried and cracked lips as he battled against the terrors that had seized his mind. His wild eyes wandered about the room that had suddenly become totally unfamiliar to him.

For days, Paul had been trying vainly to understand what was happenng to him, the frequent lapses of memory, the recollection of dreadful things that he could not possibly have experienced, the difficulty in separating in his mind a past he could not have known from a reality that was drifting swiftly away from him. There were long periods of time for which he could not account, dark hours from which he would suddenly awake as from a tortured dream, to find about him evidence of an angry violence he could not recall. Terrible, indecipherable images swept through his mind, threatening to drive him to madness. He had remained here in this frequently strange office, afraid of showing himself to others, frightened that they might sense in him the terrible darkness he knew was coming. He had a vague recollection of Linda fleeing from him, her face pale with horror, but he could not recall why she had come or why she had left with fear etched in those eyes he had loved so long.

Paul frowned and closed his eyes. He could not doubt that he was, somehow, losing his mind, and the aptness of the phrase frightened him, for he sensed it was not merely insanity that faced him, but the actual surrendering of his mind and personality to ... to what? He moaned again, and twisted slightly in the chair. What was this horror that faced him? How could he combat something he did not know or understand? How could he keep this unknown force at bay when he had no knowledge of from where it came or what it was after?

The room fell silent. A dying flicker of lightning touched the bearded face with the closed eyes and dripping perspiration, lighted the tightly clenched fists on the arms of the chair, the straining that caused the body to tremble.

Slowly, the trembling ceased and the tension eased. The white-knuckled hands released their tight grip on the chair arms, and the lines of agony faded from the face. A slight smile unpleasantly curved the dry lips and the eyes opened, clear and unshadowed either by doubt or fear.

He rose from the chair and walked with firm steps through the darkness of the outer office to the door. The perspiration on his face was washed away by the light drizzle of rain as he left the office and turned his steps in the direction of Fowles House. There was now no confusion in his strong, determined mind. He knew what had to be done.

Fowles House was dark and silent. Rain dripped from the gables, streamed from the gutters, and glistened on the empty expanse of the Widow's Walk; it ran like black sap down the twisted length of the tree near the veranda. Huge black clouds hovered over the old house like wings attempting to conceal the darkness below. Only the scarcely heard rhythm of the sea below the cliff disturbed the stillness. Small crawling creatures scrambled across the wet sands of the beach to feast upon the minute marine life cast up by the high seas and left helpless and stranded on the land. Lightning revealed the perpetually empty horizon.

No light came from within the house itself. Its rooms and corridors were dark, and only a slight lessening of the darkness marked the tall windows. The glowering portraits were lost in shadow, but the eyes of the long dead seafarers were accustomed to darkness. The ticking of the grandfather's clock was the only sound to be heard. The dying flashes of the exhausted storm weakly brightened the empty staircase leading from the foyer to the darker rooms above. So had the house greeted the darkness for many years; it might easily still have been vacant.

Ruth tossed restlessly in her uncomfortable sleep, disturbed by a series of strange dreams of which she was hardly aware. She felt herself sinking into a depthless green void, a swirling mass of sea water that was both frightening and strangely comforting. She seemed to drift effortlessly in its seething embrace, almost like the dreams of flying she had so often experienced as a child. Even the strangely twisting creatures that surrounded her, formless masses to which she could give no name, did not frighten her; they seemed to surround her with an unasked protection. Always she seemed to be moving with a purpose, towards an area of darker, more mysterious green where, she sensed, something waited for her. There was a thrill of anticipation as she moved closer to the almost unseen movement before her.

Yet still the strangely comforting dream was occasionally torn by a touch of panic, of almost paralyzing fear, when she raised her eyes to the brightness above, when she felt herself engulfed by the sea and she longed to raise her head once again above the surface of the watery world to the clear purity of a blue sky with the warm touch of the sun and the gentle carress of a soft breeze. Then she would twist and moan in her sleep, feeling the feather-like touch of unreasoning fear, and one hand would move to the green scarf about her throat. For just that brief moment, she would attempt to remove the scarf, and then suddenly the fear was gone and comfort returned, and she would clasp the scarf more closely about her throat and her doubts would disappear as once again her dream thoughts drew her ever closer to the darkness for which she was headed. It was coming closer now, ever closer, and in her sleep she felt a sense of constantly growing anticipation and excitement.

There was no sleep for Ellen that night. She lay quite motionless in the center of her bed, still fully clothed, waiting for something she sensed was about to happen, something neither she nor anyone else could hope to prevent. Her mind again went to the strongly sensed terrors of that room in the cellar of this house, its biting coldness, the aura of unimaginable evil with which that small room was filled. She had many times sensed the touch of the past, in strange and haunted places all over the world, but never so strongly as in this terrible house, and never had that feeling been so completely composed of darkness. *Evil* had been here and that evil still remained, and her grandson and his wife had become the very center of its terrifying force. She had always been intrigued by contact with the unknown world beyond, but never before had she experienced such all-consuming fear. What she sensed in this house was not simply an intriguing contact with the past. This was something powerful and above all deadly.

She ran a small, trembling hand over her perspiring forehead. Perhaps it was not yet too late. John and Ruth would have to leave this house tomorrow, as early as possible in the morning, and the house itself must, somehow, be destroyed, razed to the ground so that the evil that festered here would be left without a home.

She seemed to hear strange sounds in the darkness of that night, shiftings and movements, yet she knew the house was silent and empty save for Ruth and John and herself. There could be no sounds, save for those created by her own deeply stirred imagination, and the irritating dripping of the rain. She forced down a driving urge to rise from her bed and flee from the house, to run as far as she could go, away from the very sight of this terrible place. But she could not. There were John and Ruth to be considered. She could not leave them here to face the unknown with their total lack of experience, although she had no conception of what could be done to help them. She knew with a terrible growing certainty that something was coming to them through the gathered darkness.

Would this night never end?

John also lay awake and restless, staring uneasily at the grayness of the window, waiting for the brightening of dawn as he listened to the silence around him, broken by the trickle of the lighter rain and the dripping from the eaves. The thunder was growing louder again and the lightning brighter and more frequent. Another storm was rising. It was often like this at this time of year, one violent storm following quickly on the heels of another. The winds had been released from their confining caverns and were again beginning to howl about the lonely old house.

John had removed his shirt and thrown himself onto

the bed; for some reason, it did not occur to him to remove his trousers. The sheets under his bare back were already damp with perspiration, running over the sides of his chest and onto the bed. How could one tell what was the perspiration of humidity and what the perspiration of fear?

For fear had now become his all-pervading emotion, fear that filled his heart and mind so intensely that he thought he might yet snap under its pressure. He seemed in the very center of a vortex of terror, and during those few moments when he managed to slip into an uneasy slumber, that fear followed him and his dreams were filled with whirling faces . . . the brutal face of Fowles, laughing, his large head thrown back so that his teeth gleamed wickedly through the redness of his beard . . . the love-familiar face of Ruth, staring at him with green eyes glinting in mockery . . . the gentle face of Ellen staring with a confused mixture of pity and terror. He woke from these brief dreams writhing in the clutch of his own terror, afraid again to close his eyes and face the strange world of darkness that filled his mind.

He sat up in the bed, shifting his legs over the side, and reached for a cigarette. As he struck the lighter, his eyes fell upon the clock at the side of the bed and he saw it was not yet two in the morning. What was it that made this night seem endless?

He rose and walked over to the window, refreshed by a slight cooling breeze running over his dripping body. He could see little beyond the darkness, and felt that perhaps a fog was rolling in from the sea. A flash of lightning dispelled the illusion, and for a brief moment he could see the merging line of sea and horizon, like two worlds coming together silently under cover of the storm.

He wondered if perhaps that was what was going to happen at Fowles House, the joining of two worlds, the present with the past. He sensed that the end was coming now, the end of all this strangeness and fear, the confusion and uncertainties that had surrounded them since their arrival here. He had no conception of what that end might be, except a gut-twisting certainty that it would be something terrible. The unknown forces of the past that had again been set into motion by his and Ruth's arrival at the house were now gathered in full strength, and the end was about to come. Not even Grandmother Ellen could help them now.

John thought again of Ruth, and of the early happiness that had been theirs. He saw her once again strolling along the dark beach whe they had first met . . . lonely, sad, beautiful. He remembered those first years of their marriage, their knowing and understanding of each other, their closeness, their mutual dependence. Marriage had come to him later in life than with most, but it had come in the guise of the one person with whom he could be happy. He remembered Elinor, the final expression of their marriage, and the aching sadness that had followed her death. He saw again Fowles House as it had first appeared to them: tall, old, noble, washed by the pure sea air, and recalled their excitment at having found the ideal residence for their planned period of isolation. He recalled then their first days of happiness here, the fun of restoring the old house to a livable status, Ruth sitting upon the bluff hard at work on her painting, gayly waving to him whenever he took a break from his own work and stood at the tall window of the study to look at her, and he remembered his heart then was filled with love and the desire to protect her against any further sorrows that might come her way.

And then he remembered how Ruth had slowly changed, how she had withdrawn from him, and he saw again the coldness in her green eyes when he realized at last that she had become a stranger. There followed those bitter quarrels, his desperate attempts to under-stand. . . He thought briefly of Linda, and then forced her from his mind. There could be, there must be, only thoughts of Ruth now. The evil he had sensed in the old house surrounded her most darkly, and he cried out at the realization that he could see no way to dissipate the cloud that hovered over her.

For John still loved Ruth as deeply and sincerely as on the day of their marriage, and his hands trembled at the thought of a further life without her. He knew that regardless of what happened here on this night, their happiness was at an end. He had lost her; the house had taken her from him. He moaned slightly with the pain of that realization. When we are in the midst of happiness, we somehow feel that it will always be this way, just as the young in the midst of life can not conceive of a time when they will die. But sorrow and death are always close by, and then how desperately we wish we could for just one brief moment enjoy that lost happiness again. Perhaps the gods punish us with sorrow for not realizing that happiness is their greatest gift to man.

John started and turned abruptly when he heard the sudden noise in the corridor just outside his room, the slamming of a quickly opened door, and then the rush of running bare feet. He paused a moment, and heard nothing further. Crushing out his cigarette, he silently reached for his shirt and drew it over his shoulders. When he bent to slip his loafers onto his feet, his head in the darkness heavily struck the sharp corner of the table beside the bed and after a moment of searing pain he felt a trickle of blood run down the side of his face. Dabbing with a handkerchief at the slight wound, he stepped out into the dark corridor, pressing the light-switch near the door.

The corridor was empty, but the door of Ruth's room was just slightly ajar, as though it had banged heavily against the wall when opened, and then closed only partially.

"Ruth?" he called softly, not wanting to awaken his

grandmother, as he entered the room and turned on the light. "Ruth, are you all right?"

But the room was empty. The rumpled sheets indicated that Ruth had lain in the bed, but she now was gone. He stepped again out into the corridor and paused, confused and more than a little concerned. A banging noise drew his attention to the further end of the corridor, and he saw that the door to the Widow's Walk, which was always kept shut, was open, loudly banging against the wall in a heavy draft sweeping down the narrow stairs. Again touching with the handkerchief at the continuing trickle of blood, John took the steps three at a time and was almost thrown by the force of a sudden, unexpected gust of wind as he stepped onto the exposed platform.

Ruth stood with her back to him, facing out to sea. Her hands lightly touched the rusted iron railing that encircled the Walk, and she seemed to be encountering no difficulty in maintaining her balance despite the strength of the wind that heralded the new storm. She wore the same flimsy green negligee of earlier in the evening, and John suddenly remembered Ruth had purchased it somewhere long ago as a joke because he had jestingly compared it to the flowing negligees of women in films as they were carried away in a dangling state of fear-swoon by some inhuman laboratory creation of the power-mad scientist. The gown was whipped behind her by the wind, and her dark hair was drawn away from her face. She held her head high, as though gladly greeting the spray-drenched wind; she stood where the house dropped sheerly to the edge of the cliff above the black-rocked breakers. As John approached her, he could see on her face an expression of peculiar, indecipherable exultation.

"Ruth!" he said loudly, in a slight lull when the wind had momentarily subsided. "Ruth, are you all right?"

She turned very slowly to face him, indicating no

surprise at his sudden appearance, and her eyes seemed to glow with a smouldering green fire. It was almost as though she at first failed to recognize him. Her face seemed to shine, or perhaps that was merely the way the light glowed upon her wet skin through the open door. About her throat was the silken scarf she had taken to wearing at all times. Beyond her, all was blackness, save for the unnatural illumination of the sheets of lightning. The sound of the breakers could only faintly be heard above the howling of the wind.

"Oh, it's you, John." Her voice registered neither emotion nor surprise at seeing him there, the wind flapping his open shirt.

"What are you doing up here like this?" he demanded, angry and concerned at this self-exposure to the approaching storm. "It's dangerous up here. That railing isn't sound, and there isn't enough protection; a good strong wind could blow you right over the side. And you aren't dressed warmly enough; you'll catch your death of cold in that ridiculous outfit." He again touched his right hand to his forehead as he felt a salty trickle of blood run into the corner of his mouth. "You'd better come on downstairs."

She smiled at him and gazed indifferently at his injury. "You are bleeding."

"I struck my head," he explained impatiently. "It's nothing."

"No. Of course it isn't."

"You might show a bit more concern," he pouted like a displeased child.

Her strangely expressionless eyes looked at him for another moment and then, as though totally disinterested in what she saw, she turned away again to face the sea. Lightning sharply outlined her form, while another exceptionally strong gust of wind pressed the gown against her thighs and full breasts; he could see the erect nipples through the light fabric of the negligee. She seemed dressed to receive a lover.

"Concern?" she repeated, as though unfamiliar with the word. "Why should I feel concern over so simple a matter? Can't you see, John? It really is unimportant. You should try to rise above such trivialities."

The increasing wind, which did not disturb Ruth, pushed John back a step, and he reached out to grasp the railing for support, annoyed at this display of physical weakness; the railing gave slightly under his weight and he felt a momentary fear of falling onto the pointed black rocks far below. Ruth merely raised her head to the wind as though it injected into her a new life and energy. What was there about her that disturbed him so? He was in the presence of a total stranger. He hardly knew what to say to her, how to talk to her, but it had to be done; this strangeness merely strengthened his own determination.

"Ruth, we're going to leave this place," he said with sudden decision. "We're going back to the city. It's not good for us here. I'm going to make arrangements tomorrow; Grandmother Ellen will stay with you while I'm in town. We'll lose the balance of the rental money, but that isn't really important. . ."

Her head turned slowly; she seemed to move as though under the restraint of a dream. She looked at him with eyes that held a curious pity, as though he were a child incapable of understanding the trials and the eccentricities of adult life.

"No, John." She shook her head. Her voice was low, but fully as determined as his own; she seemed to speak in a normal tone, while he found it necessary to shout above the wind. "We're not leaving here. Not tomorrow or at any other time. We're never going to leave this place."

"But this house isn't good for either one of us," John insisted, his voice almost pleading. "Something has happened to us here, Ruth. I don't know. . . The atmosphere is all wrong. I can't work. . ."

"Perhaps you haven't really tried."

"You know I have. It's this damned house. There's something about it. I don't know," he stammered again. "Something wrong. Something evil. I can't concentrate the way I should."

Ruth shrugged her shoulders. "That's your problem, isn't it? It doesn't really concern me at all. I work very well here."

"You work very strangely here," he countered. "It's not like your work at all; I don't even recognize it. It's distorted . . . it's unnatural. . ."

"It's the work I was always meant to do," she answered him firmly. "All my work before this has neither meaning nor importance. It was all a preparation for this. I've found myself here, for the first time. For you. . . Well, the solution is simple enough. You may leave any time you wish, but I'm staying. This is my home now, and I'm never going to leave it."

"That's nonsense. I couldn't leave without you."

"Why not?" She laughed slightly, a brittle sound that was lost on the wind and contained no touch of humor. "Oh, John, you're speaking of trivialities again."

And John suddenly felt fear. This discussion was not going the way it should. It suddenly occurred to him that he might well lose the argument and his wife as well.

"I choose not to think of our marriage as a mere triviality," he said somewhat smugly.

Her laughter came again, singularly unpleasant, harsh and cold; it was as though she secretly prided herself on knowledge of matters concealed from him. Her tongue darted quickly and licked her lips, and John was unpleasantly reminded of the flicking movement of a reptile tongue.

"Can't you see it simply doesn't matter any longer, John?"

"No, I can't see that, and I don't intend to. It matters very much to me!" he insisted. He took a step towards her and reached out to touch her, but then drew it back;

somehow, he could not bring himself to touch her, even to add force to his pleading. "Ruth . . . what is it? I've been trying to understand, but I . . . can't. None of this makes any sense to me. These past days, weeks . . . what's happened to us?" He softened his voice. "You used to love me."

Ruth turned to him again, and for just a fleeting moment, almost like a shadow passing over her eyes, he saw some of the remembered warmth and tenderness in her face, a softness, a yearning and, much more alarming, a silent plea, as though something within her was asking for help but could not find the words.

But the moment passed, and the expression faded as quickly as it had come, replaced by a cold severity, as though someone had stepped into Ruth's form and was looking at him through harshly indifferent eyes.

"That's true, isn't it?" she asked, and there was a touch of wonder in her face and voice, as though at realization of an irreconcilable truth. "Yes, I did love you once, John. Oh, that seems very strange to me now! I have no time for love any longer. I'm sorry . . . for you. For me, it means nothing. You'll have to go someplace else for that sort of thing now."

"You're talking nonsense again. You're my wife, Ruth."

"No. Not any longer."

"What?"

"I don't belong to you any longer, John," she said slowly and firmly, as though wanting to impress the words on his mind. "I know you'll find that a bit difficult to accept; I'm afraid your ego will be somewhat damaged. That part of my life is over now. The best thing for you to do is simply to go away and forget all about me. It would be better for both of us that way. Find someone else. Linda, perhaps."

John moved closer to her again, and the wind sprinkled his flushed face with bitter salt spray that started to drip from his eyebrows and into his eyes.

Lightning flashed again, and its brilliant yellow light revealed a harshness and arrogance in Ruth's face. She was totally indifferent to the pain she was causing him.

"It's all wrong," he thought, shaking the spray from his eyes. "It shouldn't be happening this way." Again, he reached out his hand to her, but she moved quickly away from his touch.

"Don't touch me!" she snapped at him. "Don't touch me ever again! I'm no longer yours to touch!"

"You don't know what you're saying, Ruth," he remarked in a soothing tone. "You must be ill. The cold . . . the storm. . ."

She laughed again, and the humorless icy sound mixed and mingled and became one with the roar of the approaching storm and the heavy crash of the breakers far below them. She tossed her head back, and her long, loose hair was caught by the wind and flew about her head like the tangled, writhing serpentine locks of a Medusa.

"Why must I be ill, John? Because you don't care for my words? Truth is something that few humans can bear to face. Often it's too uncomfortable." She turned to him again and once more, for but the briefest moment, her harsh face was touched with a faintest shade of pity and, perhaps, even with sorrowful regret. "Poor John. You simply don't understand all this, do you? How can you? Don't blame yourself. This is all so very much beyond you, or anyone. You've no idea what it is I've found here."

"You've found a harsh, barren world where you can nurse your sick sorrow until it's finally driven you out of your mind!" he shouted again to make himself heard above the increasing wind.

Ruth stared at him for a moment, and suddenly her face became tremulous with fear, rippling across her features like a curtain of green water, and her eyes stared at him with the unnatural wildness of horror. Her lips moved but she made no comment; her throat was contorted with strain as she tried desperately to speak.

"He. . . He. . ." She gasped before the fear faded and was replaced by a trace of amusement in eyes that again had turned cold and indifferent. She turned away for a moment, and when she faced him again, her face was calm and lacking all emotion.

"You see, John, it wasn't mere chance that brought me to this place. My entire life has been directed to this very house, and to this very night. It has all been waiting for me here, and I never realized it. How nearly I came to missing it!"

John stared at her, scarcely believing he had heard these strange, inexplicable words. Had her mind really gone, at last? These could not be the words of a rational woman. This was not, could not be, the woman he had known and loved, with whom he had been so willing and eager to spend the remainder of his life. He shivered under a touch of fear. There was something wrong here, something completely beyond his understanding. He had somehow fallen into a terrible nightmare, with no knowledge of how to awaken himself from it.

"Ruth. . . Ruth. . ."

She seemed again to have forgotten his presence. Her face streamed with the cold wind-blown spray that had plastered her light covering to her body; he saw that she wore nothing beneath the delicate gown, yet she was untouched by the sharp sudden cold of the storm-wind as she looked out to sea, her head high, her face glowing with a peculiar ecstacy of expectation. He thought that on this same platform women long since dust had often stood on just such a stormy nights in the past, searching through the dark wildness of the lonely night for that faintest flash of white sail that would tell them the hoped-for vessel had not succumbed to the vicious batterings of the turbulent green seas, and that the captain would yet return in safety to the house on the cliff.

But no, it was Fowles himself who had stood here, tall and dark and evil, gazing anxiously out to the horizon for a sign of his next unfortunate victim. Had there been women here after the captain's death? It was difficult to believe love had ever resided in this terrible house.

And those days were long past. This was a different time, another age. What was Ruth looking for with her eyes so hopefully scanning the invisible horizon, searching avidly for something she could not hope to see? The tumbling masses of black cloud and the surging, restless seas were brightened by flashes of lightning, but this revealed only an empty world where no man would have dared to venture on so threatening a night. The great sailing vessels were long gone, a sometimes lovely, often brutal, and somehow bitter-sweet memory of a colorful and violent past. There was nothing there now. John stared into the blackness, his eyes narrowed, searching for the unseen, and it seemed to him that the black clouds gathered into strange, alien forms that hovered menacingly about the house, coming ever nearer to the two lone figures upon the Widow's Walk. . . .

John abruptly shook his head to clear it of the swirling confusion that had suddenly clouded his mind. All this was sheer foolishness. He and Ruth were alone in the storm, far from others, and Ruth was obviously extremely ill. Perhaps he had been too patient, too gentle, too weak, from the very first. It was time now for him once again to act the man and do what was needful for his wife, whether or not she was willing to accept it. This was Ruth. He did not want to lose her.

He stepped closer to her again, this time determined not to be put off by her strange words. "Ruth, you've got to come downstairs with me. You aren't well. This storm has frightened you. You've exposed yourself to the cold, and you need sleep. In the morning, we'll arrange to leave this place, and you'll feel much better."

She shook off, with an expression of distaste, the hand

he had placed on her arm. "Leave me alone."

"No. I won't leave you alone." His voice was firm again, feeling himself more of a man, more in control of the situation. "We've had enough of this foolishness. You're coming with me, Ruth, even if I have to carry you downstairs. You need help."

Ruth turned to him abruptly, almost violently, her lightning-brightened face suddenly wild with an almost inconceivable fury, her blowing hair providing a frame for a face that was almost totally unfamiliar to him. He shuddered under the look of those strange eyes in which he seemed to see the oceans of the world swirling in storm created malestroms.

"Help? Help?" Her voice, too, had changed; it was like the shushing of breaking waves on some far distant shore. "What do you know of help? What could your puny efforts do for me?" Her eyes widened with a sudden ecstacy. "I have help, John! More help than you or anyone else could ever give me, help for all my pain and sorrow and loneliness!" Her face came closer to him; her eyes had again turned to green flame. "And it's coming, now!" She reached her hand out to the horizon, her long slender fingers sweeping like streaks of fluorescent green light against the dark sky. "It's out there, John, all the help I'll ever need, and it's coming to me, to me alone, tonight, now!" She cried out to the night with a shrill, piercing scream that sent cold shivers down John's spine. "John, my life is just beginning! The petty existence of the past years will soon be forgotten, with all its sorrows, as though it had never existed! A new future glory is waiting for me known only to the chosen few!" She turned back to him, her lips unpleasantly curled, and her fiery eyes ran over him as though he were a creature beneath her notice. "Go, John, leave me alone. This is no place for you!"

"I'm not going without you, Ruth," he said firmly. "You're my wife and I love you. Your place is with me."

The laughter carried a shrill, keen edge; was it

hysteria or was it madness? He felt he was standing on that platform not with his wife, but with one of the ancient Furies. Why did glory and madness so often go together? Whom God would destroy. . . .

"My place is with you, John?" She threw her head back again and laughed to the thunder-pregnant clouds. "No, John, you're mistaken. My life is no longer yours, and my place is no longer with you." She took a step back and stared at him; he felt suddenly deeply hurt by the undisguised contempt in her face. "You pitiful, puny creature! You with your empty words of love, your childish dreams, your meaningless accomplishments, your stupid little triumphs! Master of the Earth, you call yourselves. How the insignificant race of man has managed to delude itself through the pitifully few millenia of the insignificant and unimportant existence of its form! Man!" She suddenly brought her face very close to his, and seemed to spit out the words. "Can you for one moment believe yourself in the smallest respect equal to *him* to whom I now truly belong?"

John stared at her, attempting in his confused mind to make some sense out of the rambling of her vituperative words. She spoke as though he and she belonged to two entirely different worlds, almost two different forms of life. The darkness about them seemed to have deepened. The wind flapped the legs of his trousers with the explosion of rapid pistol-fire and billowed his shirt out behind him like sails, and he was reminded of the first time he had stood on the wind-exposed bluff before the house. He wondered at the sound of the beating sticks like the black tattoo of a voodoo ritual, and then remembered the blasted tree beside the house; it was the first time the waving branches had made any sound.

"What the hell are you talking about?" he demanded, his voice hoarse with wonder and fear.

Ruth threw her arms out as though embracing the storm, in the exaggerated gesture of an actress in a Greek tragedy.

"How can you ever hope to know the wonder that is coming for me?" Her turn was swift and abrupt; her breasts moved under the wet gauze of her gown, and her twisted face was like something from an ancestral nightmare of the days when men cowered in fear behind the flickering comfort of the fires that guarded the entrance to their dark caves and kept back the unknown terrors of the night. "Get out, John! You place yourself in deadly peril by remaining here. You don't belong. I can not answer for your safety. This is not for you. He comes only for me. I tell you this for your own good. Go, before it's too late. Soon there will be no escape for you!"

Looking at the fury in her face, at the strange writhing of her supple figure, John could no longer doubt that Ruth was mad. The anger and fear left him with this terrible revelation, and he stared at her with sadness and pity . . . this woman, his wife, mistress, lover, mother of his dead child, this beautiful young woman he had met so fortuitously on a lovely tropical island paradise how many ages ago? . . . standing here now, braced against the wind, soaking with the salt spray from the storm-tossed sea, her face and body contorted into something scarcely human. He had lost her. He knew that now.

How had it happened? When? Not just now, this moment, but somewhere else, some time else. Somewhere, somehow, they had taken the wrong turning in their lives, and now it was too late to turn back. Nothing could save them now. It was finished. In a flash, he saw and remembered so many things from the happier days of their past. Oh, God, it had been so long since he'd felt the need to cry!

"Ruth. . . Oh, Ruth. . . ."

Slowly, he put out a hand to touch her hair, to soothe her, perhaps merely to let her know through the touch of his trembling fingers that he still loved her. She started at his touch as though those fingers had burned her, and he heard the hiss of her breath through tightly clenched teeth.

"Take your hands off me!" she demanded, in a voice filled with sibilants, like the angered spitting of a madly cornered serpent. "Don't you dare to touch me! I am no longer yours to touch!"

She turned quickly to escape the suddenly loathsome contact with her husband's hand, and the unexpected movement knocked John off his balance. His fingers slipped from her hair and touched the silk scarf about her throat; he clutched at it in an automatic effort to retain his balance, and by doing so tore it from her throat. The small bit of colored cloth fluttered for a moment in his hand and then was carried away by the wind into the darkness, like a wounded butterfly rushing to its doom, while John stepped back with a sharp cry, startled by what he saw on the exposed surface of Ruth's throat.

He could not see clearly in the dim light through the open door and the flickering, confusing and momentarily blinding flashes of lightning, but the smooth white skin he remembered so well, to which he had so often pressed his lips in their now forgotten moments of passion, had terribly altered. Something had spread over its surface, something with a deep tinge of green stretching from just below the jaw line into the lacy collar of the gown, that area which Ruth had, during past weeks, kept so carefully concealed with her scarf. John shuddered involuntarily as he looked at it; there seemed to be something unclean, loathsome, like a leprosy. As the lightning cast flickering shadows over the exposed surface, it almost seemed to him that he could see movement, creeping, crawling. . .

"My God, Ruth!" His cry was lifted by the wind and borne out to sea, where there was no one to hear it.

Ruth placed a hand heavily on his bare chest, a hand that felt incredibly cold, like the touch of icy waters burning through his very flesh. In her anger and hysteria, she pushed him with a strength she had never before possessed. Still off balance, John staggered and fell to the platform. For a moment he lay where he was, stunned and confused, staring unbelievingly up at his wife, who stood over him like a lightning-limbed colossus from another world, her face scarcely human, her wild eyes blazing with an insane fury and her wet lips black with anger. The sickness of her green-scummed throat glistened in the intermitent light from the sky.

"I told you to go!" Her voice was deep and throaty, nothing resembling Ruth's smooth, refined tones. "You wouldn't listen! I told you of the danger, I warned you that you placed yourself in terrible peril by remaining! You wouldn't listen! It will soon be too late. Go now, while you can! Go back to your own world. You don't belong here!" And then, for one last moment, a moment John would remember through all the remainder of his life, the face again softened and the eyes looked at him with a fleeting reminder of their old days, and the voice was once again that of the woman he had married. "And take Ellen with you. She is in far more peril than you yourself! For her sake go! Take her and go!"

John lay as if paralyzed, totally incapable of movement. The breath had been knocked from his lungs and he lay gasping painfully, cringing from what stood above him. He felt now nothing but a terrible, trembling fear. There was no strength in his limbs, and he seemed incapable of thought or decision, he could not even begin to rationalize. Something dreadful had happened. The world had changed. The unknown had entered his life.

Slowly, he began to sidle away from Ruth and crawl on hands and knees towards the promised safety of the open door leading back into the house. Ruth stood quite motionless, watching him, her hair wild and seeming to crackle with the electricity that filled the air, her suddenly brilliant green eyes lighted by a maniacal fury, her gown blown about her by the wind like the sea-moving dress of a Lorelei. John's hand at last felt the sill of the door and he threw himself over it, tumbling down the short flight of steps to the second floor corridor.

Dazed, he slowly and painfully managed to raise himself first to his knees and then to his unsteady feet, shaking his head, stretching his arms to support himself against the walls. He turned his head and looked back, up to the darkness of the open door; lightning briefly again brightened the portal, showing him only the cloud-covered sky. Was it all really true? Had it really happened, or was he still caught in the vortex of a crazy dream? Was Ruth still up there, and was it really Ruth, that strange almost demonic figure with the blowing hair and the green eyes? He thought of medieval tales of demonic possession. He had never believed in such things; possession was merely the result of hysteria and ignorance and could not apply to him and his time. He took a tentative, uncertain step towards the stairs, and then stopped. No, he could not bring himself to go back up there. He could not look at her again. . . .

The slight wound on his forehead had been reopened by his sudden fall, and he again felt the trickle of warm blood running down the side of his face; he licked at its saltiness as he staggered down the corridor, like a heathen looking for strength in the taste of blood. He was scarcely aware of his surroundings or his movements. None of this could be real. He could not have seen any of this. Things like this simply don't happen, not in a sane and rational universe, and most certainly not to him. The night, the storm, his unhappiness . . . somehow they had all combined to create this nightmare for him.

He paused when he reached the main stairway, and he was struck by a sudden blast of wind that again almost knocked him off his feet. He leaned heavily against the railing and stared unbelievingly at the chaos below.

All the doors and windows of the ground floor stood

wide open, and the foyer was dazzlingly illuminated by lightning flashing through the main entrance and the opened doors of the adjoining rooms; again and again, he was blinded by the flashes of light, followed quickly by crashing peals of thunder that caused the very house to tremble, and he wondered if the storm could possibly have broken so quickly and with such intense fury. The sea wind now had free access to all the rooms and corridors; having at last gained this unrestricted entry, it whistled and raced about the house like a thousand madmen on a rampage of brutal revenge. The curtains at the windows stood out stiffly from the walls, like waiting mortuary slabs, and the whistling of the wind, screaming its paeans of victory, was almost deafening. The foyer had become a whirlwind of papers that had blown there from his study, twisting, writhing cones flying in the wind currents like disembodied miniature spirits; bits of fabric and even small artifacts were caught in the cyclones of wind that tore gleefully through the house; the small table under the mirror near the grandfather's clock suddenly toppled with a loud crash, its slender vase smashing into a thousand pieces.

The chaotic scene seemed to swim before John's eyes, and he swayed slightly as he held tenaciously for support to the railing. He suddenly sensed the presence, the almost tangible atmosphere of *Evil* that filled the house. How had the doors and windows become suddenly opened, how could he explain the incredible violence of the storm that seemed to surround the house, striking the old timbers with an almost unearthy violence? Everything swam before his eyes, and he was filled with sudden nausea. He leaned over the railing and retched violently, his fear-tightened stomach muscles forcing the bile from his mouth; he heard the splatter of his bitter vomit hit the floor below. The wind screamed in his ears in a wild time-lost language he could not understand. He stared down into the foyer, and it seemed to him that the air was filled with moving, writhing, screaming, unsubstantial forms.

He turned dizzily when he heard a door open in the corridor, and only through a determined focusing of his swimming eyes could he see his grandmother, standing in the open doorway of her room, fully dressed, her pale face etched with horror. Convinced at last that the strange sounds she heard were not the result of her imagination, Ellen had managed to conquer her nameless fear, rise unsteadily from her bed, and step into the corridor. When she saw John leaning drunkenly against the stairway railing, his wet, smeared shirt billowing from his body by the wind in the foyer, a trickle of blood running down his right cheek and a string of vomit dangling from his mouth, with an expression of indescribable fear and horror on his face, Ellen realized the end had come at last.

"John!" she called, stretching out her trembling arms to him. "John! John!"

His mouth opened, but for a moment there was no sound; Ellen could hear the whistling of the wind in the well of the foyer. The crystal leaves of the chandelier raised a noisy cacophony of sound as they struck heavily against each other; several fell like glittering daggers to the floor. John swallowed, shook his head, and again tried to speak.

"Grandmother!" His voice was a harsh, frightened croak. "We've got to get out of here!" He swayed a moment longer, and then straightened himself, strengthened by the sight of the frightened old woman and his realization of her danger. He rushed to her and placed a protecting arm about her, guiding her towards the stairs. "We must get out of here!"

Ellen leaned heavily against him, her step weakened by fear, as they started down the stairs. They seemed not to be alone. They sensed they were surrounded by writhing, crawling, slurping things that had no right to exist in the sane world of man. Ellen cringed as she imagined a wet touch on her shoulder, and John winced as he quickly moved his free hand across his face, as though brushing away something that had fallen on him.

And yet, they were alone. There was nothing to be seen but the wind-blown debris, nothing to be heard but the incessant howling of the wind and the tumult of the storm.

They stumbled down the stairway, falling again and again against the railing or the opposite curving wall, battling the wind that seemed hungry to push them back and prevent their escape. Finally they reached the bottom step and here, with a slight cry, Ellen slipped from John's protecting arm and fell to the hard floor of the foyer. Almost without stopping, John swept his grandmother into his arms and carried her across the wind-screaming entry, through the open door, and out of the house.

The sky had gone mad. As John stepped quickly down from the veranda and carefully set Ellen on her feet once again, the wind tore at them and they could hear the old wooden house shudder under its impact. The massive tumbling clouds seemed white in the almost constant sheeting of lightning that brightened them. There was no rain, but the air was filled with terrible sound, and the very ground beneath their feet seemed to tremble with the sonic force of crashing thunder. With his arm about his grandmother's narrow waist, John guided Ellen towards the car at the far side of the veranda, using his body to protect her as much as possible from the fury of the wind.

"We'll be all right in the village," he said, almost speaking to himself. "Nothing will happen to us there."

Ellen followed him without question, and it was as though the wind that struck them fanned the fire of her own fears. She had no knowledge of what had caused their precipitate flight from the house, but she had only to look at John, his face white with shock and horror, a stream of dried blood, black in the light, running down one side of his face, his eyes wild and his lips trembling, to realize that something terrible had occurred while she had lain awake in her room, battling imagined sounds she thought were created by her own fear.

"Yes, the village. We'll be safe there," John said again, as though the repetition brought him strength. "I'll take you to Linda. She'll understand."

They paused at the car, and Ellen turned to him, able to speak at last. "But, John, Ruth, what about Ruth?"

John looked at her with wide eyes, as though the mention of his wife's name had intensified his fears. Slowly, he turned his head and looked to the house, then up, towards the gables, towards the Widow's Walk. Ellen followed his gaze and gave a sharp cry of fear when she saw the slight, green-clad figure standing upon the Widow's Walk, against the railing, staring not at them, but out to sea, the wind whipping her hair and gown into a frenzy, yet standing firm and erect as though borrowing strength from the wind that attacked her.

"Ruth!" Ellen cried out, not calling to her, but merely expressing her own shock and amazement. Then her eyes wandered down over the house and she cried out again at what she saw. "John! John! The tree!"

The dead tree beside the veranda was wrapped in a sheath of brilliant green flame that seemed to lick hungrily at the blackened, seared trunk and dripped like curtains of liquid emerald from the bare branches that beat against each other with a loud clatter in the violence of the wind that swept across the face of the bluff. The air seemed suddenly filled with the choking, acrid scent of sulphur.

And then suddenly it became clear to them that there was something bound to the dead trunk of the tree, a hazy, indistinct form struggling violently against its strictures, writhing and twisting under the touch of the green fire. At the same moment, they seemed to sense the presence of a multitude standing about them, surrounding the blazing tree, and they could hear the wildly ecstatic shouts of a mob blooded by the excitement of victory.

Ellen, one hand placed before her face to ward off the nauseating stench of sulphur, muttered, "And that's how he died! They burned him before his own devilish house!"

The indistinct figure seemed suddenly to burst its bonds, or perhaps the ropes that held him to the tree were burned away. The form fell to the ground, wrapped in green fire, and then, raising itself on the burned stumps of legs, dashed across the bluff, past the cowering figures by the car, and with wild screams and indecipherable imprecations, hurled itself, a flaming mass, over the edge of the cliff and into the sea.

John turned quickly away from the ghastly sight towards his grandmother, who leaned heavily against the side of the car, her terror-stricken face still staring towards the flaming tree. He took her hands in his.

"It's over, Grandmother," he said. "Whatever it was, it's all over!"

Ellen slowly shook her head, narrowing her eyes as she again stared towards the house. "No, John. No. Look. The veranda. There's someone there."

John followed her eyes back to the house, and in the green-shadowed darkness of the veranda he saw a tall, bearded figure, standing completely motionless, staring at them. The sick green light cast shadows upon the strong, bearded face, and with a pang of renewed fear, John thought at first it was surely Captain Fowles himself, until he realized with a start who it was standing in those green shadows.

"Paul! It's Paul!"

Ellen nodded slowly. "So, we have the catalyst!"

"Paul! Paul!"

It was not John who now cried the name, for the voice came from the roadway leading to the bluff from the beach below. He turned quickly and saw Linda standing at the entry to the bluff, her hair blown by the wind, her face pale and her eyes wide as she looked at the stern figure. Paul slowly turned his head in her direction and then, with an almost incredible swiftness, darted from the veranda and into the house.

Linda rushed to them, and as she threw herself into John's arms, he saw that her face was streaked with tears; she trembled in his grasp, then looked up into his face, her swimming eyes pleading for help.

"Stop him, John! Stop him! He's out of his mind, John! He'll kill her!"

A wild sound of laughter came to them above the howling of the wind, and all three instantly looked up to the Widow's Walk.

"No, no!" Ellen moaned, clasping her hands together in helpless frustration. "It's too late! It's too late!"

Ruth stood looking down at them, and the wind pressed her light gown against her body so that she almost appeared naked. Her lips, black in that light, were parted, and from them came peal after peal of maniacal laughter. Her body twisted and convulsed like some tentacled creature from the depths of the sea, and her throat was a swollen mass of black flecked with green. Paul stood behind her, tall and motionless, on his face an expression of triumphant mockery. It would have been difficult to tell the difference between Paul and Fowles himself.

"Ruth! Ruth!" John shouted, extending his arms upward. "Come to me, Ruth! Come down to me!"

Ruth looked down to him and tossed her head back with hysterical laughter. Ellen placed a hand on his arm.

"You can't appeal to her, John," she said. "Not any more. It's too late. She no longer knows you, or anyone. She knows only him. There's nothing we can do now."

John shook off his grandmother's restraining arm and, dashing around the car, stood directly beneath the Widow's Walk, his agonized eyes turned upward to the woman who had been his wife.

"Come back to me, Ruth!" he pleaded. "I love you! I need you!"

Ruth stared down at him for a moment, her lips twisted in mockery, and her voice seemed to come to them from a great distance, and there was in it the sound of the gurgling of the sea.

"Go away! My life is here!" She spread out her arms and cried in ecstacy, "My life is only beginning!"

Linda took her place beside John and called up to the man who had loved her. "Paul! It's Linda! Paul, come down! You love me, Paul!"

Paul looked down at her, and for a brief moment there was a touch of remembrance in his face, and the features of Fowles seemed to fade.

"Linda. . . Linda!"

But it was too late. The mockery, the triumph, the madness returned as he placed an arm about Ruth's waist.

Ellen now stepped away from the car and, standing alone on the windy bluff, firm against the attacking wind, called up to the man who stood on the platform.

"It's all over, Captain Fowles!" she cried, her voice shrill as it rose above the wind. "It has been over for centuries. You and your beliefs belong to the past. You have no right to her! Your evil has no place in this time!"

For a brief moment, he looked down at the small white-haired woman who so dared to defy him, and his face was livid with hatred. He tightened his grip about Ruth's waist, and she turned her face to him, alight with adoration and ecstasy. His voice came down to them as though it were a part of the thunder and of the violence of the night.

"She belongs to *him!*" he cried, "as all women in this House have always belonged to *him!*"

"No!" Ellen cried. "Your god is dead! He is dead!"

A moment longer, he looked at her, and there was confusion and uncertainty in his face, a fear that surely had never been there during the lifetime of the brutal captain.

"Your god is dead!" Ellen screamed.

With a low cry, then, Paul lifted Ruth into his arms and leaped with her over the side of the house and into the sea.

CHAPTER TWENTY-ONE

IT was a pleasant, beautiful day. The hot, sultry constantly stormy weather was over at long last, and there was even just the slightest touch, a mere first nip of autumn in the air again. The sun shone brilliantly upon the gilded tail-flicking whale atop the church steeple and the masts of several sailing vessels moving slowly out into the harbor, their wakes like the trailing gowns of fashionably clad women; it was reported that the fishing had suddenly and quite strangely became unusually good, and the locals were quick to take advantage of it. Children romped in the streets, their heat-engendered lassitude gone. The merchants again sunned themselves before their stores; the grocer determinedly attempted a new and novel arrangement of his apple display, then went back to the old standard triangle, his desire for creativity again destroyed by his total lack of imagination. It was as though all the recent violent weather had never been. Faces smiled again and people walked a bit more briskly down Main Street.

The gossips were seated on the park benches surrounded by flowers that bloomed late after the heavy rains, critically and perhaps enviously eyeing the too scantily clad young girls who walked about the square leaning too intimately on the arms of their boy friends, but their talk was still only about the tragedy of the recent storm, culminating in the total destruction of Fowles House, and the shocking deaths of Ruth Kendall and Paul Sanders.

Of course, none of them had known the poor dead woman at all well, having seen her only once or twice on her rare and brief excursions into the village. She was said to have been an artist, and everyone knows how peculiar such people can be! They all agreed it was a sad loss for John Kendall, who really seemed to be quite a nice and agreeable young man. Their greatest sense of pity was quite naturally reserved for Paul Sanders, who had been sincerely liked by the entire village. It was no surprise to any of them that he had died a hero's death, attempting to rescue the Kendall woman from the storm-endangered house while John Kendall saw to the safety of his aged grandmother. But Paul had been too late, and when that last incredible flash of lightning . . . its crack had been heard for miles around, you know . . . had finally struck the old house and sent it crashing into the sea, both Paul Sanders and Ruth Kendall had gone with it. Their bodies had not been found.

Nothing as dramatic as this had happened in the old village for the past two centuries, not since the violent days of that dreadful old Captain Fowles, and it would provide delicious material for the gossips for many years to come, besides providing an added bit of color that might help restore some of the lost tourist trade. People, after all, find a vicarious pleasure in visiting a spot where tragedy has occurred. No doubt some enterprising merchant . . . from out of town, of course . . . would come up with a money-making concession for the bluff where it had all happened.

There was a certain amount of sympathy for Linda as well, although some of the gossips drew their mouths into firm lines with the consideration that she had always been a bit too fast for her own good, a bit uppity besides, and it was only respect for the heroically dead

Paul that prevented them from implying there had been something perhaps not quite proper between him and his . . . secretary. Still, the girl had lost one husband and probably a prospective second one, and all women could sympathize with that. Linda would be leaving the village now, it was said, and perhaps that was just as well, for all concerned.

But it certainly did make a simply marvelous topic of conversation.

They sat silently over their coffee, lingering, waiting for the time to say goodbye. They were all returning to the city, all putting behind them the horrors of which only the three of them knew the truth. Let the village, let the world, believe Ruth and Paul had perished in a natural disaster; it would do no good to tell them otherwise. They would alone know, these three. Their dreams would be filled with it for years to come.

Linda stared into the sun-dappled square she had known so well, where she and Harry had once been so happy, and where, for a time, a different kind of happiness had come to her with Paul. From the large window, she could just see the small building where she and Paul had worked together. The shade was drawn over the window and among the faded photographs of rentable properties a FOR RENT sign now rested in one corner. Yes, they had been happy days, perhaps happier than she had then realized. She pictured Paul again . . . charming, warm, handsome, friendly, always helpful, constantly concerned about her well-being. Perhaps she had been wrong. Perhaps she had loved him, after all. It did no good to think of that now. Paul was gone.

John absently stirred his coffee and attempted to direct his own thoughts to the Ruth of earlier years, the lovely, cheerful and talented young artist he had loved. Would he ever be able to forget the fury and the horror of that beautiful face as he had last seen it, distorted by the madness that had seized her and taken her to her terrible death?

Ellen silently looked at them both, and felt a deep sadness for the sorrow that had come to these two young people. John's face was now heavily lined, and there was gray in his hair that had not been there before. Linda possessed the sadness of all those who have known love and, perhaps through their own indifference, have lost it.

The restaurant was strangely silent, although several tables were occupied, and all realized that much of the muted talk concerned them, for eyes wandered constantly and uncomfortably to their table. The *maitre* had greeted them at the doorway as though he were the director of a funeral parlor, and their waiter had spoken to them only in mournful whispers.

It would be over soon now, as far as their presence in this village was concerned. They were waiting only for the arrival of the bus that would take Linda away, and then John and Ellen would return to the city. They had offered to take Linda with them in their car, but she had firmly and politely refused, preferring to be alone on the trip she would now take with an even greater sadness than she had anticipated.

John signaled for fresh brandies, and Linda waited until the mournful waiter had filled their order, his eyes appropriately lowered, and tiptoed silently away before continuing her account of what Paul had told her about the legend of Fowles House on that terrible night of his death.

"When the villagers burst into Fowles House," she said, "it was whispered that they saw terrible things that no human had ever seen before, save for those who voluntarily lived in the black world Fowles had created for himself. The house seemed to swarm with terrifying creatures from the depths of the sea, crawling all about the house, inside and out."

Ellen nodded. "I think we sensed them, John and I, when we ran from the house. It seemed filled with . . . things . . . although we saw nothing."

"They found Fowles himself in the room in the cellar, naked, surrounded by a host of drooling devils. The room glowed with the brilliant green color of the sea, and on a small earthen mound in the very center of the floor, a naked woman, survivor of the most recent ship disappearance, had just been horrifyingly sacrificed to the *Satan of the Sea*. She had not been the first; it was said the room was filled with the mutilated bodies of women, and was foul with the hot stench of blood."

John shook his head and gazed at the peaceful scene through the window; it was difficult to believe in such horrors on this bright, sunny afternoon.

"They dragged Fowles out of the house and tied him to a stake they erected just beside the veranda in front of the house. There was no question of accusations, defense, certainly no form of trial. All were too horrified by what they had seen, and cared now only to root out the incredible obscene evil that had established itself on the bluff. They piled wooden faggots about the stake and thrust their torches into it. Fowles screamed the most incredible blasphemies, struggling at the binding ropes, while the flames licked at his body and the suddenly silent villagers stood and watched his final agonies.

"But Fowles belonged to the *Satan of the Sea*,, and he could not permit himself to die on land. When the fire burned through the ropes, he broke his bonds and, with his body a blazing torch, while the people screamed in fear and backed away from him, he dashed on the burnt stumps of his legs across the bluff and hurled himself, still screaming and shouted his obscenities, from the cliff and into the sea. Some claimed the green water seemed to rise up to seize him and drag him down. His body was never found."

Ellen closed her eyes and ran a trembling hand over her forehead. "I can still see it," she muttered. "The memory of it lived on that land for two centuries."

"A terrible way to die," John said with a slight shudder.

"No more terrible than the deaths he brought to so many others," Ellen commented firmly.

"Nothing has ever been able to grow on that bluff since then," Linda continued. "Many years later a tree was planted there, on the very spot where the stake had stood, perhaps in an attempt to erase the memory of the horror that had happened there, but it soon died; the dead tree was kept there as a ghastly memorial."

"And what of the house after then?" Ellen asked.

"It stood empty for many years after Fowles's death," Linda replied. "The captain had distant relations, but most preferred to avoid the house that had such a terrible history. A few finally did try to live in it over the next century or so, but it always ended in disaster. One woman hurled herself into the sea from the top of the bluff, another became violently insane on the Widow's Walk during a severe storm, screaming about unearthly creatures rising from the sea, and died there soon after. About a hundred years ago, a newly married couple moved in. The bride was dead within the month, in a particularly horrible manner. They found her on the floor in the cellar room; she had slashed open her abdomen with a kitchen knife. Whispers began about the inherent madness of Fowles House. The family abandoned the place until the present owners, perhaps touched by the same greed that had so strongly marked Fowles himself, decided it was foolish to have so valuable a property standing empty. They caused certain modernizations to be made, and put the house up for rent and possible sale."

"And Paul really knew nothing of all this?" John asked.

Linda shook her head. "I'm certain of it; at least, not consciously. Of course, he was aware of the vague rumors and whispers, but even if he had known, I doubt he would have taken any of it very seriously. He naturally would have put it all down to superstition, and who would expecct any problems after so long a time?"

"And the curse?" Ellen asked.

"What curse?" John asked in return.

"There must surely have been a curse," Ellen replied. "Only that could explain the continued existence of this horror after a period of two centuries."

"Yes, there was a curse, of course," Linda agreed. "It was said that as Fowles burned, he screamed that his house would forever serve as a snare for women, that all women who dared to live there would become the permanent property of his avid master, the *Satan of the Sea*, a continued sacrifice to follow those Fowles had murdered there, and in his own time and manner, this Satan would come to the house and claim his own. The woman could not hope to escape, nor would she want to. Somehow, these women would find their way into that little room in the cellar, the focal point of all the horror that had occurred in the house, forever saturated by the blood of the innocent sacrifices. There they would be surrounded by the aura of the Satan, and his presence would become their most burning desire. They would be deluded into seeing in him all the hope for the future, satisfaction of their own greatest dreams and desires. Unaware of the actual fate intended for them, they would be filled with a yearning to please him and would live only for his coming. As a sign of his favor and ownership, Satan would place upon them a mark. . ."

"The green scaliness at Ruth's throat, that she tried to conceal with her scarf," John suggested.

Linda nodded. "The green mark of the sea. A stamp embossed somewhere upon the flesh, sea green in color, that would grow until it destroyed all that was human in the woman, and she would become completely his own . . ."

"But what was Paul's place in all this?" John wondered.

"I . . . don't know," Linda remarked, a slight catch in her voice.

"I think I can tell you that," Ellen said, and they both turned to her. "The evil that festered in that house might of itself stir at the presence of a woman, but something else would have to bring it to life again. You remember I spoke of a catalyst, John. I think Paul was that catalyst."

"But how?" John asked. "Paul supposedly didn't even know about the story at the time we arrived."

"It wasn't at all necessary for him to know about it," Ellen insisted. "The knowledge would come to him when it was necessary. It's obvious that Paul was a descendant of Fowles himself. When the evil stirred again, the spirit of Fowles entered Paul's body and took over his mind and soul."

"You're talking about possession. That sounds like medieval nonsense," John complained.

"I have said before that not all the strange beliefs and superstitions of medieval times was nonsense," Ellen said quietly. "I think if we could examine the truth behind the deaths of those other, later women at Fowles House, we would find, somewhere, somehow, the spirit of Fowles was abroad. There was always a catalyst. There may always have been unknowing descendants of Fowles in this village."

"He changed so completely," Linda said quietly, remembering. "He suddenly seemed so very different, so totally unlike the Paul I had known so well. He talked like a man from a different time, and that last night I saw him, when I thought he had actually gone mad, he even looked different, older, more brutal."

"Like Captain Fowles himself," Ellen suggested with a slight nod. "John, when you saw Paul standing on the veranda, did you not, for just a brief moment, think you were actually seeing Fowles?"

John nodded slowly. "Yes. I did."

"And you were," Ellen assured him. "By that time, Paul's personality had been so completely absorbed by the spirit of Fowles that nothing whatever remained of Paul himself, as you knew him."

"Then it was not really Paul who did these terrible things?" There was in Linda's voice a note of anxiety, a terrible need for comforting.

Ellen smiled slightly, and placed her hand over Linda's where it rested on the table. "Of course not. Paul Sanders had no knowledge of what his alter-ego was forcing him to do." She hesitated for a moment, a frown creasing her forehead. "I'm quite certain that sometime close to the end, he must have realized something was happening to him, with no understanding of what it was. He probably sensed the coming danger."

"What do you mean?"

Ellen looked at Linda for a moment before replying. "My dear, he never did permit you to enter Fowles House, did he?"

Linda returned the look, and tears sprang to her eyes. "No . . . No, he never did."

"Because there were moments when he had a fleeting glimpse of the dangers that awaited you there," Ellen said confidently. "He was still able to want to spare you the horrors of which he knew nothing."

"And what of Ruth?" John asked.

"Ruth's case was even more frightening. She was caught in a terrible vortex of which she knew absolutely nothing, save for the strange yearning for something she could not understand. You remember how strangely she welcomed me to the house; unknowingly, she was welcoming another sacrifice."

John nodded slowly, understanding. "Yet even she had moments of remembrance. Almost at the very end, she urged me to go and to take you with me."

Silence fell for a moment. A ray of sunlight speared through the window and touched the cloth of the table.

"And now it's over?" John asked.

Ellen nodded. "Oh, yes, it's all over now. The house is gone, the place of evil destroyed. There is nowhere for

Fowles to go now. The bluff has been cleansed by fire from heaven."

The restaurant clock chimed three times, and Linda began to gather her things together. "I'd best be going," she said. "I don't want to miss the bus."

John made as if to move. "We'll go out with you."

She placed her hand on his arm. "No. Please. Stay here. I'd prefer it."

John rose with her, and she bent to kiss Ellen lightly on the cheek. "It would have been nice to meet you under more pleasant circumstances."

Ellen embraced her. "Times will get better, my dear. I'm certain we'll meet again. The young still have time to forget."

Linda turned to John, and her eyes glistened. "Goodbye, John. I'm sorry. This should not have happened to you."

"Nor to you," he said, as he bent forward to kiss her, fleetingly recalling their night of intimacy. "There's still happiness somewhere in the world. There has to be."

She turned, and they watched her walk smartly from the restaurant without looking back, through the door and out of sight.

"She's really quite a fine woman, John," Ellen said. "I hope you'll be seeing her again."

John nodded slowly, looking at the doorway through which Linda had passed. "I'm sure I shall. When all of this is really part of the past. . ."

Less than an hour later, they were on their way. They drove swiftly through the village, John looking neither to left nor right, and then on along the road running parallel to the sea, each busy with thoughts that could not be shared with the other. The sky was a pure blue, completely clear of clouds, and the brilliant sun shining on the sea cast daggers of light into their eyes.

They followed the curve of the road and left the sea behind them.

EPILOGUE

NIGHT had fallen, and with it came an unexpected light drizzle of rain. The street lamps were ringed by halos of mist, and the autos made a swishing sound as they moved along the wet pavement of Central Park South. The trees of the park provided a leafy barrier that moved slightly with the touch of a soft breeze. Pedestrians walked quickly by, either hugging the side of the hotel for shelter, or totally indifferent to the falling moisture. A carriage horse stood just across the way, its ears drooping. The Oak Room glowed with light, and there was a gentle comfort in the buzz of conversation from the many now occupied tables.

My gentle aged companion, her long tale completed, sat back with a gentle sigh.

"And that's the story of Ruth Kendall, young man," she said, sadly, "a strange and dreadful story of a horror from the past that destroyed a fine and talented young woman, someone very dear to me. I don't expect you really to believe it," she added with a slight, wistful sigh.

I did not dare to comment on this, but asked instead, "But what of the painting?"

"It was found on the edge of the bluff, very close to the spot where the house had tumbled into the sea, lying face down, and rather strangely unharmed. John, of course, had no wish ever to see it again and when it became for me too harsh a reminder of that terrible time, I disposed of it to the gallery."

"And your grandson? And Linda?"

"John has returned to his work," she replied with a nod of her head. "The great novel still has not been written, and I doubt it will be now. He doesn't really seem to care any longer. Linda? I don't know. Neither John nor I have heard of her since. I hope she has found her happiness."

We were silent for a moment, staring out into the rain-brightened darkness, and then Ellen Pirenne began to draw on her gloves and gather herself for departure.

"But I must be leaving now," she explained. "You have been very kind, in listening to the story of a rather lonely old woman."

I took her hand. "It has been very kind of you to tell it to me. May I take you somewhere?"

"Oh, no, no," she responded, as we both rose from the table. "As I told you, I'm staying here at the hotel. I've packing to do. I'm leaving for Vienna in the morning." Her smile was sweet, sad, and beautiful. "I spend most of my time there now. Vienna is very beautiful at this time of year."

I watched her go, an old woman from another time, leaning on her cane, nodding to acquaintances as she passed from the room, and I hoped she might yet manage to forget the horrors she had known.

I never again saw Ruth Kendall's final work. When next I inquired about it at the art gallery, Tetrollini informed me it had been sold for a rather surprisingly good price to a young woman who refused to give her name. It would be rather overly romantic of me to attempt to guess her identity.

It doesn't matter.